They Realized They Were in Each Other's Arms.

Neither wanted to be the first to pull away.

It had been a long time since he'd held a natural woman close, a woman without all the concealments of modern fashion. She wore no hoop or stays, had on no stiffened bodice; there were no girdles, laces, padding, or petticoats between herself and him. He became stunningly aware that she had on nothing but a nightgown, a thin covering of cotton; and he, nothing but his silk brocade robe. He couldn't feel his robe or hers. He couldn't feel anything for feeling all those intricate wonderful curves peaking against him, all that sweet warm womanflesh of her. No—not womanflesh. Della. His own Della. Infinitely precious, infinitely needed in this darkness—and needing. He knew it. It was in her body, in her quick, silent breaths. She said nothing.

There was nothing she could say. She would only lie against him, feeling him against her hard and real and everything she'd ever dreamed.

All too soon, he drew back. But it was only his head, tilting away from her, as he considered her. Every move he made was languid, dreamlike, easy, as he seemed to be considering her in a new, strangely exciting way. They regarded each other. His was the first move. He slowly lowered his head and brushed her lips with his. She turned her mouth blindly to his, dreaming, not wanting to be awakened.

Praise for the Wonderful Romances of Bestselling Author

EDITH LAYTON

THE WEDDING

A TRUE LADY

"Exciting action-packed tale with a fresh, innovative story line. Colorful characters, danger, sizzling passion, and crisp dialogue add an interesting dimension to the smooth and well-written tale. You'll definitely know who is a true lady at the end. A pleasure to read."

—*Rendezvous*

"Charming! Edith Layton writes a marvelous tale! *A True Lady* is truly special. Fast-paced and humorous, it carries you along on a whirlwind of emotion. Romantic! A wonderful 'opposites attract' love story. Ms. Layton delights her readers once again with characters that are larger than life. Fans of Edith Layton will be thrilled with her newest story! A most memorable tale!"

—Kristina Wright, *The Literary Times*

"An action-packed, exciting Georgian romance. Christobel is a great lady, and Magnus . . . is a classic English hunk. The supporting cast is all first-rate as they add spice to the tale. Fans of the genre will enjoy the reading experience."

—*Affaire de Coeur*

"Very funny, touching, and *highly recommended.*"

—*Manderley*

"Delightful. . . . Great plot twists. . . . I want to meet the hero! He's handsome, witty, and the epitome of a romantic lead."

—Helen Holzer, *Atlanta Journal*

Books by Edith Layton

The Wedding
A True Lady
Bound by Love

Published by POCKET BOOKS

EDITH LAYTON

Bound by Love

POCKET BOOKS

New York   London   Toronto   Sydney   Tokyo   Singapore

An *Original* Publication of POCKET BOOKS

POCKET BOOKS, a division of Simon & Schuster Inc.
1230 Avenue of the Americas, New York, NY 10020

ISBN: 0-671-53531-5

First Pocket Books printing August 1996

10 9 8 7 6 5 4 3 2 1

POCKET and colophon are registered trademarks of Simon & Schuster Inc.

Front cover illustration by Danilo Ducak

Printed in the U.S.A.

Chapter

1

1745

Virginia colony

The frail boy was staring down into the murky water as though he actually thought he might see his reflection there instead of the usual dockside bilge. His father and sister were talking with the captain of the ship that had just brought them to this new land, and because of all the bustle attending that landing—sailors unloading the huge four-masted vessel, passengers being met by friends and relatives—no one noticed the boy's fascination with the water lapping at the mossy, seaweed-scarred pilings of the dock. No one, that was, except for another boy who shouldn't have been watching at all. But, as this boy's master always said, boys are like dogs; they can always spot another of their kind in any crowd, and when they do, they pay more mind to them than to their own business. But a good wallop cured that soon enough, as it did all else that ailed them.

The boy's master clucked his tongue and gave the young

fellow a swat that nearly made him drop the heavy crate he was carrying. Used to such encouragement, the boy only staggered and didn't drop his burden. Instead, to his master's astonishment, he uttered a muffled exclamation and threw it down. Then he ran full tilt back down the dock toward the empty place where the other boy had been—before he'd lost his balance and fallen into the filthy water. The second boy followed him in, hitting the water with a splash. Then everyone else on the dock noticed what had happened.

The young boy's father grew pale, his daughter screeched, and they rushed to the dockside, calling for help as they watched the two boys struggle to stay afloat. The captain of the vessel shouted for his sailors. Some jumped in the water; others threw lifelines. There was a hullabaloo that didn't stop until the frail young boy was hauled up to the dock and, dripping, shivering, and sobbing, was restored to his father's arms. Then it was all holiday with many a cheer and a few caps thrown into the air for good measure, as the boy's servants bundled him into warm blankets and chaffed him ruddy and dry.

Hardly anyone noticed the other lad after he was hauled up to the dock again. He was only a ragged local boy. After giving him congratulatory pats on the back, the sailors left to get on with their jobs. He stood alone, wet, and shivering; the wide shoulders that showed his approaching manhood racked with shudders. But his master saw him right enough. He gave the boy a slap that sent him sprawling and then kicked him for good measure.

"Lout! And what of my pots, ye lobcock, eh?" his angry master shouted as the boy scrabbled away, readying himself for another kick. "Them china pots come all the way from England without harm—now I'll wager half of 'em will go to the rubbish heap instead of the shop. What's been broke will be took from yer dinner till they're paid for, y' young villain, y' hear?"

The boy rose to his feet and nodded. It was a windy

April day. His wet shirt clung to his thin chest. There was little enough flesh on that lean frame; his ribs could have been counted if he'd stopped shivering long enough for them to be tallied. He was a lanky boy, thin with new growth and thinner from hard usage; his fair skin showed his many bruises. But boys were far cheaper than imported pots—that was a fact of life—so the sailor who offered him a bit of old sailcloth to dry off with gave him a sympathetic smile and a shrug along with it.

"Yer no bloomin' flower; the wind's brisk enough, it'll dry ye!" the boy's master shouted, snatching the cloth from his hands. "Time's wastin'. There's what's left of my pots to see to—blast ye, get moving!"

"Hold!" A cultured voice intruded, and the boy's master looked up to see a gentleman frowning at him. "This boy should be commended rather than beaten," the gentleman said. "He saved my son's life. What's a pot compared to that, I ask you, sir?"

The boy's master looked at the man shrewdly. The fellow was middle-aged, well dressed, wearing a handsome bob wig, a good woolen greatcoat, and fine silver shoe buckles, and carrying a silver-headed walking stick. He was every inch a substantial gentleman, with a plummy English accent that showed he hadn't been in the Colonies long. Obviously this fine gent would soon be gone again. Rich he might be, but it wouldn't do the boy's master any good. His pots were gone. Unless . . .

"Ah. Ye be givin' the lad a reward then, will ye?" the boy's master asked.

"I hadn't thought . . . but yes, of course," the gentleman said. "I certainly shall give your son a reward for his valor."

"My son!" the man chortled. "That's rich. Nah. Any whelp of mine would be better lookin' than yon scrag. This lad's no more'n my bond-boy, curse him, for he's not worth the porridge in his bowl. Always with his mind on something else, and not my business, and counting the

3

hours until he's free, like all his cursed lot. But a man's only got two hands, and I needs help. Much good it does me! My pots are all a-jumble, curse him!"

"I shall pay for them," the gentleman said angrily, "but I should like to reward the boy as well." He was going to say more, but saw the boy shake his head as though to warn him. "That is . . ." the gentleman went on more slowly, "if I can be assured that he can keep his share of the reward."

"Aye," the boy's master said eagerly, delight clear on his face. "Sure. Live and let live, says I."

"My lord," the captain interrupted angrily, "the fellow's a rogue. The boy won't get a sniff of any reward. If you wish to help him, pay for the damage he's done, for I believe that if you don't, it will come out of his hide."

"And why not?" the boy's master said angrily. "He broke more'n he's worth!"

"Why, this is monstrous!" the gentleman exclaimed. "Is the lad his slave?"

"As good as—for the term of his bond," the captain explained. "He's a bonded servant. How many years left on his contract?" he asked the boy's master.

"Two," the man growled, with a menacing look at the boy that didn't bode well for his surviving those years. "His papers say a full seven years and that's what it will be. I bought him with three years already gone of it and he's been with me for two more. I want my money's worth, for a boy of twelve eats more'n one of ten, though he don't do a lick more work. He'll be free when he's fourteen and nary a second afore that, I can tell ye."

The gentleman looked perturbed and gazed down at his own son, whose small face was solemn, even as his eyes begged his father to intercede. Thomas was his father's joy in life as well as his despair, because he was small for his age and plagued by illnesses. The gentleman looked at the bond-boy again. The lad was only a year older than his own son, and though obviously mistreated, was taller and stronger, and his clear gray eyes held a wisdom far

4

beyond his meager years. His well-shaped lips were white with cold, but they bowed into a rueful smile as he shrugged his bony shoulders.

"Thank you, sir," the boy said in a soft, civil voice that sounded more educated than it had a right to be under the circumstances, "but I'll do well enough if you pay my master the damages. I don't need more, thank you."

His master grabbed the boy's arm and twisted it sharply in order to silence him. The boy's face contorted but he didn't even gasp. "He speaks nonsense. Pay him no mind!" his master snarled. "A mess of crockery a fair trade for a boy's life? Why, 'tis laughable! If yer really grateful, reward him with gold. He'll get his fair share."

The gentleman had started forward when the boy was seized, but he stopped when he saw the look in the man's eyes and realized the power he held over the boy.

"Fair share? Likely," the captain scoffed. "Save your gold, my lord. Just give the old villain his damages and pray for his soul, and there'll be an end to it."

"It would be better to pray for the boy's life," the gentleman said with decision. "I'm not a religious man, but I am a wealthy one. I want to buy the boy's papers. Name his price," he said imperiously, staring at the man, "but mind you, I'm no fool. I'll pay his bond and something over, and no more."

"I don't have to sell him to you," the boy's master said, but there was a glitter in his eyes. He was a cruel man and a petty one, but a merchant to his toes, and he smelled the possibility of profit. "I can keep the lad the whole two years if I like. 'Tis my right. I'm his lord and master."

"And I am a lord," the gentleman said, "with connections here in the Colonies. But if you don't want to—don't sell him to me." He turned away. "Get the fellow's name," he told the captain in a bored voice. "I'll see what I can do to his business if he doesn't wish to do business with me."

"Hold on. I never said I wouldn't," the boy's master cried.

"Oh?" the gentleman said, turning to look at him with interest.

The two men dickered there on the dock, with a sharp April wind coming off the wild Atlantic around them. Ordinarily the gentleman wouldn't have kept his fragile son and young daughter out in the cruel breeze any more than he'd have subjected them to the stares of a common, curious crowd. But every time the negotiations faltered, he saw how his little daughter stared wide-eyed at the bond-boy. More than that, he saw how his son and the boy continued to look at each other as their elders wrangled over the body and soul of one of them. And so the bargaining went on.

"Done!" the boy's master finally said in disgust after the same offer had been made, withdrawn, and then made once more. He shoved the boy toward the gentleman and held out his hand for his gold.

"Not quite," the gentleman said. "Here's half. Bring me his papers within the hour and you'll have the rest, plus a reward for speed—*if* it's done speedily."

The man nodded, turned, and lumbered down the dock toward shore, hurrying to get the papers back in time to earn the extra coins.

The gentleman sighed. He looked down at the shivering boy. "Well, lad," he said, "'tis all but done."

"I see," the boy said quietly. "And so you are my new master. Do we go to England, sir?"

"Gads, no!" the gentleman said in alarm. "I've just arrived. And I'm not your new master. I did this to set you free. I don't hold with bond-servants. But," he said, as he looked at his own son again and saw how young Thomas—the fortunate one, pampered and cherished since birth—nevertheless looked fragile compared to the starved, bruised bond-boy, "I wonder, have you family?"

"Yes," the boy said, "but not here, sir. In England."

"So they will take you in if I send you back?" the gentleman asked.

"I can no longer say, sir. It's been years, and they sold me into bondage," the boy said very softly.

"Ah, well then," the gentleman said thoughtfully, "I expect you're in need of gainful employment." He saw the hopeful expression on his son's face. "I've brought my son and daughter here so we can remain together as a family while I take care of my estate," he told the bond-boy. "I plan to be here for several years seeing to my property, building up the plantation, setting up export routes. I'll be hiring help. I suspect my son would be glad of company his own age. And a gentleman, no matter how young, can never have too many servants. Are you interested in working for him, lad?"

"I am," the boy said promptly.

"Well, then," the gentleman said, as he saw his son's growing smile, "'lad' will not do, then, will it? What's your name, my boy?"

"I am Jared St. Andrew Bellington," the boy said, bowing.

The gentleman frowned. "Bellington . . . but I know that name. It is very like the earl of Alveston's. Are you related?"

"More than that," the boy said drawing himself up tall, "I *am* the earl of Alveston."

"Oh lad," the gentleman said sadly, looking at the poor, daft boy. "Oh lad," he said with deeper sorrow, looking at his son. "I'll set you free, then, and God help you."

"No," the boy said with dignity. "I'll help myself, as I've always done."

"Father!" the gentleman's son cried, "No! Please. Keep him on. I believe him."

"Very well. Don't upset yourself." The gentleman told the captain with a heavy heart, "But this doesn't bode well. I've only been here an hour and I've already made a bad bargain."

"Sir," the bond-boy said proudly, "you have not. You'll see. You've made a very good one, one you'll never regret. You have my word on it."

The gentleman studied the boy who stood so tall in his rags and slowly shook his head. The lad was obviously addled and yet, in that moment, against all reason, he believed him.

But there was no time for belief or disbelief now; there were too many things to do now to waste time speculating about a servant. The boy would be loaded into the coaches with the rest of the household supplies. Before anything else was done, though, the baron of Kent had to make sure his children had their first luncheon on dry land in weeks. Then he'd finish making preparations for the trip to their new home. But before one wagon was loaded, a room had to be hired at the dockside inn, because the doctors had said his son needed a nap after each meal. That was his first priority. He didn't worry about his little girl because, although she was years younger than his son, she was a hearty little soul, as sound in health as she was in temperament.

Once assured his son was resting comfortably, the baron left his children's room—and he left it as mere Mr. Alfred Kensington. He'd researched this new land where he hoped to make his fortune and discovered that in this new country, a title didn't mean as much as title to acreage. In fact, since many important businessmen in the Colonies were here mainly because of their dislike of nobility, he decided not to take any chances. His title went into the family Bible he'd carried across the sea, and there it would stay for the duration of his years here.

When all the wagons and carriages were packed with supplies and workers he'd hired, Alfred Kensington sighed with relief. It would be a long drive, and a longer time settling in. But at least it was begun. Now to get his children and their nurse into the carriage to begin the last lap of the journey to their new home.

He helped his son into their carriage, praying the vehicle was sprung well enough to spare him discomfort on what would be rough country roads. The boy hadn't complained on the long sea voyage, though his father knew he'd suffered, his weight loss and pallor speaking eloquently of the discomforts he was too stoic to mention.

"Where's Jared?" Thomas Kensington asked his father as soon as he had seated himself in the carriage and looked around to see only his sister and their nurse already inside.

Alfred frowned, trying to remember who "Jared" was.

"My new friend," Thomas reminded him. "The one who saved my life, Father."

"Ah, yes. He's in the third carriage, with the other menservants," Alfred told him.

"I thought he was to be *my* personal servant," Thomas said.

"Well, so he will be. But we surely don't need more than Nurse here for this trip," his father explained.

"Nurse is for Della, but I'm a big boy now, Father," Thomas said with gentle persistence. He was a quiet boy, polite as the gentleman he'd been raised to be, quiet as only an invalid could be, but as insistent on getting his own way as only an indulged and cosseted young aristocrat could be.

"But we scarcely know him, son," Alfred said uncomfortably, "and it's such a long trip. . . . I'm sure the boy will be happier among his equals than with us right now."

"He says he is an earl, Father," Thomas reminded him.

Alfred grimaced. The reminder made him think of all the reasons he'd hesitated to hire the boy on.

"I want him here with me. I believe him, and even if you don't, he doesn't seem like the sort to get angry about it," Thomas said.

Alfred sighed. His son had the uncanny ability to accurately judge his elders' feelings—a gift that only a boy who'd had to pass his childhood watching instead of doing could possess.

"To be sure," Alfred murmured. He'd have to fetch the boy. If he refused, Thomas would gently but patiently keep insisting on it, until he was told to be quiet, and then he'd sit so quietly his father would feel like a monster and worry whether he was only sulking or really feeling ill.

Alfred sighed, backed out of the carriage, and walked back to the menservants' coach. But he wasn't happy about it.

He too doubted the lad would be trouble; if he was, it would be simple enough to expel him from the carriage. But it probably wouldn't come to that. The lad had seemed normal except for that wild statement about his title. And who could blame a lad for concocting a title for himself, to make his servitude more bearable? The lad had saved his son's life, after all. And it might be a fine lesson for young Thomas, too, Alfred thought with rising spirits. Maybe riding so closely with the boy would persuade him that brave as the boy had been, he wasn't a fit companion. Dogs and horses could lay down their lives for their masters, too, but that didn't mean one wanted to spend all one's time with them, after all.

But when the boy climbed down from the menservants' carriage and stood before him, Alfred frowned. The boy's skin seemed clean enough, maybe from the dunking he'd gotten when he'd saved Thomas. But he wore a shirt so threadbare it was nearly transparent, and the badly sewn rents in it were almost as appalling as the many patches on his ragged britches. And he was barefoot. Such a person couldn't sit next to Alfred's children, no matter what a service he'd done for them. But Thomas wanted him.

It was a lucky thing that harborside shops carried everything settlers in this rough land required. But even so, Alfred's three coaches and two wagons waited for nearly a half-hour while clothes and a pair of shoes were purchased for the boy. He emerged from the shop and stood before Alfred for inspection. He wore a plain linen shirt, a clean pair of britches, and a simple pair of shoes. His fair hair was combed and caught back in a neat queue. There was nothing lavish about his clothes, but there was no fault to be found in his appearance at all now. Still, his new master frowned. Although the lad was lean to the point of starvation, bruised to several colors on his thin face, and dressed in the most simple clothes money could buy, he still looked every inch an aristocrat.

It might have been in his bearing. He held his wide shoulders straight as his back, and he stood tall. It might have been in his face. His even features were calm and his light eyes watchful. It might have been his manners, as good as Alfred's own. Or his accent, which, though not quite English, was also not quite colonial and held an air of cool, reasonable conviction . . . and interest, laughter, and kindness. By the time they were an hour down the road, Alfred found that he liked the lad. He made Thomas laugh like a boy again. While Thomas laughed at the droll stories Jared told about native customs, little Della sat and stared at him, her eyes wide as her precious china doll's were.

"It sounds great fun!" Thomas said when Jared finished telling how many kinds of fish there were to catch. "I can't wait! Father, is there a stream on our land?"

"Aye, and a pond and the river nearby. But we must wait to see what the doctor says."

"But I'll dress warm," Thomas protested, hope and frustration clear in his voice. "You heard Jared. He said the summers are hot here—much hotter than at home. Why, it's warm here already, and the natives go about half clothed; you saw that for yourself."

"Aye, but you aren't a native. We'll wait on what the doctor says," Alfred answered decisively. Seeing the question in Jared's eyes as Thomas fell still, he added, "My boy has a weak chest. He wheezes summers as well as winters, though winters are the worst. One of the things that brought us here was the climate. Hot in summer and temperate the rest of the year, I heard." He paused, frowning at himself for making excuses to a boy—and a former bond-boy at that.

"Exactly," Thomas crowed, excited again, "so there can be no good reason for me not to fish with Jared as soon as can be!"

"But our summers are damp as well as hot," Jared said gently, "and sometimes that can bother people with a wheeze; it makes them sneeze and cough. It's because of

11

all the flowers. There are so many here, growing wild as well as in gardens. Higgins, my old master, had that problem. But there are remedies: drinks and potions. They use Indian herbs and flowers here. Yes, real Indian cures, and they work, too. They use flowers to cure flower fever." He paused, smiling at Della's fascinated stare, and added, "One of them is a flower blue as your eyes, my lady. Though not so pretty," he added teasingly, with a little smile.

She flushed and looked down, pretending to fuss with her doll's hair in order to avoid his eyes, though in a second she was peeking up at him again under her lashes.

Gallantry! Amazing, Alfred thought. And from what was less than a beggar boy, since a bond-boy was not valued as much as a free man, of course, or even so much as a slave. A slave was an investment to be protected, and a free man might seek other employment. A bond-servant was expendable. If he lived to work out his bond, it only profited himself. This lad had been the lowest of the low until hours ago and yet he spoke like the man he was fast becoming, and not only that, like the nobleman he'd pretended to be. *Astonishing,* Alfred thought.

"Do you have anything that cures giggles?" Thomas asked with a grin. "Because that's what my sister suffers from the most."

"No, I don't," the little girl said in a gruff voice, but tears sprang to those great blue eyes, and her thumb popped into her trembling mouth.

"But why should anyone want to cure giggles?" Jared asked with just the right amount of wonder in his voice.

Nurse beamed at him, as Della stared, her tears forgotten. Alfred sighed with relief. The boy was sound, whatever nonsense he'd spouted back on the dock. That must have been sheer bravado, whistling in the face of defeat; it showed spirit, not madness. No question that he himself still had the touch with people as well as investments. In a matter of years, he'd have the money to return to England, vastly successful, the youngest son with as much money as his fortunate brothers who'd only had to be born to get it. And with luck, this chance-met bond-boy would be a useful addition to his family. He was gently bred, whoever had raised him. And strong and clever. He obviously knew this land, too. The children would be bound to feel out of place, and Jared would be of great help to them.

But first Alfred had to give him another chance to ease out of the corner he'd painted himself into, Alfred thought. The boy had said a foolish thing, a child's boast in the face of tyranny. It was time to let him worm out of it so he could have a new beginning. "Jared, eh?" Alfred mused aloud. "Jared what? I disremember exactly what you said, lad."

"Jared St. Andrew Bellington," the boy said softly, "earl of Alveston. Exactly as I said. I'm sorry, sir," he said into the stony silence that followed his pronouncement, "but there it is. It's who I am, although I know it's hard to believe."

"Impossible to believe," Alfred said harshly, "and I'll thank you to remember it. So. You continue to claim it. I see. Is there anything else you insist upon that others would think madness? For I tell you straight, boy, it will not do. I'll brook no nonsense. My family is my life, and if you have any odd kicks to your gallop, I'll have it known here and now. I'm taking you into my house. I expect you to be a companion to my boy. I want no difficulties. None. If there are any, tell me now and I'll give you the price of a ride back to town and your next meal and we'll be done with it. It would be far better than what would await you if I discover that you in any way harmed my children, I promise you."

"There will be no other difficulties, sir," the boy said quietly, though his face had grown very pale beneath its tan, and his thin, calloused hands were clenched in tight, trembling fists on his knees. "I cannot help who I am, nor will I deny it, because my heritage is all I have left to me. If it displeases you, I'm sorry, but I will not—cannot—give it up. But I promise I'll do everything that I can to reward your trust in me. You bought my bond, but freed me in spite of it. You'll find no other fault in me. I'd like to work for you, sir," he added, gazing steadily into Alfred's eyes.

Alfred saw his son's face. "And how old are you?" he asked Jared wearily, his temper cooling. There'd be others to keep watch; the boy would be carefully observed until he proved his worth.

"Twelve, sir."

"Only a year older than I am," Thomas said with pleasure.

"And if I keep you on," Alfred asked Jared, with a warning glance to silence his son, "do you promise to always protect and defend my son?"

"Yes, I will."

"Done, then. You may stay on with us for a time. Your name is Jared Bellington—if you insist," Alfred said. "But I'll hear no more about it. Keep it to yourself. I warn you, I hold you responsible for my son's well-being. His life and happiness are your only concern."

"Father!" Thomas wailed.

"I will serve and protect him," Jared said in a low, steady voice. He said it like a sacred oath, so solemnly that Thomas grew quiet, and even Nurse turned to stare out the window in the silence that followed.

Until a foggy little voice asked plaintively, "And me, too?" Della waited for an answer.

"Oh, but of course, princess," Jared said. And they all laughed with relief.

The house was a grand one, by Virginia standards. Alfred climbed down from the coach and stood in the drive, staring at it. It was raw and new, but seemed well built, just as the letters had described: set among tall trees, itself tall and wide and whitewashed, with many windows and chimneys and a long, curving crushed-shell drive before it. It was the grandest house he'd seen since he had left the ship. It might do for a dower house at the estate where he'd grown up. He'd have to make do. This house was for a farmer and a businessman, and that was what he was determined to be. This new world had tobacco, cotton, produce, and spices that the old world wanted. He knew exactly who wanted them there. And he'd supply them—for a sizable fee, so that when he returned to his world, he could be a gentleman and pretend he'd never been anything else—and so that his children could inherit more than useless titles when he was gone. He didn't know when that would be—that was the point. When he'd lost his beloved wife and the new babe so suddenly, he'd realized how impermanent life could be. He was determined to leave Thomas and Della something more than the bittersweet memories that haunted him; he was resolved they'd never have to live on anyone's charity, not even his own brothers'.

That ambition, so odd in a nobleman, was what had brought him across the sea. But it was not so odd here. He'd noticed that same kind of ambition and pride in so many people here, even in such a lowly creature as his recently hired bond-boy. It was what drew him to the poor youth.

He turned to help his son down from the coach, and found Jared had already done it, and had taken Della out as well. The lad stood by the coach with Della in his arms as they both surveyed the house.

"Your new house," Jared told the little girl.

"Yours, too," she assured him. She drew up her legs so he wouldn't set her down and put her arms around him and snuggled up against him so he could carry her home.

Chapter

2

There were perfectly adequate servants' quarters in the new house: rooms in the attic for the females and a separate house behind the main house for the men, not to mention all the rooms above the stables. But no sooner was Thomas installed in his room than he insisted on having his new servant sleep close by.

"Jared will be happy to be in with the other lads," Alfred said. "I dare say it will be better than any quarters you've had a while, eh?" he asked Jared.

"Yes," Jared answered, "much better, thank you. I'm happy where I am, Master Thomas, believe me. I have my own mattress *and* my own pillow, and they're near the window, too."

"Della has Nurse sleeping next door, in her own room," Thomas said in the flat voice that his father knew meant he was deadly serious.

"Alcove, really," Alfred said absently, "and that crate goes there, lads—easy now, easy—it's glassware," he called, because he was trying to placate his son and at the same time direct his servants as they set up his new household. "And Della's a baby, Tom; that's why Nurse sleeps nearby."

"Am not a baby!" Della cried, outraged. "Am not! You said, you said!" she shouted. "You said I wasn't anymore."

"No, no, of course not," her father said, flustered, "and so you are not. Five years old—my goodness, not a baby at all! A grown girl. But there you are, Tom," he said a little desperately, his eyes following a crate that was being carried into the music room, "a *girl,* after all, has to have her nurse nearby. But you are almost a man."

"Yes. Exactly," Thomas said insistently. "He is my manservant, is he not? Didn't you have your valet nearby at home?"

"So I did, but that was at our old home. This is our new home; I'm not at all sure I shall even need a valet here. Lord, Thomas, be reasonable." He dropped his voice and whispered harshly, glancing over at Jared, who was standing nearby, pretending he didn't hear. "We don't know the boy. It's enough I'm giving him a roof over his head, much less house room!"

"I'm very happy where I am," Jared said stiffly. "I promise you I am, Master Thomas."

"But *I* am not," Thomas said. And kept saying it.

Alfred dressed formally for dinner and laughed aloud to himself as he did. When he had a wife, when he lived in London or in Kent, when he was on shipboard, when he was among civilized people, he had no choice but to dine in formal attire. But tonight, for the first time his life, here in this crude land and now that he was on his own, it didn't matter how he dressed. No one who mattered would see him, after all. Only servants. His daughter dined in her room with her nurse; his only companion would be his son. He supposed that after such a trying day, he could be excused for being informal. He could dine in the kitchens in his shirt sleeves if he wished.

But he was born a nobleman and had been raised a gentleman and he could no more eat in the kitchens in his shirt sleeves than he could cook himself the meal he would eat. Most of all, he told himself, as he inspected his neckpiece and decided he might need a valet after all, he had to set an example for his son. A gentleman remained a gentleman in all circumstances, whether or not there was anyone to judge him; that was what set him apart from common men. When he returned to England, he wouldn't have become a savage, and his son too would be a perfect gentleman. Everything he did now was for Thomas, after all.

And so he stepped from his room smiling, wearing a long coat, waistcoat, shirt, britches, and a carefully tied cravat: the very model of a gentleman, the picture of a marquis's son, even if he was the youngest. He was pleased with himself; He didn't look bad. In truth, he was a fine figure of a man, hardly showing his years at all—a bit thicker at the waist and thinner of hair, but hardly old—at least not as old as he'd felt in England. This really was a land of new beginnings.

He was pleased with his first night in his new home. The land didn't look savage; there were natives, of course, and crude farmers to be seen working in the fields. But the fields were lush, and the forests were being cleared at a rapid pace. There was money to be made here and a future to forge for himself and his son and daughter. There was time to make his mark, and this was the place in which to do it. It had been a dangerous gamble, a long and worrisome voyage, but now he was here, and now he had something to work for. He was content.

Until he heard his son cry out.

He ran down the hall to his son's room, fumbling at his side for the sword that wasn't there—that he hadn't worn because he hadn't thought he would need it in his own house. His heart pounded, but he vowed he would fight with his own two hands—and teeth, if he must—to defend his son against whatever danger there was that he couldn't imagine in this harsh new land.

He ran into Thomas's room. But his son wasn't there; he was standing at the door to the small anteroom beyond, staring in horror at Jared, the bond-boy. Jared stood against the far wall, white-faced, his hands trembling on the buttons to his half-open shirt as he hastily tried to do them up.

"What have you done?" Alfred shouted in rage as he seized the boy and slammed him back against the wall. "What? Tell me!" he cried, gripping the boy's shoulder and shaking him for emphasis. Visions of what the boy might have done to Thomas enraged Alfred so much that all he wanted to do was to beat him into the floor. He raised his arm so he could strike the boy with his heavy hand.

"No, no, no," Thomas wailed, but Alfred was seething with fury and seemed to hear him from a great distance. He saw the boy flinch as his head struck the wall behind him. Only then did Jared wince—as did Alfred.

Alfred's arm wavered. The blow never fell. His hand stayed arrested in the air. *Boy,* he reminded himself, trembling with the effort of holding back. *This is only a boy, whatever he has done.* Alfred let out his pent-up breath in a harsh sigh and lowered his hand to his side. Jared, he saw now, had bitten his lip when his head struck the wall. There was blood on his mouth, but he stared straight at Alfred and there was no fear in his eyes, only resignation.

"What have you done?" Alfred asked savagely. He let go of the boy. One wrong word and he knew he wouldn't be able to contain himself, no matter how much he disliked hitting a thin, defenseless youth, especially one who made no move to protect himself. Alfred's fists clenched hard at his sides as he waited for an answer.

"Father, no!" Thomas shouted. He ran to his father's side and tugged at his knotted fist.

"All right, I won't hit him. But he must go; you can have no pity," Alfred snarled, never taking his eyes from the bond-boy. "I'll have him out in a trice. You'll never have to see him again." He looked down at his son at last. "Oh my God, what did he do to you?" Alfred cried, seeing Thomas's grief and fearing the worst.

"Nothing, nothing." Thomas wept. "Oh Father, he's bleeding. Oh, he didn't do anything. Oh, look, he's bleeding."

Nurse came bustling into the little room. She held the bond-boy's face up to the light to get a closer look at the damage. "'Tis only his lip, master," she said. But the look in the boy's eyes was beyond mere pain.

Alfred straightened his coat, shook out his sleeves, and took a deep breath. Now that the fear was gone, he could see clearly again. The commotion had drawn many curious servants, aside from Nurse. They hovered in the doorway. And Della stood barefoot, in her nightclothes, clutching her doll and gazing at the bond-boy wide-eyed, her own lips trembling.

"He didn't do anything," Thomas kept sobbing. Alfred became afraid, because when Thomas flew into a passion, he often grew feverish. Alfred dropped to his knees in front of his son.

"Then why did you cry out?" he asked him. "I thought—ah, well never mind what I thought. I believed he had harmed you, and I came to stop him. . . . " He glanced up at the bond-boy and saw, in that moment, that the boy knew it was a lie. He had come to kill him. But the boy said nothing. His face was still, though his lean chest shook with the short, shallow breaths he took in reaction to the sudden, violent onslaught.

"He didn't do anything." Thomas wept, his eyes wild. "I cried out because—because he was getting dressed and I walked into his room and he didn't see me, but I saw—I saw . . ." He began sobbing again.

But now Alfred grew very still, relief giving way to a new

dread. Maybe the lad hadn't done anything to his son, but what vile thing had Thomas seen him do?

"What did you see?" Alfred asked fearfully. He had taken a strange boy into his home, a mad boy, and what he might have caused by so doing squeezed at his heart.

"I saw . . . I saw . . ." Thomas began to say, but then was overcome with emotion again and subsided into sobs.

Alfred looked up at the boy, who, for the first time, flinched, and shook his head in denial.

"I *will* know," Alfred told the boy grimly as he rose and advanced on him. "If you don't tell me of your own free will what my son saw, I'll have it from you, one way or the other. You will not leave here until I know."

Now the boy's eyes lit with a fury so brilliant that Alfred took a step back without realizing it. Then he saw pain in them, before the light was quenched and they became deadened. Without a word, the boy turned his back on his new master. While Alfred sputtered in growing outrage, the boy unbuttoned his hastily done up shirt and, without warning, let it drop from his shoulders. When Alfred saw what his son had, he himself had to bring his fist to his mouth to stifle his own outcry. But his servants gasped and murmured in shock.

The bond-boy was young, but the scars on his back were not. They crisscrossed that lean back: some were white welts, some pink, some thin, white delicate tracings, as of frost or cracked glass across the otherwise smooth clear skin of that newly broadening back, disfiguring it. He'd been beaten, savagely and often. Alfred had once seen an old cart horse with similar marks on his hide and had refused to deal with the farmer who had owned him. He'd never seen a man with such scarring. He wished he had never seen a boy with such, and remembering how he himself had almost beaten the lad made his stomach feel hollow and cold.

"You may put your shirt on again," Alfred said dully.

The boy didn't turn until he had done up his shirt, and

when he did, the look on his face made Alfred order his servants out and about their duties. Nurse stayed to cluck over the lad's torn mouth, giving him a wet rag to hold over it. She would have stayed to fuss longer if Alfred hadn't commanded her to go, too.

When she left in a huff at how rude he sounded, the room was silent except for the harsh sound of Thomas trying to get his tears under control. Alfred paced the room a few times before he spoke. "Useless to say I'm sorry. You must know that," he said, with a quick look at Jared. "I'll make it up to you."

"I'd like to leave, sir," Jared said quietly. "Thank you for saying it was a mistake. Thank you for all you've done. But I have my freedom now and I'd like to take it, if I may."

"I wish you would not!" Alfred said, this time without bothering to so much as glance at his son. "The fault was mine. I acted without thinking—or rather, I suppose, from thinking too much. It will not happen again."

"But it will," Jared said wearily. "It always does. That's how I earned my stripes," he said with a smile too old for his face. "I'm a good servant. At least I try to be, but there are some things I won't do—or can't say. That's not good when you're a bondsman. Old Higgins hated me because he said I was always looking down on him. I guess I was. He beat me some, but not as badly as my first master, who got tired of my insisting I was an earl and not just an orphan. My second master beat me harder because by then I was older and I kept trying to run away. Then I learned that even if I did get away, if I was caught, it would add more years to my contract. Whoever caught me would be rewarded, and I'd have work off that reward price, too. So I waited and learned to be quiet, although I couldn't help the way I . . . but I'm not a bond-servant anymore—or so you said?" he asked again, his face suddenly looking younger and vulnerable. "This . . . this didn't change that?"

"No, no, I told you so. You're free," Alfred said quickly. "But I would ask that you stay on with us. We'll try to make a new beginning."

"How can I?" Jared asked, old pain making him look more like Thomas than Alfred could bear. "It will only happen again. You think there's something wrong with me because I keep saying I'm an earl. I don't blame you; it does sound crazy. But it's true."

Jared let out a long, shaky breath, and when he spoke again, he addressed Alfred directly, looking in his eyes as though they were both men of the world. "After my parents died," he said, "my brother and I went to bed one night and woke to find strangers in our room. We fought, but there were three of them and they were grown men. They put us into sacks and took us from our house in a farm cart. And then . . ." He paused, then went on, stony-faced but with his eyes wild with light, "We were driven a long way, and then they tossed us into a river—like kittens they were going to drown. I'd been working at my bonds since I woke up, so when we hit the water, I managed to get free. I freed my brother, too. But he—he couldn't swim as well. I saw him go under the water. I tried to reach him, but the current carried me to shore, where they caught me again. This time, they took me to London and sold me to a soul driver—that's what they call men who buy bond-servants without asking questions, to sell in the Colonies. I've been here ever since. I guess I was lucky. Luckier than my brother, at least."

He shook his head as though to clear it of the memory. "It happened," he told Alfred imploringly, his expression hopeless and yet still insistent. "Beat me as you will, but I won't deny it. I can't. If I deny who I was, then I'll be what they wanted me to be—nobody. Someday, when I'm older, I'll put things right. It's what I'm waiting for. So now I try to be a good servant so that someday I can return to England."

"There was such a case," Alfred said, musing. "Aye. I

23

remember reading about it—a young bond-servant in the Pennsylvania colony. He claimed the same thing. Yes, now I remember—it was an evil uncle, he said. He claimed he was an Irish earl, and many believed him; in fact, he won one case—and lost another. His uncle was a powerful man; with that title and the estate in his hands, the lad didn't have a chance. Why, he fought it for years and years. I remember seeing a letter in the *Times* about it. Why, now that I recall, it was almost exactly the same story!"

"Yes," Jared said softly, "James Annersley, earl of Anglesey. Everyone knows about it here. He tried to prove who he was for twenty years. He never could. He died two years ago, still trying. That's another reason everyone thinks I'm lying; they think I'm copying him. I think that's what my uncle counted on. But James Annersley didn't have a brother. And he never won back his title. I will. I vow I will—someday. And I'm *not* mad," he said with the first hint of defiance he'd shown. Although he'd always been set on his story, he'd never been anything but polite and deferential.

In fact, Alfred realized, with a feeling of disquiet, his manners were always refined. Of course, he was only a bond-boy, whatever he claimed. It was impossible to believe he was really a kidnapped earl; that was the stuff of fairy tales, a once-in-a-lifetime thing that had already happened once, as the boy himself knew very well. *But still*, Alfred thought uneasily, *the boy is always a gentleman, even when there is no reason for him to be.* It was almost as if he too knew that a man had to act a gentleman whatever the circumstances, whoever was there to see him, or else he'd sink to being a savage. Whatever his beginnings, he behaved just as an aristocrat should.

"I'm not saying I believe you, lad," Alfred finally said, "but I'm not saying I don't. One thing I will say: whatever you are, you're not mad—at least not in the way I think of madmen. Nor do I believe you'll hurt my son. Stay on with us. It may be we can do you some good. It may be you can do us some."

"Yes, will you?" Thomas asked eagerly.

"Will you, Jared?" Della echoed in a frightened little voice, which made her father realize she'd been standing still in the shadows the whole while. He went to her side and took her small hand in his, hoping she'd remember that, and not the way he'd punished the bond-boy.

Jared grimaced when he saw her, reminding Alfred of how boys hated to let girls see their pain. But then the boy's thin shoulders finally slumped, letting them all see how tightly he'd been holding himself.

"Yes," Jared said. "I'll stay, if you want me to."

"If I want you to?" Thomas cried, "Of course. Oh, this is fine. You won't have to work all the time, either. Not with us, right, Father? We'll fish and fly kites—oh, we'll have a grand time!"

"Aye, until the autumn. Then it's schooling for you, lad," Alfred said. "But for now, aye. Jared can teach you the way of summer in this land."

Alfred and Thomas grinned. But Della looked troubled. She let go of her father's hand and walked toward Jared. Then she stopped and reached out a chubby hand toward his mouth. "Aren't you going to fix that?" she asked shyly.

"Oh, this?" Jared said, wincing as he touched his torn lip. "Yes. Don't worry. I suppose it looks bad, but it's nothing. I've had worse."

"Does it hurt?" she asked.

"Not much," he said, trying to smile. "Your nurse helped. It will be better soon, you'll see."

"No," she said worriedly, biting her own pink lip, "I mean your back. Does it hurt? Can we fix it, too?"

This time, Alfred winced. The boy's back was so hideously scarred, and with his enormous pride, it was easy to see why it was his secret and surely a humiliating subject for him. But in the way of all small children, Della had gone straight to the point: Alfred wondered how the boy would take it. Jared sat back on his heels before he answered.

"No, not anymore," Jared finally said. "It doesn't hurt now."

"Oh," Della said. She nodded and clutched her doll tighter. "I'm sorry it ever did," she said solemnly.

Jared cocked his head, and then he smiled. "Thank you," he said. "That helps."

And although Jared had smiled at them several times since they'd met, Alfred suddenly realized he'd never seen him *really* smile before.

That summer was blazingly hot. At least it was to Alfred and the servants he'd brought from England.

"All the summers we prayed for a clear sky and sun all day, and look at this," Alfred remarked to Nurse one shining July day. "The sun's so relentless, I believe I could do with a nice damp mist."

"But Master Thomas couldn't," she snapped. "Look at the boy, sir. Tan and stout, laughing all the time and breathing free. 'Tis the moistness in the air as well as the pure, sweet warmth of it. Not a cough or a fever this month," she said, knocking her gnarled knuckles on the sill of the window they were looking out. "He's just like a regular boy now, thank the Lord."

"Aye," he said, smiling, watching how Thomas capered alongside Jared as they headed down to the stream to fish. He smiled wider as he saw Della skipping to keep up behind them.

"And the baby," Nurse said, her eyes misted. "It's a treat how Jared looks out for Miss Della, sir; why he even has Master Thomas doing it these days. I don't mind telling you I wouldn't let her stir from this house if I had any worries about her. I'd be out there catching her every time she followed them, which is every time they set foot outside. But between the outside servants and Jared, who watches her like the apple of his eye, she's safer with them than with me, for I can't wade into streams after her, that I can tell you. Unless you want me to sir," she added hurriedly, "and think I ought."

"No, no," he said, laughing, watching his daughter catch up and take Jared's hand as they swung down the lane. "No need. You're right; it couldn't be better. That boy's the best investment I've made so far." Except for the house and the land, he thought smugly, thinking of his young tobacco plants flourishing in the fields.

But the sight of the young trio pleased him even more: tall, young Jared, dark and newly robust Thomas, and their little shadow with great blue eyes and ebony curls. Alfred chuckled. What a change three months had made—in his fortunes and his son. In the spring, Thomas had been pale and listless, only his eyes showing the energy a boy his age should have. But now he was growing flesh and gaining confidence in every way. With no more night fevers and days of coughing, he flourished, mind and body. It was the climate, of course—and the influence of his new servant, Alfred admitted. That lad was growing, too, on a steady diet of good food. He was becoming positively handsome. In these few months, Jared had put on weight and height, his lanky body becoming smoothly muscled. A head taller and twice as composed as Thomas, he looked years older than Alfred's son now, and acted it, too. But that was because Thomas was learning to be a boy at last, while Jared finally had the opportunity to grow more like the man he tried to be.

Alfred nodded to himself. Things were finally in hand. He'd even sent some inquiries to London. The boy's story deserved that, at least. But what with ocean travel and the way men a continent away reacted to inquiries made by an employer across a wide ocean, information traveled even slower than the post. And so, Alfred thought, he might be ready to return to England richer than a king by the time he found out if the lad really was an earl. It didn't matter. Now, they all had time.

Or so he thought that sparkling July morning.

* * *

August came damp and surly that year, with the heat less a blessing than a presence now that the novelty of it had worn off for the newly arrived Englishmen at Alfred's plantation. They discovered a New World August had bugs in its teeth and sweat in its armpits and was so hot and humid the only things that wanted to move were the crops in the field as they strained toward the sun that tried to bake them into the earth.

But Jared showed Thomas how to cool his ankles in the creek as he fished and showed Della how to sip the nectar from the tip of the honeysuckle horn instead of gathering flowers in the sweltering heat, and let them both lie in deep grass and watch clouds when it got too hot to do anything but dream aloud.

"Father's hired a schoolmaster for me," Thomas said drowsily one afternoon as they watched clouds gather to thunderheads.

"Ah," Jared said, "so you won't be going to the school-house in September?"

"I am to be a gentleman," Thomas reproved him. "I shall have separate lessons. You can take them with me."

There was a silence. Jared ran a blade of grass through his fingers. "I don't think so," he said gently. "I'm a servant, Tom. I'm here to work, not take lessons."

"Nonsense," Thomas said, sounding very like his father. "It will be good for both of us."

"No," Jared said quietly, lying back with his arm behind his head, "I don't think so."

"Jared," Thomas said with a hint of humor, "I'm your employer and I say yes and so there's an end to it. If it makes you feel better, we'll tell Father you're helping me with my lessons, and that's how you'll be working."

Jared was quiet so long Thomas thought he had fallen asleep. But Della was watching, as she always was, and she saw the pain in Jared's wide-open eyes. "No," Jared finally said, "because it wouldn't be true. I wouldn't be learning the same things you were. I couldn't. I'm probably leagues behind you, Master Thomas." Thomas sat up. These days,

Jared only called him that when he was angry with him. "Truth is," Jared went on, "I did well with my lessons until I stopped having them—that was five years ago, when I was only seven. I know my letters, Tom, and my numerals, and I can write my name and read some of Della's books. But that's about all. Bond-boys aren't tutored in anything but how to use their backs, you see."

"But you know everything," Della said passionately.

Both boys laughed. "So I do," Jared said sadly. "But not how to read and write and calculate."

"You will," Thomas said with determination.

"Hooray!" Della cried.

Lessons started in September, and by October, when the crops were coming in, Jared could calculate how rich his new master was going to be and write up an account of it for his own diary. Della lost a tooth and was horrified by how she looked, until Thomas gave her a shilling for it and Jared told her the tooth fairy would give her another. The next morning Della awoke to find that she had indeed received another coin, and then jiggled all her other teeth so much hoping for another that both boys couldn't stop laughing. Thomas grew another inch and gained more weight, and everyone saw that he'd likely be the image of his father one day.

But then November came.

It was not so cold as England had been in the autumn. But it was chilly and damp. Still, Thomas refused to wrap himself up like the invalid he used to be, no matter what Nurse said, even when he stole out with Jared and some other boys on the plantation for an All Hallow's Eve frolic. They carried hollowed gourds filled with candles to light their way down the back paths to the back of the barn. Once there, they told delicious ghost stories and ate roasted nuts and crisp new apples, then dared each other to run through the new graveyard behind the church. And then, stifling laughter, they slipped back into their houses again.

Nor did Thomas let Nurse bundle him in blankets when they drove back from church the following Sunday, even though she had pointed out so many of the boys there who were coughing and sneezing. Now that Thomas was a real boy, he passionately hated the trappings of the invalid he'd been.

But what he hated didn't matter, because he was back in bed before the week was out. And this time, all Nurse's potions, as well as the local doctor's, couldn't bring the fever down.

At least it was a brief illness. There wasn't time for Thomas to be as afraid as his father was. Sometime in the night, while his father and his new servant and friend kept watch, Thomas's painfully sawing breaths stopped and he slipped into a deep sleep. As Jared looked up in sudden hope and Alfred began to smile with relief, Thomas let out what sounded like a natural sigh at last. And then, though the man and boy at his bedside waited at first in hope and then in despair, he never breathed in again.

When the funeral was over, Nurse took Della into her room, and Master Alfred took to his room alone. Jared roamed the house and fields like a wraith, as though he thought he might meet Thomas's wandering spirit there. All he found was himself, twice bereaved. Once he'd lost a brother, and now he'd lost a boy who had been like a brother. It was even harder this time, because now he was old enough to feel more pain. The first time, he'd had fear and confusion to keep him company; now he had nothing but sorrow. He'd never been so alone, because he didn't even have a tormentor now to take up his attention. All he had was loneliness, and though he'd learned to live with physical pain, he didn't know how to bear this kind of pain, in part because he hadn't loved anyone in so long.

Jared met Alfred by accident one windy evening a week after the funeral. Jared was at the graveyard by the church, where he liked to sit and remember how good life had been before Thomas had gone, when he glanced up and saw Alfred standing nearby. He was about to speak, to say something, because he hadn't seen his master since the day of the funeral. But the look in Alfred Kensington's eyes froze him. He rose slowly and slowly backed away, without a word. He hadn't survived the last seven years by not recognizing hatred when he saw it.

Alfred begrudged him the air he breathed; that was clear enough in his eyes as he looked at the tall, fair-haired boy he'd bought—the boy who lived, though his own son did not. The words were clear as if they were spoken aloud—at least to Jared, who had learned to duck when he saw a blow coming. He knew what he had to do.

"Sir?" Jared said. "Sir, I've come to say good-bye."

"What?" Alfred said, distracted. He'd been standing by the window in his study, mourning. That's what he'd been doing every day since Thomas had died. He worked very hard at it, not doing much else, except eating when his stomach hurt and sleeping when he couldn't stay up any longer. He didn't know what else to do. The reason for his life, the reason why he'd come all these miles to start anew, was gone.

"I'll be leaving, if I may, since there's nothing for me to do here now," Jared said.

Alfred nodded agreement. The boy spoke truth. There was nothing for anyone to do now.

"Thank you for everything," Jared said carefully. "My freedom, the clothing. But . . . could you write something to show I'm a freed man, sir? I'm going back to town; I'll need something to show so they can't put me back in bondage."

"You could stay on here," Alfred said, though he didn't know why.

"No, sir," Jared said, shaking his head. "You wouldn't like that. I'd only remind you of him."

Alfred nodded.

"He was a good boy, sir," Jared said suddenly, passionately, "one of the best I've ever known. He would have been a very good man."

31

"Aye, he would have," Alfred cried in a bitter, choked voice, "if I hadn't taken him to this damned place."

"No," Jared said in astonishment. "He loved it here, sir. He always said he did. He said he never had any fun in England. He said he was always sick and never was allowed to go out by himself there—not like here. We did so many things together, sir, things that mightn't seem much to other people but meant a great deal to us—fishing, pretending to hunt for treasure, gathering berries. Nothing much to some, perhaps, but it meant everything to us. I could never do anything but work before, and Thomas said he always was too sick to play. He loved it here. Here, he was free."

"Here," Alfred said savagely, wheeling around to glare at Jared, "he died."

"Yes, sir," Jared said quietly, "but here, he lived, too. Good-bye, sir." And he left without his papers and his recommendation.

Jared had one more place to stop before he took the long road back to town. When he saw Della and Nurse there, he was both glad and shamed, realizing he hadn't seen them since the day they'd buried Thomas. However painful it was, he knew he'd be a coward if he didn't say good-bye to the little girl who had accepted him so warmly.

Nurse nodded at Jared, and then, overcome with emotion, went to sit on a small stone bench. Della stayed still and sad by Jared's side, looking down at Thomas's grave.

"Hello, Jared," she said soberly in her husky little voice. She was wrapped in a cloak, and though a brisk breeze blew her ebony curls, it didn't bring life to her small, pale face. She was quiet and troubled. "Jared," she said after a moment, "do you think it's right that we leave him here? It's very cold, and Nurse said it may snow."

"He's not here," Jared said, swallowing hard. "I mean, what he lived in when he was with us is here. But Thomas isn't. He's somewhere better and warmer and happier. So it doesn't matter if it snows."

"Oh," Della said thoughtfully, "that's what Nurse says.

That's what the minister said. But I can't understand it. This is where we *put* him, Jared. He's still here."

"Oh Della," Jared said in a shaky voice. He owed her more than a good-bye. He ran a hand over his face, and then paused, struck by a sudden inspiration. He quickly knelt and dug his hands into the fresh-turned earth near Thomas's stone. When he found what he wanted, he turned and opened his hands to show it to Della. "What's this?" he asked her.

She frowned. His hands were blue with cold and covered with dirt. That was what she noticed first. Then she saw he held a knotted wizened root.

Her nose wrinkled. "An onion, but it went bad," she said.

"No," he said and smiled. "Clever little Della, usually so right. But this time you're wrong. It's a flower. No, I haven't gone mad. It's a daffodil. It's alive, though it looks dead. And though it's ugly now, it will be beautiful in April; I swear it. Now I'll put it back and cover it with dirt, and next spring, right where it is, there'll be a bright yellow flower. It sounds unbelievable, but it's so. You'll see," he said, dropping it back and patting the earth over it.

"What looks dead is not," he said carefully, kneeling by Della again. "I know, because I'm older and I've seen it happen again and again. It's not a miracle; it's only a thing that *is,* one that we have to learn about because we can only see here and now. If we could live long enough, I think we'd see what people become when they leave us here and go on to someplace better. Wise men say they do, and since you see that we can't trust our own eyes, we have to trust those wise men. I believe it."

She stared at him. "Then so do I," she said solemnly.

"Don't worry about Thomas," he said. "Promise me."

She nodded. "But oh, Jared," she said, her chin trembling, "I miss him so much!"

He caught her up and held her close. He'd made himself forget how to cry years before, but it had been an eternity since another human being had actually touched him, without hurting him or trying to. The feel of her small, warm body trembling in his arms almost undid him. "Oh, Della," he whispered, "so do I."

She stopped crying and pushed away from him so she could see his face. "But you have me," she said.

"And you have . . ." He paused, and then, gently, with infinite sadness, he only said, "Thank you, Della."

He rose and waited for the right words to come to him. She deserved more than a mere farewell. She'd already lost one brother. Before he could speak, he heard someone call his name.

"Jared," Alfred said gruffly, "a word, in private, if you please. I'll speak with you in a moment, puss," he promised Della. He walked a little way away from the grave with Jared. Jared noted he'd shaved at last and had put on new, neat clothes.

"I've been looking for you," Alfred said. "I'm glad you haven't left yet. I think it would be a mistake for you to go. There's work here for you—we still need you here."

"Ah," Jared said carefully, because life had taught him to be careful of what looked like miracles. "But Thomas— Thomas is gone, sir, and he was the one I worked for."

Jared saw the pain flash in his eyes before Alfred shook his head. "No, lad, you always worked for me, companioning my boy." He paused, cleared his throat, and went on more forcefully, "But there's still a lot of work to be done on a plantation, you know, and now that you're almost a man, it's time to do a man's work. I need help, lad . . . with accounts and in dealing with the workers and suchlike. I think you'd be the fellow for the job—you speak well and learn quickly, you see."

Jared's spirits rose. But he'd learned hard lessons in his short life and couldn't allow himself to believe he really still had a place here, in the best place he'd lived since he'd been cast from home. He knew there was still a very good reason why he couldn't stay. That reason lay not ten feet from where they stood.

"Yes, sir," Jared said slowly, "but . . ."

Alfred stopped walking and turned to face him. "Yes, I know," he said briskly. "You are not Thomas, are you?"

"No, sir," Jared said warily.

"But you remind me of him."

Jared sighed, his heart leaden again. "Yes, sir," he said.

"But I want you to remind me of him," Alfred said. "I need you to help me remember him, you see."

"Oh," Jared said, and thought a moment. He was a boy who knew the pain of bitter remembrance as well as he knew the infinite pleasure of warm memories in a cold world, and he understood Alfred very well. "Yes," he said, "I want to remember him, too."

"Then it's time to go home," Alfred said briskly, rubbing his hands together. "Frightfully cold out here today, don't you know."

Jared was so numb with relief, he didn't feel the cold. But he said, "Yes, sir," and they went to collect Della and Nurse. Together, they headed back down the hill to home.

Chapter

3

❧

1760

The house was high and wide and white and it gleamed in the bright Virginia sunlight. The trees beside it were still young, and the house seemed like a castle rising from the fields, heavy with crops, that surrounded it. The man who rode up the long, curved shell path must have thought so, for he galloped up to the front of the house and slid from his horse the moment he brought it to a stop.

"Ho, Alf!" he cried as he tossed the reins to the stable-boy who came running toward him. "I didn't forget the barley sugar," he said as he threw a small bag to the boy. "But mind Captain here doesn't nab it from you; he likes it as much as you do. Well, well," he commented, glancing at the stables as he took his carpetbag from the saddle. "We have visitors, do we?"

"Perkins," the boy said as he took the bag and the reins.

"Perkins?" the man said, raising one tawny eyebrow. "Well, well, well."

He was a tall man and wide-shouldered. When he swept

36

off his three-cornered hat, his thick, long honey-colored hair, drawn back and tied at the base of his strong neck, caught the sunlight and tamed it to dark gold. His sun-burnished skin showed he was a man used to the outdoors, and the breadth of his chest and narrowness of his hips showed he was no stranger to hard work. But though he wore clothes for travel, he was well dressed in a long coat worn over fawn breeches, and his soft, high boots were of fine leather. Nothing he wore, however, was as handsome as his lean face. Obviously as confident as he was affluent, he looked every inch the master of his realm, glad to be returning from some errand that had called him away. It was odd that his face grew a quirked smile when he saw the older man who came to the door, odd that he greeted the man by sketching a bow and saying, "Hello, master."

"Welcome home, lad," Alfred Kensington said as he clapped him on the shoulder.

"It's good to be home again," Jared admitted, looking around the hall as he strode into the house with Alfred. "It took forever this time because of the weather. Not here— but halfway 'cross the Atlantic, or so they said when I got to Williamsburg. Several ships were delayed. I wanted to get the best prices, and since nothing spurs competition like many bidders, I couldn't start the bidding until they all arrived. But it was worth it—I got top money. I think you'll be pleased. I've been gone only a month, but it feels like a year," he said as he stopped and stretched the weariness of the trip from his long body. "Must have been two," he murmured, stopping in midmotion and cocking his head as he heard noises coming from the parlor. "Is that *Stephen* Perkins our lady is entertaining?"

"None other," Alfred admitted.

"Lord! Did she fall on her head while I was gone?"

"He seems to be courting her."

"And she didn't fall down laughing? Correct me if I'm wrong, Alfred, but isn't he the one she used to call 'snake-eyed' because he didn't have any eyelashes? Or was that his brother?"

"The same; his brother was 'fish-faced,' but he's already married."

"But she's laughing, as though she's really amused," Jared said, his head tilted toward the lilting sound. "She *did* fall on her head," he said with mock horror.

"She's of an age to court," Alfred said with a little smile, "and it may be she's considering him. There's money there, you know."

"As if our little terror cares for that," Jared said, striding into the parlor and ending all the laughter.

The petite young woman who had been laughing caught her breath when she saw him. Her face lit with joy. "Jared!" she cried with surprised pleasure. She snatched up handfuls of her wide skirt to raise its hem so she could hurry across the room to him, leaving the young man she'd been talking to standing open-mouthed, stranded in midsentence.

Jared put his hands around her narrow waist and swung her high in the air, the way he had done every time he returned from a trip since she'd been a girl. But this time she didn't squeal with pleasure.

"Down! Please, Jared," she cried, wriggling in his hands. "Thank you," she said as her feet touched the floor again. She looked ruffled—both delighted and flushed with confusion as she tried to regain her composure. She also looked adorable to him, her ebony curls all in disarray, though her elaborate gown seemed untouched by his exuberant greeting.

He forgot his surprise at her embarrassment when he saw her new gown. It was tapestried silk, the color of old roses, with a flounced overskirt and a frivolous little pretence of a lace apron tied at her narrow waist. Tight sleeves had cascades of old lace falling from her elbows to her wrists. He frowned when he saw how much the low, square neckline showed of her high, white breasts. But it was the latest fashion, and a merchant to his bones now, he knew how much it cost. French, and made by a master at that. His eyebrows went up. She usually wore simple cotton, wool, or muslin.

"A party?" he asked with a quizzical smile, looking around. "But there's no one but Perkins here—hello, Stephen—am I invited, too? What's the occasion? Not—" He stared hard at young Perkins, who looked unhappy. "Not a matter of an announcement, is it?" *She might have consulted me before she consented to a fellow's proposal,* he thought, offended. Then he remembered what he could never forget, that he was, after all, nothing to her, really, though he considered himself a brother.

Della's white cheeks grew pink, but her blue eyes blazed. "No party, no occasion, certainly no announcement of *anything,* Jared. Can't a lady dress up once in a while?"

He smiled, remembering the last time he'd heard her say that. That time she'd come down from the attic in dress-up, Nurse's best gown trailing all around her, shedding various plumes and odd bits of jewelry as she'd tripped down the stairs—literally. She'd landed in a heap at the bottom and cried until he'd picked her up, dried her tears, and told her she looked wonderful. She'd been six then.

"Certainly," he said, with a tender smile. "And I'll wager it's much better now that you're dressed in your own clothes, isn't it?"

Her smile was strained; it almost seemed as though she were gritting her small, even teeth. "Thank you for the compliment, Jared," she said tersely. "Yes, I do think I look lovely in it, thank you."

"Of course you look fine in it. You know that. You don't need flowery compliments from me, do you?"

"No, of course not. But what kept you?" she asked, changing the subject. "You were gone so long we worried."

"I know, and I'm sorry about that. But I did very well for us. As I just told Alfred, shipping was held up by a storm and I had to wait to start the bidding."

"I'm sure you hated waiting around in Williamsburg, with nothing but taverns and shops, theaters, and friends to occupy you," she said, teasing, though her husky voice made the suggestion sound much less innocent.

"I'm happier to be home," he said quietly. "I'm always happy to be home; you know that, Della. I leave because I must. We're lucky enough to be able to get shipments here from upriver, but we have to go downriver to decide who to ship to."

"I know. I was only joking. . . . Well, then, tell us all about it," she said eagerly.

There was the sound of a throat being cleared, very hesitantly, but very loudly. "Ah, but we—you said we—I thought—we were supposed to go for a ride this afternoon, Mistress Della," said the gangly young man, who had watched everything, with a sudden burst of bravery, though he darted nervous glances at Jared as he did.

"But Jared's home, and he was gone for a month!" Della said, looking at him with dismay.

"And I'll be home when you get back," Jared said. "It was a long, dusty trip. I could use a few hours to wash and dress. Run along with Stephen and have a good time."

"Most kind. Thank you," the young man said, flustered. When he finished bowing, he offered Della his arm.

"Go on," Jared urged her. "Don't worry. I'll be here when you get back, and you're all dressed up for your ride anyway."

"And very nicely, too. That gown is lovely. We'll take the road down to the mill and back again, if that suits," Stephen chattered as he led Della from the house. She looked back once, like a lamb getting a last glance at a sunlit meadow before being led into the slaughterhouse.

"What's that all about? She's not seriously interested in him, is she?" Jared asked Alfred when they'd gone.

"I don't know. But she is twenty years old, after all," Alfred said too casually. "Time she was interested in someone, don't you think?"

"Twenty," Jared said, shaking his head. "Lord, it's hard to believe. But I'm seven and twenty myself now, and by the end of this summer, I'll be a year older. That's what I wanted to talk to you about, Alfred. It's what I've been thinking about all the way home."

"Longer than that, lad, I'll warrant. I think I know what you have to say from the tone of your voice. I've been waiting for it," Alfred said with a heavy sigh. "But come, first refresh yourself, and then we'll talk it out. We've a few hours, at least, until Della gets back. Stephen's been waiting to take her for a ride for three years now; I doubt he'll return her very soon."

"Poor Della, but she made her own bed," Jared said, laughing as he went up the stairs. "All I have to do is change clothes, so I'll be down soon. I must speak to you," he said, pausing to look back, his face suddenly still and serious, "and the sooner the better."

The sooner she got home, the better it would be, Della thought impatiently. She adjusted her bonnet, squirmed on the hard carriage seat, and sighed. She wished she knew the time, because although the sun hadn't moved much, she felt like they'd been driving for hours. Stephen didn't seem to notice. He was so busy talking about himself she believed she could have dragged the tall case clock from the hall with her if she'd wanted to count the hours, and he wouldn't have noticed. They sat high on his carriage and jounced down familiar country roads, the dust and the humidity making her glorious dress as limp as her spirits as he blathered on.

It was her own fault. She'd agreed to come, after all. She'd been ignoring her suitors for years, and now there were few eligible ones left. Not that it mattered. But she'd promised her father she'd give them a chance, remembering there was also a chance Jared might return in time to see her in all her glory. That was why she was enduring this afternoon with Stephen Perkins, of all people, who still didn't have any more brains than he did eyelashes. But at least he was a man—a man who goggled at her in her new gown and then stammered praise: "Awfully pretty, wonderfully fetching."

"I never guessed, I never dreamed, I never knew. Ah, Della, you look beyond beautiful—you look like the woman I've been seeking all my life. What a fool I've been not to see what was under my very nose," was what Jared should have said.

Della fidgeted again. "Goodness!" she said, interrupting Stephen's story. "Just look at the sun! We must have been out for hours. Don't you think it's time we turned back?"

Stephen consulted his watch. "No, I don't think so," he said. "Only an hour, actually. But I'll turn 'round if you like. Anxious to see your brother again, eh? Understandable, absolutely. Family loyalty is an excellent trait in a girl."

"He's not my brother," Della said quickly.

"Yes, yes, one knows, but one tends to forget," he said, "since everyone thinks of him as such."

Yes, everyone but me, Della thought sadly.

"Still, I imagine he is the perfect brother," Stephen said, and this time he wasn't just trying to please her. She knew how awed he was by Jared, as most young men in the area were.

"Yes," Della said with a sigh, because that was exactly the problem. He was the perfect brother. But she didn't want him as a brother.

It had always been Jared, from the moment she'd seen him standing there on the docks, blue with cold, shivering, ragged, bruised and beaten, and proud as an angel. He had saved her brother, and then went on to give dimension to her life. He'd been friend, counselor, protector, and teacher in turn. Knowing him had shaped her, and she knew she was shaped for him. Her feelings for Jared might have begun as infatuation or fascination, but they had grown into something different, and they'd deepened as she'd grown to know him as a man. That was why **he was** the only man she'd ever wanted. Not that she thou**ght he** was perfect; she knew him too well for that. He was still proud as the devil and still driven by that obsession to prove who he was. But that didn't bother her; he was human after all, and that humanity called to her.

That wasn't all that drew her to him. When he'd come into the room today, she'd looked up to see him suddenly there—tall, bronzed, radiating strength and that wonderful attraction that always made all others in the room fade away, and it took her breath away. He did that to her. He made her dizzy with desire. And why not? His shining hair was the color of honey in the comb, his eyes were changeable gray—sometimes bright as rain in sunlight, sometimes soft as autumn mist. He had a long jaw and a strong nose in a lean face; in truth, there were handsomer fellows. But none who glowed with masculine power the way he did. His very presence made her feel as though she'd taken a fever. And she wasn't the only one. Every girl she knew envied her—for all the wrong reasons. Being near him didn't bring him nearer to her.

She was twenty years old now, and her love for him was a longing nothing could ease. It made her ache, heart and body. When she'd been a girl, she'd often crawled into his arms for comfort. She wished she could take more than comfort there now, but she didn't dare touch him, because she knew she'd betray herself if she did. She couldn't risk that. The only thing worse than loving him without being loved in return would be loving him and having him know it, and his still not loving her in return. He'd feel sorry for her, or be uncomfortable with her, and their easy intimacy would be lost. Nothing could be worse than that.

Other men had offered more. And why not? She came from good family and her father had money. She could sew and cook and manage a household, as well as dance, read, and write in a fine hand. She admitted she might be a trifle spoiled and used to getting her way—but that would be good for him, because her way would always be his. Other men found her alluring. She had clear skin and a small, straight nose—she took careful inventory and tried to be fair about it—and blue eyes, and if her hair wasn't as beautiful as Jared's, she thought—hers being as midnight black as his was sunlit—at least she had plenty of it and it curled. She had a small waist and a slender but curved body with high, pert breasts, and if she craned her neck enough, her looking glass showed that her rear was in similar shape . . .

. . . and she could have been a dumpling or a beanpole for all it mattered. All she could see was tender affection in his eyes when he looked at her.

What did it take? she wondered morosely. She'd danced out of the house on the arm of that foolish young English soldier the week before Jared left, tittering like a mad thing, because giggles and admiration seemed to be what men in uniform liked best in a woman. Jared had been amused. Lieutenant Evers had been wonderfully pleased. He'd tried to steal a kiss and then apologized and asked her to walk with him again, so he could try to steal another. She decided not to bother. She had kissed some young men. But there was a wrongness to it that had nothing to do with morals. And if she closed her eyes and thought of Jared, it only made it worse.

Jared loved her as a sister, and she had to accept that it might never be more, even if he did one day— miraculously—look up and see her as a woman—before he found another woman. Because she knew instinctively that once Jared gave his heart, it would be given completely, exclusively, and forever. Just the way she'd given hers to him.

So far he hadn't found that woman. Della suspected it was because he was so busy making his fortune. But Jared was getting to a susceptible age. He had no lady love, but she knew he had loved women. Most men did, when they went to town. Ruby Fairchild, whose uncle owned an inn in town, told her years ago that Jared visited late at night and had gotten into the habit of taking one particular tavern wench to her room above the taproom after hours. Well, so be it. Men were men, Della had supposed, and though she'd been hurt, the pain had faded because she'd been just a girl. But now some nights she lay abed, hungering and despairing because she knew that if Jared lay in his bed feeling that way too, he'd go to a stranger in town rather than to her. He didn't realize she was a woman, too—or he could never think of her that way.

Maybe there was nothing she could do except stay by his side as his loving friend and hope someday he'd look down and see her there and want more. She lived for that day. She had time, if nothing else, on her side.

"Home again!" Stephen announced as he pulled the horses up in her drive.

"Wonderful!" she sang and leapt to her feet. "I mean, it was a wonderful drive, Stephen, the carriage being so well sprung and . . ." She searched for some other nice thing to say because she was always fair. He couldn't help it if he was not only plain and dull but unknowingly competing with the best man in the world. ". . . and the horses so well trained," she said. "Thank you for asking me."

"We can go again, any time. Tomorrow, then?" he asked eagerly.

There was such a thing as being too nice, she thought as he helped her down from the high seat. "Ah, I can't. But thank you. Good-bye," she said quickly, and bobbed a little curtsy before she turned and hurried into the house.

She held up her skirts and raced into the parlor, only stopping when she saw the two men there, talking quietly together. What stopped her heart was their expressions. They were stilled and sober. Usually, when Jared came home from doing business, they were jolly, sharing laughter as well as a drink to good fortune together.

"Ah, Della," her father said heavily. "Did you have a good time? Young Perkins gone already? Just as well. We've something to tell you. Come in, come in."

She came into the room slowly, her steps weighted by dread, her mind busy. What awful thing could they have to tell her? She tried to prepare herself. She took in a deep breath and steadied herself. The only two people that mattered to her in the world were here before her, safe and sound. So then, whatever else they'd have to say might be bad, but whether it was that they'd lost their fortune or even the roof over their heads, it wouldn't matter. She'd still have the only things that mattered. She let out her breath in relief. She was ready for whatever they had to tell her.

"Jared here," Alfred said, "has decided to return to England."

Della couldn't hear what else they had to say. Not above the sudden roaring sound in her ears. Nor could she see their expressions, because, for some reason, everything was growing black.

"It was sitting in the sun all that time," she insisted, as they hovered over the couch where Jared had laid her down. "I ought to have worn a bigger bonnet, that's all. I'm much better now. Do stop fanning me, Nurse; I'll catch cold if you don't, and then you'll be sorry." She saw the corners of Jared's mouth kick up, and, relieved, she struggled to sit up. When she had, she went on petulantly, "I didn't keel over, I—just faltered. I'm fine now. No need for those salts, either. But a cup of tea would be wonderful, just wonderful."

Nurse hurried from the room, and Della smiled. "Sometimes her remedies are worse than my complaints. Oh, don't look like that, Jared. I mean it—I'm fine. But are you? *England?* You're going back to England? Why?"

She was proud of the way she handled herself, except for that last word, which sounded like a wail to her.

"It's time," he said, as he paced the room as though it were already too small for him, as though he'd outgrown their house since he'd left it. "I thought about it all the way home. Maybe it was meeting an English captain who reminded me of the one on the ship I took on my voyage here. Maybe it was just because it's almost my birthday and it started me thinking about time. But I suddenly realized that if I don't go now, I might never go—and I must. Della," he said, with a bright glance at her, "you defended me when I was a boy and I insisted I was really an earl. Lately, I think you and Alfred have tried to forget it altogether, as though it were some kind of childhood illness I'd outgrown or some blemish that would go away if you ignored it. You did it so well you almost made me forget. But I can't. Nor should I."

He took another turn around the room. "I stopped talking about it long ago, but that doesn't change it," he murmured. "I never stopped thinking about it. I *am* the earl of Alveston. I *was* taken from my home and sold into bondage. At first, the only thing that kept me alive was anger and my determination to make someone believe me. When I realized no one would, I worked to live, so that someday I could go back and prove it for myself—and take vengeance. Then I met you."

He stopped, and looked from Alfred to Della. He smiled. "I was very lucky. Don't think I don't know that. You gave me much more to live for. But even then, well fed and well cared for, I'd lay awake at night dreaming the same dream. It was still there—but changed. I didn't dream of revenge so much as I did of proving that I never lied to you."

"I've come to believe you, lad," Alfred said. "You know that. It's just that there's no point in belaboring a dead issue. It's done, and it was well done, damn their eyes. You know what I found out all those years ago: yes, there were a pair of brothers, but both died in some accident. Or so they said, and so no one could prove differently—not without papers, and from across an ocean. It's hard to find out more. There was considerable confusion surrounding the tragedy, and the family drew together around it. The new earl keeps to himself. I doubt it's your uncle, though, because they say the title passed to a younger man."

"Then he's my cousin," Jared muttered.

"Whoever he is, that's all I could discover," Alfred said, raising his hands in a gesture of despair. "It's a reclusive family with enough power to hide from vulgar inquiries, and they're far from London, at that. You know it; you've tried yourself. So what do you hope to gain by going back now?"

"The truth," Jared said in a tight voice. "An admission of the truth."

"You have no proof," Della cried, "no way of making them admit it—unless you try to force them, and then what's the point? You'll go to prison. You'll lose everything you've worked for. We'll lose you!" She paused, unable to go on without crying.

"Aye, she's right," Alfred muttered. "You've become the son I lost, lad. Don't—I'd ask that you don't make me grieve for another. And for such a senseless reason."

"Loss is always senseless," Jared said, "but I don't intend to die. And I'm not such a fool as to do them any injury that will harm me."

"Well, but who can say who'll win a duel?" Della cried. "You're very good with sword and pistol, but maybe they'll cheat."

"Dear ferocious Della," Jared said, smiling, "I'm not going to challenge anyone to a duel. Your father's made me a rich man, and his training made me a clever one, too, I hope. There are other ways to destroy an enemy than with swords or pistols. Pounds and shillings will do the trick very nicely, too."

Alfred looked up with hope. "Aye," he said with more confidence, "that's so. And you're the lad to do it. But I don't know, my boy. If you can't get the title or the confession, you'd settle for revenge? That's not good business. It's costly, and in the end, you'll have nothing to show for your investment of time and money. Revenge is a poor reward: it has a bitter taste, lad."

"Does it?" Jared said, musing. "I wonder. If you could destroy that which took Thomas from us, would you call that a bitter victory? I didn't think so. I don't take his memory lightly," he said softly, placing a hand on Alfred's shoulder as the older man lowered his head. "I mention it because I once lost a brother, too. I can't do anything to bring back Thomas, but I can do something for my brother's memory. And mine. What I want isn't revenge—really. Call it justice."

"I call it stupid!" Della raged. "You'll only get into trouble. You could lose all your money and your life. Stay here. We believe you—why care about the rest of the world?"

"You've always believed me, little Della. And I won't lose my money; I'm too shrewd for that. And I'll come home when I'm done. But I will have it done. The rest of the world can go hang, but justice must be done."

And knowing Jared as they did, Alfred and Della fell silent. There was no sense arguing. He was always as good as his word, and his plan was already as good as done.

The ship was at anchor, but the wind was rising, and everyone on the dock knew it was almost time to go.

"You have all your autumn clothing?" Della asked again anxiously. "England will be very chilly by the time you get there."

"Yes, yes, and I'll write often, eat regularly, and wash, too. Don't fret," Jared said, laughing.

But she did fret, because she just realized she sounded exactly like Nurse—or the way Nurse might have sounded if she could stop sniffling and dabbing at her eyes long enough to speak.

The wind ruffled Jared's bright hair as he stood before them with his hat in his hand. Della knew his mind was already far away across the sea he would soon cross. Even as he said good-bye to them, he was already gone from them. But when the call came to board, he turned and took her hand in his.

"Don't worry about me, Della," he said softly, his clear eyes searching hers. "I'm a very big man now. Rich and well connected, too, thanks to your father. I'll do what I have to, and then I'll return." He saw her surprise and smiled. "No, I don't really think I'll ever get back what I lost. But I have to let them know that I survived, and that I know what they did. They'll never draw an easy breath again. Let me at least see justice done, and I promise I'll come back to you. My life is here."

As her heart soared, he sank it again by adding, "I owe that much to your father and you."

He hugged her hard and kissed her cheek. Then, without a word, he clasped Alfred's hand and gave an unsteady laugh before he shrugged, hauled Alfred close, and hugged him hard, too. He embraced Nurse, gave them all another quick smile, and then he was gone up the gangplank.

"He'll do—" Alfred told Della in a thick voice, as he tried to clear his throat. "You'll see, he'll do fine."

"I know he will," she said sadly. Would she?

Della looked up at the deck of the tall-masted ship, hoping to catch a last glance of Jared as he made his way through the sailors and other boarding passengers. She thought she saw a glimpse of his bright hair, but it was someone else. She craned her neck, searching for him. It reminded her of a Greek myth she had once read. A nymph fell hopelessly in love with Apollo, the sun god, and suffered because he didn't return her love. And so out of pity, she was turned into a sunflower, so she could at least watch Apollo every day. That was supposedly why sunflowers always turn their heads to follow the sun as it crosses the sky. She'd seen it happen herself, even when the sun was covered by clouds. But what happened when the sun left the sky?

He said he'd be back. But if he didn't come home? How long should she wait? Della drew a deep breath and wrapped her arms around herself to try to hold herself together. A woman's place was in the home, and an unmarried one's place, in the bosom of her family. But he was her family, as well as her life. She was Della Kensington, after all. If he didn't come back, she would follow him.

But he'd come back, she told herself. Because he said he would.

Chapter 4

Jared had crossed this ocean once before, but it might have been in another life. The closer he got to England, the more he wondered which of his lives was real.

He lay in his cabin and knew he was at sea because he felt the dreamy roll and pitch of his comfortable bed as he seemed to float with it. As a boy, he'd lain in a huddle at the bottom of the ship, and the only way he'd known he was on the sea was by the stench of the bilge, the sway of the darkness as it lurched around him. It had taken him a while to understand what the strange and terrible slurping sounds he kept hearing were. When he realized it was the sea outside, it was even worse. It had seemed like the sea was smacking its lips, already tasting the boy who was kept from it only by the hard floor he huddled on. The other bond-servants, each in their own private misery, mostly ignored him. He'd lived alone for the first time in his life, and that was harder than the stale bread they fed him and more bitter even than the salt of his tears.

He hadn't known where he was going and couldn't believe they'd actually taken him from his home. He'd been very young, he thought now. But that was what had kept him going. That, and the determination to get back home again. It was what still kept him going.

Now he was grown and had strength and money, position and experience. And love—he mustn't forget that, he reminded himself, because Alfred and Della had become the family he had lost. *No,* he thought, rising from his bed in agitation, *nothing had ever replaced them.* He paced the cabin as he'd done every night since he'd set sail, as though by walking he could get to England faster. But it was no use—his real family wouldn't be there when he returned.

His father had been the tallest man in the world; wide-shouldered and with a hearty laugh, he'd smelled of tobacco and horses, and nothing had ever smelled so delicious, except for the rose scent of his mother. The memory of that scent had come to him in the ship in the darkness in that terrible time, and it had sustained him. There had been a grand house and stables—he remembered the stables so well, he knew he must have spent a lot of time there. He remembered a library and great double stairs in the center of the house that Nurse was always cautioning him and his brother not to race up or down. And there were the kitchens, full of noise and steam and scented with wonderful things that Cook always let them taste, and the stream and the pond, and the geese, and that monkey puzzle tree in the front that even small boys could try to climb, if no one caught them at it. And the laughter, he'd always remembered the laughter. That memory too had kept him going.

But then Father had died, and after Mother died of the same sickness, the darkness started to fall. Then uncles and aunts had come to console the orphaned children. They looked so nearly like his parents that it made his heart ache, but they were nothing like Mother and Father at all. He had kept trying to find a bond, in hopes he'd find what he had lost. He had been seven then, his brother Justin, six. How could they guess one of the uncles would kill one of his brother's sons and try to kill the other?

There were many uncles, but was it Uncle George or Uncle Roland? Jared wondered now, as he had for so many years. He discounted Uncles John, Lawrence, and Martin; they were Mother's brothers and would inherit nothing from the crime. But his father's brothers . . . Uncle George could become the earl. If he never married, then Uncle Roland could inherit the title, the estate, and all the honors. Either man could profit—if their elder brother's children were to disappear—as they conveniently did.

Whoever had inherited had obviously died soon after, so Jared supposed there was such a thing as divine retribution. He regretted it. If the man had lived, Jared could have had his revenge, whatever the cost. But how innocent was the heir of this man, his son who now lived Jared's lost life? No inquiries had turned up more. The earl was a reclusive man. It was as though he was still hiding something—guilt or shame? Jared vowed that he'd feel much more than that after he met him—just as he'd vowed on this same ocean, a lifetime ago. But that was all he could do.

It seemed a paltry revenge for such a crime. But these were modern times; it was 1760, after all. A man couldn't reclaim his title with his sword anymore. He thought he might win a duel, but even if he did, he'd probably only lose his own life for killing a nobleman. He was rich and well connected now, but still only a commoner and a foreigner. He wanted revenge, not suicide. But he could cause scandal.

Still, that was all he could do, and Jared knew it. He had no papers; the only proof of his claim was written on his face and in his blood. He could be the image of his father and it wouldn't matter; there were such things as bastards. England's nobility was littered with them: lost princes and missing heirs, bitter men, seething with jealousy, men who would lie about their heritage if their faces would allow it.

No, his uncle had done his work too well. The boy he had been had been carried off in the night, and though he had lived, his claim to his title died that night—along with his brother. Jared muttered a curse as he stalked the cabin, the loss still fresh after all these years. It all was.

He still woke in the night, suffocating, thrashing, and kicking off his covers, trying to get out of the sack they'd put him in. He still woke sometimes in empty triumph to find himself free and swimming up to the light—years too late. In feverish nightmares, he still swam against the current, trying to save his brother. He still saw Justin's face, so like his own, clear blue eyes fixed on his—waiting to be saved. And then he woke on the banks of dawn, lost and empty, seeing the emptiness where Justin had been before he'd been swept away. All the beatings Jared had endured from all his various masters were nothing to that pain. It never faded. It was as though he had a hole in the center of his soul.

To regain his title had been a boy's dream of glory, and it had kept him alive during the worst years of his life. Now that he was a man, he knew he could never hope to regain his title—any more than he could hope to restore his brother. But he'd have his revenge, somehow.

Then, he thought wearily, when it was done, he supposed he'd return to his second home. To Alfred. And dear little Della, who had shown him unconditional love when he'd lost all hope. But now, halfway between yesterdays, it seemed to Jared that his lost brother's face was as clear to him as Della's, and just as unreal: two beloved children lost in the stream of time. As he himself was. He was between two lives, with nothing resolved.

He had to settle a score before he could go on. And so he paced the miles away, walking back to England, planning and plotting. Only now, he wasn't dreaming.

* * *

He was unprepared, and that startled him. He didn't like not being in control. But as Jared stood on the deck and looked out at London, he realized for the first time exactly how hard a job lay ahead of him. A boy had left and a man had returned. He knew that. But he had not expected the world he now faced. This was a country that had ruled the known world for hundreds of years. He had forgotten the sheer size of its capital.

He'd never really known this city. He'd lived in the countryside and had been brought to London and the docks by night all those years ago. Jared remembered only darkness shattered by flaring torches. He remembered the stink of brine, rough hands pushing him aboard the ship that would carry him into bondage, and that was all. Now he stood and stared at the land he'd been exiled from. And was amazed.

The port was clogged with ships of every stripe and size. There were mighty East Indiamen, bulging with goods from every exotic port of call, loading, unloading, or waiting in their slips for customs men. Coastal barks and brigs, lowly herring buses, coal carriers, and fishing boats were docked there, too. And of course, men-of-war, from frigates to sloops—there was a war on, after all. But beyond that—! From the high deck, Jared could see London itself. He stared. The sheer number of houses, crammed together, the number of streets, the number of people in them! He could see bridges and towers, the names of which were written in his history books, rising above the tumult like titans. The Colonies were growing, but the tallest things in them were still the trees.

Jared scowled. He'd sworn never to be surprised by anything again. And certainly never to be afraid again. So he planted his feet apart and prepared himself for landing by trying to calm his heart and watching carefully before setting a boot on English soil again.

"Come in, come in, sir. I dare say you are exhausted," the elderly man said as he showed Jared to a chair in his office. "Three weeks to cross the sea—with a fair wind in your sails. And I understand you arrived only yesterday? Would you like a cup of coffee? Or tea? Ah, coffee, is it? Midgins, bring Mr. Blessingham a cup of coffee," he told his clerk when Jared nodded.

"The name is Bellington," Jared said quietly, but with such emphasis that the old man stopped and gave him a sharp look of appraisal.

"Bellington,—ah!" the old man said, tasting the word and staring at Jared.

He knew the name, of course. He was a lawyer, and it was his business to know all the names of all the nobility, whether they were in London or not. An old family, dating from the dawn of nobility, with a huge estate. Reclusive, but still . . . He tried to fit the name to his visitor. Oddly, it suited, though the man was clearly a colonial. His visitor was a tall, muscular young man, golden-haired, broad-shouldered, and lean as a Viking invader, and with such a look of pride and danger on his high-nosed, handsome face. But there was something behind the pride, and the light eyes held keen intelligence as well as warning. Well dressed by provincial standards, the lawyer thought, and well heeled by the look of him, too. And yes, he seemed well spoken and well bred, and there was the look of nobility in his fine bones. But *Bellington?*

"I see," the lawyer said as Jared accepted his cup of coffee, and the clerk bowed out of the room.

"I doubt you do," Jared said dryly. "But it doesn't matter, now. It might, later on, however. That's why I'm here. You came well recommended to me, and so I've letters to leave in your care. If you don't hear from me in three months' time—How long does it take to get to Hawkstone Hall?" he asked suddenly.

"Hawkstone Hall, up north, near the abbey? Ah, well, a week by mail coach; more by private coach, but it's a far more comfortable journey. The roads are deplorable—"

"On horseback," Jared said, cutting him off.

"Ah, well then, less than a week, if you change horses often."

"Three months, then, from today," Jared said decisively. "If you don't hear from me by then, open the first letter and contact the men and the newspapers I've listed there and make the contents of the second letter known to them. And," he said, reaching into his pocket, "if I don't return to you by then, send this letter to the Virginia colony, as well." He tossed gold coins onto the man's desk.

The old man fingered the sealed letters and eyed the money. "And for this," he asked quietly, "you will pay me such a high fee?"

"It's an important commission," Jared said as quietly, "because if I don't return, you can safely bet I can't return to anyplace else on earth, either. Well, sir? Can you do it?"

"Of course, of course," the old man said thoughtfully as he weighed the letters in his hand. Useless to ask the young man why or wherefore; his ice-gray eyes forbade it.

"Oh," Jared said, as he rose from his chair, "and if you think about opening either letter before time, I'd think again. If I don't return, it doesn't matter, but if I do . . ." He shrugged one shoulder and let the threat go unspoken, since his face made it clear enough. "Not that I think you might not keep your end of the bargain, but I think it's only fair to mention that I've left similar letters with another well-connected man here in London, as well as with a lawyer in the Virginia colony."

The old man gave a cough of a laugh. "You mistrust me, sir?"

Jared didn't smile in return. "No," he said seriously, "I'm just being prudent. As you are a man of law, I'm sure you see my point."

"I see and admire it," the old man said bluntly. He reassessed the younger man. Whatever the lad did, it would be done with forethought and intelligence. But it was probably dangerous and might be illegal. He couldn't stop it, didn't know if he should, and would be well paid to do his bit in any case. "Done then, sir," he finally said. "I hope to see you again—and if I don't, be assured I will carry out your wishes."

Jared bowed and left. He was satisfied. If all else failed, he believed the old man would carry out his wishes.

"For this fee," the jovial man said, laughing, "I will carry these letters in my teeth for you, sir!" When he finished chortling, he wiped his eyes and added, "And you may say your name is *Hanover,* for all I care, my dear sir. But you may trust me; there's no jest in that. I'm a man of my word. Now, what else can I do for you?"

Jared relaxed. "I'd like the names of some men here in town who are good at making inquiries of a personal nature—men who are as good at keeping their word as you are and who are able to keep their mouths closed about it as well."

The jovial man grew serious. "I don't wish to know the nature of your business, sir, and that's a fact. But I am a man of the world, and London is my world. I know of such men. The one I recommend would sooner kiss the hangman than tell a tale. In his line of work, you understand, telling tales leads to the hangman. Here," he said as he scrawled something on a piece of paper. "His name, and directions. But I'd ask you to forget who recommended him, if you would be so kind."

"What were you saying?" Jared asked, as he pocketed the piece of paper.

"I dunno what else I kin do, sir," the man said, shifting in his seat in the corner of the darkened tavern. "They be a close-mouthed lot up there. Protect their young earl like the eyes in their 'eads, they do. 'E's that favorite with them. They don't trust strangers 'cause I 'ear they lost a young'n afore him, years past. Still, I seen 'im right enough. 'E's big, good looking, too, much like yerself, now I think on it. 'E ain't much for the London life, though 'e's come here, time to time. What else?" He scratched his chin and Jared could hear the rasping sound of his whiskers as he did. "Well, 'tis said the young earl of Alveston be a bruisin' rider, a man for sport, good to his servants, a good landlord, aye, a fair man, when all's said."

A man I would like, Jared thought bitterly. *And why not? He's my cousin. But still, he should know he's a usurper and sits on a throne made of skulls.*

"Not married?" Jared asked.

"Nah, though the ladies be after 'im somethin' fierce. 'Andsome as 'e can be, that lad."

No dependents, and so he'll give up the title with a bow and a smile, Jared thought with a mirthless grin.

"How old is he?"

"Yer age or so, I'd guess. I di'n't look at no church records."

And so how will he know me? Jared thought with a heavy sigh. *I don't know who he is. God knows how many sons my uncles had. Twenty years have passed. . . .*

"Well done," Jared said, passing the man a purse. "Thank you."

This news was the same as the other informants had reported. The man had taken Jared's title and his brother Justin's name. He was said to be charming and handsome and very well liked. A man who liked the countryside more than the city, who liked a good jest and a fair lady, a fellow, Jared thought again, he could like—if the man hadn't stolen his birthright, if the man weren't the son of a thief and murderer and so, however innocently, a party to murder and kidnapping.

There was only one thing left to do. But strangely, Jared was loathe to do it. He sat in the dim tavern and knew what he should do now—what he'd planned to do for years. Now that the time was come, he didn't feel ready. It wasn't because of the danger, although there'd be some— no man with any spine would take such an accusation passively—and there'd be more danger if the false earl himself was guilty. That didn't bother Jared; the only thing he'd feared in years was that he wouldn't survive to this day to make this accusation. But now he found himself curiously unwilling to seek his revenge.

He was beginning to realize that once it was done, it would all be over—everything he'd lived for the last twenty years. And revenge wouldn't bring back his brother or his childhood.

He shook his head to clear it. *Strong ale,* he thought. He drained his tankard so he could order another and forget what he had to do. He'd tried in many ways to forget in the past week as he'd waited for information to come rolling in. He'd walked the streets of London like any visitor from the Colonies, as though he had nothing more than entertainment on his mind. The city had fascinated him in spite of his dire mission. Why not? This was London town, and what a town it was!

He'd visited cathedrals and buildings of state, seen the tower and the menagerie, walked the city from Fleet Prison to the palace. He hadn't stopped to gawk at the hangings at Tyburn Hill the way so many Londoners did, because he found death no more thrilling in England than it was at home, although there was so much more of it here. Nor did he have the heart to go to the theaters or pleasure gardens, or cockfights or bear baitings, or any of London's many gambling houses. He hadn't come here to amuse himself. The thought of making money and gaining power was still uppermost in his mind, and he found that, in London, moneymaking was amusement enough.

His merchant's instincts took him to the markets, from Covent Garden to Leadenhall to Billingsgate, Haymarket, and Whitechapel, to marvel at the wild variety of goods offered there. He found a different world of commerce on every street in London, too. Craftsmen and their apprentices lived and worked in their own districts, making each one a unique world of weavers or watchmakers, tailors, coach builders, or any of dozens of different occupations.

And everywhere, London's army of street vendors pushed their barrows and sang or shouted about their wares—everything from silks to smelts, and often sold side by side. He woke in the morning to shrill songs about milk and coal, and shaved to the tune of "Scissors sharpened here!" or "Oysters, alive, alive, oh!" He'd felt like a man of the world before he'd come here; now he felt like a wilderness savage.

He stayed at a comfortable inn and ate in coffeehouses where men of business traded goods from the Colonies, so he could keep up with the dealings of Lloyds and the East India and Hudson Bay companies. He turned a few pretty pennies for Alfred as he waited, and bought bolts of beautiful silks for Della. He met his informants at taverns in parts of town where anything could be bought or sold. Watching that process was amusing, too.

In fact, he enjoyed himself so much, he felt guilty about it. But the truth was that he felt even guiltier thinking about how Della would enjoy it. Just imagining her reactions made him smile. He wished he could have her there, chirping merrily at his side. He found himself lingering in the street watching a Punch and Judy show so he could tell her about it; just yesterday he'd caught himself pausing in a cathedral, trying to put the glory of a stained-glass window into words for a letter to her. She loved to go to town; she was thrilled when she got a chance to go to Williamsburg. But as he wrote her, one could put a dozen Williamsburgs down in London and its inhabitants might not notice. He decided that one day, if he could, he'd show her London—but not everything in it.

He would have gone into the mouth of hell itself to get the information he needed, and sometimes he thought that he had. He was glad of his size and the sword at his side when his wanderings took him to places where he saw human degradation such as he'd never seen in Virginia, even when he'd been a bond-boy. At least then he was the only one suffering. There were poor people in the New World, desperately poor ones who had arrived there with only their two hands and the skin on their backs. But they'd come for work, and most had found it. They were so proud of their successes that they made themselves and their homes advertisements for their achievements. Not here.

Here, there were thousands who had given up. Whole districts were filled with such poverty and misery that for the first time he began to understand why free men might sell themselves into servitude in a strange land. He, more than most, knew the value of owning his own skin. But if he had to live in London's rookeries? Then, he thought, he too might risk his life with strangers for a chance of escaping the certain death that freedom in such slums would bring. It made him see how lucky he'd been, which only made him remember how he'd been unlucky, too.

He was alone again, he realized, for the first time in years, with only his mission to keep him company. He felt as out of place here as he did in his adopted land, even though he had Alfred and Della there. But what had he expected?

He passed his hand over his eyes. The ale was too strong, he thought, as he put up his hand to call for another.

"Is there anythin' else y' be needin', kind sir?" the soft voice asked. "We'll be closin' soon, but I got all night."

Candles provided unreliable light, but he didn't need light to know what she was offering; it was in her voice, even if he couldn't make out the expression in her eyes. Her sort thronged the nighttime streets; he'd turned down dozens of better-looking wenches since he'd got to London. A furtive fellow had stopped him in the street this very night and handed him a printed sheet. It was a listing of London whores, their addresses, and a brief description of their looks and talents. He'd laughed and dropped the paper in the gutter where it belonged. He didn't like to go to strangers . . . but he was in a strange place, he reasoned—as best he could after three orders of the landlord's finest ale—and he was definitely alone again.

More completely alone than he'd been in years. He stared at the table, not really seeing it. He didn't want to remember those years, but couldn't stop himself. The memories were worse here than in Virginia because his ghosts lived *here*. He was haunted tonight.

The woman waited patiently for his answer. She smelled of ale and cooking smoke, peat and tobacco, like the rest of the inn. But he thought he also caught the scent of faint flowers.

She had dark hair and pale skin, and smiled to show she had all her teeth. She was plain but soft-spoken, and her simple gown showed she was buxom—not a beauty, but a comfortable-looking woman.

He was no stranger to women. But oddly, he felt guilty as he rose and pulled out a chair for her. For no reason, he told himself. He had made no promises to any other woman; it was only that he'd been thinking of home, he told himself, of Della. He frowned. He refused to even think about Della when he was thinking of what he might do with this woman.

But this woman was, after all, only offering her company now. And he found there was nothing on earth he wanted more than company tonight. He didn't want to think about tomorrow, especially since he wondered if he'd have many more days after it. He was about to fulfill a life's dream, but in so doing, he knew he was risking his life. No man wanted to be accused of being party to kidnapping and murder, and this was a powerful nobleman he was about to confront. He didn't doubt that a man who had once killed for a title would try it again, if pushed too far. And Jared intended to push. He wasn't afraid, but he wasn't fool enough to deny there might be consequences to his actions. That was another thing he decided not to think about tonight. He spoke to the woman instead.

They talked little, in the way of such things. She cast down her eyes when she saw how he was evaluating her, as though she didn't know he was, as though they both didn't know it wasn't conversation she was offering. He needed to find her attractive and so he did. But there was something he needed more than beauty or physical satisfaction tonight, and she was offering it. When she put one warm hand over his on the table, he shivered at her touch and realized it didn't matter how attractive she was. She seemed gentle. It was enough.

She had a room nearby, of course. He hesitated, thinking of possible traps and ploys, men working with her, waiting in the alley outside.

"Ask the landlord, if y' like," she said softly, standing so close to him he could smelled the scent of her warm skin, feel the curve of her hip against his. "I'm honest and clean. Aye, and lonely."

That last was the word that decided him. Yes, that he understood. He would take the risk; his need was overwhelming.

"Don't you want to take off your shirt?" she whispered when they got to her small room, after he removed his long coat, turned to her, and slid her gown down from her shoulders. "No," he said, as he always did with such women, taking her two hands in his. "No, and please don't touch my back."

She paused, then shrugged. Men had asked much stranger things of her. She smiled with real pleasure when she ran her hands up his chest, because his body was as good as his face, his chest lightly furred, his skin smooth and clean, the muscles beneath her hands rock hard. It seemed he held his breath.

Then he let it out in a long sigh. *This* was what he'd come for, something even better than the miracle of female contours that his body was responding to, something his heart needed far more. His body could do without; his soul could not—not tonight.

It was the touching, of course, the feeling of another's hands soft upon him, a touch that didn't bring pain, a touch that had a semblance of care in it. He needed that— and to hold another person close. That was what he needed more than the brief moment of physical release she offered. Because, he thought with muttered approval as she stroked him, this closeness, this wonderful caressing, was such a rarity, such a necessity. It was what he'd been deprived of all those years when he hadn't been considered fit for touching, only beating, when he'd had nothing but his sorrow to comfort him as he'd lain alone, aching in the dark. A simple caress was what he'd yearned for then. It was what a man might risk everything for, even if he had to pay for it. It was what he needed tonight, his last night in London—perhaps one of his last on earth.

He was grateful to her. And so for the first time in a long time, the woman he held forgot he'd paid a price for her attentions. But he could do no less for any woman who would actually touch him, a man who was less than a man because he'd been a slave. They sank to her bed together and made a kind of love, though they both knew it was something far less.

He left her sleeping and hurried down her stairs to the teeming London streets. He had to go find a stranger now and accuse him of being a liar and a cheat and tell him that he intended to do everything in his power to see that he lost his home, his good name, and his fortune.

Jared considered how he'd spent his night. It might have been the last thing he'd ever do in London, but all in all, he reckoned it wasn't such a bad thing. At least there was a mimicry of love in it. What he had to do now had to do only with hate.

Chapter

5

❧

He came riding in through a side path, but even so, it wasn't long before he was challenged. There were too many workers on the grounds for him to go unnoticed for very long.

"Yer pardon, sir," the old man said, sweeping off his cap just in case the intruder was of the quality, "but 'tis private land yer on now."

"Hawkstone Hall. Yes, I know," Jared answered, though he never took his eyes from the great house in the distance.

The old man stood, considering. The intruder didn't wear a proper wig beneath his tricorner hat, but his clothing spoke of money, and his voice, though strangely accented, spoke of breeding. He was young and well proportioned and rode a fine horse. Still, he was a stranger . . . and then the young stranger inclined his head and looked the old man straight in the eye.

"Ah! A relative of the earl's, is it, then?" the old man said in sudden comprehension.

A twisted half-smile appeared on the intruder's lips. "Yes," he said softly. "Exactly right, a relative."

"Begging pardon, sir," the old man said, touching his forehead, bowing, and standing aside so the fellow could ride through. He watched the young man ride on, but frowned, puzzled, when he saw him halt his horse halfway to the hall. The young fellow sat still as one of the statues in the formal gardens, looking at Hawkstone Hall as though there was nothing else in the world to see. *But after all, there are few finer sights in the kingdom,* the old man thought before he turned and went on his own way. He looked back once, to see the young man still sitting there, staring as though time itself was standing still as his horse and he. *But then, young men have all the time in the world,* the old man thought on a sigh as he went about his own errands again.

Jared had thought it would be smaller, because children think all things are bigger than they really are, and he remembered being a child here. But it was still enormous. He had thought it wouldn't hurt so much, either, but the sight of his lost home sliced through him more keenly than any lash. As he sat his horse and stared, he saw at once everything that for years, he'd glimpsed only in dreams. He felt tears come to his eyes and was astonished, because he'd banished the tears long ago, after he himself had been banished.

Mine, damn it, he thought savagely, sitting upright in his saddle as he stared at the great golden stone house, hands fisted tight over the reins. *Mine.* No matter what man ruled here now, no matter what would happen here, this was as much his home now as it was then.

He gazed at the mansion hungrily. Many men had done so. It was a magnificent house, not a forbidding castle or one of those cold piles of brick that stood naked and alone, dominating the land around it, like some he'd seen as he'd traveled here. It was a deceptively simple-looking house, made of glowing golden stone. There were formal gardens in front, but it didn't need anything to enhance its unique beauty. Wide and long and meandering, with many roofs and entrances, it had been built in the days of Queen Bess, though it was said that men had lived on the site since the dawn of time. It had no one style; it had its own style. Horseshoe shaped, with two wings on either side in front, it had an enclosed courtyard that welcomed a man into its province even before he walked up the great stairs to its front door.

There was no home like this in the Colonies. There hadn't been enough time for something like this there; the people who lived in the Colonies before the English came had built houses they could carry away with them when the seasons changed. This home had been built to outlast time and seasons. It had grown over the years, like the great trees in the drive that led to it, each generation adding something. His father had said it wasn't finished yet and never would be, because it had to grow and change with their family. His father had been right. But the house was the same now as it had been when Jared had last seen it, because the family had ended with him.

Mine, Jared thought as he sat and stared. *Mine.* Everything in it was his, from the peacocks that strolled over the scythed grass to every last chimney that studded the long rooftops, to the mullioned windows that showed prim faces to the sun and then took the sunlight and fractured it into prisms of stunning color inside. He remembered that. As he sat looking at his heart's home, he remembered everything else about it. In fact, he was so lost in remembrance that he wasn't aware of horsemen approaching.

The hounds' baying woke him from his daydreams. Jared looked up to see a string of dogs prancing around three horsemen coming toward him. He discounted two of them the moment he saw the man in the middle—the lord of the hall. Jared knew it. His stomach tensed. His hands closed to white-knuckled fists, and he could feel his heart quicken and then slow to long, thunderous beats as his eyes narrowed on the man who claimed to own his home.

The man was dressed in princely fashion, all in gold and brown; he rode a cream-colored horse and wore a fine, dark-gold long coat, blinding white linen, and brown breeches. He was young, wide-shouldered, long-legged, and lean-hipped. Like his companions, he wore a simple white wig, pulled back in a queue. His eyebrows were dark gold, and his face was lightly tanned, not sun-bitten as Jared's own. A lord of the manor, Jared thought bitterly, didn't work in the sun the way a man who had to work to prove his worth every day did. But it wasn't just his face or clothes that convinced Jared of who he was, it was the easy way he sat his horse, the way the other two men rode with him. His pride, confidence, and absolute surety marked him as lord and master here as surely as his comfortable smile did.

When he came within distance to see Jared close up, that smile slipped. Jared nodded. His cousin. It could be no other. The resemblance was eerie, although the face was not as lean as his. There were other differences. On closer inspection, Jared could see that the imperious nose was thinner than his own, that this chin had a definite cleft that his own only hinted at, that these brows were darker and the long eyes were vivid blue, not gray. The man was younger than himself, maybe a little shorter, and though lean and fit, there was a sleekness to him that Jared lacked. *Of course,* Jared thought bitterly, *this man has never lived in hell.* Still, the likeness was unsettling; he could swear he'd seen this man before, almost as he saw himself each day in his mirror.

"Good day," the man said cordially, as he brought his horse to a stop. "Have you lost your way, sir?"

"No," Jared said, "I have found my way back, sir."

There was a moment of silence. "Have you?" the man asked Jared thoughtfully.

He knows! Damn his soul, he knows, Jared thought with a mixture of fury and jubilation. *And why not? All his life, he's had nightmares about someone riding up to his house and saying this to him.*

"Well then, sir. I am Alveston, of Hawkstone Hall," the man said quietly.

"No," Jared said, tensing so much that his horse danced a step in reaction to the clenching of the muscles in his thighs. "I don't think so. *I* am Alveston of Hawkstone Hall."

"Is he mad?" one of the other men cried, as the other brought his horse close to his host and shouted, "I'll help run him off, Alveston!"

"No," the man who had called himself Alveston said, raising one hand to quiet them. He didn't take his eyes off Jared. "Tell me, sir. You don't seem to be a madman. I am Alveston. This is my home; these are my friends. You are a stranger here. Why should you say that you are me?"

"No, I am not mad," Jared sneered. "And I am not you, thank God, nor would I want to be."

"The effrontery!" one of the other men cried, but was silenced when he saw the look in Jared's eyes and the deadly serious, fixed expression that grew on the face of the man who called himself Alveston.

"Indeed? And why so?" the earl of Alveston asked too calmly.

"Because I don't claim a title that is not mine. I did not inherit the title through the kidnapping of the rightful earl and the murder of his brother."

Everything grew very still. All Jared could hear, above the pounding of the blood in his ears, was far-off birdsong and the restless sounds of the horses held still as the three men stared at him.

"No," the man who looked so much like Jared told him, his blue eyes infinitely sad, "I imagine you did not. I did, however. And though I regret my brother's death to this day, I'm the only one who deserves to succeed him, although God knows," he said quietly, "no one on this earth could succeed him. He was the best boy I ever knew and would have been a greater man than I could ever hope to be. Come, friend," he said, returning from wherever he'd been in his mind, "enough of this. What is your quarrel with me?"

But now Jared was ashen beneath his tan. His hand went beneath his coat to where his pocket pistol lay concealed. His voice came out a harsh whisper. "Do you claim to have lost your brother, too? God's teeth! Do you take everything from me—name, title, and now, my poor lost brother, too? They gave you a fine tale to tell, didn't they? You get everything—tragedy and all? No, no, that I won't allow. It is bad enough that I was banished and my brother killed—but to have you take our story, too? Your father, may he rot in hell, whoever he was, may have done his best to erase me from the face of the earth, but I won't let him twist history. *I* am Jared Bellington, earl of Alveston. My brother Justin died that night. You are not he. If I have to fight you for the rest of my life, I will. But you will not kill me twice—and I would warn you not to make your second attempt now," he said, drawing out his pistol.

Though he'd grown pale, the other man didn't flinch. Instead, he stared at Jared.

"Jared?" he said in a hollow voice. "But Jared was swept away in the water and never seen again. He was trying to save me and was drowned."

"No," Jared said, staring just as hard. "It was Justin who was swept away—gone, before my eyes."

"No, it was Jared. He was never seen again."

"Not in England, no," Jared said. "I was washed to the shore, and when they found me, they bound me again and took me to London. They sold me to a soul driver and he sold me into bondage. In the Colonies. The Virginia colony. I've come back at last. But Justin drowned. I saw him disappear," he said uncertainly, because the look on the other man's face unnerved him. It was too close to blinding joy to believe.

"No, no. *I* was washed ashore, and they didn't find me, though I could hear them searching in the dark," the other man said as he kept staring at Jared in wonder. "When they finally gave up and left, I dragged myself to a nearby farmhouse and told my story. I was lucky. The farmer was an intelligent man. He asked about my family. After he thought awhile, he asked if my mother had any brothers and then was smart enough to return me to one of them— my uncle John—and not to my home, where I obviously had enemies."

"Uncle John?" Jared echoed, lowering the pistol.

The other man nodded, and said in a shaking voice, "Yes. He was the one who faced my guilty uncle on the dueling field—it was my father's brother, my uncle Roland—and killed him for it. Then he exiled Roland's family to the Continent, where they still are, I suppose, God rot them. He kept the whole thing quiet, as have I— the scandal, the family name. . . . But that doesn't matter now," he said, impatient with himself, "I called my brother—What did I call my brother, sir?"

"'Jard'—at least my brother called me Jard,'" Jared said, shaking his head, refusing to believe what his eyes were now telling him, "but anyone would know that."

"Yes. And he called me 'Just.' 'In Jard and Just I place my trust,' my father jested, and so did we. But yes, you are right, anyone else might know."

The two men faced each other, their horses prancing in place. The other two riders held their breath as well as their horse's reins, they didn't want to miss hearing a word of this strange meeting.

"But no one would know what we did that day, the day before we were carried away," the other man finally said.

"No, because it was forbidden," Jared said, "so we couldn't tell anyone."

"Because no one wanted us to go to the old mill alone. . . ."

"But there was a grouse's nest. . . ."

"The number of eggs?"

"Four," Jared whispered, "but the amazing thing was that . . ."

"Only three hatched, though we stayed most of the afternoon. . . ."

They fell still. Then, without taking their eyes off each other, each man slipped down from his horse. They stood facing each other, their heads cocked, like men squinting into a clouded mirror.

"Jared? Are you truly Jared, returned to me?" the man said uncertainly.

Jared could only nod. And then they fell into each other's arms and embraced, rocking back and forth together. When they stepped apart, each man's face was wet, but no one could say with whose tears.

"Brother," they said at the same time. And then they both laughed.

"And here's the blue room—yes, still yellow—we couldn't understand it then, and I still don't. Lord, Jared! It's you, my God, it's you!" Justin said, for the twentieth time that day.

"Yes, I'm here, though I still don't believe it," Jared answered, as he did with each exclamation from Justin. He felt they both must sound like drunken fools, but though they'd toasted each other often since they'd met that morning, what percolated through his veins now was astonishment, dizzying gratitude, and bliss, not wine.

They walked through the house, arms around each other's shoulders: one golden-haired, the other, wigless now, had tobacco-hued hair that hadn't been sun-baked to gold; both were tall, broad-shouldered, and slender. They were laughing, remembering, and still testing each other— because the truth was so blindingly good that neither of them could accept it all at once. It was both wonderful and terrible. It was like a noose that tightened the more they struggled: The more they believed each other, the more they rejoiced; yet they knew the happier they became, the harder it would be for them if they found it was a lie.

"And here's the drawing room," Justin said, flinging the door wide, watching Jared carefully.

Jared stood and stared. It was more beautiful than he

remembered, and he hadn't thought that was possible. The glow of this room had lit his dreams even in the darkest places. It was a long, high room, with a domed ceiling timbered with oak. Long mullioned windows took up the whole wall facing the front drive. Above them, set in dark oak, were many little shamrock-shaped trefoil windows, filled with brightly colored glass, making the day more brilliant than a starry night by casting long spears of radiantly tinted sunbeams down on the polished wooden floors.

"I didn't remember this," Jared whispered, and Justin tensed. "I didn't know then that the walls and floors were oak," Jared said in wonder, "and that the fireplace had an obsidian mantel. I knew it was wonderful, but I didn't realize how expensive it was," he said, laughing. "Forgive me, my lord brother, but it's the merchant in me talking now."

Justin smiled, but his smile was taut. He took his hand off Jared's shoulder as they strolled into the room. He ran his hand down a long, dark oak side table. "Remember this?" he asked Jared casually.

Jared grew quiet. "Yes," he finally said. "It used to be in the main hall, by the staircase. And if you crawl under it, you might see our initials. But I'm not sure anymore. Back then, it seemed to me that they were an inch deep and a mile high, and I thought we'd be killed for carving them there. But now? They might only be scratches; we were very young and very afraid Nurse would catch us at it. Any more tests, brother?"

Before Justin could answer, Jared went on, "I don't expect you to kill the fatted calf yet, but I hoped—no," he said, shrugging, "to be honest, I never hoped to find you, so how could I know what you'd think? I never thought anyone would question me, either. I didn't think anyone but the guilty one would know me, and he certainly wouldn't want to prove who I was. Truthfully, I thought *I* might be killed," he said ruefully, "much less the fatted calf. So ask away; I would if I were you. It's just . . ." He laughed humorlessly. "It's just that I don't know *what* I expect you to do."

"Nor do I," Justin admitted. His expression was sober. "Jared, if it *is* you, you know this means my world is completely turned around."

"I know," Jared said. "Mine, too. I don't know what to do any more than you do. I was going to take vengeance. But Uncle John did that for me."

"Years ago," Justin said. "And to be on the safe side, he cautioned Uncle Roland's younger brother George to never even dream of interfering with me—not that he had to. George was afraid of his own shadow, and terrified of Roland, to boot. He was so grateful to Uncle John for—ah—removing Uncle Roland from the scene that he was practically in tears. Everyone at the funeral thought he was grieving for his brother, not crying from relief. He died five years ago, poor old fellow, and being very accommodating, he never married to leave behind jealous cousins to trouble me." Justin chuckled.

Jared's smile slipped when he heard the word *me*. His face grew grave. Head down, he paced a few steps before he stopped and looked up at Justin. "You should have said 'to trouble *us*,'" he said.

Before Justin could answer, Jared went on. "I can never prove who I am, you know, never. Not even to you, obviously. And I've made a new life for myself in Virginia. I'm prosperous now. Alfred made me a full partner. Don't turn up your aristocratic nose, brother; it's a thriving business. I'm rich now. What I'm trying to say . . ."—he ran a hand through his hair—". . . is that the wind's been taken from my sails. I came here to right a wrong. I found it was already done for me. Better yet, it wasn't as bad as I thought, because you're here. Do you know what that means to me?" He grinned, but then his smile faded again, and he paced a few steps away.

When he looked at Justin again, his gray eyes were bleak. "I was prepared to take vengeance; I lived for it. But this? I'm trying to reason it out; it's not easy, so bear with me. The way I see it, I can't realistically hope to regain my place. When I grew up, I realized it was impossible. I—I'd like to stay awhile if it's all right with you—and then I'll go."

"What?"

"I said I'll go. Well, look at it," Jared said angrily. "I appear from out of the past and say I'm Jared—which I am—but how can I prove it? I can't, and that's the truth. I can tell you everything we did together years ago because they're bright in my memory—my memories were the only things that kept me going for a long time. But so what? You're the only one who can remember most of them with me, and you were just a boy then. And here you are, an earl of the realm and a well-respected one. And I? I was a bond-boy. Do you know what that means, brother? Do you? Let me tell you, then: a bond-boy is the lowest of the low in every way. A boy is less than a man because he can't work as hard, and a bond-servant is less than a slave. If a slave dies, you lose a sizable investment. You lose nothing but time and a little money if your bond-servant dies, and that only because they expect you to bury him. In fact, it's cheaper if he does die, because if he lives to work out his bond, you have to let him go with some money in his pocket.

"And so here I am, a bond-boy from the Colonies jumped up to a wealthy merchant—and claiming to be an earl? In short, brother," Jared said harshly, "dreams might have kept me going, but I'm a realist now. I'm a merchant; I deal in facts and figures. You're the earl of Alveston. I appear and claim to be your brother. So what? No court of law can prove it. There are no papers, no pictures, no witnesses. You yourself told me the men who kidnapped us were disposed of by other men our damned uncle hired immediately afterward. I can't say who the man was who sold me into bondage. I can't prove who I am now any more than I could then. I was beaten for saying it then. Now, I'd be mocked."

He put up his hands like a man surrendering in a duel.

"At least let's remain friends. I'll go quietly, but first I'd like to see it all again. That's all."

Justin stared at him. "Are you mad?" he asked incredulously. "Go? When you've just returned? When you're the rightful earl, not I? I don't doubt it anymore. Aside from your face, there's too much no one else could know. *No one*. We were close—closer when our parents died. You know things no fraud could. Suppose you or some collaborator of yours *had* met Jared somewhere, sometime—they might know what kind of knot was used to tie us up that night or how cold the water was. But would they know our favorite place to swim? Not the pond, but that muddy little duck wallow we would run off to. We'd come home filthy, and no one knew why. We did. You did."

Justin faced his brother and challenged him, but not the way Jared thought he would. "If you were a pretender, you'd ask the name of Jared's pet dog in case anyone ever asked you about it," Justin said. "But would you even think of asking Jared what his favorite name for our old long-nosed vicar was? His favorite color, maybe even his favorite dessert—but our secret names for our least favorite things? Ye gods, man! Even Nurse didn't know we called the vicar 'Punch' because of his nose. She'd have skinned us for it. But you knew. And then after all of that," he said triumphantly, "you just offered to leave!"

Justin smiled. "I doubted you at first. I was shocked. I think I was afraid of being disappointed. But I don't doubt you anymore."

"But if I was clever, I *would* offer to go—knowing that you are indeed 'Just,'" Jared said wryly.

"Jared," his brother said, looking at the hard face of the man before him, so like his own, but with eyes that had seen too much pain and privation. "I no longer doubt you. Take your rightful place."

"You would give all this up without a battle?" Jared asked in amazement.

"It was never mine," Justin said soberly. "I never flaunted the title; I developed a reputation for being a bit of a recluse, in fact. I think I never felt I really deserved it or the title. You do. It was always yours: you are the earl of Alveston. It's as simple as that."

It wasn't, of course. The uncles were of two minds about it.

"He has the look of Maria, no doubt about it," said Uncle John, the youngest and most reasonable of Jared's mother's brothers.

"Well, but so do all the Fentons, and God knows there are dozens of them—breed like rabbits," Uncle Lawrence grumbled from the depths of his chair by the fire in the drawing room.

"Bad lot, the Essex Fentons," Uncle Martin grunted.

Jared and Justin exchanged a bright glance, as though they were boys again, listening to their uncles discussing the world in their usual cantankerous way.

"Maria was the beauty of the family," Uncle John said with a sigh, and his brothers nodded in silent tribute to their dead sister. "And Charles was a likely rogue," he added, and they rumbled agreement. "But a fair man, a good man, not like his brother—ah, but what's done's done. Now, as to the lad."

"Got the look, all right," Uncle Martin muttered.

"And Alveston here—ah, Justin here—he's all set to hand over his coronet to him," Uncle Lawrence said.

"Alveston's a *boy*," Uncle Martin countered, and they all muttered agreement. A man with only twenty-six years to his name was a mere infant to them.

"But the lad remembers him. Swears it's him. I dare say I tend to agree," Uncle Lawrence conceded. "Knows every detail of the story of that terrible night they was carried off, and the devil knows we hushed it up after, didn't we? But he knows things we didn't and that young Alveston—ah, Justin—had forgotten about, too."

"Has the look, the manner," Uncle Martin put in, *"and he remembers what I gave him on his sixth birthday—not* only that, but what he said about it, too. Cheeky fellow. Every inch the nobleman, and only six then."

Jared and Justin dared not look at each other because they both remembered Jared's reaction to the shiny penny piece his uncle had given him when he'd wanted toy soldiers.

"Manners don't make the man," Uncle Martin said.

"Neither do brothers who are looking for long-lost brothers," Uncle John said worriedly. "We must go on what is before our eyes. But wait—what of birthmarks? What of scars, Justin? Can you remember any that your brother had that we might be interested in and can look for now?"

Jared seemed to startle, or at least it looked like his wide shoulders leaped and he flinched. But the firelight played such large and disturbing shadows over them all that before anyone could be sure, he was quiet again, standing so still by the mantel that it seemed impossible he'd moved at all since they'd started discussing his fate.

"He was seven, Uncle. I was six," Justin said with a small smile. "I remember he fell and scraped his knees. I remember he cut his thumb once. Will that do?"

"No sense looking for scars," Uncle Lawrence scoffed. "Any man may scar himself. Ha! For an earldom, there's some who'll take off an ear."

"True, true," Uncle John said and sighed. "So there's no more we can learn here. But my man's making inquiries in London."

Jared stood by the fireside, the light playing such shadows on his lean face none of the uncles could know what he was thinking, even if they cared any more than they had when he'd been a boy. Jared understood that. Because whether he turned out to be an earl or not, he was still a boy to them, and they were his elders. In fact, it spoke volumes for how much they had already accepted him that they took no extra care to be polite to him. But they had come to see him as soon as they'd gotten word of him, and the sight of them moved him almost as much as the sight of his house did. The sound of their voices brought back his childhood as vividly as anything in this house did. He could give them no less than the absolute truth.

"I'm afraid your man won't find out much," Jared said simply. "I remember the name of the ship that I was taken away on—I'd like to forget it, but the good ship *Fair Fortune* will never leave my mind. But I doubt they put bond-boys on ship manifests. Even if they did, I don't think they put down the name I insisted on: the earl of Alveston. They cuffed me for saying it and then starved me until I stopped. But it worked against them"—he grinned wryly—"because they didn't make much money on me when we reached the Colonies. I was too scrawny by then.

"Everyone wants boys who look like they can do a good day's work. That's why I was bought by a city trader," he told Justin. "Farmers want sturdier lads. But in the long run, it worked against me, too, because I found out it was easier to escape from the plantations. They're in the middle of nowhere, and if you run far enough, you can start again as a free man. Many did. It's harder in the cities. It's not easy to get far when everyone on the street knows just whose bond-boy you are and how much they'll get for bringing you back. There's always a reward for escaped bond-servants. No, I should have eaten more on the journey and revenged myself later. All I ever got from my attempts at escape were beatings."

Justin didn't know what to answer. Even the uncles sat still. Jared winced when he realized what silenced them. He hated pity. It reminded him how pitiable he had been.

"Still," he added lightly, "I suppose I was lucky, after all. Because Alfred bought my papers and freed me—if I hadn't been in the city and on the docks that day, it never would have happened. The way things were going, believe me, if it hadn't, I wouldn't be here today to trouble you."

"But you are, and we'll deal with it—justly, never fear," Uncle John said quickly. "Because before I even left my house—in fact, as soon as I got the message from Alveston—ah—Justin here—I set inquiries in motion. If Justin here acknowledges you—yes, yes, Justin, I know you've said it often enough, but please let me go on—and if we can find out more to prove it to our satisfaction, or more to the point, if nothing is found to disclaim it, we will support you. We'll see your claim's made valid as smoothly as possible."

"Won't be that smooth outside the courts," Uncle Lawrence commented.

"Aye," Uncle Martin said gruffly. "Be a scandal any which way. John will take care of the legal etcetera, all right. We'll see to the rest. But if it comes to pass, the gossips will have a party, lad, and there's naught we can do about it. Still, if it does happen that you are Alveston returned to us, we stand ready to take you to London to let the world know we acknowledge you. That's what counts."

"I didn't come here to go to London," Jared said quickly. "I wanted only to come see the hall."

"Nonsense," Justin said. "I myself will take you 'round, introduce you. . . ."

"We're being a bit anticipatory," Uncle John said quickly. "Nothing has happened yet. As I said, I expect to hear from my man any day."

"I don't think he'll find much," Jared said, "but thank you for trying. Thank you all," he said carefully, "for listening."

They shifted in their chairs. They were old men and rich ones, from a family old as the kingdom, and in their time they had heard everything. But this—the story of a boy sold into slavery, whether he was one of theirs or not—bothered them.

"Never fear," Uncle John said staunchly. "We'll soon know."

Jared nodded, though he didn't think they'd ever know much more. He was wrong.

Chapter

6

It took another week, a week in which Jared and Justin rode out every day, exploring the neighborhood together the way they had when they were boys. They visited all the old places, recalling all the mischief they'd done. In those hours, the last of Justin's doubts faded away. And if Jared had harbored any about this man who claimed to be his brother, he had no more, either. Whatever the world decided, they knew who they were. Each felt more complete than he had in years, even though they both soon realized they had led such different lives that they had grown into different men than they might have been if their greedy uncle hadn't interfered.

But now they were as close as though they'd never been apart. It amazed them both how quickly that happened.

"Where to today?" Justin asked idly as they finished breakfast a week after Jared had come home.

"The village, I think," Jared said. "Last time, I was too

amazed at how it had grown to notice much more about it."

Justin grinned. Only one new shop had opened there since he'd been a boy. "The tavern does have good cider," he agreed, "and Sally is the prettiest barmaid in the district."

"Oh?" Jared asked, one golden eyebrow arcing in surprise. "You have designs there?"

"Lord, no!" Justin said. "The worst thing a man can do is to dally with a local lass, especially if her father is as big as James Rutledge is. Don't tell me you're interested?"

"No, but I'd like to see what's offered in the shops. I need some new clothes. No, save your breath, I meant it: I won't wear yours. I was a beggar long enough," he said, and that silenced his brother's protests. "Anyway, more than what they have, I'd like to see what they might need in the stores. I'm a merchant, you know. So, shall we?"

"I am at your disposal," Justin said, rising from the table.

"Well," Jared said, hesitating, "I'm not taking you away from your usual duties, am I? Because, if I am, I can go by myself."

"There's nothing I have to do—there's nothing I'd rather do," Justin said.

They left the house and headed for the stables. The stable men rushed to do their bidding, smiling and bowing. There was a rumor that the young colonial was the rightful earl returned—gossip was faster than summer lightning in the countryside and just as truly aimed. If it was so, then they were content. Young Alveston was a good master; this new man looked like he would be just as good. They stood and smiled at the two handsome young men as they rode off together. Either or both would do them proud.

But as they rode away, Jared marveled at what had happened in just one week's time. Whether he knew it or not, Justin had already slipped back into being the younger brother, ready to follow Jared anywhere, the way he'd always done. Jared had always wondered what would have happened, what sort of man he would have been, if he hadn't been stolen away all those years ago. But now he wondered what would have happened to Justin. Would he ever have escaped from his older brother's shadow?

Today, from all Jared could see, his brother was an estimable man. He'd been to university, which Jared deeply envied, but Justin wore his education lightly. He was a sportsman and a scholar and, though gentle and soft-spoken, he had an unconscious air of command. Would it have been so if he'd had an older brother to dominate him? Jared didn't know, any more than he knew whether he'd been right to come back and make his claim, if it meant his brother might be displaced. But since there was little chance that he himself would become earl, he relaxed and vowed to enjoy visiting his past again for these few days.

"Alfred and I grow and sell tobacco," Jared said. "We work hard at it—not all by ourselves, of course. But neither do we have slaves or bond-boys, unless we've bought their freedom and given it back to them, since Alfred is sensitive to such things." He added with a proud grin, "We trade, too. There are things I can broker for our neighbors: sugar, cotton, beets, other produce, things a village like yours can use. The New World's blessed with rich soil and good climate, though as in everything else, it's wilder. That's good, too; I can get my hands on furs, everything from beaver to fox—and fine, thick pelts at that. So if I can make a few contacts here and there, build up a market for Alfred, then I'll feel I've done something more than bother you on my visit here."

He grinned, but didn't laugh. Justin had noticed that Jared didn't laugh aloud very much—not the way he'd used to. That was the greatest difference from the boy Justin remembered. He stole a glance at his brother, sitting tall and straight in his saddle. *Strong and strong-minded, then as now.* Justin thought with the envy and wonder he always felt when he considered his brother. He'd mourned him most of his life, for Jared had been his ideal. When he'd understood the evil that had been done, he wished Uncle Roland were alive so he could kill him again. And yet, even so, lately there were times when he wondered if Jared's sad adventures hadn't given him even another advantage. It was almost as though the suffering Uncle Roland had visited on him had also been a gift. Jared had always been clever and strong, even as a boy. Now, he seemed invincible.

"I'll tell them what I have to offer, and buy a few shirts while I'm at it. Buying always sweetens selling," Jared added.

"You won't find decent clothes in town. You need London for that. Or my wardrobe. All right, I don't understand, but I will obey," Justin said with a laugh as Jared began to protest again. "So be it. I won't lend you any clothing. But I'll give you the name of my tailor, and he can visit, measure you, and make up some clothing for you. Bespoke linen is better than ready-made. You're an English gentleman now, brother."

"I don't like being fitted and fussed over," Jared said abruptly. "If they don't have what I want, I can wait until my reinforcements come. I know Della will pack everything I need, and she's due here in a month, if she doesn't decide to swim here herself—she'll be that eager to get here," he said, chuckling.

"A child packing? They do things very differently in the New World."

"No, no, did I give that impression? No, she's all of twenty now, as I was reminded recently. She's all grown up, but I swear I still see little Della whenever I look at her. It's always that way when you've known someone since they were little—why, I still half expect to have to help you hold your glass so you don't spill your drink down your chin when we get to the inn, little brother."

"If you have enough of that cider, I'll have to help you with yours, brother," Justin said, laughing.

"I doubt it. I'm weaned on home brew, and they use New World liquor to stop pain, revive dead mules, and start fires."

"Shall I like your Della?"

"I don't see how you can't," Jared answered. "Be careful of your heart."

"Oh, but I don't have to be," Justin said, "because it's not mine anymore."

"Really?" Jared asked. "Do you know, with everything that's happened, I hadn't thought to ask. But you are six and twenty, aren't you? Have you got a woman, lad?"

"Better, I've a fiancée."

"No!" Jared whispered, reining in sharply and turning in his saddle to stare at his brother. "I never thought—I never asked. . . ."

"You don't have to; you'll soon see." Justin laughed at his brother's shocked expression. "She's visiting in London, but I wrote to her about you, so be sure she'll be here any day now. But wait! I never asked you, either. Is there someone in Virginia waiting for you?"

"Only my little Della," Jared said lightly, "and she doesn't count. No, I've been too busy—plotting and planning to come here, I suppose—to think about a life's mate. But you . . . I shouldn't be surprised, but I am, although of course you're old enough. Still, I never thought . . . tell me more about your lady."

"No, I'll say no more," Justin said, grinning like a boy. "But trust me. You're in for a great surprise—in several ways."

But the greatest surprise came when they returned to the hall at the end of the day. The uncles were waiting for them. They were smiling.

"Here you are!" Uncle John said triumphantly, waving the papers he'd just received. "The *Fair Fortune*'s captain was a good seaman and a scrupulous officer—navy-trained, don't you know. He wrote down everything, even that he'd taken on a difficult passenger on fourth August,

1740, before he set sail from London for the Virginia colony. What does he say? Ah, yes, here." He scanned the paper, and then read out, with pride:

Also taken aboard this night, a poor, daft bonded servant, a lad, aged seven, fair and well developed, who nonetheless claims to be his lordship, the rightful earl of Alveston. Confined to quarters for the length of the voyage, because he is quite mad.

"Ah. There you are. Well, then, greetings, my lord Alveston," Justin said with a twisted smile as he bowed low to his dazed brother. "Or shall I say, greetings, my poor, daft lord?"

"I can't do it," Jared said as he paced the room, head down, hands behind his back. "No," he said again, shaking his head, "I can't take your life away from you. It's not right."

Justin sat, head back, watching the morning sunlight that filtered through the window. "It's right," he said calmly, "and it is just."

"Life's not that simple," Jared snarled. "Besides, I wouldn't do it right. You've been trained for it. Being earl of Alveston, managing these estates, being responsible for all your tenants is a job. And you've done it well."

"Managing an estate should be child's play for a merchant," Justin said easily.

"It's more than being in trade. It's the people, dealing with them, high and low. There's our name to be considered. Let's face it, brother, I can't do it justice. Do you think I don't remember Father? He was a gentleman as well as a country squire. He knew the ways of the gentry in London, too. I don't even know this country! Do you think I didn't notice the way fashionable people looked at me in London? My coat is of a good cut, but not Continental enough. My face is too tanned. Men don't

87

wear their swords in the street here anymore, it seems. Even my pistol is made by the wrong man. Everything I do marks me as a colonial—quaint and amusing.

"The truth is, I don't know your ways. I didn't even know how to amuse myself in London. I don't know opera or theater, and I've never taken the grand tour. Do you think that would go unnoticed in your circles? Worst of all, I haven't the education you have," Jared added bitterly. "I had some before I left here. The rest, I snatched and stole from books I found when I could find them—and the time to read. Then Alfred hired tutors for me. But I'm a wilderness savage compared to you."

"Not quite," Justin said with a little smile. "You do read; most of my schoolmates went near books only when threatened with expulsion. As for being taken for a wilderness savage, whatever you wear, you look every inch the earl, you know."

Jared threw him a bright look. "Flatterer—it's only because I look so much like you."

They laughed. But Justin meant what he said. It was true his brother was taller and tougher-looking than he was, more a warrior than a courtier. It was also true he didn't sound like an Englishman; his words were slightly drawled, he used different slang, and had a colonial accent now. But his grace and dignity were unmistakable, as was his air of decisiveness. The only thing Justin didn't understand was why no one had believed him all those years ago. Man or boy, colonial or Englishman, his brother looked every inch a nobleman.

"Have done, brother," Justin said suddenly. "You would have taken the title like a shot if I weren't here."

Sunlight glinted off Jared's gray eyes, making them cold and clear as ice as he looked at his brother. "Aye," he said bluntly, "I would have. But you *are* here. I won't supplant you."

"But I supplanted you," Justin said calmly, "and do you know," he said with deceptive mildness, because this was a thing that his brother had to believe, "it's always made me uneasy because I knew I didn't deserve the title and that you'd have been a better earl than I was. You saved my life that night, and I thought you'd died doing it. Then I was rewarded by taking over your place. It stuck in my throat.

"Why do you think I go to London so seldom? They say I'm reclusive, and it was true that for those first years, I was made to stay close to home. The uncles insisted. They were afraid for my safety and for the family reputation. They wanted everything kept hushed until they discovered the culprit, and after they did, they had to be sure there were no more plots or danger to my life. That's likely why your Alfred could never find out about me; we discouraged inquiries. But afterward, when I was a grown man and it was clear there'd be no more attempts? Then it was my choice. I hesitated to prance about London as the earl of Alveston. Because I always felt like I was an imposter."

Jared stopped pacing and gazed at his brother with disbelief. They were in the guest bedchamber he'd been given when he came to Hawkstone Hall. He himself was still in a dressing robe, as was Justin, and Justin wore no wig. But he looked like the lord of the manor, even so. It was in his gentle, confident smile, Jared thought with pride and despair; it was in the way he spoke to the servants—softly, but with command, in the way he did everything—with patience, humor, and ease. Sleek and well balanced, he was exactly what he should be, and what Jared, who had clung to life by his wits and prayers, knew he could never be.

"Why do you think I never added on to the hall?" Justin persisted.

"And you wanted to? Not enough room for a single man here—is that what you want me to think? Cut line, brother," Jared said with a wry smile.

"But I *was* going to marry. I didn't build, because I never felt it was my place to. That doesn't matter; there's no point to this argument. Believe me, there's no way on earth I'll keep the title now that you've come back. Ye gods, Jared, what do you think I am? You're the rightful heir. You must take the title and all that goes with it."

"But all that goes with it is yours—this house, the land—"

"Yours, and have been since birth. But don't think I'm *that* noble," Justin said with a small smile, "I'm not exactly destitute. I have my own money, properties, a snug manor house in Shropshire, all left to me as second son— and my bride will bring a good portion to me, too. Take what's yours, Jared. It's only right. Besides, you have no choice. I renounce the title."

"Renounce away," Jared muttered. "It makes no difference. I have a life waiting for me; I'll go back to it. I'll be gone before I'm missed, believe me. I only want to show Alfred and Della that I never lied to them, and then I'll leave. It's too late. This is your place in life now. Now— you said your lady's coming today? Would you please leave and let me dress for her?" He reached for the belt to his robe.

"You can't run away from your birthright."

"I'm not running, I'm walking. Look, Justin," Jared said, his hands on his belt, his face sober and sad, "I'm only talking sense. Life treated me badly—how badly, you can't know—I hope you never do. But I survived, and returned to find what I lost can't be mine anymore. That was another life. It's useless to talk about it. I'm a rough, blunt man now, a merchant and a trader, and a good one. I'd be a bad earl. If I were taking the name from someone who didn't deserve it, I'd do it gladly even if it meant making an ass of myself. But you are the earl of Alveston, to perfection. Stay that way."

"I'm your younger brother; you are whatever you want to be. I—" Justin stopped in midsentence as Jared muttered a curse and abruptly turned his back on him. He shrugged the robe from his shoulders and let it drop to the floor, exposing his naked backside to his brother.

Justin started to smile at such an expression of impudence, but then he saw beyond his brother's brazen display and gasped. It was hard to believe his eyes. The long, lean, muscled back above those firm buttocks was crisscrossed by jagged white and pink welts, from the nape of the neck all the way to the waist. Some of the scars looked like licks of flame flashing across his brother's back, some were thick as ropes, some were fine as hairs.

It was an abomination, especially on that cleanly tapered torso. Jared had obviously been brutally savaged.

"By God, Jared! What happened to you?" Justin cried in horror. "A wildcat? Some accident, some animal in the New World . . . ?" His voice tapered off as he realized that some of the deep, clawed marks were obviously from different times than others, being overlaid in places, and all were too random to have come from a single attack. As he gazed at them, he slowly began to understand that the animal that had done this to his brother was one of their own kind.

"Yes," Jared said as he jerked a shirt down over his head and let it drop to cover himself, "an accident—of birth. I couldn't forget it, you see, and should have when I became a slave. I was disobedient, 'uppity.' My first master beat me for it, but he used only fists. My second master was a more determined man. Eventually I stopped trying to convince him of who I was. But then he got tired of my crying at night. He decided to rid me of the habit. He beat it out of me. The remedy worked. Though I'd wept for my lost life, I wouldn't give him the satisfaction of crying over my wounds—which only got him angrier and started the beatings." He shrugged. "It became a contest, after a while. I'd have won, you know, which means that if he hadn't found a buyer for me, I don't think I'd be here today. Still, I was lucky; my third master didn't use a whip. He was wise enough to know a badly aching back cuts down on work. He punched and kicked, but I learned how to curl into a ball of knees and elbows. Occasionally, I was beaten for that, though, because I understood it smarts when you go to punch a lad's face and connect with his shin instead.

"I told you I was less than a slave. In truth, I was less than human," Jared said with deadly coldness as he saw his brother's ashen face. "Some bonded servants were lucky and found good homes, as I eventually did with Alfred. But by then it was too late. This is not a man who should be earl, Justin," he said with sad conviction. "I was lucky to have survived, much less make my fortune. Do I know how to take tea with a duchess? Chat with a duke? Take my place in the House of Lords? All I know is what I managed to read piecemeal over the years."

"Our late lamented king couldn't even speak English," Justin scoffed, but his voice was shaken. "And I know English noblemen who can't speak coherently, much less read."

"And how many bear scars from constant beatings, like disobedient dogs?"

"What do your scars have to do with it?" Justin cried. "They were honorably earned."

"No," Jared said with deadly calm, his eyes ice, "they were not. If I had any honor, I would have killed them or let them kill me. Sometimes I wept, so they'd stop. I can't forget that. Still, I'm glad of my back; it reminds me of what I am, and when there's a damp wind from the west, it reminds me of where I'll go when I return home."

"You are home," Justin said angrily. "If you don't take the title, one of Roland's damned exiled sons will get it after all, because I won't take what isn't mine—I will not. I have honor, too—or do you think I would live my brother's life, the life of the boy who saved my own, once I knew he still lived? You think very well of me, don't you?" he said with heavy sarcasm.

Jared's face flushed, and he was still. But then a wide, humorless grin showed white in his tanned face. "No, but I'll bet your fiancée will agree with me."

Justin grinned wider and he relaxed. "Do you? How much? Rich as you are, I don't think you have that much. But you'll see. Wait until you meet my Fiona. I have some surprises for you today, brother. No more time for argument now. You have to get dressed," he said, rising from his chair. "And so do I. We've got company coming. I won't offer you the services of my valet again, but don't worry, we don't live high here in the countryside, and whatever you wear, you look well. Meet me downstairs. In the meanwhile, think about what we discussed long and hard, because I won't be swayed in this."

Jared nodded. He would think about it; he couldn't help it—he hadn't been able to stop since he'd gotten here. The arguments kept turning in his mind as he put on a shirt and dark breeches, buttoned his best salmon silk vest, and then shrugged into a dark-blue long coat. He straightened his neckpiece, brushed and retied his hair neatly at the nape of his neck, and then surveyed himself in the looking glass. He looked good, he thought, but he was still sure he didn't look like an earl. His brother looked like an earl.

Jared left his room, but didn't go downstairs immediately. He suddenly realized this was the first time he'd been alone in the great house since he'd come here. Justin had been with him every waking minute since then. But now—it was too good an opportunity to miss. He roamed the corridors of the old house, nodding absently at any giggling housemaids he passed, smiling absently at any footmen, and when there was no one nearby to see, running his fingertips lightly along tabletops and mantelpieces, as though he could take it all in by touch. His mind still couldn't take in the grandeur of his lost home—and his heart dared not.

It was more than he'd expected. Since boyhood, his eyes had been trained on New World luxury, which was a far cry from this. In Virginia, every good piece of furniture, every expensive carpet or work of art—even silverware for the table—had to be brought from across the Atlantic to be considered beautiful. He'd seen some good pieces that were beginning to be turned out in Boston and New York, but no one in any of the Colonies considered them half so elegant as something that had come from home—and nearly everyone in the Colonies thought of some land across the sea as home. Nowhere had he seen so many wonderful things as this house had, and more than that, had in casual, everyday use.

The fireplaces and mantelpieces, the clocks, windows, carpets, vases, and chinaware—there wasn't a room that didn't have something his merchant's eye couldn't appraise as priceless. Beyond that, he stood in a hallway and let the warmth of the house wash over him. There were centuries here—he could feel as well as sense them. He took a deep breath and smelled the wood lovingly polished over the decades, the scent of antiquity itself. He loved the aroma of fresh-cut wood, and there was nothing like knowing you were the first to tame a piece of land and build a house on it to call your own. He looked forward to it. But there was nothing like standing in a house and feeling the weight of your ancestors around you, knowing you were one in the link of a long, unbreakable chain.

Jared was two men, and he knew it. One of them responded to this house with a love that was close to pain, and the other could only stand back, jealous and amazed.

This was his. But it could no longer be his. It was where he'd dreamed of being, but now that he was here, he didn't belong anymore. It was like finding a rare jewel cruelly marred. And his brother, the perfect English gentleman, noble in every way—how could he even think of dispossessing Justin, depriving him of everything he'd thought was his for most of his life? But that was what he was supposed to do, the house whispered to him, because he was the earl, and he had ancestors who had died without blinking for that honor.

And so did I die, in a way, Jared thought sadly. *I was the earl, but I can never be that boy again. So be it,* he thought with resignation and despair.

He took another deep breath. Then he made his way quickly down the great stairs, but not as quickly, he thought ruefully, as he and his brother had flown down it all those many long, lost years before. Because he was grown now, he couldn't do that, like so many other things, again.

"Ah, my lord," Justin said with great pride when Jared appeared in the drawing room. "At last."

Jared stopped and stared at the woman at Justin's side. She was hardly more than a girl, but she was dressed as the great lady she obviously was. She wore a white wig, with ringlets framing her lovely face. Tilted amber eyes smiled at him, and he held his breath. His reaction seemed to make her smile all the more, producing a dimple to the side of her shapely mouth. Her delicately featured face had thin, arched brows, a straight nose, and cheeks lightly blushed with peach. She wore an elaborate rose gown with panniers and a low, square-cut neckline that showed the bounty of two perfect white breasts. Her waist was tiny, but she was not, the top of her head came to the partial cleft in Justin's chin. There was laughter in her eyes as Jared stood staring at her. It wasn't mocking laughter. It was as if they shared a joke together.

"Jared," Justin said with pride, "allow me to present my fiancée, the honorable Fiona Trusham."

The lady curtsied and Jared bowed, woodenly, because he was dazed by the sight of her. She was every inch the elegant noblewoman he imagined belonged in this house: she fit it in just the way that she fit on Justin's arm, gracefully, as neatly as though a master painter had placed her there.

Justin helped her up from her low curtsy and then lifted her hand and brushed the back of it with his lips.

"Fiona, this is my long-lost brother, to whom I cede everything: house, holdings, and title, all that is his birthright—all, in fact," Justin said with a growing grin, looking like the boy Jared remembered in his mischievous glee, "except for one thing, of course: your own sweet self, my dear."

"Too kind of you, my dear," she said teasingly, "but what if he insists?" She smiled at Jared, waiting for his reaction, but he could only frown at them both in confusion.

She pretended to swat Justin with her lacy fan. "Fie, Justin. He doesn't know, does he? You see, my lord," she told Jared in a soft, sweet voice, "I am part of your birthright. By all rights, I should go with the house, the holdings, and the title. When I was born, I was promised to the earl of Alveston."

"So you see brother, I'm not *that* noble," Justin said. "There are some things that come with the title that I am not giving up."

"As if you have any say in the matter," Fiona joked, although her warm brown eyes considered Jared thoughtfully. "After all, it was specifically agreed upon by your father and mine at my birth, just months before your father's death and the tragedy of the kidnappings: I am the promised bride of the earl of Alveston."

Then she laughed, and so did both men. But suddenly, neither brother was really smiling.

Her hands were shaking so much that the paper in it crackled. Della stood by the packing cases and trunks that were heaped in the hallway and reread the letter that had just been delivered. Then she raised her head and shouted.

"Oh, this is beyond anything I ever dreamed. *Father!*" she cried, whirling with the letter in her hand. *"Father!"*

Alfred came running from his room, his face white, a pistol in his hand.

"What is it? Oh, by the rood, girl, I didn't know whether to bring my pistol or a physician, you frightened me so. What is it, a letter? Oh!" he said, suddenly even whiter. "Nothing's happened to the boy, has it?"

"Yes," she whispered, her eyes wide and dazzled. "Oh yes, Father, something has—something wonderful. He

96

writes, he says, that he hoped the letter would arrive before we left, but—but why am I dithering? Oh, Father, he's decided there's no use denying it anymore. He's going to take his rightful place. He's going to be named earl of Alveston!"

Chapter

7

He was tall, with wonderfully wide shoulders and a slim waist, and with his lean jaw and piercing eyes, he was altogether about as handsome as a fellow could be without being objectionable about it, Della thought. Not that she thought that the first mate, Master Jack Kelly, *could* be objectionable to any female. He was as slick as he was handsome, and that was saying a lot. She sighed. He was used to that reaction coming from his female passengers, and a small smile began to play around the edges of his hard, handsome mouth when he heard that little stifled sound. He gazed into her eyes. His, she thought sadly, were almost bluer than her own, and his eyelashes seemed just as long as hers were, too.

"What have I said to make you sad?" he asked in his deep, manly voice, with just the right touch of teasing in it.

Oh, the lad was a rare handful, all right, she thought unhappily.

"No, it's nothing you said," she said, turning to face the

sea and not his eyes, which were bluer, since the Atlantic was gray and grouchy today. They'd been aboard the ship the *Boston Boy* for almost three weeks. England was supposed to heave into sight any hour now, and it seemed Master Kelly was ready to make a move now.

"Maybe it's something I haven't said," he murmured, smiling. "Mistress Della," he went on in as quiet a voice as he could and still be heard above the snapping sails and the soughing sound of the sea washing against the keel of the great ship as it sliced through the waves, "I've walked with you on several evenings, although a turn or two around the deck is not my idea of a proper walk, you understand. I'd have had the privacy of tree-shaded lanes to go with the starry skies, had I my way—but needs must do as the devil drives. Still, believe me, it has been my delight to accompany you whenever I could on this journey, for as many days or nights as I could free myself from my work. We've dined together, albeit at the captain's table, under his watchful eyes. But we haven't always had to deal with watchful eyes," he reminded her, his voice growing lower and huskier, "for we did manage to kiss last night, if you recall. I can't forget, nor do I ever want to. And so I have a thing I'd ask you now, if I may. Don't worry," he added with a satisfied smile in his voice. "I've spoken to your father."

"I know," she said sorrowfully.

"I live in Boston town," he said. "While that's not far from Virginia by ship and coastal lanes, it's a way too far for a seafaring man to come a-courting the way he should. And you're off on a visit to London now, and who knows how long it will be before we can meet again. I set sail back for the Colonies as soon as we unload and take on more cargo. And as I don't think there's more that I can possibly know about you than I do now, and as you have the most beautiful face, kissable lips, and charming disposition of any girl I've ever met . . ."

And the richest father, don't forget—not that I doubt you have, Della thought.

". . . I'd like to ask for your hand, my dear, since you already have my heart," he said, and clasped her hand in his and held it against his broad chest as he waited for her answer.

She looked up at him. He was a grand sight. His curly black hair emphasized his deeply tanned face, and his growing smile was showing strong, white, even teeth. *A prize, no doubt about it,* Della thought. He wasn't a bad fellow, and if he was a little too full of himself, why, he had ample cause to be. But with all that he was, there was one thing he wasn't.

"I am deeply honored," she said carefully, making sure to get the wording right. She knew the proper form; she'd had to say it to many other men in the past. "But I cannot accept. But thank you very much," she added impulsively. "I'm sure that if I could accept, you would be one of the first fellows I'd consider."

His hand clenched on hers in a sudden spasm and he stared at her, dumbfounded.

"I dare say no one ever said no to you before," she said mournfully.

"I never asked," he said in astonishment.

"Well, I'm honored, but there it is," she said. She was acutely uncomfortable, and when she glanced up at the helm, she thought she could see the captain himself looking down at them in fatherly fashion and all the sailors smiling. She felt like a cheat and a rogue, and so she stared out to sea. But she nibbled at her lip and her small chin quivered. It made Jack Kelly think a moment before he spoke again, and he didn't give her up hand.

"My father's been after me to pick a lass and settle down," he said. "He's after all of us boys, to be sure, but I bear the brunt, since I bear his own name. It's that way with fellows who were wild in their youth; they get to be regular Puritans when it comes to their families. Before he met my mother, he was a roaring fellow; aye, they even called him Black Jack for his deeds, though my mother is quick to blush and say it's for his hair." He grinned, and

Della almost regretted her resolve—it was that charming a grin.

"Still, it's no secret that it was piracy that first sent my father to the Colonies to seek snug harbor and lick his wounds," he went on. "But once there, he found working for his fortune better than making war for it. I have great prospects, you know. I'm training with Captain Mason now because my own father's not sailing anymore, only building ships. But soon as he feels I'm qualified, I'll be piloting my own vessel and building my own trade."

"And my father's a merchant. I know a marriage between us would have been grand and profitable for all concerned," she said. He began to protest, mentioning her eyes and her nose and what all, so she wouldn't think it was her father's gold that prompted his offer, she thought, so she cut in to say decisively, "But it cannot be."

"Then there's someone else?" he asked immediately. He couldn't imagine it had anything to do with him, she thought. But there was someone else, so she nodded.

"Ah!" he said, thinking furiously, "but you liked my kiss."

"Oh yes," she said, for she had. His mouth had been firm and warm and his arms, infinitely comforting. But there hadn't been anything else but a mild sort of panic as she realized that she'd led him on. She'd led herself on, too. She'd led herself into a shipboard romance with a dashing sailor because she'd wanted to feel another man's desire, as well as his kiss—mostly because she'd wanted to feel more when he kissed her.

But he wasn't Jared—not his fault. Not really hers—and the fellow whose fault it was didn't have a clue about his guilt. Not his fault, either, for being so strong and smart and noble and handsome and the only man whose hands—not to mention mouth and whatever else she could imagine—she wanted upon her.

"Ah," he finally said, his brow unfurrowing, "so he is already wed."

"I should say not!" she said angrily. "What do you think I am?"

"But if you care for him, why else would you still be unmarried?" he asked with such genuine puzzlement that she warmed to him again.

"That's very kind of you," she said, "but the truth is that he doesn't think I'm such a prize as you do. Oh, he likes me, to be sure. But not as a woman, exactly."

"Then what exactly does he think you are?"

"The truth is," she said sadly, "he doesn't think of me much at all."

He paused. Then he brought her hand to his lips before he let go of it. "And you're going to wait forever?" he asked.

"I don't know. I don't think so," she said quietly, looking down at her shoes as she shifted her feet, "but I'm only twenty, you know."

"My sister is twenty and she is married, with a babe and another on the way," he said, "but I see. So there's no hope for me?"

She gazed up at him then. And had she been able to see herself through his eyes, it was possible that she'd have acted differently in everything she did. But she couldn't see what he did: a lovely young woman with startling blue eyes, white skin, a tiny, tilted nose, and the warmest rosy pink mouth he'd ever seen or tasted. Her hood had fallen back to show that she wore her own hair, black as a fashionable wig would have been white, and the sea wind had tossed it into a tangle of shining curls. Autumn was in the air, and she wore her cape closed against it, but he remembered the look of that shapely little form and how glorious it had felt in his arms. He sighed.

"Della, m'dear," he said, so overcome with emotion that he echoed his father's speech patterns, "the man's a fool—or worse, he's blind and has no heart atall. You're every man's desiring, and there's truth itself. Tell you what, m'dear. If it's all right with you, I'll say good-bye to you in London town, but look in on you in the Virginia colony one year from today. Who knows? He may have come to his senses by then, and if he has, I'll be lost, but at least I'll know it and give up dreaming. But you may have come to *your* senses, and if you have, why then, I'll be the happiest man on earth, and the rest of my life will be a dream. Is that all right with you?"

She nodded. She couldn't believe that Jared would come to his senses, any more than she believed she'd ever come to hers. But it would have been too cruel to say no to Jack—or to herself.

"Then we'll say no more now," he said, taking her hand and placing it on his sleeve, with his own covering it. "But may I write?"

"I'd like that," she said.

"Where shall I send the letters in England? And how long do you stay?"

"We're off to Hawkstone Hall," she said and then paused. "But for how long, truly I can't say. I don't know."

"I'll write to you there anyway, and if you've gone, they can send the letter on," he said, as he began to stroll with her. "I know how it is with relatives: they're mad to see you, and then two days later they're remembering why they moved away in the first place." He laughed.

She didn't. "We're not visiting relatives," she said. "We're visiting the earl of Alveston."

"Indeed?" he asked with interest. "But Alfred said you were staying with a fellow that was like his own son."

"That's true . . ." she said sadly, "but he is not my brother."

"Seeing all this," Alfred said, pushing himself back from the table and gesturing at the bare goose bones on his dinner plate, "makes me regret having raised you in the wilderness, child."

Della knew he wasn't talking about the remains of his dinner, because they were in a fine restaurant on one of the best streets in London. She'd spent most of her dinner staring out the window of their snug private parlor, watching the street. She'd been so entranced she hadn't had a bite to eat.

"Virginia's not wilderness," she murmured, distracted by the sight of two grand ladies exiting from a coach outside. She held her breath at the ease with which they held their huge panniered skirts, tilting them gracefully to the side so that they could sweep out of their carriage and daintily pick their way down the little stairs the footmen had let down for them. They did it just right, in the process exposing only a glimpse of fine white stockings covering trim calves and ankles. She was getting the hang of it just by watching. But she still didn't see how they managed not to knock the tiny hats off their high dressed wigs.

It was a chilly evening, so they wore capes, but Della could step outside her private parlor and see how the fashionable ladies of London looked without them. Their gowns were so exquisite they nearly took her breath away, and she was sure they'd do just that if she had to wear them. The ladies' bodices were so tightly fitted, so straight and firm all the way down to the V where they ended at the waist, that Della knew their corsets must have been made in hell.

No wonder colonials made so much money whale hunting, Della thought with a giggle. There must be a whole whaleful of stays on every fine lady in London. It made them walk stiffly, with only their hoops swaying— and their bosoms jiggling, of course. The square necklines were so low that every step a lady took in her high-heeled shoes made the tops of her breasts bounce and quiver alarmingly above those unbending torsos. But the fabrics! The embroidered silks and satins, the figured brocades and ribbons and rich colors and swags of fine lace! Della had seen well-dressed women at home. Now she saw that their finest would be exactly what London's finest ladies wore—at home.

She fingered the silk of her own cherry-striped gown. It had modest panniers and a decent neckline. It was one of her best dresses and was barely adequate to qualify her as a lady here. She put up her chin. She didn't care. She cared nothing for London. She was on her way to see Jared. That was why she was here.

But now Alfred was gazing out the window to see what she was watching. "Aye," he said, nodding as he saw the ladies descending from their carriage. "You can do some shopping. There will be time to have some new gowns fitted, never fear. You may even be able to get some done in time to take with us before we leave for Hawkstone Hall. The rest, we'll send on. But in the meanwhile, you can tog yourself out with new fans and shoes, hats and muffs—yes, you must get a slew of them—and some new capes and . . ."

"What?" Della asked in astonishment. "What are you talking about, Papa? There's no time at all."

He chuckled. "Time and to spare, my honey. I've business to do while I'm here. But as they say, all work and no play makes Alfred a dull fellow, and we can't have that, can we?" he asked playfully. "Don't worry, we'll have time for fun, too, puss. Show you the sights first, of course—the tower and the palace, and more. Every street has a surprise. You know how you marveled at the fact that they've houses built on the top of London Bridge, like it was a regular street at home? Well, there are shops there, too—fine ones. . . . Aye, I hear you—no more talk of shopping, but surely some evenings at the theater. London has the best in the world. If the weather holds—and I wonder about that because October's coming in and it can be cruelly cold—we'll have a look at some of the pleasure gardens, too. I remember them from my youth."

He sighed. "Your mama and I passed many happy hours at London's pleasure gardens. There were fireworks and concerts, dancing. . . . I wonder if Vauxhall is the same? And Ranelagh? No matter, it can only be better. And wait till you see an opera presented the way it ought to be! And a ballet—oh yes, we'll attend some of those, to be sure.

"We might get invitations to private balls as well," he

said happily. "I'm going to pay a call on our old friend Dr. Franklin. He's been renting a house here since '57, not far from here, I understand. He's officially in London for diplomatic reasons, but he's always on the lookout for a good bit of trade, and not too lofty even now to meet with old friends. A merchant's as good as a philosopher to him. Aye, our 'Poor Richard' is rich in friends; he's a very social fellow. He loves London. Colonials are all the rage here because of him, they say.

"So," he said comfortably, "I expect we'll be asked everywhere once I call on him. Of course, until then, there are always the public masquerades. You wouldn't meet anyone at them, because a lady must go masked if she has any reputation, but they're wonderful fun, and if I'm with you . . ."

He stopped because of the open-mouthed way she was staring at him. Her eyes were open almost as wide and were as startlingly blue as the tops of the flames of their table candles.

"What?" she asked incredulously. "What are you thinking of? We have no time for such nonsense. We have no time at all. I don't want to sit here in London when we're only miles away from Jared. It would be wrong for us to delay, to idle here when he's been waiting for us so long. He's *expecting* us, Papa," she said urgently. "We have to get there as soon as we can."

"Nonsense! Jared knows better than that."

"But I don't," she cried. "I traveled all this way—weeks on the ocean aboard a rocking ship, sleeping in a cramped little room, worrying about whales and whatall every minute—and all to get here. Now we're here at last and you say you want to linger in London, as though we have nothing to do!" She bounced in her seat, she was so agitated. "We have to go on *now.*"

"He'd expect me to take care of business here," Alfred protested. "He'd want us to take in the town a bit. He'd want you to get some new finery—Jared would want you to look nice for his friends."

Della smiled a smug smile. "Do you really think that matters to him? Do you think how he's dressed matters to me?"

But now her father grew solemn. He dabbed at his mouth with his napkin a few times before he finally answered. Then he dabbed at his forehead. "Della, my dear . . ." He paused, searching for words. He reached out and took her hand in his. "It's altogether possible that it does matter to him now. He's an earl now. And then, too . . ." His eyes, blue as her own, grew sad. "Understand, my dear, that it's also altogether possible that he will never see you as you see him."

She blinked. She'd never told her father how she felt about Jared and had foolishly thought he didn't know. She'd believed it her own secret, daydreaming of the wonderful day when her love would be reciprocated and she could announce it to her father and the world. But she never told him, because what if it never happened? Her father's sympathy would only make it worse. Her happiness was everything to him. She shuddered to think about what might happen if he knew and told Jared how she felt. Jared loved him and she knew how indebted he felt. What if Jared then got the notion he could repay Alfred by offering for her? That would be worse than losing him to another woman: the shame and pain of having a love returned by obligation would be unendurable.

"How *I* see him?" she squeaked, desperate to deny what she now knew her father knew. "How *should* I see him? He's—he's Jared, that's all, Papa. I just want to see him now."

He sighed again. "All right then, so you shall. I'll take care of business on our return to London, before we go home again. And Della," he said gently, "we shall go home again. We must eventually, you know."

"Oh, I know," she said with false brightness. But she prayed it would not be so. At least for herself. Jared had found his home at last, but she knew too well that wherever he was, was her home.

It was more than the fact that she'd worshipped him when she'd been a little girl. She wasn't a child anymore. She'd compared him to other men since she'd become a woman and had found all other men lacking. She'd seen her fair share of them, too, she reassured herself, more than most girls, in fact. She'd seen American men and was now seeing English gentlemen. Everything she'd seen of colonial men had only pointed up Jared's elegance, manners, and grace. And so far, all she could see in English gentlemen *was* their elegance, manners, and grace.

Colonial men came in two breeds. One type was so busily making a point of how rough, tough, and ready he was for the New World that he smelled like a savage and dressed like a bear and spoke about nothing but trapping and planting, building, or exploring. He needed a woman only to breed with, and didn't mince words about it. Still, some of this type were dangerously attractive. But she was the pampered daughter of a successful Virginia trader, and so, however exciting, they were simply not the sort for her.

The other kind of colonial man was worse, she thought. He was a townsman who aped the English while saying that he himself was better, and so he didn't come out looking even as good as the woodsmen. Of course, she had to admit that some colonial men, like the handsome and charming first mate on the *Boston Boy,* for example, were neither type. But then, they weren't Jared, either.

Soldiers—and she had seen a lot of them, owing to the recent wars—were in an entirely different class. Wise fathers didn't let their daughters near them, and clever girls soon learned that it took more than a uniform to make a man. Della was a very clever girl.

If she felt a little guilty about rejecting a man like handsome Jack Kelly, she had no hesitation about belittling the Englishmen she'd seen so far. She actually enjoyed sneering at them. Although she'd been born in England, she'd been brought up in the New World and felt just as unsure of herself as she was proud of herself for being a colonial. But who could resist mocking fine

English gentlemen? The ones she'd seen so far in London were outrageous. They wore high heels and minced in them. They wore furs, satins, and lace, and smelled like flowers. If her nose didn't deceive her, they wore as much amber perfume in their powdered wigs as their ladies did, and their wigs were often even more elegant. They carried fans and used them; they cradled fancy little snuff boxes in their white hands; they spoke in such nasal, artificial accents that she could hardly understand them. They were hardly men at all to her.

But Jared—he was elegant without airs, graceful without being womanly, tough without being crude. He was perfect. And he always would be, to her. Her father was right—London was a fascinating city, and she wished she could see more of it. But there was only one thing she had to see now.

"So when shall we leave, Papa?"

"It's a long trip," he said, musing. "There's your maid and my man and all our luggage to take with us, too. We'll need to hire two carriages and several changes of horses along the way, and good, reliable coachmen and outriders, too—they have bold highwaymen here. It's not safe on the roads. This isn't America, you know."

"How long?" she asked impatiently.

"Well, between this and that, say a week. . . ."

She groaned.

"Say three days, then," he said in surrender. "It can't be done sooner."

"Well, then," she said brightly, "do you know, I'd like some of that delicious-looking syllabub now. Oh, but maybe some of that rarebit first. And toast; it smelled so good before. And some of that joint of beef you said was so good—the rare part. And ale—yes, definitely—now I'd like some ale, too."

"Oh, Della," he said and sighed.

"It will be all right, Papa; you'll see." She grinned at him. But he only sighed again. "It will be fine," she promised. "We're going to see Jared. He's gotten what he's wanted all his life, what he deserved—so how can it be bad?"

Della dropped her towel and gazed at herself in the looking glass for long, silent moments. She hadn't taken stock of her appearance much since she'd come to womanhood, but she felt the need to do it now. She hadn't been able to on shipboard, not with her maid living as close to her as her own shadow. But this was a fine inn and the girl had her own alcove now, and the door between them was shut firmly. So Della contemplated herself in the glass. It was a thing she found as necessary as the long soak in the hot tub from which she'd just climbed. After all those weeks at sea, her hair had felt like kelp and she had sworn she leaked brine from every pore. Now she smelled like lavender and her hair hung in damp, silken coils. And now she stood naked in front of her mirror and ruthlessly assessed herself.

Her breasts were nice, she thought dispassionately; they were high and firm and full, and tilted very nicely down to rosy tips. Her waist was small; her stomach was almost flat; her hips rounded then tapered to shapely legs. Surely, she thought, men must see more, because she wasn't awfully impressed herself. In fact, only her breasts pleased her a little; the rest looked fairly commonplace. Her faults seemed glaring. Her skin was perhaps too white, because she could see blue veins here and there. And her hair . . . She sighed. She'd never minded having black hair—on her head, at least; she'd thought it a nice contrast to her complexion. But that jet-black triangle, that inky patch on all that whiteness of her body? It looked silly, at best—ugly, actually—not what she would have liked at all.

Jared's body hair was golden. She knew because sometimes in the summertime when he worked outdoors, his shirt would gape a little. Men on a farm weren't modest, but Jared never took his shirt off in public and had always been very circumspect around the house, even when he'd been young. She'd seen his bare torso only once, all those years ago, that terrible, painful time after he'd first come to them. She tried not to remember that. Instead, she remembered the glory.

Once, when he'd been helping with the haying, his shirt had slipped aside and she'd seen golden hair on golden skin moving over smooth, hard muscles. Actually, that was the day she'd learned what lust was. *The preachers were right,* she thought. She'd been punished for it, all right: she'd been stricken with incurable longing every time she remembered the sight of his handsome body. And she couldn't forget.

Now she frowned at her reflection. She placed a hand over that dark thatch and stared at herself in the glass. Then she turned and looked at herself from over her shoulder. She turned again, angled a leg, bent a knee, sucked in her stomach, and jogged a few steps in place. Then she sighed, picked up her nightshift, and pulled it over her head. Enough was enough—it wasn't as if there was anything she could do about her looks.

But as she scrambled up into her high bed, she decided she would waste a day tomorrow after all. She'd go to the finest fashionable dressmaker she could find and order herself the most extravagant gown in London town.

But she wasn't wearing that wonderful gown when her carriage finally approached Hawkstone Hall. First, the dressmaker wasn't able to finish it on time. Second, the dressmaker had then explained it wouldn't have been good to wear on a long trip anyway. In order to travel in such a fashionable gown, with a hoop and wide panniers, a lady wouldn't be able to sit on a seat in a coach. She'd have to travel crouched down between the two seats. That was what beautifully dressed ladies did in London when they had to travel from house party to house party. But they had to travel only a few streets, after all. And then, they were London ladies, who usually traveled only from upstairs to downstairs.

Della wore a green silk gown with only a drape of fabric

to hint at panniers, with no hoop at all, and without so much as a rib of whalebone to support her ribs. Although she guessed she looked provincial, she was very comfortable. But she got so excited when the carriage finally turned into the drive that she couldn't breathe any better than she could have if she'd been wearing a corset made of spikes.

"It's the most beautiful house I've ever seen!" she said, gasping as she stared at the golden stones of the hall.

"Aye, our lad's done himself proud," Alfred said with a trace of sadness in his voice. He remembered the beaten but proud boy on the dock as he looked at the grand house before him, and he had to blow his nose before he could speak again. "Done fine, our lad has; that's a fact."

When the coach stopped in the drive and what seemed to be dozens of servants appeared to help unload it, Della hesitated to step out. But then she remembered who she would see inside the wonderful house, and she forgot to be awed. She emerged from the coach and hurried down the little stairs, looking around for Jared.

When the tall man came running lightly down the steps to the courtyard, Della stopped breathing. She poised herself on her toes, ready to launch herself at him—and caught herself just in time. Because though this man had Jared's height and shoulders and looked like him from afar, the nearer he came, the more Della saw the resemblance was like a glance into an old, wavy mirror. Jared's head, but not his face; Jared's mouth, but not his eyes. And this man wore a white wig pulled back into a queue and tied with a black velvet ribbon. That should have told her immediately, but she'd been so eager to see him, she hadn't thought.

Della stood and smoothed her gloves as she waited for the man to approach. This wasn't Jared. Of course—it was his brother, Justin, the man who had been earl until Jared's return.

She eyed him openly as he came nearer. He wore a long

coat with bold brass buttons over a fancy long vest, a ruffled white neckcloth, and shiny silk breeches, and there was lace at his wrists. But fashionable as he was, he looked more manly than any English gentleman she'd seen so far. Maybe that was because she knew who he was, but it seemed to her that this man was so full of vital energy, just as Jared was, that the lace and powder only made him look more masculine by contrast—the way the contradiction of a pirate wearing a single golden earring made his tanned face look even more manly. He was a handsome fellow, with an air of easy command. She looked over his broad shoulder for Jared.

"My dear sir," Jared's brother greeted Alfred. "How good to see you. We hadn't expected you so soon! But I know Jared will be delighted. I'm his brother, Justin. And this must be Della! I'm amazed," he said, taking her hand as she dipped into a curtsy. "The way Jared speaks, I thought I'd have to get a nanny for you—and look at you. A most welcome surprise—a grown and beautiful lady."

Nothing at all like Jared, Della thought with sad irony as she rose from her curtsy and smiled at his brother.

"But where's the lad?" Alfred said, and then laughed. "I mean to say, where is the earl?"

"Out riding. I expect him back shortly. As I said, we didn't know you were coming so soon, or I'm sure he'd have been here to greet you himself. Allow me to do the honors. Please, come in; your rooms are ready. Wash the dust of travel from your hands and then join me for something to wash the dust from your throat," Justin said with a sweep of his hand as he showed them the house like a lord of the manor, welcoming them in.

Della smiled and followed him, marveling at how pleasant he was. After all, it *had* been his house; he had ruled here until a few months ago. *I would have been mad as fire,* she thought. But then, she told herself, relaxing, *he's giving it* back *to Jared after all.*

Still, as she climbed the grand staircase to her room, she

wasn't so much awed by the magnificence of the house as she was worried about Jared's being here. His elegant brother, with his lacy cuffs and white-wigged head, seemed to belong here, but Jared, with all his virtues, was still a plain, no-nonsense man from the Colonies. Della wondered if this return of his was such a good thing after all. *Just look at King Midas,* she thought. *All the gold in the world isn't worth much if you can't use it properly.*

Her room was twice the size of the one she had at home, and she'd thought her home the nicest on their side of the river. The furnishings made her revise further her view of home—there was so much gilt and glass here. Her traveling dress looked very plain in comparison to the draperies at her window, not to mention her bedhangings. She had her maid unpack and help her slip into her second-best gown, one she'd saved for an important dinner, because she now felt the hall demanded such finery. And she wanted Jared to see her at her best, after all.

Still, once she'd put on the blue silk gown with lighter panels and had fidgeted with the dollop of lace at each elbow, she sighed. It didn't look that fancy, after all—at least not here. She picked up her favorite fan, the one with a painted scene of Arcadia on it, and rebound her hair into a high tumble of curls. Nothing helped.

Her sense of the ridiculous saved her. Here she was, she told herself, in the grandest house she'd ever seen, halfway across the world from home, about to see Jared again— and she was staring into a mirror? There were so many things to see and she was only looking at herself? *Blockhead!* she chided herself, and, grinning, left the room.

She went down the wonderful double stairs she'd come up, the sweep and breadth of it making her wish she could simply keep going up and down it all day: up the right stairs, across the hall, and then down the left stairs again. She was so busily staring up at the high domed skylight that bathed it all in white light that she almost stumbled when she heard her name called. She paused, momentarily blinded by that light, and couldn't see where Jared was, although she knew he had called her. She stood midway on the stairs, squinting down into the hall below.

The tall man with the white wig was Justin; she remembered the cut of his coat. There, by his side, was her father. There was a beautiful lady, all in rose silk, there, too. And then, aside from a footman, she saw only another elegant, white-wigged gentleman. But where was Jared? She looked for a glint of golden hair and that familiar tanned face.

"Della, you wretch!" Jared called. "Has sea travel made you blind? Come down so I can welcome you to my new home."

"Jared?" Della asked in an awed voice.

He was the elegant gentleman next to the beautiful lady! His glorious golden hair was hidden under a white wig, tied back with velvet ribbon. He wore lace at his throat, with more frothing out from his wide, turned-back cuffs, and his vest was gray-striped silk. His riding coat was long in back and cut close in front in the latest style, so his muscular, buckskin-clad thighs could be shown to best advantage. His face was only lightly gilded by the sun now. She ventured down the stairs, half afraid of what she'd find at the bottom.

When she got there, he put two hands around her waist. She caught her breath and looked up into his warm, gray gaze. It was Jared, her Jared. She sighed with relief, her heart warmed. A smile tugged at his lips. He lowered his head; she dared not breath, but her lips parted. And then he laughed and bent his knees so he could swing her up in the air, the way he'd done when he'd returned from his travels, ever since she'd been a child.

"Della!" he cried exuberantly, holding her a little off the floor so he could see her eye to eye, as she rested her hands on his shoulders. "My own little Della. Welcome! Welcome to my home," he said with pride.

Then he put her gently down, hugged her hard, kissed her cheek, and took her hand in his.

"Brother," he said, "Mistress Fiona," he said in a softer voice, "here's my dear little Della, who's been like a sister to me, come all the way from the Colonies to see me."

Della smiled and curtsied to them, glad of the chance to bow her head for a minute. It seemed that in spite of all her fears and hopes, Jared hadn't changed at all.

Chapter

8

They were all much too polite. Della wanted to put down her fork and knife and shout at the earl, the man she'd known as Jared, "Where's Jared? Who are you? What in the world has happened?"

She sat at his table and dined. Dined! But Della longed to laugh, to rejoice with Jared at meeting again, to tell him everything that had happened since he'd left and hear everything that had happened to him. She wanted to be natural and free, the way they used to be—certainly not to be treated like "company," the way she was now. She desperately needed to look into his eyes and be his Della, and not his "little Della"—or yes, even "little Della," if she could have her Jared back again in place of this charming, pleasant, happy man who looked more like his brother than her Jared and whom she hardly knew at all. Who was this stranger who greeted her, introduced her to his brother and friends, and then sat down to "dine" with her?

117

But she was too polite to do more now—too tired, confused, and disappointed, too. And much too proud to cry. Instead, she looked from face to face and hoped she'd pinned a nice smile on her own as she listened to them chatting. She drank her wine every time they refilled her cup, and if they weren't fast enough, she raised it to get the footman's attention. But she was too distressed even to get tipsy.

They sat at a long table in a long room with tall windows overlooking the grounds. It was early evening, and dusk was slowly shading everything outside the same shade of gray as Jared's eyes. He sat at the head of the table, his brother at the foot, and when they grinned across at each other, it was eerie, because they were so alike and unalike, all at once. The beautiful Fiona sat next to her fiancé, but she watched Jared and kept jesting with him to make him smile at her. He did, and often.

But why shouldn't he? Della thought with growing unease. Fiona Trusham could make any man smile. She was as charming as she was lovely, young, and fresh-faced, with classical features and pansy-brown eyes that were always smiling. Her brows were light, so Della assumed her hair was, too, but whatever color it was, her fashionably curled snow-white wig made her creamy skin glow like a pearl. Her manners were perfect, her voice was low and pleasing, and she laughed at everything the gentlemen said to her. And they had a lot to say. In fact, she made every man at the table feel he had all her attention. She wasn't mistress of this house or promised to its master anymore, not since Jared had come home, but even so, she queened it there at the foot of the table, as though the foot were the head and she and Justin were lord and lady of the manor. It made Della uncomfortable, but neither Jared nor Justin nor the lady herself seemed to care.

Fiona's mother, a plump, placid lady with a comfortable smile, sat on the other side of Justin. Her husband, Baron Trusham, a slender, clever-looking man, too well dressed to be the countrified gentleman he claimed to be, sat beside her. He passed his time watching Jared carefully, his mild smile concealing whatever he thought of the man who had taken his prospective son-in-law's—and so too his daughter's—place at the head of the table.

The three uncles, whom Della still couldn't get straight in her mind, ranged round the table. The one beside Della was polite to her, but was more interested in talking to his wife. The other wives, each separated by an uncle, kept talking to each other across the hapless gentlemen throughout the meal. The housekeeper, pressed into service as a dinner guest because otherwise the company made the unlucky number of thirteen, sat across from Della— and no matter how hard anyone tried to talk with her, she knew her place too well to do more than nod. Della sat at Jared's side, but because he was host, he said little to her aside from "Try this lamb; it's delicious."

So in a sense, she sat alone. Della didn't feel like eating. She tried to keep her eyes on her plate anyway, so she wouldn't be caught staring hungrily at Jared, the way she found herself doing when she wasn't thinking. But Justin saw it. She was sure he did, and she ducked her head when he gave her a sudden understanding smile. His eyes seldom left his brother, though. The few things Della had eaten had stuck in her throat when she thought about that.

After all, the man had been king here. Now he'd been deposed. Della remembered how the English nobility were famous for scratching and clawing their way to power. Stories about clever, ambitious, deadly Tudors and Plantagenets—various Henrys and Edwards and Richards—and then Jared's own wicked uncle—began to spin in her head. She put down her fork and knife, her appetite completely gone.

Jared sat at the head of the table and surveyed his guests—*his* guests—in his great house, and his heart swelled. His brother, his uncles, his home—all here, all restored to him at last. Alfred and Della were here now, too, to share in his glory. He'd never felt such contentment, such pride, not in his whole life. He wondered if it was true that a man had to lose what he had before he really appreciated it, or if he'd have been just as happy if he'd never known those years of helpless longing for what he had lost. He doubted it.

One cloud shadowed his happiness. Once again, he wondered what his brother was really thinking. How could he just hand over all of this without pain, resentment, and anger? His expression grew grave as he met his brother's somber eyes across the long table.

And Della saw it and her heart clenched.

She thought of the Borgias and ambitious brothers and grew colder. Then she saw Jared's hand on his glass. It was a strong and yet elegant hand, a hand she knew was capable of both hard work and fine letters. She relaxed again. She'd been about to defend Jared from imaginary enemies, but he needed protection the way a tiger needed teeth. Then he laughed at something Fiona said, and she saw the admiration in his eyes as he gazed at the lady at his brother's side. Della realized there were things other than enemies for her to fear.

"A toast!" Justin said, rising from his seat, holding his glass high. "I know we've had many before, but we were starving then and not so eloquent. So I propose one more now—one made on comfortable stomachs and full hearts. My friends, I give you a toast: to Jared, earl of Alveston, who's home at last, thank God."

They cried, "Hear, hear!" and downed their drinks. But as Justin sat, Jared stood. "I give you another toast," he said, smiling at his brother. "To a truly just man. Having him returned to me means more than any title could. My lords, ladies, friends, and relatives: I give you a toast to my brother, Justin, restored to me at last, thank God!"

They were still smiling when dinner was over and the ladies went into the drawing room to wait for the gentlemen to join them. Della made her way to a corner seat, and Fiona came and immediately sat beside her. She smiled, and Della finally understood the force of that smile as well as Jared's reaction to it, because it melted half her hurt and some of her confusion. The lady's beautiful brown eyes sparkled and were filled with lively curiosity.

"You must tell me about the Colonies," Fiona said, angling herself as close to Della as she could, considering both of them were wearing enormous skirts. "I've never been farther from home than the front gates—" She giggled. "Well, not really. I've been to London, to see the queen—and king—but never farther. I've met people from the Continent, of course. But you've come from across an ocean! From a whole new world! Tell me all about it, please! And Jared—I mean the earl—tell me about him, too, if you please; he says you were like a sister to him, so you must know everything. Was he really a *servant?* What did he do? He won't talk about it to me. It must have been terribly sad. Oh, please, tell me all."

The oddest thing was that Della found herself almost ready to confide everything to her—until she remembered the way the lady and Justin had sat at their part of the table and behaved as though they still had the right to command all of it.

"Mistress Fiona," Della said quietly, "it's not my place. . . ."

"Oh, pooh!" Fiona said. "Don't stand on ceremony with me! Jared said your father has a title, though he doesn't use it, and so you're a gentlewoman, too, even if you don't call yourself one. So let's be colonial and dispense with formalities. Is it true that hardly anyone uses their titles there? How do you know who comes from good families?"

Della grinned in spite of herself, because the woman was so ingenuous.

"Well, some people do use them, but most don't," Della told her. "We judge a person on how they behave, not on how their ancestors did," she said piously. Seeing Fiona's expression, she relented and laughed. "That's what we *say,* but I think it's really because it would be too confusing. We don't give out titles in the Colonies, so no one could be 'the earl of Philadelphia,' for example. Even if someone called himself the earl of Alveston, there, it would sound fine, but it wouldn't matter much because no one would know who or what he was. We're not all English, you see. We have people from many countries—more arriving each day—from so many places it would be hard for anyone to care about any one particular country's titles. And honestly, I don't think it would help a man's business one bit if he made a fur trapper or an Indian call him 'my lord.' And business is what the Colonies are all about.

"Don't misunderstand me," Della said quickly. "We have heaps of titled men at home. We're quite civilized, you know. But the new settlers wouldn't take to it. They might even resent it. After all, most are coming to the Colonies to make a fresh start. Everyone thinks he has a chance to live like a lord even if he wasn't born one. But if he works hard enough, he really can. Not in such houses, of course," she said in embarrassment, looking around the elegant room, "but very nicely, even so. We have so much land and so few people on it, so a title doesn't mean as much as a full purse does. You see, at home, people are making their fortunes now the way our ancestors did here in England long ago. But it's harder because we don't have serfs—only slaves and bondsmen."

"Which is what he was," Fiona said eagerly, "so tell me about it, please. He worked for you, didn't he?"

Della hesitated. She could discuss Jared for hours, but his harsh past wasn't Fiona's business. She wanted to say it, but she was beginning to like the girl.

"You're going to say it isn't my business," Fiona said promptly. "But it is. After all, he could be my husband if I insisted." She giggled at Della's shocked expression. "It's true," she explained with a mischievous grin. "It's not just my vanity. You see, our land touches on the hall's on the southwest side. Our fathers were friends, and so when I was born, they agreed that I should wed the next earl when I came of age so that the two properties could become one. It's in a marriage contract.

"Jared vanished the very year I was born. It didn't make any difference to the settlement, because there was Justin to take his place. I grew up with him; we've both always known what our fate was going to be. The only reason we aren't married now is because he's kindly agreed to let me have a little fun before I start filling his nursery for him. I'm only nineteen, you see. And though I dote on Justin, no girl is going to rush into marrying a man she's known forever, is she?"

Della sighed, thinking of why a girl would do just that, as Fiona went on, with a devilish gleam in her eye. "And just look at our *new* earl of Alveston. He's like a brother to you, so I suppose you don't see him the way a girl does. But just look at him!" she whispered, as the gentlemen came into the room to join them.

Their gazes immediately arrowed to Jared. He was smiling at something Justin had said. It didn't matter that he was the topic of conversation; side by side with his brother, he was the one who would draw the eye. Della's dark-blue gaze locked on him because she could never look anywhere else when he was in the room. Fiona's brown eyes widened as she looked at him, because he was new and somehow more vivid to her than Justin was. His was the more intense coloring, the darkness of his tanned skin making his smile whiter, and his gray eyes clear as ice. As he led the gentlemen into the room, it could be seen that he was an inch taller, leaner, and more muscled; in everything, he seemed more than his brother now.

"Mmm. See what I mean?" Fiona purred. "Justin will have to look to his laurels, don't you think?" She laughed, showing little white teeth. She looked just like a cat, Della thought in dismay, an adorable, silken little cat that one couldn't blame for what it thought anymore than one could stop it from thinking it. Yes, Della thought, as Fiona stared at Jared, she looked just like a sleek little cat that had just found something fascinating to play with and then devour.

* * *

Della couldn't sleep. And it wasn't because she was in a new bed in a new house. She hadn't slept in her own bed for a month, and exhaustion had claimed her swiftly all those nights. She couldn't sleep now because she was so near Jared and yet he was further away from her than he'd ever been. The man who wore Jared's face was a stranger to her now, and it troubled her as much as it frightened her. She got up from her bed and went to her window. There was nothing but starkly moonlit gardens to be seen. She turned and paced her room once, and then drew on a robe. She felt trapped.

Her nightshift had no hoops; her hair was gathered in a simple tie at the back of her neck, just like a fashionable young man's. She was without corset and bodice; she was unfettered and yet chained to her room for the night. She was where she'd yearned to be and not at all where she needed to be. She was moonstruck and longing—and so unhappy she knew she had to find human company.

Not him, of course—she was moon-mad, not entirely mad. He was probably sleeping, as she should be. There was no one she really could talk to now, she knew that. Her father would only be frightened if she tapped on his door to wake him. Her hardworking maid lay snoring in deserved sleep in her trundle bed. But there might be a servant who could direct her to the library, Della thought hopefully. Once there, she could hold a book in her hands and pretend to be reading, and he might hear of it, and she might see him. . . . No. Della sternly banished the fantasy because she hadn't had any luck so far, and so there was no reason to think she'd suddenly find some this eerily bone-white night. But if she stayed alone in her room, she'd howl at the moon, she was sure of that.

She left her room, tiptoed across the hall, and then skimmed down the stairway, which was bright as day beneath the glass dome above it and cold as the stars in this endless night. She wished she'd thought of wearing slippers. There were no footmen awake downstairs, but she eventually found the library anyway—after several toe stubbings and brief, painful encounters with tables and chairs that hid their sharp edges in the deeper shadows.

It was a grand room, with a cool, polished wood floor and not half enough carpets to cover it for her comfort. She saw a massive fireplace on the far wall that held a great gaping mouthful of shadows. She wished she could light a fire, because she wasn't used to such cold Octobers in Virginia. But she knew it wasn't really that frigid—half the chill was in her own heart.

The moonlight had looked bright enough to read by, but it wasn't. She sat curled up in a chair by the window anyway, holding a book and staring at it, seeing only her own problem on the strangely bleached white pages.

"You'll ruin your eyes. We'll have to get you a walking stick and a begging bowl if you keep that up. If you want to read, I'll get a light."

She sat up sharply, clutching the book to her breast. "No! Don't," she said. He stood in the doorway, tall and fair, in a long robe that came to his feet. In that moment, she didn't know if it was really him or just his brother or her longing to see him that had produced a vision of him.

"Why aren't you sleeping, Dell?" Jared asked, coming into the room.

Her heart picked up its steady beat. "Can't," she said breathlessly. "New house, new room, new bed, you know."

"Don't I just?" he murmured, putting his hands into the deep pockets of his robe and staring out the long windows to the moon-drenched grounds beyond. "Isn't this place something, though?" he asked, gesturing at the window, the room. "Is this not *something*, Della?"

She nodded.

"I couldn't sleep, either," he said. "I tried. But then I came downstairs. I often do. I roam this place at night, Dell. I still do, after a month. I can't believe it's true. I guess I'm still afraid that if I fall asleep, I'll wake to find it was all a dream." He sounded so lost that he stopped talking when he heard himself. When he spoke again, his voice was lighter. "I heard you—or someone—making noise and trying to hush it immediately after. I came to see who was bumping into everything that had a corner on it and swearing like a sailor as she did. Traveling by sea has been educational, hasn't it? If Alfred heard you, he'd wash out your mouth. Shall I?"

"Just try," she said in the rough little voice she had always used against his teasing threats.

"What do you think of it, Dell?" he asked suddenly.

She knew just what he meant. Her spirits rose. This was Jared talking to her now, Jared as she'd always known him—not the earl of Alveston, whom she didn't know. "It's everything you said," she answered promptly, "and more. I didn't understand the grandeur of being an English nobleman before. It's like—it's like you're a king or something here."

"I know, I know. Sometimes it's too much, but sometimes, I admit, I wallow in it." He spoke to her there in the low light, and it was like talking with himself, only better, because he knew she understood him. "I don't know if I'll ever get used to it," he admitted. "By God, Della, do you understand the differences I've known? From being considered a piece of human rubbish to being treated like a king—and all in one lifetime? Sometimes I think both extremes are absurd. Sometimes I don't—and that worries me. Thank God you're here."

Her eyes flew open wide and she began to smile.

"You and Alfred put things into perspective for me," he went on, as her smile faded. "I can never get too far above myself with you two around. You're living reminders of what I was."

"You might come to hate us for that," she said in a small voice.

His big hand came down on her head and rested there lightly before he ruffled her curls, as he would a child's. "Yes. Likely," he scoffed. "Oh, very likely, isn't it? I meant only that you make all this real to me, because none of it seemed real until you and Alfred got here."

"You're happy?" she asked, feeling the chill in the night as his hand left her hair.

"Happy?" he laughed. "What an inadequate word. It can't hold all I feel. I suppose I was happy once before, before they stole me away. But I didn't know it then. But this? This is much more than 'happy.' I'm home, Della. Do you know what that means?"

She couldn't answer because of the lump rising in her throat, so she only nodded, not even knowing if he could see her head move. But he could see her clearly, only as though she were a silhouette cut from paper, all in black and white. Her hair was darker than the darkness in the room, and it formed an inky frame for her white face. When she moved her head, it moved the shadows, showing her in flashes of high drama, as though he were watching her during a lightning storm. But he didn't have to see clearly; he knew her expressions better than his own. And he felt her warmth from where he stood. He smelled the fresh floral scent she always wore, and his heart grew full. She was here—his Della was here. Things seemed right at last.

She saw him glowing golden in the dim light, the brightest, warmest thing in the chilly room. He wore such a colorful robe that the shadows couldn't extinguish it, and his hair was loosed and fell in soft golden waves to his wide shoulders. He was tall and straight and strong and everything she remembered, everything she wanted. She felt all the old stirrings and more. But though they were so close and alone together in the moonlight, there was no romance in it for him and thus only sorrow in it for her. She clasped her hands tight over the book to keep them still and to keep herself together, so he wouldn't know.

He was so relieved to be with her that he relaxed and spoke of things he usually didn't.

"Those days, before I met Alfred and you," he said, his voice soft and dreamy as the night, "how can I explain it? I knew I'd been someone once—I almost got myself killed for insisting on it more than once—but the truth is, sometimes I myself wondered if I'd only imagined it."

"We believed you," she said, keeping her voice even, fearful of ruining the intimacy of the moment. He seldom spoke of those days, even with her.

"Yes, and I thank God for it. I don't think I'd have lasted much longer, Dell. I was getting to the point that I didn't care. Nothing hurt anymore. That was the worst part. If you feel pain, you try to avoid it. But I was getting to the point where I didn't. It seemed to me that if I'd only imagined I'd been an earl, then I was mad and didn't deserve to live. If I had really been one, then it was too degrading to live the way I did."

Della was glad it was too dark to see the pain that must be in his eyes.

"I could always take the beatings and the humiliation," he said thoughtfully, "because I knew I was better than my master was. If you fill up a boy with a sense of his worth early on, it's like filling a camel with water: it keeps him going later when everything else has gone. But I was coming to manhood, and there were other dangers. Old Higgins was threatening to sell me to a man who wanted— It doesn't matter," he said abruptly. "I don't think I'd have survived much longer. No one believed me; I even doubted myself."

"Thomas believed you the moment he heard what you said."

"Thomas," he said softly. "By God, I wish he could be here to see this. You were lucky to have such a brother. I've always tried to take his place for you, even though I knew I never could."

She went very still. "Don't worry about it," she managed to say. "I don't need another brother . . . but I can always use a friend. So," she said more briskly, "my lord Alveston, what next?"

"What, indeed? Learn the estate, learn my duties, begin

where I left off and hope I don't make a botch of it, I suppose."

"You'll never come back?" she asked, and swallowed hard.

"Back? Oh. Virginia. Well, to visit—of course. This is my home now . . . but what's this talk about going back? You just got here. I want you and Alfred to stay on and on, to share this with me. It's nothing without you, you know."

"If I were going to be with *you,* then I would stay. But . . . but the earl of Alveston makes me nervous," she said in a rush.

He laughed.

"No, I mean it," she said, looking for a light way to put a hard thing. "Take the wig you wore today—I mean, I know it's all the rage, but it's not the Jared I know. You have such beautiful hair," she said wistfully. "What I wouldn't give to have such . . . I hate to see it covered over with white curls like a sheep's. Or like old Mr. Peterson's, at home."

He put back his head and roared with laughter. Old Peterson was a miserly shopkeeper whose flea-bitten old wig was the joke of town.

"So bad?" he said gasping with laughter.

"No," she admitted, "not really. But not Jared, either."

He grew sober. "I'm not precisely Jared anymore, Della. I'm the earl of Alveston now."

"Oh, I see," she said, "and so then I guess we'll soon see you rigged out with silver-headed walking sticks and china snuffboxes and very high heels that make you totter, and you'll paint your face a bit, and wear a fan at your belt, and start to drawl when you speak?"

"No, no," he said, laughing. "My brother doesn't, does he?"

"But he's not the earl now, either, Jared."

"No, he's not. That bothers me as much as it does you," Jared said seriously. "That's the one flaw, isn't it?" he asked, raking his hand through his hair in his distress. "The one thing that makes it less wonderful. But two men can't wear the same title. Sometimes I wonder if I should just return to Virginia and let things go back to the way they were for him. He makes a better earl than I do, doesn't he?"

"No," Della said simply, "You are the earl, and you can't change that. You shouldn't, because then you'd just be finishing what your uncle started."

"But if he is better suited . . ."

"He's not, brother," Justin said.

Della and Jared both started and turned to look at the man who stepped out of the shadows by the door. Justin wore a robe, too, but his hair was cropped short, and without his wig, he looked less like Jared.

"I'm not eavesdropping," he said. "I didn't even bring along a pistol to see who was sneaking around the house in the dead of night, because I think you two were trying to wake the dead. Is this what you do in Virginia? Is that why you people are so marvelously productive? You never sleep?"

"A new house . . ." Della tried to explain.

"New burdens," Jared said decisively, and they were all quiet for a moment.

"You make too much of it, you know," Justin said calmly as he strolled into the room. "It's not really like having a kingdom, brother. There are no decisions of any importance to the nation to be made here, nothing beyond what to plant next spring or how to fix a tenant's roof. It's not like the old days, when we had to muster forces and ride off on crusades or protect the villagers against the Vikings or get together with the barons to plot against our least-favorite kings. No, now it's merely a nice property with an old title. It's true that every year, you have to preside over the village fair, and you have to go to a few christenings for goodwill. They'll nag you to take your place in the House of Lords, and if you feel like shopping in London, you'll go. But it should be nothing for you. In fact, you may find it dull. After all, you managed a thriving business as well as a plantation in the Colonies."

"Yes. But no man could come along and take that from me by simply saying he was my brother," Jared said with equal calm.

Della held her breath as the two men spoke, because there in the black and white shadows, she sensed the tension between them over their new roles.

"No. You're wrong. He could, even in the Colonies, if it was his," Justin said. "There's the crux of it. It is *yours*. Yes, I enjoyed being earl in your place—what man would not? But I always knew it was your place, not mine. That's not a good way to live. Don't try to make me do it again. I give it back to you with an open hand. Our uncle showed us brothers can be worst enemies. Let me show you they can be best friends. Don't make this harder for us both, brother. Take what's yours, leave me what's mine, and rejoice with me for it. And then sleep easy, because it's the right thing to do."

There was silence in the room. Then in a voice made unsteady by either laughter or tears, Jared said, "Now look what you've done. You've made Della cry."

She was glad that her tears diverted them, so she let the few sentimental tears become a stream.

"Little sister, I never meant to do that," Justin said, as he knelt by her side and produced a handkerchief from his sleeve.

"I'm . . . not . . . anyone's . . . sister," she said through gritted teeth as she snatched at the handkerchief, her tears forgotten in her annoyance.

"See?" Jared said as he knelt at her other side, "that's how a real earl behaves. He carries a handkerchief with him everywhere. All I can offer you is my sleeve."

She giggled.

"Earls and magicians, yes," Justin said with a straight face. "Don't worry, brother, I'll teach you the way of it; it's all done with mirrors."

They laughed at that, and then so much more when

Della blew her nose and Jared said they could use her on foggy nights to warn ships instead of the Eddystone Light. They laughed so hard they had to hush each other, and then ended up laughing even more.

Giggling so much she was breathless, Della let the two of them finally accompany her back up the stairs. At the top, Justin bowed over her hand and wished her a good night. When he left, Jared stood smiling down at her. The glass dome above the stairs made a circle of broad, bleached light for them to stand in.

"Little Della," Jared said tenderly, "always the right touch for the right moment. Thank you, you little rogue." He pretended to cuff her chin, but his fist only brushed it, like a lion reaching out with blunted claws to play. "I remember too well how easily you can make yourself cry. Lord, remember the time you started wailing when Alfred was about to kill you for spilling ink all over his important papers? You said you'd cut yourself on the broken inkwell, and you cried so hard, we all thought you were bleeding ink and wound up frantically trying to comfort you for your crime. The inkwell wasn't even broken," he chuckled. "I knew how easy it was for you, and yet I believed you, too. Tonight, downstairs, you lightened a difficult moment for us. Little Mistress Mischief," he said gently. "Thank you."

His eyes were the exact color of the moonlight, and just as shadowed as he gathered her in his arms in that moon-drenched circle. He held her tight against his hard body and hugged her fiercely, though his embrace was soft. He bent his head and brushed a kiss against her cheek. She closed her eyes and was sure her heart stopped even though it was beating as though it would leap from her breast. His soft hair brushed her face, and it smelled like good soap and warmth and man and Jared, and she breathed in hard so her lungs would burst. And wished . . . .

"Good night, Della," he said, releasing her.

She stepped away from him. It was the hardest step

she'd ever taken in her life, because every instinct begged her to stay. But now she worried. She wore no corset or stiffened bodice, so surely he must have felt how her breasts had peaked in excitement, how her body had heated against his—she felt she'd blazed like a candle in his arms. She was afraid to speak as she backed away, staring up at him.

He paused, for in that second after he let her go, he felt empty and alone again. She'd felt so very good in his arms. Too good—in the wrong way. He'd been looking for his little sister, but it was as if he held a stranger, a tantalizing stranger. It put him off balance, made him uneasy. He frowned, but a heartbeat later he smiled, realizing it was a natural reaction. He'd have to remember she was grown up now. Very grown, he thought ruefully—he'd felt every one of her supple curves pressed close, her firm breasts growing taut against his chest. He'd felt more than that— was why he'd stepped away so fast.

But it was simply explained, he told himself. Neither of them had on much clothing, and bodies were traitors, responding even when hearts and minds were otherwise inclined. He, of all men, knew that. Further, he reminded himself, a woman's breasts were sensitive to things like cold. A man's body was sensitive to a woman. Her body had reacted to natural stimuli, as had his. He hoped he hadn't embarrassed her; he knew he'd shocked himself. He'd cut off his arm before he'd offend or upset her or betray her and Alfred's trust in him. She looked upon him as brother and protector; whether he was nobleman or bond-boy, he could never let her down.

He'd have to remember to be less free with his embraces so as not to embarrass either one of them again. They were both adults now, after all, not able to snuggle like puppies in a litter, no matter how much familial affection they felt for each other.

But even so, the embrace had comforted him. Just being close to her did that. He realized it was because she would always understand who he was and where he'd come from and try to help him cope with it.

"And thank you again," he said with feeling, "for being Della—when I most needed her."

"Oh. But there's nothing I could do about that. Good night, my lord," she said breathlessly, sweeping him the deepest curtsy she could, so deep as to be a mockery. She hoped he'd laugh enough to forget, in case he'd guessed her emotions, so that he wouldn't hesitate to hug her again someday.

He grinned. " 'Night, love," he said. "Now go to bed."

She did, smiling all the way, because he'd said *love,* and for tonight, she would believe it, even though she was too smart to fool herself very long. For tonight, she would sleep with his words echoing in her ear.

Chapter

9

There was the smell of apples—not a good smell, because they were rotting, fermenting, too sweet and too acid and too heavy in the air. The stink of cider mash was not the sweet scent of cider. But that was how a cider press smelled. Otherwise, it was pleasant, cool and damp, as a cellar ought to be in summer. Then why was he so cold and yet slick with sweat? He listened, hoping he wouldn't hear anything. But he did.

A thumping, or was it his heart? Jared twisted in his bed, knowing he was dreaming, and struggled to awaken. But then he was back in the cellar again—only now it was a cupboard in the back of the kitchen—and the smell of apples was stronger, and he remembered there was a cider press he should be tending to. In the way of such dreams, he worked the handle of the press, sweating, straining, bearing down with all his insubstantial weight, and yet he was in the cupboard at the same time, listening.

"I got his contract for a full seven years," Jared heard the

135

man at the table say to the man opposite him, as he jerked a thumb toward Jared, who strained at the cider press and listened from his cupboard. "I've only had him for a few months of them. That's good time left to go. I'll sell you his papers for a song, but I ain't givin' him away."

"A song, is it? Ha! A dirge is what you mean," the other man said and laughed. "He's not worth two coppers, Smith. He's a runt, and you know it. Thin as a lathe. You're in luck; I need a runt—a sizable boy won't fit in chimneys. But I don't know if he'll suit, even so; I'm taking a chance. There's talk he's weak-minded, too. We all know you beat him black and blue. You ought to jump at my offer. Why, I believe you couldn't trade him for a good dog."

"A fat lot you know, Brown. I beat him 'cause he's new to the work and rambunctious, like all boys, rot them. But he'll train up good. He'll fatten fine, too, if anyone wants him to; he ain't sick, just off his feed. 'Sides, I paid good money for him and I ain't givin' him away. You want him? You got to pay for him."

Jared listened to the two men arguing about him. He trembled, as much with indignation as with fear.

"Your name, boy?" the huge man demanded, as he led him away, down twisting streets that tilted and changed as they walked on them, as streets do in dreams. But he knew this was no dream, because he'd tried to wake up so many times and could not.

"I am Alveston," he said. "Jared Bellington, earl of Alveston," the boy said in a proud but fearful voice. "I was stolen away, sir, taken in the night and sold into bondage. If you return me to England and Hawkstone Hall, you'll be rewarded, I swear it. Please believe me, sir; I speak the truth."

He groaned in pain now, as he had not then, as he felt the lash on his back, but his tears stung worse, because they were tears of shame. A Bellington did not cry; the earl of Alveston did not cry. If he did, then he would never return to his home again. If he didn't, then there was a chance he'd be discovered for what he was and everything would be *made right again.* It was a boy's magical incantation to keep his mind off the pain, to keep his mind together, but it was a man who groaned now as the dream cast him back to the days and nights of his despair again.

"See, the way I'm seein' it," the hairy man said craftily, *as he drained his glass and plunked it down on yet another table, "ye'll be killin' him soon. Now, that's yer business, Brown, to be sure it is. Still, if the guvner hears of it . . . it be illegal to kill indentured boys, bad as they may be. Ain't like he's exactly a slave—worse, to my way of thinkin', 'cause yer held accountable fer his life. It'll cost ye a bundle to keep out of the lock-up, do ye kill him, to say nothin' of the fine! But, say, do ye be sellin' him to me . . . ye'll use yer coins to buy 'nother lad's papers, or maybe even get yerself a slave. I'm a poor man; I got no choice. I need a lad for me shop. This one ain't much, to be sure, and addled, to boot. An earl, he says! Why not a duke, while he's at it? Ha!*

"But it ain't funny fer long," he said, wagging a dirty finger, *"and ye can't beat it out of him, can ye? 'Cause if ye could, Gawd knows ye'd have been the man to do it. We hears him yellin' sometimes, and sometimes we just hear yer old belt singin' as ye go at him. But still, I need a boy, and I ain't got much coin. Solve yer problem and mine at one stroke. That's a fierce temper ye got on ye, Brown. Ye'll be killin' him afore long, and we all knows it. What do ye say?"*

"And I suppose that if he does meet with a misfortune, you'll be the one to inform on me? Ah—take him and both of you be damned!"

They were buying and selling him. He couldn't bear it, but he had to. He was alone in the darkness, hiding, shamed, but doing it to avoid a beating.

But it was the shame and not the pain that made him twist and turn in his bed now, an ocean away from the place of his dreaming, a lifetime away from the boy who was weeping.

Jared woke in a tangled welter of bedclothes, damp with

sweat. He sat bolt upright, gulping great breaths of air until he felt his heartbeat slow and his body begin to dry in the cool morning air. He looked around the room, still unsure of where he was and if he was really awake. Dawn's first gray light was the only thing to illuminate the room; the fire was out in the grate. He'd left orders to be sure no servant came in while he slept to rekindle it before he awoke, the way servants commonly did for men of rank. Keeping his secret was well worth a cold awakening. It didn't happen often, but often enough. The earl of Alveston could not be known to weep in his sleep. *The great earl of Alveston,* he mocked himself, *in his great mahogany bed, covered in silks and satins—and the cold, damp sweat of defeat—because he had been a slave in all but name once and knew in his heart that he could never be a proper nobleman again.*

But he had to be. Was that to be the story of this life—to always be what he knew he was not, while others insisted that he was?

Jared rose and paced the room, a massively muscled man at home in his naked body, wearing it like a princely garment. He was as used to his nudity as other men were to their long nightshirts, because unlike them, he always slept without clothes, knowing the toll the dreams took when they came.

He paced and counted his blessings, as though to be sure of them: He was back home. He had been very lucky in his ill luck, finding Alfred and Della, working to make a fortune, and then, finally, the ultimate triumph—becoming himself again and finding a brother he thought was lost—but he'd taken everything from him by doing so.

Jared stood by his window with his weight braced on his two hands and stared out as dawn raised a filmy curtain of mist from the landscape. *And what a landscape!* he thought in wonder. He saw his manicured gardens, his statuary, and, in the distance, his orchards and his pond glittering beneath the rising sun. His spirits rose, too. But then he cracked the window open and breathed deeply. There was a faint scent of windfall apples on the autumn breeze, and he remembered his dream and his life again.

He rang for his bath but was glum and abrupt with the valet his brother insisted on sharing with him. When the man handed him a towel so he could dry himself before the newly laid fire, Jared happened to glance out his window again.

As the morning fog lifted, he could see early workers hurrying on their way, milkmaids from his dairy, farm workers going to his fields—and a lady in belled skirts strolling in the formal gardens. Della. He recognized her immediately by the way her lilting step made her skirt sway even before he saw that inky hair, unmistakable even from a distance. He grinned, forgetting the night as he saw the day and Della walking out to enjoy it. It would be good to talk with her; they hadn't had much time together since she'd come to his new home. He'd missed their talks.

She was with another woman who was too elegantly dressed to be her maid, too slender to be any of the aunts. She wore a tiny hat perched on a jaunty white wig, wearing a gown as rosy as the dawn—Fiona! Jared's smile grew and he dropped his towel. It was time to be dressed and out, leaving the night and all its pain behind him.

Fiona's laughter lit the morning; just hearing it made Jared pause to listen, because it sounded like dulcet bells. Then he heard Della laughing along with her. It was her usual rich, full-throated laughter; just hearing *it* made him grin.

"Ladies," he said, as he came up behind them, "may I join you?"

"Jared!" Della cried in delight as she spun around to see him.

"Why, of course," Fiona said with a growing smile that she hid behind her floral fan. "But we're the ones who should ask if we may join you—it's your house, after all."

"One forgets," he murmured.

"We two do not," Fiona said, laughing. "We dare not. Good morning to you, my lord. But what are you doing up so early? Don't you know that a grand English nobleman should be just getting to sleep around now?"

"Forgive me. I see I'll need a little time to become adjusted," he said with a crooked grin.

"Never fear," Fiona said, eyes alight with mischief above her fluttering fan. "We'll guide you every step of the way."

It pinched at Della's heart to stand beside Jared and watch him being flirtatious with another girl. She'd thought it might happen one day, and now that dreaded day had come. Fiona was too well brought up to simper, but she smiled and batted her eyelashes and gave Jared a roguish look. He stood smiling, his gray eyes taking in Fiona with such appreciation that Della felt she was in the way. No, worse than that, she didn't feel in the way at all—just entirely out of the picture. And Fiona was Justin's fiancée! But Della wasn't worried about Justin now.

"Is Justin still sleeping . . . I mean to say . . . like an English gentleman?" Della blurted. She hadn't asked where he was when she'd met Fiona earlier; she'd just been enjoying her company then. Fiona had been a charming companion, pointing out the various outbuildings of the hall, showing Della the gardens, nodding greetings to all the workers they passed as they strolled along together. They all knew Fiona, even though she lived miles away on her own estate. Della thought they were having fun together until Jared appeared. Then Fiona forgot her and focused all her attention on him with stunning swiftness.

"Oh, Justin?" Fiona said carelessly. "He's out riding, since the break of day, or so I'd guess—it's what he does when the weather's good—and when it's bad—whether I'm here visiting or not. Leaving me alone and to my own devices, as usual. I don't know why we're going to all the bother of getting married," she said, laughing up at Jared.

"After all, we're already behaving like an old married couple. Thank heavens I met up with your little Della, or I'd have been bored to pieces."

"But Fiona, we're almost the same height, and the same age, and I am not 'little' in any sense of the word," Della declared. *There,* she thought, *I've said it, and I'm glad.*

"Oh no, you're wrong about one thing, at least," Fiona said, tapping her lightly with her fan. "Jared said you were a year older than I."

"Age doesn't matter," Jared said. Della smiled with relief, because although she'd never thought twenty was a great age, Fiona somehow made it sound like she was an ancient spinster compared to her. "Or height either," he went on. "'Little Della' is just what I'm used to calling you; I think I'll still do it when you're ninety, Dell."

"Just so!" Fiona said on a gurgle of laughter. "It's because he's known you forever. But don't fret. It's a charming name, like Little John, an English fellow who also wasn't little in any sense."

"Or Chicken Little," Jared joked. "And don't look at me like that, Della, my girl, because when you're a little older, I'll bet you'll be grateful for being called 'little.'"

"But I am *not* grateful now," Della said mutinously.

"I didn't realize it rankled so much. I'll never say it again. I promise," he said, looking down at her with concern.

"That's exactly how it is with old friends," Fiona said merrily. "Why I packed an entire wardrobe for this visit, and yet I vow I could wear the same gown day after day as far as my own fiancée is concerned. He just doesn't see me anymore. Don't fret, Della; it's just that the years work like vanishing cream on us where the gentlemen are concerned."

"Now you have me worried. I have to see that my brother gets his eyes examined," Jared said gallantly, offering Fiona his arm.

He offered Della his other one, and they all strolled on that way together. Fiona joked and laughed, her fan fluttering as much as her eyelashes as she looked up at him, acting as though there was nothing on his other arm but a piece of lint.

That's what Della felt like. She didn't say a word. It would be rude to interrupt, and what could she say, after all? She didn't know anything about the hall and felt she'd sound stupid interjecting 'Oh really' or 'Is that so?' whenever Fiona stopped for breath. Anyway, she was becoming too unhappy to speak at all. Jared knew her moods too well; she didn't want him to think she was jealous or hurt. And she was so jealous and it hurt so much, she didn't know what to do.

She tried to cheer herself up as they walked on. It probably didn't mean anything; what did she know about English ladies? Maybe they all acted like that with men. As for Jared, Fiona was going to marry his brother; she'd soon be family, so it was only clever of him to try to get to know her better. It wouldn't be a bad idea for him to flatter her, too. *Clever Jared,* Della thought glumly as she heard Fiona's lilting laughter in response to something he said.

Then there was the fact that Fiona looked lovely as a blooming rose this morning in a glowing pink gown. Della wore green. It was a pretty gown, but it made her feel as if she were the leaves that set off the beauty of the rose. She was a perfect complement to Fiona's looks, and her silence was a perfect background for Fiona's voice and laughter. *The only good thing about being in the background is that no one notices how unhappy you are,* Della thought wretchedly.

She is delightful! Jared thought as he listened to Fiona and watched her stop to admire a rose arbor. He gazed at her with pleasure. She belonged here at the hall as much as the rose arbor did. She fit in perfectly, so cultured, such a lady in every sense of the word—at ease in any company, obviously pampered since birth, sure of herself, and yet not spoiled—she had as wide a smile for his gardeners as for him.

"M'lord, lady, Mistress Fiona," one of them said as he paused, his hoe on his shoulder.

"Griffin," Fiona replied with a glowing smile. "I was just telling his lordship about your roses. Just see how your work pleases him."

The man beamed, bent his head, touched a lock of hair on his forehead with one hand, and then trudged away with a lighter step. Justin was very lucky, Jared thought. It wasn't just her manner. Her face and figure were as pure and perfect as that of a porcelain shepherdess he'd seen on a table in the drawing room. Remembering the figurine made him frown; he had to go over everything in the house in detail with Justin as soon as he could, because he wouldn't take what wasn't his. But which of the treasures he'd seen in the hall had come down through the years, and which were ones Justin himself had picked? He'd never take those; they were Justin's taste, his prizes, a part of his life, and so they were his, no matter who had paid for them.

He gazed at Fiona as she leaned to inhale the fragrance of one of the roses. She was way above the likes of him, he knew. But he could admire her, and he did. He drank in the sight of the lovely girl with the snow-white wig that only emphasized her youth and beauty. He stared at her laughing mouth, her alabaster skin, her gown showing so much of it above her small, high breasts. The roses near her face showed how their subtle colors were echoed in her cheeks. She too was Justin's choice.

But then, the traitor thought came creeping in: no, she wasn't, not really. If Justin had been the one they'd found in the underbrush that night, if Justin had been the one sold into bondage and shipped to the Colonies, not him, then Fiona would be his. The thought was startling. But once thought, it was there: if he had never been taken from his bed that night, she might even now be in his. He'd never have waited years to marry such a beauty, the way his brother had.

She would have been mine, Jared thought, accepting the

reality of it for the first time. *So it was written. Fiona herself said so.*

Denial came fast on the heels of that thought. Jared recoiled from the whole idea, as if it were the deed and he'd somehow cuckolded his brother. He was appalled by his ugly, ignoble musings. That was exactly it—it wasn't noble. Whatever their father's plan had been, it was impossible now, because Fiona was Justin's beloved. And even if she weren't, he himself wasn't worthy of such a lady anymore. He was earl now with all that entailed, but Justin was the true nobleman. *As for me,* Jared thought resignedly, *I'll have to keep trying to be one the rest of my life. Still . . . if I had such a lady wife, no one would ever doubt me, maybe not even myself. . . .*

Jared didn't like the way his thoughts were running, so he looked at Della, hoping to catch her eye. She could always divert him.

But she was oddly silent and her mouth was grim. He studied her with sudden concern. She didn't look sick. In fact, she looked fresh and lovely. He knew her: if she were sick, her pale complexion would be sallow, not glowing with banked light the way it was now. No, Jared realized, she was only ill at ease. She seemed uncomfortable with Fiona, because she kept eyeing her strangely—enviously. Jared sighed. Of course. Fiona was a fine English lady, and Della was a colonial girl.

She was a very pretty colonial girl, to be sure, Jared thought. Fiona might be a milk-white porcelain lady, but Della was vivid: dark and white, with dusky rose lips and unforgettable blue eyes. He had forgotten just how lovely she'd grown to be. The new setting he found himself in must have changed his perceptions of the whole world. In fact, he hadn't even recognized Della after only weeks away from her.

He'd come in from riding, been told there were guests, and looked up the stairs to see an enchanting young woman standing there, staring down into the hall. She'd looked straight into his eyes without recognition, and he hadn't recognized her, either—maybe because he hadn't been expecting to see her, but in that strange instant, he hadn't known her. He'd only been dazzled by the fresh beauty of the lovely little creature gazing curiously at them all. When her intent blue gaze swept past him as she searched for another face, he'd been deeply disturbed, struck by a pang of terrible loneliness and anxiety. No wonder, he thought now; it was mad for him to forget his friend. A second later, the world had gone right again and he'd recognized his dear little Della.

His dear *unhappy* little Della. She was obviously uncomfortable with the world she found herself in now. Alfred had made his fortune in Virginia, but living in the Colonies had obviously hampered Della socially. That was a pity, because there was so much she could enjoy here. But there was no reason she couldn't grow to be as fine a lady as Fiona. He'd see to it, Jared decided. That was one good thing his new title could do for him immediately. He'd take her to London, see she was introduced to the right people. She was quick; she'd get used to it. She could take her rightful place, too. The thought pleased him. Being around Fiona would help. He'd make sure that continued, too.

"How long are you staying with us?" he asked Fiona suddenly.

Della's eyes widened. Not because of the question, but because of the way he'd said 'with us,' as though he was again the earl she didn't know.

"Tired of me so soon?" Fiona asked playfully.

"Tired? Mistress Trusham, if the men of England haven't let you know by now how impossible that would be, I think I really did come home in time."

Fiona's fan wagged in front of her sparkling eyes. "I usually stay on until I think of someplace more diverting to go, but now that you're here, I wouldn't want to be in your way."

"You think that's possible? No, you're in exactly the right place. I want you to behave just as you would with Justin."

"*Just* as I would with him?" she asked, her fan fluttering and muting her giggles. "My goodness! What would people say?"

" 'Lucky fellow,' probably," Jared said, grinning. Her flirting went beyond that of any decent girl he'd ever met at home—in the Colonies, he corrected himself. But he couldn't judge her by those standards. This was her world: she was protected by family and friends, and she was promised to Justin. Surely she wouldn't think his brother would ever overstep his bounds. In her world, men of breeding did not. Jared was deeply flattered she even considered him such.

Della had to remind herself to close her mouth as she listened.

"I just wondered if you would come to London with us," Jared said. "I have to go sooner or later; it might as well be sooner. Justin and the uncles have been nagging me to go, and Della would enjoy it, too. It would be nice for her to have some feminine company on the trip."

"London! Oh, delightful!" Fiona said, her eyes shining. "It's the best place to be in the autumn. So much to see, so much to do!"

"Well, I haven't said yes or no yet," Jared said, "but Justin says I have to take my place eventually. He wants to introduce me around, and I'd like to see my town-house. . . . Della doesn't know the city any better than I do. I wondered . . . I thought you might take her to some dressmakers—maybe come with us to some social events, too."

"Say no more!" Fiona said excitedly, letting her fan drop and swing from her wrist, entirely forgotten in her honest excitement. "Yes, of course I will. Oh, won't we have fun!"

"London?" Della said, looking from one of them to the other. "No one said anything about that to me."

"I was going to," Jared said.

"But we just came from London," Della said nervously, remembering that her next step from London was to go home. "I thought we were going to stay on here for a while."

"Oh, pooh!" Fiona said, stamping a little foot. "What's here? Cows and sheep and vegetables." She laughed. "But in London? Musicales and theaters, masquerades and balls, not to mention shops! My goodness, do you call that a choice?" she asked, looking up at Jared, her face alight.

She could hardly defend vegetables, Della thought miserably. But a spark of rebellion flared to life. She raised her chin. "Fine," she said, "but don't bother taking me around, Fiona. I don't need a dressmaker, Jared. You may have forgotten, but we don't exactly live in a cave at home. I have more than buckskin dresses and loincloths in my wardrobe. I've brought some fine gowns along."

"*Loin*cloths!" Fiona said, with a faint blush showing on her cheeks. "My goodness. I've never seen them. But if they're coming in, London will have them, never fear." She laughed at her own joke, and then grew serious. "Much of the fun of going to London is getting new clothes, Della. I don't know about the Colonies, but the fashion changes every season here. I hear skirts are rising in front to show the ankle and hair is rising to show off how big the hats are going to be this year, too. Mustard yellow's still the rage, but white is coming in as never before for gowns. . . .

"You must think I'm trivial," she told Jared with a pretty pout, as if daring him to agree. "But it's so comforting to know the lace at one's sleeve is exactly the right length." And then she burst into laughter at the absurdity of it all.

Jared smiled. Della sighed. She might as well be angry at a butterfly. It wasn't Fiona's fault that she cast a spell over Jared even as she cast other women into the shadows with her brilliant smile.

"And as for you, my lord," Fiona said merrily, "even if

you don't care a fig about fashion, you must be a teeny bit excited about going about town, showing the world you are returned. It's one thing to come back to the hall, but if you return to London as earl, you will be returning to the world! I thought you wanted that."

"I do," Jared said, but then he hesitated, dark-gold eyebrows lowering over troubled gray eyes. He thought of what his reception might be in the clubs and halls of power in London. The story would have gotten out by now. They'd know he had been an indentured servant, lower than any of their valets and footmen; lower even than the men who toiled in their fields at home, because at least those men were free. Yet now he was an earl, preparing to sit at their sides in their houses, at their tables. Would they accept him? Should he care? Was he ready to find out? That was why he'd put off the trip to London. Maybe it could wait. . . .

"She's right," Della said suddenly, seeing his face and guessing his reasons for hesitating, and knowing he would do a thing for her father that he wouldn't for himself. "You should go. We will, too. Father will be delighted; he has unfinished business there. He couldn't take care of it before because we were in such a rush to see you. And . . . I do want some new clothes, actually, and I'd like to really see London once before I die—go home again."

"Die?" Jared said, laughing again. "I don't think so, Della. Virginia's not the end of the world, or of life. We're not talking about Virginia, anyway; we're talking about London. If you want to go, we will—soon as we can."

It was decided then, and he was glad. It was easier if he was doing it for Alfred and Della. But he wondered why Della didn't look happier now. His heart grew heavy as he gazed at her. She was his family as much as Justin was. He'd longed to show her the hall and his triumph. He had, but it wasn't the way he'd thought it would be.

She wasn't happy here, and her unhappiness clouded his pleasure. With that ebony hair and her bluebell eyes, she was as lovely now as she'd been when she was the little girl he'd promised to protect and care for. But much of her darkling beauty came from her vivaciousness, and that was gone now.

He found himself remembering a fawn he'd once found and taken from the forest after its mother had been killed for meat. In spite of all his care, it had faded and was gone before the end of a week. He'd never enjoyed venison again or forgotten those sad, knowing eyes, filled with a wisdom of how futile his efforts were, filled with a knowledge far beyond his.

"Do you have a blue gown?" he asked Della suddenly. "I mean something blue as bluebells—or the wild asters we have at home?"

She looked up hopefully. He'd said *home* again, but this time he was talking about her home. "I have a blue dress, yes, but not the exact shade you mention," she said, thinking hard.

"Well then," he said, "that's what you have to find in London. You had such a ribbon once, remember? I got it for you in Charleston. I saw the flowers by the roadside on the way there and they made me think of you; so when I saw the ribbon, I knew I had to get it for you."

"Yes! I loved it. You brought it back from your very first trip there alone," she said, pleased that he remembered.

"Deep blue will be difficult to find this year," Fiona said thoughtfully, "As I said, white is all the rage. But don't worry! I will contrive to find what you seek. But such a gown won't be very fashionable in London. I fear you'll have to keep it for when you're back in Virginia, Della, dear."

Della grew quiet, thinking of Virginia, thinking of how she wished she were there now—and how she wished she never had to go back. Jared would be here from now on.

Jared grew thoughtful, too. If Della found a life for herself in London, she would never have to go home again. . . . He stopped, frowning, wondering what in God's name he meant by *home* now.

Fiona was thinking of something clever to say to make

him laugh again when the morning peace was broken by the sounds of barking dogs and thudding hoofbeats.

"I think there's our Justin," Jared said, looking across the park to see a single horseman racing across the fields toward the hall, followed by excited dogs. "And he's riding like a madman. Ho, Justin!" he called, waving his arms.

They met Justin in the drive. His horse was lathered and he leapt from its back as soon as he'd halted it.

"Such news!" he said breathlessly. "The king is dead!"

Jared went very still, not knowing what that meant for his plans. He looked at Fiona.

"Long live the king!" she said simply.

Della gasped audibly.

"Out with the old, on with the new," Fiona said, laughing at her expression.

"He was struck down while going about his business—literally—in his water closet, they say. Or rather, whisper," Justin reported. Fiona giggled as Della and Jared simply stared. "Some say it was a fitting end. He wasn't particularly well loved," Justin explained. "Especially by his grandson, and his grandson is a reasonable fellow, or so we all think. Young George is the first of his line to be born on English soil; thank God for that at last. So he's also going to be the first king in his line to speak English without an accent. That will be nice for a change. He's young and open to change, too, just the man to deal with a growing world like ours—and yours, brother. If any man knows the value of a man being himself, as you say they do in the Colonies, why then it's certainly a prince who saw his own father waiting around all of his life for *his* father to hand down the title and never doing it."

"We were planning to go to London, but now I wonder," Jared said, "what with the funeral and the public mourning. . . ."

Justin and Fiona looked at each other and burst into laughter.

"Brother," Justin said, "you do have a lot to learn. We're a practical people. They'll be more fireworks for the coronation than tears for the funeral. You won't want to miss it, believe me. As Fiona said, the king is dead; long live the king. We'll celebrate the last much more than grieve about the first."

"Yes," Fiona said, capturing Jared's arm as they strolled back to the house. "My goodness, you don't think there'll be public mourning and grieving in Virginia when they get the news, do you?"

"No," Jared said.

She replied, "You'll see—there will be even less mourning here, because we knew him better than did the colonials."

Jared threw back his head and laughed, which made Fiona look very satisfied.

But Della didn't look satisfied, nor did she know that her heart was in her eyes as she watched Fiona stroll back to the hall on Jared's arm.

Justin handed his reins to a stable boy and took Della's hand. He placed it on his arm and looked down at her with concern. "Fiona is—well, Fiona," he said carefully, watching Della's face. "She sparkles. She needs to see approval for it, too. It's her personality. I think nothing of it, nor should you."

Della stared up at him in surprise. His strong, handsome face was filled with tender concern for her. But seeing his face was almost as unsettling as hearing what he said. His was so nearly and yet so completely not the face she needed to see, though he said the words she wanted to hear. Worst of all, he seemed to know her secret, so she hurried to find a different subject to talk about.

"But is London the place to go now?" she blurted. "I mean, we were talking about going to plays and parties and balls."

He understood and let it go. He just nodded, patted her hand, and said, "As you should, because that's exactly what you'll find there when we arrive. But let us tell the uncles of our trip."

* * *

The uncles agreed with him, taking the news with their dinner, and drinking to it together, many times. And, in light of the astonishing news about the king, they took their port with the ladies immediately after dinner this memorable night.

"To a happy coincidence," one of the uncles said, rising to unsteady feet. It was his eighth toast of the night. "To a new king of England, and a new earl of Alveston!"

No one drank, and a sudden shocked inhalation made him open bleary eyes and fogged ears to his own awkward toast. "Ah, I meant—" he began, but never got the chance to finish, because Justin spoke up.

"The king is dead, long live the king," Justin said, raising his glass. "The earl is gone, long live the earl. So it is, and so it must be. Off with the old and on with the new. To the king! And my brother! And why not? For at least, my friends, they don't plan to bury *me* before they raise him up! Or so I hope," he added with a wry smile, looking at the settee by the fire, where Fiona sat smiling, at the right hand of his brother. And where Della sat, at the other, worrying.

Chapter

10

~⁓

She would look like this on her deathbed, she thought in horror. Della stared back at her reflection.

"Oh my! Don't you look wonderful!" Fiona cried, clapping her hands together in delight.

"No. I look dead," Della said woodenly.

Fair-haired girls looked wonderful with a head of fleecy white curls, as did redheads, of course, because of their unfortunate natural hair color, she thought numbly. But girls with gypsy-black hair that suddenly turned white as snow? It was like taking the color from a rose. She looked drab and drained, Della thought, and not only was she not as pretty as Fiona, but she looked twice as old, and sick besides. Della stared at her newly powdered hair with loathing, as though she'd seen something moving in it.

"No," she said, rising to her feet. "I'll wash it out."

"After all our work?" Fiona cried. "When it's so late? We haven't time. No, you mustn't; it's perfect."

"It's perfectly awful on me," Della said.

There were many things she'd accepted about London fashion in the week she'd been a guest at Jared's townhouse here. She now wore a gown whose square neck was so low she was afraid to cough, whose side panniers were so wide she had to walk sideways to get through doors, whose bodice was so narrow and tight she swore she could feel an olive going down when she swallowed it—and she was sure everyone else could see it in transit, too. She could hardly breath and could see her toes only if she sat and stuck her feet way out in front of her. Enough was enough.

She would wash the powder out. And if Jared didn't want to wait for her to go with him to their first social engagement here in London, well, then, she thought defiantly, let him not—let him just go everywhere with Fiona. It seemed he wanted that anyway. She stared at the ghost of the woman she'd been and rubbed away a tear, pretending it was a stray eyelash. She was wondering what she'd pretend the next one would be when she heard his voice.

"Where's Della?" Jared asked quietly from the doorway of her room.

She spun around to see him and felt dizzy.

She gasped. "Oh. But where's Jared?" She was surprised she could even say that. He took her breath away.

"Here," he said.

He stood in splendor. He wore a dark-blue velvet long coat fitted tight across his wide shoulders, with a froth of lace at the wide sleeves. He had on dark velvet breeches with silver buckles at the knee, over white hose that showed his strong, straight legs. His coat opened to show an embroidered waistcoat of gold and gray. His powdered hair, held with a velvet ribbon at the base of his neck, made his skin look golden and his eyes gleam gray as an evening storm. He looked regal and powerful; tall, lean, freshly shaved, and immaculate. She sighed at the sight of such a magnificent male. But she had spoken the truth. He wasn't her Jared. Nor was he Justin, who stood beside him, equally splendid in black and wine-colored velvet brocade.

"Here I am, but where's our Della, I wonder?" Jared murmured, coming in and walking around her, inspecting her gown, her face, her hair.

His lips twitched when he saw her defiance and obvious misery. He'd seen that guilty, shamed, but brave expression before—a long time ago, when she'd filched a pie from Cook, shared it with a stray dog before dinner, and come home jammy and defiant, with the mutt on a string. Otherwise, she looked lovely. But also white, very white. In her white gown and whitened hair, the only color in her face was the flashing blue of her eyes, the berry red of her lips, and the slash of her black brows as they dipped in a ferocious scowl.

"She hates the powder on her hair," Fiona complained, "but how can she go without it? She can't. Absolutely no lady of fashion would. Perhaps if she were blond, she might just get away with it . . . but not with those masses of black curls. I know we're not going to the assembly rooms or a ball, only to a house party. But there'll be important people there. Look Della, Jared refuses to wear a wig anymore, and he's had a regrettable influence on his brother in that respect, too, but even they had their hair powdered for tonight! You tell her, gentlemen."

"She's right, Della," Justin said, "and you look lovely."

"You'd look *odd* without powder," Fiona insisted.

"She looks odd with it," Jared said.

They all stared at him. He circled Della again.

"I agree with Della," he declared. "Pretty," he said, his head to the side as he considered her as she stood mutinous and ashamed under his scrutiny. "No, not pretty—beautiful, I think, but not like Della. Not any more than I look like me," he told her with a tilted smile. "You see? Now that the shoe is on your foot, it pinches, doesn't it? What she means, I think," he told Fiona, "is that *Della* is black and white and vivid. This Della is white and beautiful, but she doesn't feel like herself and she doesn't like it. We don't stand on so much fashion at home."

"Pooh," Fiona said, fanning herself rapidly. "Your Dr. Benjamin Franklin wears the most ornate wigs. I've never seen him without powder. He's the picture of fashion, as are all the ladies he entertains here in London."

"He isn't at home now," Jared said, "and he's a man who loves London and the ladies and wants to be accepted by both."

"Della must be accepted by London, too!" Fiona snapped. "I know I sound miffed, but I am," she wailed. "I worked *so* hard to get her looking like that. My seamstress had to sit up day and night to get the gown ready, we took *hours* doing her hair, and it's growing so late. You don't want to arrive when everyone's jaded and weary. But we can't go at all if she wears her own hair! She'll look eccentric, or worse, like she doesn't know any better."

"So I won't go," Della said, shrugging. "It's not that important to me."

"All because of your hair?" Justin asked, bemused.

"I want to feel like myself. I must be true to myself," Della said. It sounded virtuous, but she realized it was more for her vanity that she wanted to dress her own way. She knew she could look so much better as herself without all these trappings—especially now when she saw that even when she was gotten up to look like a lady of ice and sugar, as was the fashion, it was still Fiona's fashion, not hers. And she was tired of feeling inferior.

Fiona was dressed all in white, too, but she glowed with it and was not overwhelmed. She wore white on white, with diamonds and brilliants to make her white gown glisten. Her topaz eyes sparkled as much as the shining pearly dust she'd sprinkled over her elaborately curled fair hair. She was a few inches taller than Della, and a little more slender, but the main difference was her delicate complexion, which was all subtle shades of winter, fashioned by nature to suit fair hair. Della's camellia skin was meant to be enlivened by the contrast with her own ebony hair.

"But we're supposed to introduce our new earl to London tonight!" Fiona said in vexation, stamping her foot. "To show we support him and give him our blessing. I suppose if Della wants to stay home, she may, but we must go. It's getting late!"

"I won't go without you," Jared told Della simply. "You know that. Can you see me leaving you sitting alone, Dell? For any reason? I can't. I won't. I don't know why it's so important to you, but so be it. We'll stay home."

Della's eyes widened, and then her lashes fell over them. She turned away from the hateful image in the glass, picked up her fan, and gripped it tightly. "No," she said ungraciously, "I'll go. I won't sit here knowing I kept you from going somewhere you should be. No, I'll go."

She'd stay home if she could, but she wouldn't hurt Jared in any way. And he knew it, his knowing eyes be damned, she thought rebelliously. The anger brought high color to her cheeks, and she glowered at him as she swept past him to the door.

"Very nice," Jared murmured for her ears only, as she passed him. "Temper is your best cosmetic, Mistress Mischief."

"Thank you, Master Rat," she murmured sweetly, just as though they were home again, teasing the way they used to. Before he became a lord, she thought sadly, and she became a lady—but not enough of a lady for him, obviously.

If Jared hadn't seen her as a woman before, he'd certainly never see her as one tonight. It wasn't what she'd dreamed of at all. Still, she raised her head and took the arm he offered her, because it was near his heart. She smiled at last. At least she was close to him—but not for long.

A footman intercepted them in the hall. "A message for you, my lord," he told Jared.

"I'll be with you in a moment," Jared told Della absently, gazing at the sealed letter on the footman's silver tray.

He stepped to the side of the hall and, beneath the dim light of a flickering wall sconce, unfolded the letter. He scanned it quickly, made a sound somewhere between a cough and a laugh, crushed the note in his big hand, and then dropped it like something loathsome.

"Bad news?" Justin asked curiously, noting his brother's thunderous expression.

"More of the usual," Jared said quickly. "Someone else eager to take advantage of another fellow's good luck. Nothing to concern yourself with, brother."

Jared walked back to Della and offered her his arm again.

"What was it?" she asked worriedly. "The note, I mean?"

"Nothing but an attempt to pry money out of me. I get many such letters these days," he said casually, but his eyes were still dark. "Don't trouble yourself about it."

She regarded him gravely. But then her father came to meet them, and she was walked to the carriage between them, as though they were making sure she wouldn't bolt. She looked back only once, to see Justin scanning the crumpled note his brother had discarded, wearing almost the same look of bitter fury on his face.

But nothing could distress her for too long tonight. She couldn't worry about problems with all the wonderful things that were soon to be displayed before her.

The party was held in a high stone house on a fashionable street. It was filled to the doors with exquisitely dressed people. Della couldn't stop staring. She'd never seen such jewels, such ornate hairstyles, such a lot of face paint—and that was only on the gentlemen!

White was popular in London this year, just as Fiona had said. But though all the ladies did wear their hair powdered, some wore brightly colored gowns. Others had radiant patterns on theirs. Della would have been pleased to have a sprig of green on her gown, instead of looking like Fiona's anemic shadow.

She wondered if Fiona had insisted she wear white because she knew no one else could look as wonderful in it as she herself did. Then she dismissed the thought. Fiona simply didn't worry about competition—she didn't have to. Della knew that as surely as she knew she was out of place here. She wanted to turn and leave; she wanted to see how long Fiona's wonderful gown stayed white after she threw her glass of wine at it. She wanted to shout at the injustice of it all. She wanted to go home. But home came to her instead.

"You do me proud," Alfred said in a voice thick with emotion as he bowed over her hand. "May I have this dance, my dear?"

Della bowed her heavy head, curtsied, put her hand on her father's arm, and let him lead her into the dance.

She danced well, as did her father. It was one of the things they often did together at parties at home. They crossed and recrossed each other's paths in the intricate steps of the stately pavane and had time for a word now and then in the middle as they met. But they didn't speak much, because Della was so busily watching the steps of the dance—not hers, but others'.

"It's politeness, nothing more. She's his brother's fiancée," Alfred said at last, when the dance brought them together, "and Justin doesn't mind."

"I know," she said simply, and then she added lightly, "He says she *sparkles*," before the pattern of the dance led her away from him again. Her eyes didn't stray far from the couple they spoke of, and neither did anyone else's. It was true that the appearance of a new earl, returned from abroad to reclaim his title, would make for a prodigious amount of gossip.

But Della felt it was more than that: Jared danced with Fiona, and they looked too right together.

Justin danced with another lady, but he watched them, too, his handsome face sober, his eyes dark and considering. And Fiona tossed back her head and laughed. Tall and graceful, Jared moved with her in the pattern of the dance: accepting her, releasing her—but never entirely—preening, courting, flirting, fascinating each other, all in the spirit of the dance, her hand in his, his eyes always on her. And he never stopped smiling down at her.

It might have been only courtesy, but Della couldn't bear it. As soon as the music stopped, she murmured something about finding the withdrawing room and hurried to escape from the pain of the sympathy in her father's knowing eyes. She didn't go to the withdrawing room, because she knew women sought more than chamber pots there, and she dreaded facing a roomful of gossip. There were things she didn't want to hear.

She fled to the long doors that led to the garden behind the house, but sighed in defeat after she slipped outside. As she had feared, the garden was crowded, too. There were already several romance-minded young women standing by themselves there. They turned to see her and then looked away again, disappointed. They were pretending to be there for a breath of air. Each was really hoping for an encounter with some dashing stranger, some exciting man who might ask them why they were there, all alone in the night. Della knew that dream; she was young, too. Girls did that at home, escaping their mothers and maids, looking for adventure. She guessed it was the same in London. Sometimes it worked; most of the time there were too many girls and not enough dashing strangers. It was a chilly night; all they'd probably catch would be colds. She stepped back into the house again.

There were old gentlemen dozing in the library, the kitchens were bustling with sweating servants who stared up at her in surprise when she peeked in, and footmen guarded all the other doors. But there was a long, dimly lit hall, and so she stood by the stairs and caught her breath, trying to find some excuse to get herself home without a fuss.

"There you are," Jared said from behind her. "It's my dance, remember?"

"No," she said, her shoulders going up, though she didn't dare look up at him. "You never asked."

"I was about to, but you ran away as soon as the music ended. What's the matter?"

"Too much party."

"Really? We just got here. At home, I seem to remember you dancing until dawn," he said, "and dancing all the way to the coach when I insisted we leave, and then humming everything you'd danced to until you finally fell asleep."

On your shoulder, she thought, remembering that long-past night at home, feeling a thrill now as she had then at the secret joy of it. She hadn't really been asleep. She'd been tired, half dozing in her corner of the coach, but when he'd gathered her close and put her head on his shoulder, every sense had awakened. How could she sleep when it was so glorious being that close to him? Breathing in his scent, hearing his voice rumbling up from his deep chest as he'd spoken low to her father, so as not to wake her? Once, he'd absently stroked back a curl from her forehead. Such a light touch, but every inch of her had felt it. He hadn't awakened her; he'd aroused her. She knew then she could never sleep comfortably without him again.

"That was then," she said.

"Della," he said, putting his hands on her shoulders and turning her to face him, his eyes troubled as her heart was. "What is it?"

She couldn't look at him, much less answer him.

"Too much party? Or too much London?" he asked quietly. "Ah, I know all of this is confusing, after home—I mean after Virginia," he said, frowning at his slip. "Or do I? Lord, I don't know which is home now. But you told me I have to stay here and assume my rightful place, didn't you? I'm trying. You have to help me. Sometimes this place—this opulence, these people—sometimes it seems too much for me, too. But then sometimes it feels so good, Dell, I can't hold it all in. When I was alone in the world, I needed you and Alfred because you gave me a home and a family. Now I have all those things, but I still need you here with me to convince me of the reality of it. Sometimes I find myself so happy, I can't believe it. I know it's hard, but please, stay the course, for me. And be happy for me. Can you, Della?"

She couldn't help but be, when he said it like that. She nodded. He took her hand in his and led her back to the dance . . .

. . . where he danced with Fiona again.

This time, Della danced with Justin and acted as though that was exactly where she wanted to be. Then he introduced her to dozens of gentlemen who smiled at her accent and all asked the same questions of her—mostly about Jared. She danced with half of them and laughed and dined and drank with the others until the sun began to rise and fashionable London knew it was time to go home. Then she got into the coach again, as sleepy now as she had been on that long-ago night a world away from these London streets. But this time Jared had no shoulder to offer her, because he had to keep turning in order to answer Fiona, who kept claiming his attention, talking and laughing with him.

Justin was silent, all his attention on his brother and his fiancée. Della sat watching them, too, looking at their eyes and lips as if she could read more in both, in the dim light, than either of them was saying. She was suddenly wide awake and very afraid. She couldn't keep her word. Clearly, he was happy, but she couldn't be happy for him.

"You are very taken with my brother," Justin said simply. He waited for Fiona's answer. They had left Jared and Della so he could escort her home, and now they stood in the hallway of her parents' townhouse alone together, as was their right as an engaged couple.

"Am I? Who isn't?" she answered gaily. "Everyone says how charming he is."

"Yes," Justin said. He let out a deep breath and gazed down at her. She sparkled. Even in the dim dawn light, her every slight movement made the brilliants on her gown tremble and shimmer. Lovely, he thought, even to a man who had known her, as she liked to say, forever. Perhaps she had known him that long—he'd known her since she'd been a baby, and she'd been adorable even then.

He remembered the little girl, pampered and willful, stamping her foot if she couldn't get her way—which wasn't often—and getting amused smiles for her tantrums instead of rebuke. He remembered the young girl, lovely and seemingly unaware of it, although she was never unaware of her effect on people—especially men. She was her father's pet and was closer to him than to her mother; but then he and every other man she knew found her coquettishly adorable, as perhaps women would not. Her father's companionship may have been what made her more forthright and more at ease with men than other young women her age. She had few female friends, but never seemed to mind the lack of them. But it was not so with men: from noblemen to stableboys, all fell over themselves for her smallest smiles. Fiona had never had an awkward stage in her life. She had never been cruel or unkind, either—not that he'd been aware of. But then, he realized, they'd both sailed through life making only easy choices, hadn't they? Until now. Now his whole world was righted and yet turned upside down.

She was very lovely and still quite young, but they were supposed to marry soon. Now, after all these years, he suddenly wondered whether he really knew her.

"Fiona," he said carefully, "we've never really talked about what's happened, have we? Jared's return, and everything it led to, happened so quickly. I should have discussed it with you immediately; I see that now. I'm sorry. I didn't think. I never asked your advice, but there was no reason to, and I really had no choice—I never wanted one, actually. He's my long-lost brother: there was no way on earth I could deny him anything. But I think we have to discuss it now. Does it make a great deal of difference to you, his coming back and taking the title, I mean?"

"Father's very upset," she said, tilting her head to the side, as though thinking about it. "Mother's not much more pleased."

"I see," he said stiffly, suddenly chilled, for the first time wondering if he had taken too much for granted after all. "And so—they want the engagement ended?"

She waited a heartbeat to answer. "I don't think so," she said seriously, and then burst into giggles. "Oh, your face! No, they never said it. And why should they?" she asked teasingly, cocking her head to the side and touching his chin lightly with the tip of her fan. "Who's to say he would want me anyway?"

He knew the right answer and spoke it automatically, while he thought furiously. "Who would not?"

She snapped her fan closed. "Don't patronize me, Justin," she said angrily. "I flirt, but I do have a brain *and* a heart, believe it or not. Fine greedy thing I'd look if I dropped you and took him! It was a shock, and not just to my father. He was the one who made the plans for my marriage in the first place, so of course he's distressed. But I thought I was going to be a countess, too. I've thought it since—well, forever. Now I find I'm to be merely a lady— for the rest of my life. The hall won't be ours, and I'd always thought it would. I had some plans, some changes in mind. . . . I don't like it, of course—I don't. But what can be done?"

"I see," he said, and he did—and was ashamed of himself for not realizing it sooner. "Then of course I'll understand if you want to end our engagement. We're not really legally bound anymore, are we?"

She went very still, so still that even the sparkling powder on her breasts didn't move with her breath. When she spoke again, her voice was oddly solemn. It hardly sounded like her usual light tone.

"No, I suppose not," she said. "Nor are we bound in any other way, are we? Justin, we never really courted, did we? I mean, there were no love notes or stolen kisses for us. No declarations of passion either, now I come to think of it. We just always knew what we would do, didn't we? And that was that."

He paused. "You're right. I suppose I never thought of it before, either," he said with perfect honesty, "but nevertheless I always thought you were beautiful, desirable, all the things men write love notes about. I never stole kisses, because I knew they would be freely offered. And they were, and I was very well pleased with them."

"Very . . . well . . . pleased . . . with . . . them," she said consideringly, dropping each word into place between them. "I see."

He wanted to take her into his arms and kiss her hard, the way he had every so often when he let his body rule his mind and forgot himself with her. Those few times, the feel of her in his arms made him forget to be patient and bide his time because their time was coming and he'd always known it. But for the first time since he'd known her—which was, as she'd said, forever—he wondered if his kiss would be welcome to her. It was like doubting his own reflection in the mirror. He groped for words.

"Well, then," he said, hesitating.

"Do you wish to end it?" she asked.

"I?" he asked, astonished. "Why would I?"

"Why, indeed?" she said, and listened to the silence between them for another moment before she laughed, a little artificially. "Well then. I think we ought to go on the way we were, don't you?"

"No," he said, "I think not. I think I should try some— courtship—don't you?"

She smiled. He took her in his arms, bent his head, and kissed her. But he couldn't stop wondering, for the first time, if it was to her liking. And so it wasn't—not for either of them. It was a cool kiss, for all that their mouths and their tongues met. And a cold kiss, for all that they held each other so close. When they parted, they looked at each other in the dim light and neither knew what to say. But she knew how to prattle; she had it down to an art.

"Good night, sweet prince," she said lightly. "I'll see you tomorrow, I suppose. We go to the theater, do we not? With Jared?"

"And Della," he said.

"Of course. I only meant—do you still want me to accompany him everywhere when we all go out together? Dance with him, dine with him, show the world that I accept him gladly? Or are you going to complain about it again? That is to say, if you're going to make a fuss over it, I'll ignore him. I just thought you wanted me to show what a wonderfully happy family we shall be."

"Is it a difficult duty?" he asked quietly.

She lowered her eyes. "No," she said, "I quite like it. He's charming, as I said—as you know. And he's very . . . *different.*"

"I see," he said.

"Do you?" she asked, looking up at him again. "I hope so, because I dislike quarreling. It's not like us. I can't remember the last time we did."

"No, I don't know that we ever did," he said thoughtfully. "I remember only how you used to carry on when I teased you."

"That was years ago," she said.

"So it was," he said.

"Yes," she said.

"I'll say good night then." He bowed and left her, thinking that he'd left something else unsaid.

London had the gayest parties, the most elegant balls, the most opulent pleasure gardens, and altogether the best entertainments in the English-speaking world. Everyone knew that. Young women in Virginia who were happy with their families and lives nevertheless dreamed of someday seeing the nightlife of London. Most didn't dare dream of seeing it in the company of the cream of London society, though. Della should have been ecstatic—especially since Jared obviously was.

She shifted in her seat and sighed, and then put her hand to her mouth in guilty surprise, because it had been a long, loud sigh. But the theater was so noisy that she could have shouted and no one might have heard her. Even the smell of it was loud; the air reeked of tart oranges and heavy perfume, pitch torches and too many people packed together. She was glad her shyness had made Justin and Fiona arrange for their seats to be with the rest of the audience, because although the fops and some fine ladies insisted on sitting right on the side of the stage itself, Della was sure she'd have died of embarrassment if she had. She was happy to be on the audience side of the stenchy torches that ringed the stage, in a box a little above the stage.

Happy was not exactly the right word. She was, she thought, satisfied with her seat, at least.

This way, at least, she could try to watch the stage—or the audience, which was equally entertaining—instead of the play that was going on inches from her nose between Jared and Fiona. The stage, after all, had only one singer gamely trying to finish her song now. The stage had iron pickets to protect it from any ruckus in the audience, which was a sea of gentlemen, common men, and poor men, ladies, common women, and tarts. They were all so colorful and noisy that the only way a person could tell one class from the other was by personal introduction—or by listening to the fascinating commentary supplied by Fiona. She talked through all the performances and was actually more amusing than anything presented on the stage. Or so Jared seemed to think.

Fiona had a clever mind and a sense of humor, as well as beauty, Della thought sadly. It was no wonder Jared never looked away from Fiona even when she was pointing out amusing things to him. He sat with her and Justin sat with

Della, in order to let the world see how happily they were both accepted. Jared and Fiona sat in front of Della. All she could see of Jared was his strong profile as he studied Fiona's face. It hurt Della to see it, so she looked away. But then she always looked back because she couldn't help it any more than Jared could stop watching Fiona, it seemed.

All Della could see of Fiona's profile were her eyelashes, her fan, and her smiling mouth, whenever she took her fan away from it to tap Jared when he said something that pleased her. They sat close, but Fiona's wide skirts kept them somewhat apart, so they had to bend their fair heads, like flowers, toward each other. Della could hear only every other word they said, and she was glad of it. It was bad enough hearing Jared's deep laughter and Fiona's trills of merriment.

"This is not a good evening," Justin said to her.

Della turned to look at him. He was sitting beside her, but she'd forgotten him because he hadn't said anything all evening. He too had been looking straight ahead. His handsome face was carefully expressionless.

"I mean to say that usually the theater is more entertaining," Justin said. "We should have taken you to a Shakespearean play, something with Garrick, not a night of clowns, fire-eaters, and jugglers, like this. Next time we'll take you to something finer."

"Why bother?" she answered without thinking. "Wild colonials are supposed to like simpler pleasures, things like spectacle and farce, aren't they? I guess that's exactly why we're here."

"Of course," he said smoothly, "that's why there are so many wild colonials here tonight, aren't there? But I'm curious. How many do you see? Fiona's mentioned at least two dozen noblemen and -women who are here. But not one colonial."

"There are only two of us," Della admitted with a small smile. "You can't count my father; he grew up here."

"Yes. Which is probably why he's learned to sleep

through everything." Justin said, looking over to where Alfred sat, hands folded over his stomach, peacefully dozing.

She laughed as Justin smiled at her.

"I only meant that there are better things to see in our theaters," he said. "Don't judge us by tonight. And don't be so quick to take offense, little firebrand. I'll be the first to tell you when to be insulted and whom to be annoyed with. That's what we're here for, you know."

For the first time she saw how warm his smile was, rather than how much like Jared's, and for the first time, she felt he was really looking at her.

"Is that what you're here for?" she echoed, with a touch of sadness, looking at Jared as he laughed at something else clever Fiona whispered to him.

Justin's smile faded as he saw what she was looking at. "Yes," he said slowly. "Or so I believe."

She bowed her head, sorry to have embarrassed him. When she looked back at him, she saw his dark-blue eyes were as sad as her own. He leaned closer so she could hear his every word.

"They say the theater is a mirror to life," he said. "What jaded theatergoers look for is novelty above anything else. It brings in the audiences and gets talked about the next day. But it doesn't last. By its very nature, it doesn't last."

She knew he wasn't talking about the theater, and she could only hope he was right. He stayed close by her side as they watched the end of the performance—neither of them watched the one on stage. Yet somehow, even though she knew it was wrong to take any kind of comfort from someone else's unhappiness, still Della felt a little better knowing she was no longer alone.

Chapter

11

⟋⟍

Jared was the earl of Alveston. Everyone in the room with him acknowledged it. The room was lavishly furnished, in the heart of London, and filled with some of the most influential men and women in all England. A beautiful woman, promised to him since birth, stood at his side; his lost brother was grown up, alive and well, and smiling at him in the same room, where he stood with the girl Jared had thought of as his sister since he'd met her. Her father, the man who had bought him out of bondage, was there, too, smiling encouragement at him. And Jared himself was grown tall and strong, and he was dressed elegantly. His breeches alone cost more than most men's weekly wages.

But the most amazing thing was that no matter how hot the food he ate or how tight his new shoes or how often he secretly pinched his own arm, nothing woke him from this dream. *This must be real,* he thought in a daze of happiness. He doubted it only because it was so much more glorious than his dream had been.

There were flaws in the realization of the dream, of course, if only because it was no longer a dream, but only one flaw he could think of right now: Fiona was his brother's fiancée. Yet tonight, the way she laughed with him and hung on his arm and smiled at him as she introduced him proudly around the room, even that relationship seemed flexible, as capable of change as anything else in a dream would be. And yet this was reality. No, it was better than reality—it was happiness. He hadn't known much of it in his life. He'd never guessed how good this would feel; there was more to it than he could have imagined, because there were more triumphs in life than a poor abused boy could have known about and included in his dreams of glory.

For example, Jared thought with pleasure, Dr. Franklin, the most famous man in the Colonies, stood only steps away, with his son, holding court. Jared knew both of them from home—from the place he'd been exiled to and had come to think of as home, he corrected himself. Jared straddled both worlds. He knew the unofficial guest of honor and he was meeting the finest gentlemen and fairest ladies in Mrs. Cornely's elegant assembly rooms, the most fashionable place to be in all of London at the moment. And all of them were waiting breathlessly for his every word, hoping for a clever saying they could repeat the next day, as if he were the celebrated Benjamin Franklin himself.

The gentleman from Philadelphia had been the rage in London for three years, ever since he'd come here on some mission from the Colonies and stayed on. But the new earl of Alveston was the latest rage. Jared was interested by the first fact, but was overwhelmed by the other. All he wanted to do now was to share the joy of it.

"They've turned Poor Richard's head," he whispered to Fiona from where they stood watching Alfred chatting with Dr. Franklin, waiting for a chance to introduce the ladies to him. "Which is a pity for us—for everyone in the Colonies. They say he's looking for a permanent home here. He finds more birds of a feather in London than at ho—than in Philadelphia—" To Della, he said, "So I'm a little confused—stop giggling at me. Go—Alfred's beckoning to you; time to make your curtsy, Mistress Torment."

"You, too. Come with me," she whispered back, tugging his hand. "Or do you think he won't want to talk to you now that you're not a colonial anymore?" She teased him, knowing everyone in London was dying to talk to the new-found earl. Dr. Franklin himself hadn't been able to take his eyes off Jared since they'd come in.

Jared's story was popular knowledge now; the news had spread like wildfire. It was a staggering story, romantic as it was exciting, and everyone in Jared's party was being stared at and whispered about—Jared and Justin especially. Everyone wanted a look at the fellow who'd come out of nowhere to replace his brother. And everyone else wanted to see his brother's reaction. They seemed to think it was astonishing that Justin accepted Jared so well. Della heard one man whisper to another, "Giving up an earldom, after all, to a fellow who just walked in and said, 'Howdja do'?"

In the few days they'd been in London, the table in the hall of their townhouse had been flooded with invitations, and Justin was set on Jared's accepting every one of them. And Jared tried to, making sure that Della came along with him wherever women were included.

Now Della grinned up at Jared, took his arm, and went to meet her father's famous friend. Justin and Fiona followed. They went everywhere Jared went. But Della felt better about herself tonight, in every way, than she had at her first party. Only a week had passed since then, but many things had changed. Now, a new low-necked, dark-red gown flattered her, and she'd gotten used to the foolish notion of powdered hair—had even begun to like it a little for fancy occasions, if the truth was told, because it made her seem so sophisticated. Justin had become an amusing friend, and she needed one. And best of all, he was keeping Fiona close by his side tonight.

Della felt like an actress on a bright stage as she stepped beneath a glittering chandelier filled with flaring candles, all the guests ringed around them. She and Jared joined her father, but Fiona stood behind them in a circle outside their own bright one, with her fiancée, where she belonged.

Della knew it was mean-spirited of her to be pleased with that, but knowing it didn't change it. Tonight she could be truly happy for Jared; there was nothing to mar her pleasure at seeing his joy at taking his place in the world to which he belonged. He tried to act as though it were something he was doing for Justin's sake. But she knew him better. He radiated happiness. It showed in his easy smile, his posture, the way he moved. She rejoiced for him. Tonight she didn't have to share him with anyone, just everyone. That was easy.

She made a low curtsy and looked up into Dr. Franklin's eyes, which were twinkling with interest behind his spectacles. He was a stockily built middle-aged man with a kind face. He was dressed in the height of fashion, with rings on his fingers and silver buckles on his shoes. His mouth was narrow, his cheeks round, his chin double, and his eyes alive with humor. He smiled at her; she grinned at him. And then by mutual silent consent, they played the game. Colonials were considered interesting specimens, so the two of them had to prove they were more than that.

"My dear, how lovely you look," Dr. Franklin said as he took her hand and raised her up. "Here is my son; William, what do you think of this little beauty? You were too slow, my boy, not finding her in Virginia, whilst you had a chance. Now you must fight all the English gentlemen for so much as a minute of her time. Alfred, she's grown to be a beauty! How are you, my old friend? And how do the two of you do here in wicked London town?"

Della smiled; she knew every comment and question was for the benefit of his audience. Benjamin Franklin was many things, and the most famous man in the Colonies, but he was a diplomat first and a celebrity foremost. She answered sweetly and was careful to say everything in a low soft voice, with perfect diction. She too would try to show these English how cultured a colonial could be.

"So," Dr. Franklin said, looking beyond her, "the fellow I knew as the most clever tobacco and sugar trader in all the Colonies now appears to be the luckiest one, too. Do I behold my friend Master Jared Bellington of Virginia—who is also the famous earl of Alveston, restored to his homeland at last?"

Jared smiled and opened his mouth to answer, but another voice spoke first, from a dim recess of the room.

"So *he* says, at least."

The room fell still. All chatter from those who hadn't heard the statement stopped as they were told of the words that had just been uttered. Jared froze. Then he spun around, his head to the side, listening to something no one else had heard. His eyes narrowed, and Della noticed that he was suddenly sickly white beneath his tan and that a fine dew of moisture appeared on his upper lip.

"Now, I'm from Virginia, too," the voice drawled, "and I have a different tale to tell. Indeed, I do. *The earl* here and I, we know each other well. Oh, very well, indeed. That's my boy, you see."

Several in the company gasped, and Jared bared his teeth in something like a snarl. His hand went to his side, but he wore no sword tonight, so his hand curled into a white-knuckled fist instead. His eyes were narrowed, glittering, searching the crowd for the man who had spoken.

Jared drew in a breath when he saw the man at last. "Yes. So I thought. Tonight's my lucky night. I'll kill you," he said conversationally as he strode toward him. "Now that I can, I will."

"Yes, of course; fancied you would say that," the man drawled insolently, with an arrogant smile on his thick lips. He was a big man, tall and broad and beefy, and his eyes were reddened, with pouches under them. He was a man who clearly loved the bottle and the serving board. While there was something coarse about him, he wore good clothes and had a heavy, opulent, gold-headed walking stick in his thick hand. He gripped the stick tightly and stood his ground as Jared neared him. But when Jared got close, the man saw his eyes and broke and ran to the door, pushing astonished guests out of his way.

"Yes, I will certainly kill you, but not quickly," Jared snarled.

He reached the fellow in three long strides, grabbed him by his shoulder, spun him around, and hit him hard in the face. The man's head snapped back and he staggered, but he didn't fall, though he'd taken a heavy blow. He took another, and another, as Jared's fist crashed into his face again and again. Then everyone saw that the only reason he didn't fall was because Jared was holding him up with one hand as he kept smashing the man with his other hand, which was knotted into a fist.

Women screamed, and men murmured, and some shouted for Jared to stop. But it was Justin who thrust through the crowd and caught Jared's arm and forcibly held it back. When Jared swung around with a growl to see who was holding him, he let go of his prey and the man dropped like a stone to the floor at his feet. Justin grappled with Jared but managed to hold him fast, for although he struggled, Jared didn't seem willing to hit his brother. Then Justin shouted for help. Strong as he was, he realized it would take three men to hold his brother—or this crazed man who resembled his brother—who was fighting like a mad creature to be free so he could kill the one who'd challenged him.

The guests gaped, watching avidly and with open mouths. It was Della who finally stopped it all. She picked up her heavy skirt and raced through the room, elbowing people aside, shoving them out of her way, pushing at chests and stomachs, stepping on toes, clearing a path for herself. She stopped only when she was in front of Jared. Then she cried, "Jared! Stop—stop it!"

And he did—instantly. He paused, panting, his hair disheveled, his knuckles covered with blood, the wildness dying in his crystalline eyes. It was replaced with a look of pain and fury and something too deep and lost for her to understand, but even through it, he saw her.

"It's him," he told her in a strangled voice. "Brown."

Della's hand flew to her mouth.

Jared looked at Justin. "Let me kill him," he said, and it was a plea.

"But everyone will think it's because of what he said," Justin said hurriedly in a low voice, turning so that he put himself in front of his brother, trying to shield him from all the curious eyes. "Think it over. Rest awhile and take it slowly. You don't want everyone to believe what he said, do you?"

"Why not?" Jared said, anguished. "It's true."

Many in the crowd gasped, then shuffled their feet and muttered to one other.

"I *was* his boy," Jared said with a mixture of shame and hate, clenching and unclenching his fists with the force of his inner agony. "He was my master. *That* master."

Justin grew very still. "Oh," he said, understanding more than had been said. "No, brother," he said, looking down at the man at his feet as he began to dare to try to crawl away. "No. I can't let you kill him. Let me."

They got the man into the library. Once there, they promptly threw out as many onlookers as they could and closed the doors so they could have privacy with him. Jared hovered over the man where he sat crumpled in a chair. Justin stood by Jared to watch over him so his passion wouldn't get out of hand again.

"Steady, steady, brother," he told Jared in a low, urgent voice, "we don't want to kill the bastard just yet, only question him. Punishment will come later, I promise."

Alfred had been allowed to stay, because he was family; Della, because they couldn't remove her with hot pliers, as she said. The uncles stayed, along with Dr. Franklin, because he was so fascinated nothing on earth could keep him away—and his son remained with him. Four English noblemen were there, too—one because he was a magistrate, the others because they were too influential to remove. Fiona had been too terrified to move. When at last she did, her father stopped her and stepped forward himself. But by the time he got to the doors, they were firmly locked.

The man Jared had called Brown sat in the chair they had thrown him into, holding a hastily obtained towel to his bleeding mouth. But his eyes were now bright and rat yellow, filled with fury along with pain. And they were fixed on Jared.

"So, now you know how good it feels, too, don't you? *Boy,*" the man spat at Jared.

"Mind your manners, fellow," the magistrate said harshly. "You are addressing an earl of the realm."

"Oh, to be sure," Brown mumbled through his broken mouth. "I was only congratulating his lordship for finally discovering the pleasure of dealing out what he used to receive."

Jared's face went white, but his mouth curled in disgust. "I made a mistake," he told the man fiercely. "I should have killed you straight out. I'd forgotten why it was I hated you more than anyone on earth."

"Forgotten?" the man asked with a chuckle. "Why, lad, I had hoped you'd never forget me. I certainly haven't forgotten you; you provided some of my only happy moments in that God-rotted place," he added with a leer.

Della shuddered at the expression on the man's face, and looking at Jared, she swore she could feel the tremor that passed through him, too. His hands had closed to fists again, not to strike Brown, but to conceal their fine trembling at the sound of Brown's voice and the secretive smile the man gave him, as though they shared something.

Now Jared remembered what had been worse than the pain of the beatings. He remembered what still happened in his most awful nightmares, the thing some kindly portion of his brain made him forget each morning. Now, as Brown's voice met his ears again, he remembered the man's sawing breaths, his growing excitement, the ultimate pleasure he gave voice to whenever the pain in Jared's back had become too much for Jared to bear—when the boy Jared had been finally broken and sobbed or cried out at last, and in that way gave his tormentor his own release.

It was why Jared had endured so much, why he had so many scars. Each time that moment came—when the whip fell to the floor and not on his back, when he heard his persecutor suddenly cry out in wild mingled pain and pleasure, he hated himself for causing that cry as much as he hated the man who had had the legal right to call himself Jared's master. Jared had been too young to fully understand the meaning of that cry, but had known on some level, even then, that it was a shameful thing, and that he was in some way party to it.

Thus, whenever he was beaten, Jared had always tried to suppress his outcries out of shame. And so he suffered more, and provided more pleasure by doing so. It was a wonder, he thought now, that he had ever lived to be sold to someone else.

Brown and he had never touched, except through the lash. Although Jared had felt nothing more than blessed surcease from pain when the beating ended, he'd known something very wrong had happened. Even more than that, he knew that he'd given a man he hated something that man wanted, something that still made him feel filthy.

"The man took his pleasure through beating others," he said wearily now, because there was no hope of hiding it all with Brown here, and because bad as it was, he didn't want Justin to think it was worse. "I'd forgotten how he enjoys it—or else I'd never have beaten him."

"But I don't like being beaten myself," Brown said slyly. "I quite understand your lack of enthusiasm now, my lord."

"Be quiet!" the magistrate shouted. "Oh, I will hang him high, my lord, given half a chance."

"I was seven," Jared said abruptly. "I'd never have been eight unless he sold my papers to Higgins, the man Alfred bought me from. Brown knew he'd have some trouble with the law if I died. I think I was coming close to it. He'd have had to pay more than he had to cover it up. Bond-boys are cheap, as you know, doctor," he told Dr. Franklin, who had made a strangled sound, "but not free, in any sense."

Dr. Franklin looked down at his silver-buckled shoes. He had begun his career as a shopkeeper as well as a printer, and it was well known that he had once traded in indentures, buying and selling papers of unfortunate people who still had time to go in their terms of servitude.

"We have much land to be worked at home, industry to be built and run," Dr. Franklin said quickly. "We need helping hands, as many as we can get. But bond-servants are not slaves. They gain their freedom in time, by dint of work and by way of payment for it. Most come from far worse circumstances and most are not treated ill. Many prosper. They are given a nice bit of money to start out in life when they leave their servitude. Many get even more. Why, I've a friend at home whose mother was such a servant. She married a rich man when she had worked out her bond. There are many such."

Jared said nothing, but his lip curled. He knew many women who were not so lucky.

Dr. Franklin saw his expression and went on hastily. "Peter Williamson, from Philadelphia, was just such a fellow—you know who I mean," he told his son. "He wrote that book about it, too. He prospered in time, but first he was kidnapped and sold into bonded service— why, he's even now in Scotland, seeking a way to sue the very shipowners who carried him to Philadelphia when he was a lad. Some servants have a hard row to hoe, to be sure, indentured or not. But no man—no sane man," he said with a glowering look at Brown, "holds with the beating of children."

"Maybe not," Jared said with a shrug, "but the law does, so long as they aren't killed outright."

"Not economical," Brown said smugly.

Dr. Franklin turned to scowl at him. "What were you doing here tonight?" he demanded, glad to change the subject, one he felt uncomfortable discussing among his English friends. The practice of buying indentures had gotten its start in England, but it wasn't common there now. England didn't need workers as badly as the Colonies did. Pennsylvania still had many bonded servants, but it wasn't something on which a man sent to England to promote the progress and plenty in his homeland wanted to dwell.

"I was paid handsomely to be here tonight," Brown said, wincing as he tongued a loose tooth. "Not handsomely enough, as it turns out. I left Virginia years ago; couldn't prosper there. I came home and am known to turn a hand at what I can. I heard about the new earl of Alveston. Who has not? Once, when I was in a tavern, I spoke about my knowledge of the boy he had been. I became instantly famous for it; many men bought me dinners on the strength of the tale. One offered me gold to come here tonight and tell it again. I did offer you the chance to pay more gold and stop me," he told Jared, "but you never answered any of my notes."

"I'm a man of business," Jared said tightly. "I know that silence is the most expensive and the most impossible thing to buy. Blackmail's a bad bargain all around. And then, there was nothing left but to tell the truth, and everyone already knows that."

"Some of your fine friends mightn't like that truth," Brown said slyly. "Men have gotten rich on less."

"Men have been hanged for far less," the magistrate commented.

"Why didn't you tell me?" Justin asked his brother.

Jared shrugged. "Why bother you with such slime?"

"Perhaps he thought you were the one who sent the notes," Brown suggested, and this time it was Jared who stepped in front of his brother to prevent him from attacking the man.

"How did you get in?" an irate nobleman demanded imperiously. The assembly rooms were popular because they were so selective.

"An invitation was secured for me, and I was admitted," Brown said, shrugging. "I can *look* the gentleman."

"You were just supposed to tell the tale?" Justin asked.

Brown gave an evil grin. "No, *his lordship* is right; that wouldn't do more than cause gossip. But since I knew him when he was young, I was supposed to come here and debunk his identity entirely. I tried. He almost killed me—you saw it. I decided to run rather than be killed. My life is worth more to me than money."

"If so, it's the only thing that is," Jared said bitterly.

"What man gave you gold?" Justin persisted.

"Now, he'd tell me his name, wouldn't he?" Brown mocked. "He paid handsomely. Promised more if I did it right. It was done in the dark, so I couldn't even describe him—it could be any of you." He laughed derisively as he looked at them all.

"There is no crime we can prove now, and there is no punishment bad enough for this fellow!" one of the uncles said passionately.

"Oh, I shall find a place for him," the magistrate said furiously. "I doubt he'll see the light of day again, one way or another, after this night's work. Blackmailing a peer of the realm is a hanging offense—at least in my court, it is. And there I shall see him, to be sure. Don't worry—I give you my word that none of you shall ever see him again."

As he was led away; Brown looked uneasy for the first time.

Nearly all the others left with him, to go pour cold water on the gossip, as Dr. Franklin put it. But Jared and Justin remained in the room, unable to face the guests yet. Della lingered, watching them.

"Who do you think it was?" Justin asked.

"Oh, it could be anyone," Jared said, but his voice

sounded far away and his eyes were on the fire as though he saw something there besides the flames. "Anyone who would like to see me discredited, that is. Do any of our evil uncles' sons still harbor hopes? It could be one of them. Have you any enemies, Justin? It could be one of them. As for me, I don't know—maybe someone I slighted once. What man has no enemies? It could be anyone, as my former master said."

"But it is specifically someone who doesn't want you to be earl," Justin said thoughtfully. "Maybe even old Trusham. He's charming, but also determined, and he hates to be crossed. His daughter was going to be a countess, with all that it involved. Your coming has put his nose in a knot, you know."

"Fiona's father?" Jared asked, looking up in shock. "I didn't know—well, maybe I did. But do you really think . . . ?"

"It's possible. Trusham's a man of high ambition who suddenly found his daughter was promised to a man with fewer prospects than he wished for her. Who knows?" Justin shrugged his wide shoulders. "It won't help him now, whoever it is—not anymore. You could certainly see that tonight, yourself. It's too late: you're the earl now, legally and in the eyes of society. I've acknowledged it, as have the uncles. The lawyers have noted it. It's done. The story will mean nothing."

"Nothing?" Jared asked with a crooked smile. "I doubt that. It's too good a story. Our ancestors must be spinning in their graves—an earl of Alveston beaten, screaming with it, and giving some pervert his pleasure that way. Wonderful."

"An earl? No, a seven-year-old boy!" Della cried, rushing to his side.

Jared turned to look at her. His face was suddenly flushed, and not from the fire. He stepped back from her, but not before she could see the sudden look of horrified dismay he tried to hide. "Blast! I didn't remember you were here, Dell," he said in a shaken voice. "It's not a tale for a lady's ears."

"I'm not a lady!" she cried. "I'm Della. And so what if I know? There's nothing for you to be ashamed of. So he beat you—he was an evil man."

She saw the muscles in his lean jaw working as he clenched his teeth against his immediate answer. She hated the way the light had gone from his eyes; he seemed dazed, like a man who had taken a heavy blow. And when he'd been so proud, on the night he thought would be his greatest triumph—it wasn't fair. Her heart ached for him.

But Jared was a man who knew the value of discipline. When he spoke again, his voice was deep and the anger in it controlled.

"The man did more than beat me—he took pleasure from it," he said. "You may not know—damn it, you shouldn't know!—but such things make the victim feel as shamed at the villain."

She saw the despair on his face and shuddered; she'd seen nothing like it since the day she'd seen his poor scarred back, all those years ago. There were things in her childhood she'd forgotten, but that sight of his back was as vivid to her now as it was then—perhaps even more so now that she loved him so much. She stood tall as she could for such a small woman. When she spoke, her words were as cold and precise as his had been, but her hands were closed to even tighter fists than his.

"Well, I do know about such things. What woman doesn't—whether she's a lady or not? If some beast here in London should grab me one fine night, drag me off, and have his way with me—which happens, Jared, don't pretend it doesn't—should I feel as shamed as that villain? You're saying I should? And so then if that ever happened to me, it would be my fault for being there when he felt lustful—is that right?"

"Lord, no, Dell," he said quickly. "Only a fool would think— Ah, I see: Della at her healing again. You're right,

but it isn't the same. He never touched me otherwise . . . "
He paused, ran his hand through his hair, and nodded in
surrender. "And yet here I am, shouting and storming,
carrying on as though he had, aren't I? As though it were
yesterday—which it wasn't. I see. Yes, of course. You're
right, I *was* a child. I wasn't even sure then of what was
happening, exactly. I just knew it was ugly and somehow
wrong. Not my fault at all, was it? I'm sorry, Della. I've
been acting like a violated virgin, haven't I?"

He looked at her, stalwart, steadfast, lovely little Della,
who stood watching him with her heart in her vivid blue
eyes, always faithful, ever true, his sister in all but name.
His face relaxed and he smiled at her.

She exhaled her pent-up breath and nodded back at
him, her hands unfurling like flowers.

Justin stood quietly watching them both. It seemed to
him that Jared hadn't been carrying on at all. He'd been
upset, yes. But all Justin had seen was his pallor and
tension. Della had seen far more—she'd seen what Jared
felt, she'd heard his unvoiced anguish. He wondered if
either of them really knew how deep was their bond, and
yet knew he could never tell either of them that. Because
looking at the yearning in Della's eyes, he also saw what
Jared evidently didn't, and he knew she wouldn't want
anyone else to see it. He, of all people, understood what
she was going through.

"No apologies, and no thanks either, please," Della said
briskly, "not unless you want to listen to all those I owe
you. You helped me when I lost everything, a long time
ago—remember? And then about a million times since."

"Two million," he said with a smile, once more himself.
But when he looked at the door to the library, he tensed,
realizing that although he could weather the rest of the
night, its dreamlike beauty was gone. True, he was the earl
of Alveston, returned to his land and his family again. But
there was a blot on the glorious dream now, a terrible tale
that would be whispered behind his back for all his life.

"Well then," he said, "to battle. Let's go in and talk about wicked masters and poor bond-boys and give them a story to remember. Maybe they won't slap their valets and lady's maids quite as hard tonight."

"More likely they will, by tomorrow night," Justin said dryly. "They lose interest in lessons as fast as they learn them."

"But they'll never forget my story," Jared said.

"What of it?" Justin asked lightly, but he went to the door and opened it quickly because he knew there was no answer.

The brothers walked out together, but were immediately separated by eager questioners. Fiona flew to Jared's side, her eyes wide. Della was asked questions, too, but she could hardly listen because she was so intent on Jared as he looked down at Fiona gravely.

"It's a disaster. I'm sorry," Jared told her. "No sense denying it. You knew I was a bond-boy. That man was my old master. He was a degenerate, and he did beat me. He had the right to, because he owned my papers. I'm sorry you have to be involved with this in any way. But Justin is blameless, so it shouldn't affect you too much."

"Affect me?" Fiona asked. "Why, all it has done is get me more invitations than I've ever gotten in one night. Poor fellow," she said, tapping him with her fan, "I never knew you had such woes. But they're over now. You're an earl, and no one can harm you anymore. They say that beast will go to Newgate for daring to harm an earl of the realm. They say he'll hang, but I won't even go to see it. Now then—the most important thing." She smiled at him. "Are you going to come to the Bedfords' ball with us next week? Or do you prefer the duke of Torquay's? Because wherever you go, we shall, too. You're the lion of the moment!"

He looked down at her in bewilderment. She wasn't joking; her eyes were shining. She was laughing up at him, without malice, without censure. The ugliness he had faced in the other room might have been on another planet from hers. What he had been meant nothing to her. She had no idea of what a bond-boy was, what servitude was, how debased he'd been and felt. It was of no importance to her; it was a thing that had happened in the New World, not her own. He realized that it always would be so, whatever she heard. He had no shameful history with her. With her, he'd always be free of that past and the pathetic, abused child he'd been.

She was as beautiful as an angel, glittering and shining with innocence and merriment. She was promised to his brother, the man whose house and title he'd taken, and yet she didn't shun him for that or for his appalling past life. She came from a different world and would never understand his old one . . . or cause him to remember it. He looked at her with wonder. Then he smiled, picked up her hand, and put it on his arm. He straightened his shoulders and walked into that other world with her as his guide.

Della stared after them, distracted. She felt a hand at her own elbow.

"Della?" Justin asked pleasantly. "Will you come to dinner now? I hear they have lobster patties, the latest thing. Come, you must be hungry."

She looked up at him and he saw a hunger no dinner could appease. "You don't care?" she asked in a whisper, the hurt naked in her eyes.

"I don't know what I can do about it," he answered just as bluntly, "or if I should do anything. She has free will. And so do you and I. Come."

"If it was her father who arranged this tonight, he needn't have bothered," she whispered, her face pale. "One earl or the other, it seems to make no difference, does it?"

"Perhaps," he said, smiling and nodding as he walked with her toward the dining room, as though it was his dinner and not his life and heart they were talking about. "Perhaps not."

She almost stumbled.

"What would you have me say? Or do?" he asked in a low, savage voice.

She looked up at him, startled by his anger. It was then that she saw that Jared's brother was not so bland and controlled as she had thought, but was as upset by what was happening as she. He was not, she thought as she felt the iron tension in his arm and looked into those blazing eyes, so very different from his brother after all.

Chapter

12

❧

Jared paced the study of his London townhouse. Justin sat in a chair by the fireplace, watching him. Alfred and Della were upstairs sleeping, the way most people were at this hour of the night. But the brothers were awake and talking. They had come home from the assembly rooms and talked over the events of the night until it began to turn into a new day.

"You think it really might have been Trusham?" Jared asked again now, shaking his head. "He seemed to be one of the most outraged about what Brown did. Yes, yes, I know he would be if he was the one responsible—because the plan failed. . . ."

"More than failed," Justin commented. "You got so much sympathy that anyone who said anything against you would have been thrown into Newgate with Brown."

"But Fiona's father was more than angry; he seemed really concerned. It's hard to believe he holds my taking the title against me."

"Not now—not any longer, of course not," Justin said quietly. "But Brown may have been paid for his lies before Trusham realized tonight what had been happening under his nose. Sometimes it's difficult to see what is exactly under one's nose, you know."

Jared stopped pacing. He didn't face his brother; instead, he stood by the fireplace, head down, stirring the dead ashes with his foot.

"I will never hold her back," Justin finally said into the stillness of the room. "I've known her too long and I have too much pride for that."

Jared bit off a muttered curse. "Who says you have to?" he asked angrily.

"Her face tonight, for one thing," Justin said simply. "Yours, for another."

"Damn, I didn't mean to—" Jared said harshly, but his brother cut him off with a simple, quiet word.

"Indeed," Justin said. "Who does?" he went on, not letting Jared speak. "I understand such things are beyond one's control. I wouldn't know—I never looked at another woman. . . . No, that's not true; I did a deal more than look when I was up at university. But that was considered part of a young man's education, and I never regarded the females I visited as women, precisely. It was more in the nature of—nature studies. I'm sure you understand, brother. She was a child then, but once she was grown, I never looked at another woman seriously because I always had her in mind for my wife. Because she was, in effect, my wife, from the day you were lost. We both knew it."

"As she is now," Jared said.

"Is she? I wonder," Justin answered, looking down into his goblet of port.

"Do you think I came back to take your title, your home, *and* your promised wife?" Jared asked, turning to stare at his brother at last. "I won't take her. I took the title because it was my birthright, and you were the one who insisted. The estate and all that entailed came with it. But that's all I expect to get. People are not included in the legacy. They're not negotiable." He laughed bitterly. "You should know how I, of all people, feel about that. We traded names and places. We can trade beds, too, brother—and we will do exactly that one day, I suppose, although I don't think I'll ever sleep easy in your room when you leave it, and I think you know that—but we can't trade bedmates. I'm used to barter; it's lifeblood in the Colonies. Sometimes a man hasn't got the money to buy what he needs and so he trades goods for goods with his neighbor, to their mutual benefit. We call it 'swapping.' But we can't swap people, brother."

"Ah, yes," Justin said calmly, "but if you insist people have free will, sometimes we must, mustn't we? I won't hold her back. I won't have a wife who wishes I had 'swapped' her along with my bed. Would you?"

"Plain talk," Jared muttered distractedly, "and premature, at that."

"Is it?"

"Another 'swap' then—plain talk for plain talk," Jared said. "Do you love her?"

"Of course. I grew up with her, I have known her forever, as she jests. You, of all people should know how it is with a girl you've grown up with." Justin said it casually, but his blue eyes were intent as he watched his brother's face.

Jared nodded. "Yes. I understand. But do you love her as a woman?"

"Enough to want her to be happy," Justin said carefully.

Jared knew it was an answer that was no answer. But he didn't ask another question—maybe because he didn't want to hear another answer.

"By God!" he said instead, glancing at the window where the flat black of night that had darkened it had turned silvery. "Morning already? And we're supposed to accompany the ladies on a walking tour of London tomorrow—or rather, today."

"We'll make it a short walk, then," Justin said, equally casual, rising and stretching his long body as though he didn't have a care in the world except for his stiffness, "and pray for rain. Meanwhile, we have a few hours to sleep. This isn't the countryside; no one who is anyone in London goes anywhere till noon."

They went out the door together. They said good night, and each went to his own room. But neither went to sleep. Jared lay staring at the canopy above his bed, wondering if it could possibly be true that everything he dreamed of was really his, and wondering why there had to be hard choices mixed in with the wonder and joy of it.

Justin lay awake, wide-eyed, seeing nothing but a blank future, wondering how it was that now that he'd gotten what he'd regretted losing all his life, he was going to lose everything else he ever had because of it. He wondered how it was that a man could hate and love at the same time and with the same intensity, and whether it would really tear him apart, as it seemed to be doing now.

It did rain. So instead of suggesting a stroll through the park, a stop at a coffeehouse, and then their usual goggling at the sights of London, Jared called a coach for Della. He took her to the inn, where Justin said he'd join them after he fetched Fiona from her townhouse.

"There's so much to do in London at night and nothing to do but eat and drink during the daytime," Della grumbled after they'd been shown to their private parlor and the proprietor had produced the menu with a flourish.

"Yes, but Fiona says that when the weather's good, there's nothing like the pleasure gardens. She says there's music and dancing, plays and promenades there, fireworks on summer evenings, strolling musicians—I can't wait until spring to see for myself," Jared said absently as he glanced over the menu and so missed seeing Della's face. But she grew so quiet that he put the menu down and looked at her.

"Something I said?" he asked.

She shrugged. It was a pretty gesture, he thought. She

wore a blue gown and her own unpowdered hair today; her vivid coloring was good to look at on such a gray day.

"Nothing," she said, and then blurted, "My father says so, too. Only I won't be here then—not in the spring. You'll have to write and tell me all about it."

He frowned.

"I'll be going home soon—we can't stay forever," she said quickly. "We came to see you, to see how you were doing for yourself—because you wrote and asked us to and because we wanted to be sure everything was as you said. And it is. But my father has a business to see to, and there's our house—we have another life, you know."

"I know," he said, still frowning. If she left, he thought, he would be alone in his new life. The thought left him feeling edgy and uneasy. "But there's no reason to hurry back, is there?" he asked. "I mean, Hoyt can take care of the business from Virginia; I trained him to do it myself. Tully and Cutler can run the plantation; they do anyway. Alfred and I are better traders than farmers. And Alfred can use the time to find some more lucrative connections here. What's the hurry?"

"Hurry?" She gave an artificial laugh. "I'd hardly call staying months *hurrying*. There are things to do at home, my dear sir."

He raised one golden brow. She blushed. "You understand—commitments and so on," she said, dropping her high-nosed manner, because she could never fool him.

"Oh. I see. Stephen Perkins won't keep? Or Jasper Threadwell?"

She flushed more rosily. He'd just named her least favorite suitors.

"Or Master Jack Kelly," she said sweetly, on an inspiration, and saw Jared's brow swoop down at hearing the new name. "The first mate on the *Boston Boy,* the ship I came here on. He said he'd call on me when I got home. I can't expect him to wait a whole year. Or I suppose I should say I can't expect the women he meets to let him wait that long, whatever he promised. He's much too young and handsome. *And* his father owns the ship."

There, she thought with pleasure, seeing his thoughtful expression, hoping the name itself conjured up in Jared's mind the image of an ardent suitor. She was very glad she'd suddenly thought of Jack Kelly, but she was also surprised she could think of any other man when Jared was with her.

She thought he looked weary this morning; he obviously wasn't used to the long hours London gentlemen kept, rolling in at dawn after a riotous night, sleeping until noon, and then rolling out on the town again. She hoped he never would be. Late hours always showed quickly in his face, although she had to admit fatigue became him, making his handsome face look even more romantic.

As he continued to gaze at her, she found she couldn't look away—she'd be leaving soon, so she wanted to look her fill at him now.

He looked at her as though taking inventory. "Have you strong feelings for this wonderfully rich, handsome, lucky sailor lad? Why haven't you mentioned him before?" he asked, his voice slow and pensive.

She was delighted. She was about to tell Jared a fine story she'd just made up about her new suitor when he leapt to his feet and smiled, Della and her new admirer forgotten. Della turned to see Fiona walking toward them, shaking herself like an angry, wet kitten.

"Only for you!" she cried immediately, shaking out her parasol. Justin, who'd come in behind her, helped her off with her cape. She wore a rich gown as warm and pink as Della's was blue. Mist made shimmering cobwebs in her high, dressed, pale hair. She shook again to get rid of the few raindrops that clung like crystals to the hem of her wide skirt, and because her stiff bodice didn't bend, the tops of her fine white breasts swayed as she, seemingly unaware, did that erotic little jiggling dance. "You're the only reason I would go out in a deluge for my dinner!" she scolded Jared.

"It's only a light mist now," Justin said patiently.

"Come, sit by the fire," Jared said, drawing up a chair for her.

Della watched as the two tall brothers settled Fiona near the fire, got her a glass of wine, and tried to stop her complaining. It was so foolish, such a lot of fuss over a little bit of rain, that a small smile began to play around the edges of Fiona's pretty mouth. But neither of the men were smiling, and they did not look at each other as they hurried to help her.

"We're very grateful that you braved a hurricane to get here today, Fiona," Della said in a pinched voice. "Not many women would dare put a foot outside in this terrible weather. I'm honored."

"Of course not," Fiona said, dimpling. "We melt, you know, in the rain." And then after that outrageous statement, she giggled.

As the men laughed, Della sighed. There was no way to fight someone who laughed at herself. No reason to fight her, either. *Might as well fight a flower for attracting a bee,* she thought despondently. Then she settled back in her seat to watch as Fiona took charge of the day.

The inn had French aspirations, serving turtle soup and pheasant with salads and green vegetables in all sorts of rich dressings, along with the usual ham, venison, veal, fish, rabbit, and chicken—and twelve kinds of wine, along with spa waters and beer. The men ate the rich food while Fiona prattled and made them laugh.

Della watched, not smiling or eating, until Jared noticed her plate and asked if she was feeling sick. Sick with jealousy but nothing else, she managed to get a few bites down around the lump that seemed to have lodged in her throat, then murmured something about being full to put him off. If she couldn't have his honest attention, she didn't want his sympathy. She wanted to watch what was happening and mark it well in her mind and heart, so that she could never tell herself in the long years to come that Jared's interest in Fiona wasn't strong and real and there from the start, and so she could remind herself that there was nothing she could have done about it.

So she sat and toyed with her food and watched her dreams die. She didn't notice how quiet Justin too had become, until he spoke to her.

"Have you truly had your fill of food?" he asked.

But his sympathetic eyes asked about more. She said simply, "I'm not used to how much you Englishmen eat at noon. If you worked on a farm all morning, I could understand it. But you've all only just awakened."

"Ah, but we don't eat breakfast," he said. "We pick at the little biscuits our servants bring us in bed and sluice them down with sips of chocolate. Then we spend an hour or two dressing so we can go out to really eat. That's when we stoke up for the hours of exhausting visiting, gossiping, and parading to show off our clothing that we have to do—before we go back home, change our clothes, and go out again to delight ourselves and our friends until dawn. The only chance we actually get to eat is at noon. We only have time to drink, dance, go to plays and parties, and gamble until dawn after that."

"And flirt," she said sadly, watching Jared and Fiona laughing over something together.

"Yes. And flirt," he said. "It's an art with us, you see. Haven't you noticed? Here in London, married folks as well as single ones do it. Engaged ones, as well. It's the style."

"From what I've been told," she said slowly, turning worried blue eyes on him, "the married folks here do more than flirt. And no one minds or cares."

"Some do. Some mind *and* care. But don't forget, sometimes flirting is only that."

"And sometimes it's not. Sometimes it's more," she said, looking at him steadily.

"Yes," he said, "that's so. So sometimes all we can do is to wait and see."

"Or leave," she said abruptly. "Did I tell you? We're going home soon, my father and I."

"No," he said quickly. "I think it would be a bad idea. Anyway, I didn't think you the sort of girl to run."

She blinked. "Run, walk, tiptoe," she finally said. He knew, and there was no more sense denying it. She was leaving soon anyway and didn't care anymore. "Does it matter how I leave? If it did matter, I might not go. But I don't want to look p-pitiful." She lowered her head as though studying her plate full of congealing soup. She hoped she wouldn't cry into it—that would be too pathetic.

"Take care!" Justin whispered urgently. "Not one tear, please, because if you salt the soup, the chef will get very angry. He'll come raging out of the kitchen with a cleaver. In the old days, it would be fine even if you spit into the soup—it might even improve it—but he's pretending to be French to lure in customers, and he thinks Frenchmen are supposed to be temperamental."

A corner of her trembling mouth tilted up, in spite of herself.

"He's got *jambon* and *mouton* on the menu," Justin went on, "but he couldn't bring himself to put a frog on the card any which way you spell it. Couldn't touch one, actually. English to the marrow, he is. Calls himself Jacques around here, but call him that and he won't even turn around, because he was born a right honest old Alf. He doesn't know how to say that in French, you see."

She giggled.

"He did try Alphonse," Justin said sadly, "but the first time anyone called him that, he hit them a good chop, so . . ."

She began to laugh. It was such an unexpected bright, free, whole-heartedly happy sound coming from her that Jared and Fiona stopped talking to see what had caused it. Jared seemed surprised that it was his brother.

Della smiled at Justin and said, "Justin was just explaining some of the finer points of being English to me."

"As I was to Jared," Fiona said brightly. "Isn't this fun!"

"Indeed. I don't know what we did for diversion before you came," Justin said, but this time it was hard to tell if he was joking.

They dined until there were no dishes left for the waiters to carry out. Then the men excused themselves, saying they were going to secure a coach or some sedan chairs for the ladies.

"It's their way of saying they have to use the withdrawing room," Fiona said merrily. "Do you?"

Della shook her head and Fiona went on with a sigh, "Well, I do, but I'll wait until I get home. *Such* trouble using those teeny chamber pots they supply when you've *such* a lot of skirt on, isn't it? How I envy the gentlemen. They just open a flap, stand in the right direction, and—oh! Have I shocked you?"

She had, but not by *what* she'd said, only that she'd *said* it. But then Della realized most of the English nobles she'd met here were freer in speech than the people were at home. She supposed it had something to do with the fact that when the Puritans had left England to settle the Colonies, they'd taken their sober influence with them. Whatever the reason, Fiona's comment wasn't so much vulgar as it was amusing, like the woman herself was. It was impossible to dislike her, Della thought sadly, even though she purely hated her. She gave up.

"No," she told Fiona with a faint smile, "you haven't shocked me. It's just that it's odd to hear an English lady say such things."

"Well, English men are equipped the same as colonial ones, I dare say," Fiona said. "Unless you know otherwise?" she asked with a giggle.

Della could only smile and shake her head.

"How I envy you!" Fiona said, and Della stared. "You've known Jared all these years and I'm only just getting to know him. What a charming man! How unusual he is, so full of spirit and experience, but with such good manners. Even his voice is different from most men's—

oh, not to you, of course. But his accent is not like Justin's, even though they are brothers. Their voices are the same, but different, like their faces. They look alike in some ways, but are totally different looking. Do you know, I believe there is no way they are alike at heart. Jared is so—adventuresome."

She spoke about Jared the way any infatuated chit at home might, Della thought, and quickly said, "Because he had to be. And he talks the way most men do at home. Now, to me, it's Justin's voice that's more unusual, even though my own father is from England—as I am, when you get right down to it. Life in the Colonies changes people, I guess. It will be interesting to see if life here changes a man back again."

"Won't it?" Fiona said eagerly. "I can't wait to see."

There was only so much Della could take. She was tired and sad, and the thought that she was going to leave this place soon made her reckless in ways she wouldn't have been if she'd planned to stay on. She knew that all of this, including Fiona, would soon be only a memory.

"Yes, everything about Jared is interesting. But you're going to marry Justin, aren't you?" she said bluntly.

Fiona looked amused, not dismayed. She laughed, a little silvery laugh. "I am going to marry the earl of Alveston, everyone knows that."

"But Justin . . ." Della said, and then didn't say more, because she belatedly remembered it wasn't polite, or her place, and it probably wouldn't do any good anyway.

"Justin is a very nice man. And I do love him—dearly. But Della, you of all people know how it is with men you've known since you were tiny! Jared's like a beloved brother to you—as Justin is to me," Fiona said with simple wisdom. "But unlike you, I am supposed to marry the man I grew up with." She made a little sad face, and then looked at Della, her eyes twinkling. "I suppose I would have without a murmur, if Jared hadn't returned, for I am a very good girl and wouldn't want to cause my father distress, any more than you'd want to cause yours any. Can you blame me for wanting some spice in my life?"

It was hard for Della to listen, she was so busily dreaming of what it might be like to be expected to marry Jared.

"I never thought things could be different, but now just look at this," Fiona purred. "All of a sudden, and in the nick of time, there arrives on the scene a man as good as Justin, every bit as handsome, clever, and even more exciting—and it turns out that he is the true earl, the man I was supposed to marry in the first place. Oh Della, dear, isn't that just wonderful?"

Fiona sat back, her pretty face aglow. She was only a year younger in age than Della herself was, Della realized, but she was very much younger in every other way. She was charming and thoughtless, but no more cruel than a child who wants only to get her way. She couldn't guess the pain she inflicted, nor would she care very much, probably, if she did. She was content as long as she got what she wanted.

But it mightn't even be that, Della realized. Fiona might think Della would be proud or even delighted at the idea of a fine English lady wanting Jared, because it was clear she, like Jared, thought Della loved him like a brother. There was no power on earth that would make Della tell Fiona otherwise.

"But . . . Justin?" Della finally asked, because she didn't know what else to say.

"Oh, who knows? We'll see. Nothing's settled. Oh, here they are. Gentlemen," Fiona said, smiling at the brothers, "have you gotten us a coach or a sedan chair to cram ourselves into?"

"Neither," Justin said. "The rain has stopped, and I believe you ought to walk off that meal. You devoured three cream puffs—not that I was counting."

"Oh, pooh!" Fiona said with a saucy grin. Placing her

hand on Jared's arm, she put her nose in the air and said, "In that case, I'll walk with *this* fellow. He's far more polite. *You* weren't counting, were you, my lord?"

"Only your smiles," Jared said with enough oily mock courtesy to make even Justin and Della laugh, whether or not they felt like it.

They strolled the few blocks to Fiona's house. It was late afternoon, and early autumn shadows were creeping down the avenue with them. Della walked behind Fiona and Jared and couldn't stop watching how their heads tilted close as they chatted. Or the way Fiona's gloved hand rested so possessively on Jared's arm. Or the way he held his own hand over hers when he guided her across a street in the wake of the street sweeper's broom, as though only he could protect the delicate lady with whom he walked.

Della stared at Jared's back, seeing his rakish new hat and how his neatly tied hair, resting on his strong, wide shoulders, glowed gold with the last sunlight. Afterward, she never remembered exactly what she had talked about with Justin as they trailed along in Jared and Fiona's shadow, but they did speak and laugh and act as though they were having just as good a time as the couple in front of them obviously were.

"Father will be so glad to see you!" Fiona said gaily when they got to her house. And though she didn't specify whom he'd be so glad to see, it was clear when the baron came out to greet them.

"My lord! I give you good day, Alveston!" he said with pleasure when he took Jared's hand. "Oh, hello, Justin," he added when he saw whom Della was with. He absently sketched a bow to Della, but never took his eyes from Jared as he did. "I've something to show you, my lord," he told Jared.

"Alveston will do," Jared said curtly, because he was so aware of Justin, silent, at his side. He was uneasy with the way the baron so quickly accepted his new title and so casually renamed the man who would soon be his son-in-law. "I have always been Alveston," Jared went on, drawing himself up to his full, imposing height, "but the 'my lord' still doesn't sound right to me."

"You'll soon get used to it," Fiona's father said. "But wait until you see what I unearthed for you! Letters from your mother. Notes from your father. And a miniature of them both. We grew up together, you know. Justin has seen them, but I'll wager you never have."

Jared's eyes widened. He hadn't seen his parents' faces in over twenty years. They'd had their portraits painted as infants; he'd seen the painting in the gallery at Hawkstone. But they'd not lived long enough to have them done as adults—or so he'd thought. He held them in his mind's eye only: his father, tall as a tree, with deep gray eyes; his mother, fair and blue-eyed and always smiling. He remembered the sound and smell and feel of them much better.

"I'd like to see the pictures," he said eagerly, all haughtiness forgotten.

"They don't look much like our parents," Justin commented. "They are just beautifully colored paintings. They could be of anyone."

But Jared wasn't listening as the baron led him into his library.

"Do you think he minds?" Della asked nervously, as they walked back through evening shadows.

Justin didn't answer right away, and so she knew Justin thought that Jared not only didn't mind, but that he probably didn't even notice they'd left.

"He has other things to occupy him," Justin said carefully.

She could only nod. She knew it wasn't only the papers and pictures Fiona's father had to show Jared that Justin was talking about. Fiona had been hanging on Jared's arm even as he'd looked down at the two tiny, brightly colored insipid portraits that were supposed to be of his parents. Justin was right; they were nothing like any real people Della had ever seen. But she understood why Jared stared at them so long and held them like holy objects—for

Fiona to see. Fiona had even shared that with him, Della thought numbly, resenting every scrap of Jared's past that she was being locked out of.

"This all may pass," Justin said as they went up the stairs to what had been his townhouse and was now his brother's. He didn't say more as the footman opened the door and let them in. In fact, he didn't speak again until he and Della were alone in the drawing room. Then he paced as restlessly as his brother usually did. That was one of the major differences between them, Della noted bemusedly: Jared was the one who was always tense—even when he stood still, he seemed filled with nervous energy. Justin always appeared calm and composed. Until tonight.

"But it may not pass. Or will it? You'd know better than I," Justin said, stopping to look at her.

She didn't pretend to misunderstand. It seemed they had come to some kind of unspoken alliance. She owed him better than coyly pretending ignorance of what he was talking about. Besides, she wanted to know the truth for herself, and he could help.

"I don't know," she told him honestly. "I never saw him like this. He was very infatuated with Sarah Pope when he was sixteen. All the boys were. But I'd never say he was in love with her; he teased her more than flattered her, and turned red when I jollied him about his interest in her. This—this fascination—I don't know. He never discussed such things with me. I didn't know the other women he visited in town, or at least I never saw him with them," she added scrupulously. "So I don't know what this is, or if it will pass."

"Nor I. It appears I know very little of love or of my intended bride," Justin said with a strange laugh. "As for my brother, I know the boy he once was, but too many years have passed since then. The boy I knew was perceptive and sensitive, as well as bold and responsible. Only a year older than I, but my superior in every way. Or so I thought then. I wanted nothing more than to be like him.

When I lost him—through his saving me—I knew I could never measure up to what had been lost. Now, I don't think that I know him at all. All I do know is that he still inspires hero worship, doesn't he?"

"It's more than that!" Della cried. "He's still sensitive and responsible and perceptive and whatever else it was you said he was. All of it. It's just that a man can't help whom he falls in love with. I'm as sorry I had to say it as I am that it's true, but I had to, and I'm glad I did," she said all in a jumble.

"Della," Justin said quickly, coming up to her. "Della," he said sadly, taking her hand in one of his and putting his other alongside her flushed cheek. "No, don't look away. Everyone doesn't see it—really. I do, but only because I'm watching Fiona as closely as you watch him. There's nothing wrong with what you feel. He *is* an admirable man. And you're right, it's not his fault."

"It must be awful for you," Della said straight out, before she could think better of it. She saw the infinite sadness in his eyes, which made her realize that she'd been too full of her own misery to see his. "I mean, to lose the woman you love to the man who's already taken everything else from you. . . ."

"Everything else was his to begin with," he told her, just as he'd told himself so many times, "even the lady. And I'm not sure I've lost her. But if I have, I'm not at all sure it's such a terrible thing," he said with a sad smile. "We took each other for granted for so long that we stopped truly seeing each other. Now I wonder if that was a good way to start out a lifetime together—as though we'd already spent one together. I don't think so, not if we didn't want a marriage à la mode, that is. And I never did.

"Sometimes blessings come in the disguise of disaster," he said, thinking aloud. He still cradled her face in his hand, but his thumb now caressed the line of her jaw. "I have my brother back, after all. I'm not landless or penniless, and what I have now was always rightfully mine. And certainly, if the woman I wanted to marry doesn't want me, it's no bad thing not to marry her. There are other women in the world. It's just that I never took the time to look at them carefully," he said, gazing into her dark-blue eyes, looking at her flawless skin and pink mouth, studying every nuance of expression on her upturned face.

She stood very still, listening more to his voice than his words. Fiona was right. His voice was like Jared's, but the accent was different. If she closed her eyes, she would never mistake his voice for Jared's, but it sounded so much like him that it struck her to the heart. It was as if she knew this man very well, and yet not at all. She opened her eyes and saw his solemn ones watching her. His face too was very like and yet altogether not like Jared's. It made her feel good and bad and lost and found, all together.

His hair had been growing longer during her stay in England, and he wore it without powder now, like his brother. But his long eyes were a clear light blue, not foggy gray; his skin was not as sun-bitten as his brother's, but just as clear and fine. She noticed he had a faint, long, thin scar on his forehead that ran into his eyebrow, and she wondered how such a fine gentleman had ever gotten hurt. But his eyes told her he could feel hurt, and did. They told her something else too as they considered her. She looked down hastily to his firm mouth, and saw that his lips were a little less full than his brother's, but well shaped, and much, much more close to her own than they had been a moment before. She wondered if they would feel like Jared's—and then realized she didn't know what Jared's kiss was like, beyond a brotherly touch. She also realized she was thinking a strange and dangerous thing. She stepped back, suddenly alarmed and ashamed.

He gazed at her, his face impassive, unreadable, but his long fingers brushed an inky curl back from her brow. "No," he said softly, "I am not he. And I am not thinking about consoling myself now, either. Or you. Nor do I believe you are my sister. Not for a minute. I think we both must begin to think about that."

She nodded because she didn't know what else to do. But it seemed to please him, and he took her hand, kissed it gently, then bowed and left her there, standing, staring after him, not knowing what to think or say.

There were voices in the hall after he'd left her, but she hardly heard them, so intently was she listening to the ones in her own head.

"Back already, I see," her father said briskly as he came into the room, taking off his gloves. "I met Justin as he was leaving; Jared not back yet? Just as well, just as well. I needed to talk with you alone, puss. Speaking of brothers, remember mine?"

"Your brothers?" she asked, getting her jumbled thoughts in order again, delighted to be diverted by the question. "Terrible Terrence? Dreadful David and Monstrous Martin?" She laughed. "Of course. I loved the story about them; it was like a fairy tale. I loved hearing about how they got their comeuppance. They were cruel to you because they'd inherited and you hadn't. They wouldn't share or help you when Mama died. And then they were mad as fire when you went to the Colonies and wound up richer than any of them—so mad that they never wrote to you again. Those brothers?"

"Well, yes," he said, uneasily.

"What of them?" She gasped. "Don't tell me you ran into one of them!"

"Well, no," he said, avoiding her eyes, "it's just that— well, I've a notion to see them."

"What?"

"Actually, I wrote to them, from here. And now they want to see me again."

"What?" she asked again, amazed. "Why? After all these years? Do they want to see you, too? Don't trust them," she said indignantly. "They probably only want money from you, because you know how to make it and they only knew how to take it."

"I know," he said, in a strangely quiet tone, "but even so, I want to see them again. Jared's not the only one to miss his family and want to visit his birthplace again. All people do, sometime, I think, whether their family's worthy or not. I know very well what my brothers are, but I confess I have this strange desire to see it for myself again, so I'm going north to visit them."

She looked at her father as she had not for years. Although he was heavier than he'd been when she'd been young, he was straight and well proportioned, and still had his hair and his charming smile. He'd never remarried, but she knew he had a "special friend," a widow in town he visited now and then. But now, seeing how uncomfortable he was with whatever emotion he was suppressing, she saw him as a man separate from her father, and suddenly realized he might have missed much more than his wife all those years of her childhood.

Although she'd joked about it, it was terrible thinking about how his family had treated him. It was worse to think about how they might try to take advantage of him now. But because his first thoughts had always been of her, how could she argue with him about his wishes now? If he felt the need of his family, then it was cruel of her to point out how selfish they'd been.

"They're very influential up there, have been there for generations," he went on, with a note of false good humor that her ears picked up. "They all have huge families. You have tons of cousins, puss. Some are your age, some a bit older—men and women. Lots of gay times there, I suspect. Lots of young men friends hanging about the place, too, no doubt."

Her eyes narrowed.

"To be brief, what do you say you come up north with me now, puss, eh?"

"Father, I—" she began to say.

He interrupted, saying gruffly, "Aye, I think it's a good time for you to go, lass. Leave here with a smile and a wave of farewell, and come with me. Leave a good impression at least. Don't see what else you can do. And I can't bear to see you hurt anymore, either, and there's the truth of it."

"Oh!" she said, her breath leaving her. She wondered if he had heard anything from the hallway, or if he was just talking about everything he'd seen in all the days before. As brave as she was, it was a thing she didn't dare ask him.

Chapter

13

Her eyes opened so wide at what he'd said, Alfred thought she looked like the child she'd been rather than the fashionable young woman she was now.

"But—I thought you taught me never to run away," she managed to say.

"I?" he asked. "Nonsense. Where did you get such a foolish idea? Not from me. There's no better answer for some problems than to run away from them. What do you think I was doing when I took you and your brother across an ocean into the wilderness? I was running away. Aye, and think—there wouldn't be anyone but Indians in all the Colonies now if people didn't run away from their problems. Who do you think is settling the place? Contented people? No, people who have run out of answers, that's who. People who are wise enough to run away and start over again—as I believe you should."

She looked at him with such wild sorrow in her deep blue eyes that he felt his heart turn over. She no longer reminded him of her mother, though she was her image. She reminded him of himself and everything he held dear. He folded her into his arms. It was easier to say what he had to without looking at her, so he rested his chin atop her head of curly hair and spoke softly, staring at the wall, the windows, anywhere but at the girl he held so tenderly.

"I'm sorry for what I had to say, my honey, but glad I've said it. You're the eyes in my head and the beat of my heart and have been since the day you were born. That I never said it so plainly before doesn't mean I didn't feel it. I can't bear to see you unhappy, and that's the truth." He stroked her silky curls and sighed. "I suppose going up north is my way of running again, but it worked last time and might again. I want to take you with me."

"But Jared . . ." she said.

He sighed more heavily. "Aye, Jared. That's the crux of it—Jared. I love the lad, too. Dearly. He's everything a man could want in a son. It was almost like the Lord sent me another after he took my only one. I confess, I had the same hopes you did. But now? He's acting like he's found the girl for him, and that's the truth with no bark on it."

He felt her stiffen, and he went on sadly, "I can't say for sure that he has, or if he really knows himself yet, either. But he's interested, and that's a fact. And she and that father of hers are getting less interested in his brother by the hour. As for Jared, he's flattered, and why not? The way I see it, she's everything he feels they took from him, along with his childhood and the life he was supposed to lead. I can't say she's good for him, and that's not just because I believe you'd be the best thing for any man anywhere on this old earth. She's so young in ways—and flighty. Pretty, and pretty manners, too, it's true, but too full of herself in that prettiness, with not a thought in her head for anything but frippery. But maybe that's what he wants and needs after the life he's led. Maybe he wants nothing from a woman but laughter and silliness now, to make him forget.

"He's had a terrible life, Della. We tried to make it up to

him, but no one could. He deserves the best, but he has to choose what that is."

"And you think that won't be me?" she asked, too wise and too sad now to bother to deny the truth anymore.

"I don't know," he confessed, "and I can't stand to think of how you'll feel if it is to be her, after all. Being here with him while he decides isn't going to make any difference. Maybe he'll even miss you more when you're gone—but no, that's not likely, and I shouldn't try to sell you a fish story," he admitted. "Absence *doesn't* make the heart grow fonder; were that so, then every sailor would come home to marry his sweetheart, wouldn't he? I don't want to see you hurt. So why not come north with me?"

He stepped back and lifted her chin with one hand. His eyes were candid as he studied her face. "That bit about my missing the old place, why there really is truth in that," he said. "I would like to see it again. That, and all the people, too, just one last time. And I want you happy. So, two birds with one stone. What do you say?"

"I don't know."

"Time for plain pound dealing," he said roughly. "Is it the brother? Justin?" She averted her eyes as color flew to her cheeks. "A nice likely lad, to be sure," he said, nodding, "but I don't know if you see that—or just the resemblance to Jared. That isn't fair, child."

"I know. Don't worry about that—*that* I do know. But Papa, I don't think I do want to go away just yet. It's like— like watching someone you love die, I guess," she said with a quavering smile. "You have to see the thing out so you can go on with the rest of your life without pretending. There has to be an ending, and I must see it for myself. Can you understand that?"

He nodded.

"And so if it hurts, why then, it does. It's not like I have no one waiting for me at home," she said with a jaunty show of bravado that just about broke his heart. "You remember I told you about Jack Kelly? Don't make such a face; he's not just a sailor. His father owns the whole shipyard. And there are other men—it's just that I've never been able to see them for Jared. But maybe once I know it's over, well and truly and forever, I'll be able to see them. Do you think that could be so?"

She asked him hopefully, and he could give her no less than his own hope for an answer. "Aye, it could be," he said. "And it might be so," he said with more energy as he thought about it. "You're as strong as you can be, child. It may well be so," he said with growing enthusiasm. "I suppose I'll cancel the trip north."

"Why do that?"

"Think: how can I leave you here alone?" He chuckled at her confusion. "I can't leave precisely because you are no longer a child. You're not his sister, after all, so you can't stay in his house by yourself without a proper chaperone. The upper classes here are pretty wild; they have more manners than morals. But even they would talk about such a thing."

"There must be some way we can work it out. I could stay in a respectable inn, with a maidservant, couldn't I?"

"A lovely young girl alone in the middle of this wicked town, with no one to protect her but a maidservant—or a man who's not even related to her, and he a man who's interested in someone else?" Alfred sputtered and then stopped to consider what he'd just said. What *if* Jared was forced to realize Della wasn't really his sister? What if he saw that the rest of the world wouldn't consider her such? And then had to think about her being alone for the first time in her life, realizing that if anything happened to her father, she would always be so? "Aye," Alfred said slowly, "puss, there might be something in it, after all. Now what inn is fine enough for my dear Della, I wonder?"

"An *inn?* Impossible. What are you thinking of, Alfred? Leave Della by herself in the heart of London in an *inn?*"

Jared was shocked. But Alfred didn't seem upset by his reaction. Instead, he shook back his cuff, inspected it, and answered airily, "She won't be by herself. The girl will be with her."

"A maid? Leave her alone in an inn with no one but a servant girl? If we were home, I'd say you'd been out riding too long in the fields without a hat!"

"Della's a level-headed miss," Alfred answered, "not flighty or easily led. And she'll be close by you. The Saracen's Head isn't a stone's throw from here. The Peacock is older, true, but it caters to travelers. The Saracen's Head has more of a residential air about it. They have fine food and a good cellar, not to mention snug rooms and proper private dining parlors—and their prices show it, but nothing's too good for my girl."

"But she could be in danger!" An image of how Della had looked that morning flashed through Jared's mind. She'd worn another new blue gown, the color that always reminded him of her eyes. But it wasn't just her eyes the gown had flattered: the color showed up her creamy skin, while the fit showed off her pert breasts, tiny waist, the graceful turning of her arms . . . *Lord!* Jared thought. *Even her elbows looked delicious today. . . .* He shuddered to think about what the men of London would think, seeing such a girl alone. Thinking about that was easier than analyzing his own reaction to her tempting appearance.

"Much too much danger. What are you thinking of?" Jared muttered. He took a walk around the room to calm himself, running his hand repeatedly through his hair, stopping only to scowl when he realized he'd pulled it from its neat tie.

"I'm thinking of her," Alfred said. "She doesn't want to come north with me, and though I regret it, I can't blame her. She hates my family. If she comes, there'll be trouble, and there's been trouble enough. You know her temper— and her tongue."

Jared did, and smiled in spite of himself.

"It's my fault, entirely, for talking against them for so many years," Alfred went on, "but I did dislike them. For years, that dislike served me well. I think it made me work harder and accounts for my accomplishment. I couldn't let them see me fail. I couldn't wait to rub their noses in my success. But now I don't want to do that, after all. Funny, how one's dreams change as one ages. For I got to thinking: I'm not getting any younger, and neither are they. Why, I'm a totally different man from the one who left England all those years ago. Maybe they are, too."

He watched Jared's changing expression and went on, "The bottom line—which is the most important one for a merchant, as I taught you—is that whatever they are, they are my family, after all. I want one last look at them before I leave England; it also occurred to me that I may never pass this way again," he said more heavily, noting Jared's expression with a satisfaction he didn't show.

"Bad news?" Justin said, strolling into the room with Fiona and seeing the same expression on his brother's face that Alfred saw.

The brothers were supposed to go for an afternoon walk with the ladies. But Alfred had come into the drawing room to talk with Jared first. He knew Della would be late—he'd made her promise to be.

"Bad news?" Jared said through clenched teeth. "Depends on how you look at it. Only that Alfred has gone mad and decided to go up north to visit his long-lost family—and leave Della here by herself—in an *inn*—until he comes back."

"Not by herself," Alfred said patiently, "with a maid. And not just any inn—the Saracen's Head."

Justin whistled.

"Why can't she just stay on here?" Fiona asked.

"With two bachelors?" Alfred asked her.

"Oh, but Jared's like a brother to her, and she knows that Justin is promised . . ." Fiona paused, blushed, stole a peek at Jared, and then went on quickly. "I mean to say, she knows Justin is an honorable man."

"I have no doubt he is," Alfred said, patiently, "but I

can't trust the world to know it, can I? We're off to Virginia on the first fair tide after I return, but gossip can cross an ocean, too. I have her reputation to think of. And, I remind you, my dear, that she *has* no brother. She did, but he died many years ago. Jared is my partner and her friend. *Not* her brother. And the world knows it, too."

"Why then, where's the problem?" Fiona asked merrily. "She shall stay with me!"

"I don't think she'll feel comfortable doing that," Alfred said hastily, thinking of Della's reaction. "She's fiercely independent. It might be different if you were *Jared's* fiancée," he said innocently enough, though he watched Jared from the corner of his eye. "But as it is, she's only met Justin and you recently, and neither of us would wish to impose."

Before a reasonable argument could be voiced, and Alfred knew there were too many that could be, he added, in all honesty at last, "Jared, if you're going to carry on, and Della, too, why then, I think I'll forget it. I'll try one last time to talk her into going with me because there are some young men there eager to meet her, and who knows? But if she sets up too much of a ruckus, we'll go home now, and none the worse for it. I can always invite my brothers to my home . . . why, I think I like the sound of that even better! Let them see for themselves. If Della doesn't like it, why then, there'll be no problem, because there are a dozen places she can take herself off to if she wants to avoid them at home."

"Too bad. She hasn't seen half of London," Fiona said sadly.

"I don't think she'll mind. She doesn't care for London really, no more than I do," Justin commented.

"Oh yes, she's a country girl, too," Fiona said. "I forgot—it's Jared and I who adore London. I shall be sorry to see her go, but perhaps I can visit her someday, too! Jared, you said you'd be going back from time to time," she said, looking at him from beneath her lashes. "Maybe I could come along. I should love to see it with you as my guide! You've told me so much about the New World. I want to see everything you saw, but for myself."

The brothers were silent. Even Alfred didn't know what to say in the face of this artlessness—or artfulness. So they all ignored it.

"I wish you'd think it over, sir," Justin told Alfred. "Please. Della may not like London, but we like her."

"There's nothing to think over," Jared said quickly. "I'm not so mad about London, either. It's interesting, but it will keep. It's time for me to learn more about the estate. There's no problem, Alfred. Della can stay with me and Justin at the hall, because—Fiona, if you'd be so kind—could you see your way to leaving London now and staying on with us there, with your mother or father, of course, the way you did when I first arrived?"

"Of course. Why not?" she said merrily. "What a good idea! The holidays are coming—we always spend them together. It will be grand! Yes, of course, I'm sure my father will agree. It will be delightful. I came to London because I thought we'd have ourselves a coronation, and that's something no one would ever want to miss. But who knows when that will be now? It's not even scheduled. Everyone says the prince is waiting to find a bride first. He wants to marry and take the throne at the same time. Pity," she said, dimpling, "for I'd hopes myself—he's only a few years older than I, and he looks nothing like his father—yet. Just think! If I leave London now, I might just be giving up a throne myself, mightn't I?" Her eyes twinkled up at them; she was as amused with herself as she hoped they would be.

Alfred and Jared laughed at her pretty foolishness. Justin didn't. "Indeed?" he drawled. "And what of me?— your fiancée? Was I supposed to have challenged him to a duel for your hand?"

"Oh, Justin," she said without missing a beat with her fan as it stirred her fair curls. "You're so honorable. You'd step aside for your king, wouldn't you?"

"If you wanted me to step aside, I would," Justin said

with utter seriousness, "for whatever man—or reason—you give."

There was a startled gasp from the doorway. Della stood there. She wore the blue gown Jared had remembered, but her face was white.

"What's this?" she asked in fear, her eyes flying to Jared's face. She'd heard only what Justin had just said, and looking around she saw the tension in the group before her.

"Aha. The cause of all our troubles. What is this, you ask?" Jared said. "*This* is a demand, cloaked as an invitation. Alfred's going north to visit his wonderful family. You are not going to the Saracen's Head. Or the Peacock. You are coming to Hawkstone Hall with us, whether the menu there is as good or not. There you will stay until Alfred comes to collect you, Mistress Mischief—just try and not!"

She relaxed. "Double-dog dare me, do you?" she asked, her head to the side.

Jared laughed, but his brother and Fiona didn't; they didn't know what the two were talking about.

"No. Triple-dog," he said, putting his legs apart and his hands on his hips as he stared at her. "So?"

"Biting and scratching allowed?" she asked.

"No, and no mud balls, either," he said, remembering her fight with a neighbor boy who had insulted him—a fight he'd had to rescue her from a dozen years ago, a world away.

Her eyes sparkled. She put her small fists on her hips, gave her rear a tiny waggle that set her skirt shimmying, and threw back her head. "I'm mad as a bull, and fierce as a black b'ar," she cried in her huskiest voice, mimicking the accent of every brawling river man she'd ever heard. "I'm a high-tailed rooster and a ring-tailed 'coon, and I can fight a pack of wolves with one hand . . . but what can I do?" She finished in her normal voice. "You're bigger and meaner. All right, you win. I quit."

"She means," Alfred said as he laughed out loud at the

expressions on Justin's and Fiona's faces, "that she'll go, but Jared had better watch out!"

"You're sure?" Alfred had asked as he'd stood at the door with his traveling case. He'd stared into her eyes worriedly.

"I'm sure," Della had said, lifting her chin. "I have to see it out."

He'd nodded, assured. Then he'd kissed her good-bye and left.

Only now did she allow herself doubts. The coach she traveled in was comfortable, with plush seats, heavy silk on the walls to keep out the cold, and hot bricks at her feet to stave off any chill that seeped through the floorboards beneath the carpeting there. There were even hothouse flowers in holders affixed to the walls by the windows. It was like a traveling parlor, down to the baskets of food provided. The only thing lacking was a roaring fire in a fireplace, stillness—and real comfort. Her bottom ached almost as much as her heart as she watched Jared being entertained by Fiona.

Traveling was traveling no matter how you tried to conceal it, and the body knew it even if the eyes were fooled, Della thought sadly—just as a man's attraction to a woman was basically a matter of lust, no matter how good his manners were.

Fiona's eyes sparkled, and she never seemed to get tired or cross—not with such an appreciative audience. Jared sat across from Della, but he might have already been across the ocean from her, because as Della watched only him, she could see nothing but Fiona in his eyes. Fiona never allowed his thoughts or his eyes to wander from her. If his attention wavered for so much as a minute, she called him back to her with a question, a trill of laughter, or, sometimes, even a flirtatious tap of her fan. And though Justin seemed to spend his time looking out the window, Della could see that he was watching Fiona's reflection in it and not the scenery beyond.

"This is foolish," Justin suddenly murmured.

"What?" Della asked.

He turned and smiled a crooked smile very like Jared's. "I spoke aloud? Forgive me. I was thinking of something else. But why should I be? For here we sit, bored to near death, when if we were at a ball, we'd be talking each other's ears off, wouldn't we?"

Bored? Della didn't think he looked bored. A bored man didn't sit with his teeth and hands clenched. But now she saw his smile was gracious and genuine.

"But perhaps you wouldn't be chattering at a ball whether or not you had anything to say, as is the fashion, because you're more of a woman than a lady. I mean that as a compliment," he said quickly, "because you are a lady born, but lucky enough to be a woman bred. But I don't know much about that, do I? I've heard my brother's story, but not yours."

"There's not much to tell." She shrugged. "I was born here, but don't remember much of it because I grew up in the Virginia colony, raised like any other girl there. Jared's the one with all the adventures. I guess my life was shaped by his."

"But I don't know what it's like for any other girl there," he persisted.

"Oh," she said. "Well, let's see. I live in a big house—not big by Hawkstone Hall standards, you understand. And it's new—so new that like most places at home, we have more trouble with sap than with dust on our walls."

His eyebrows rose. He couldn't have voiced his confusion more clearly. "I mean," she said, "that the wood at home, even aged wood, is still fairly new. Or at least you can't count on its being old. And so even if we lay plaster over it, we don't cover our walls with stretched silk the way you do, at least not right away, because sometimes the wood oozes. So we paint and pray."

"I'd heard they were religious in the Colonies," he murmured with a smile.

"No, no." Della laughed, and Fiona cocked an ear when

she heard it, because she hadn't been saying anything amusing just then.

"Not us," Della went on. "Most Puritans are up north, and even they aren't that Puritan anymore. Anyway, my house is very handsome, by our standards. We live by a broad river, so we get to see something of the world, what with so much trade going on. And it's a busy, growing world. But for me, the most interesting difference between our countries, I guess, is that I grew up reading about England's bosky forests and shady dells—Sherwood Forest and that sort of thing. But now I see your forests are so . . . tame, compared to ours. Ours are thick and wild and we have so many of them, with trees so tall their tops can't be seen; some have never been seen by white men. Not like here; your forests look as civilized as your cities. And you have farms everywhere that have been tended for centuries. I read about England and wolves, unicorns and bears, but we're the ones who have all that—except for the unicorns, of course."

"Really? Then I'll have to talk to your father about exporting some," Justin said promptly. "They're such a nuisance here; they devour all our roses and run off with the best maidens. But if we can turn a profit and get rid of them at the same time, it would be wonderful. You say there'd be a market for them?"

She laughed again, her whole, deep, full-hearted laugh, not the stifled tittering she'd been doing in Fiona's presence, because she'd thought that was what Jared liked. This time it was Jared who stopped talking to watch her and his brother.

That wasn't lost on Della, so she turned her shoulder, gave Justin her full attention, and proceeded to tell him about her life in the most amusing way she could. He couldn't have been a better audience, meeting her every anecdote with a sly quip, asking all the best questions, laughing with her and making her laugh, and making it appear as though he weren't watching the dumbstruck Fiona out of the side of his eye, either.

In time, Jared joined in, and then Fiona began to play the game. The rest of the journey went well, filled with shared laughter. Still, Della and Justin were the most amused because they'd been the most upset before they'd started their conversation. They had a good time as they drove to the hall, and by the time they arrived, they felt like comrades in arms, although by then, they were cheered enough that neither wanted to think about who the enemy was.

When they got there, Jared waylaid Della in the hall. He looked so grave and troubled that she quickly reviewed everything she'd said in the carriage, wondering if she'd accidentally said something to offend him. There was so much of his past life he seemed to want to forget now.

"I'm sorry," he said abruptly. "I've neglected you, Della. I never meant to. It was rude—no, it was stupid to just let you sit there with nothing to do but watch me. I realized it when I saw what fun you were having with Justin. You and I used to have fun like that. I think sometimes I take this earl business too seriously. I'm glad you're here to remind me."

She looked up into his eyes, delighted to be the entire focus of them for once. But she promptly ruined it for herself. "I don't think you were being too much of an earl," she said thoughtlessly. "I think you were just having your own fun with Fiona."

His eyes brightened. A corner of his mouth kicked up. "She is fun to be with, isn't she?" he asked. As her spirits fell, he grinned and said, "Thank you, Dell. I can always count on you to say the right thing, can't I?"

"But *I* can't always count on *you* to do the right thing!" Fiona cut in to say jokingly as she came up to them. She pouted prettily. "You promised you'd see me to my room yourself, my lord, and I am so exhausted, and yet still waiting—so patiently."

He laughed. "Forgive me," he said to Fiona. "You're right. A promise is a promise. This way, if you please, my lady." He offered her his arm, and she put her hand on it and gazed up into his eyes. He bowed absently to Della, as though he'd forgotten who the pretty little stranger he'd been talking to was, and walked off with Fiona.

This was what I stayed for, isn't it? Della asked herself savagely. She'd have to see it and see it again, and then maybe she'd be free. But it would take a long time to kill the dream, she thought with dull sorrow as she watched that tall, straight figure go up the stairs with Fiona. It had been such a wonderful dream, and so near, although so far. She told herself she had to be rid of it by the time she herself was far away, and so she'd watch, and hurt, and watch some more. Even the stupidest, lowliest animal eventually removed itself from something that hurt; she could only hope she'd eventually be able to do the same.

Justin kept Della laughing all through dinner. Her face was lit with laughter as she jested with him, and it suited her looks perfectly. Hers was a face made for laughter, Jared thought. He hadn't seen her looking so happy in a long while. He'd missed her before she came to England, but now he realized that since she'd arrived, he'd missed seeing her in such high spirits.

Fiona hung on Jared's every word, but he had few of them because he was busy watching Della laugh and busy listening to what Justin was saying. He had never known his brother could be so clever. He'd remembered an adoring boy, had met a charming man, but he'd never guessed Justin could be so amazingly funny. Justin's humor was dry and sly, and when Jared wasn't laughing, he found himself wondering if he too would have grown up with such a gift if his life hadn't taken him down such dark roads.

Justin was so successful in his attempts to make Della laugh that even Fiona's father, who had joined them at the hall with his wife, seemed to be genuinely smiling at him. That was such an unusual sight that it made Jared realize he'd never seen the man look at Justin with favor—or, come to think of it, look at him very much at all—at least since he'd arrived to take back the title of earl. It couldn't always have been that way. That thought, and its natural conclusions, sobered Jared so much that even Justin's jokes couldn't distract him.

Everyone decided bedtime would be early tonight because of their long journey. The company parted after dinner, instead of sitting together talking, singing, or playing cards, as they would usually do in the countryside.

"Thank you for coming," Jared told the baron as he said good night to him and his wife. "I couldn't let Della stay alone in London, and I'm grateful you've come to stay until her father returns. I hope it hasn't inconvenienced you too much."

The baron smiled. "My dear Alveston, don't stand on ceremony with us. We are at your disposal. Fiona's wishes are always paramount with us. And yours, second only to hers."

Some perversity made Jared blurt, "She's number one and I'm two? High honor, indeed, sir. But where does my brother fit in?"

"Ah. Justin . . ." the baron said. "He knows where he stands with us—like a son, of course, so much part of our family that it doesn't require thinking about. So Fiona has always thought of him, too, which is not always wonderful, if you take my meaning."

Jared thought he did, but said nothing.

After a pause, the baron went on smoothly, "You ought to have seen them as children, fighting all the time, like littermates. Or perhaps you ought not have. . . . Good night, then."

Jared looked after the couple after they left him. The baron's comments made him think, and he was sure it was exactly what the baron wanted. But he didn't like being made to think about what he'd been trying to ignore. He finally went upstairs himself.

He was halfway up the long, curving stairway when he glanced up and saw Fiona looking down at him. He paused, hand on the rail, wondering why she waited there.

"Jared?" she asked in a trembling whisper.

He quickly joined her under the high dome at the top of the stairs.

"What's the matter?" he asked, taking her cold hands in his.

"Just what I was going to ask you! You were so glum tonight. Is it anything I said?"

"Glum?"

"Well, not attentive, I suppose," she said with a pretty shrug of her pale shoulders. "I know I'm spoiled and conceited and terribly vain, and I prattle like a magpie, but tonight you didn't even pretend to listen. Have I offended?"

Her eyes searched his. She stood bathed in the light of the full moon that shone down through the great dome. Those worried eyes were the only dark things in her face, because the moonlight had blanched the rest of her to a slight, white figure. She usually looked beautiful all in white, but, oddly, she wasn't flattered by the strange illumination. It was because she was all pastels to begin with, and so the light leached the last of her color from her, Jared thought absently. He remembered then that he had met another girl here once, in this exact spot, but she had glowed in the moonlight—probably because Della was more vivid to begin with, he thought. Mentally shaking himself, he firmly dismissed the thought and concentrated on the beautiful vision before him.

The light might not become her, but she did look fragile and fair as she stood before him. Her face might be indistinct, but he could clearly see her slender form, her smooth white shoulders, and the tops of her white breasts. She looked like a porcelain princess. Jared felt more than flattered; he was humbled by the incredible fact that this perfect lady sought his approval. *His* approval! He, the man whose ragged back still bore the shameful evidence of his debasement; he, who had been a boy who would have been considered too lowly to hold this lady's cloak for her.

Her hands shook in his. He leaned closer to inhale the sweet, elusive floral fragrance of her.

"I couldn't go to sleep for worrying," she whispered. "I asked Father, and he said I ought not go to sleep, then. He said I should seek you out and ask you about it right now."

Jared let go of her hands and stepped back. "Did he?" he asked.

"Yes. So what have I done to offend?" she asked again, stepping nearer to close the narrow space between them and staring up into his eyes.

She was slight, but not a small woman. He realized he could easily bend his head to touch that delightfully curved mouth. He wondered if it would taste as sweet and fresh as he suspected it might, and if it would tremble beneath his. He wondered if those alabaster breasts would rise to his hand, the way a real woman's would. He began to bend to her, and the light fell from the sky to show him that she'd closed her eyes and tipped that pretty mouth up to his.

And then, as though her shuttering those eyes had suddenly broken some strange midnight spell, he caught himself.

His head jerked back as his thoughts became clear. This wouldn't be like holding that other girl in the moonlight; this could never be written off as midnight madness. This would set into motion a trail of events too profound to stop. This girl was not an adorable little friend who was like a sister to him—This was his brother's fiancée!

. . . who could be his. He'd been reminded of that so often lately that he couldn't forget it now, even in the sweetly scented, maddening moonlight. But now he could think of nothing except that this would be more than an embrace—it would be a commitment. . . .

. . . and a betrayal, he reminded himself, and grew cold.

He stepped back. "You said nothing to offend me," he said abruptly. "I was only distracted by all the things I know I have to do now that I'm back here. Don't worry about it. Go to sleep."

Her eyes snapped open, and he read confusion and disappointment in their depths before she laughed again. "Why, what a goose I've been," she said so lightly he wondered if he'd imagined her unspoken invitation a minute before. "Good night. See you in the morning, my lord."

He watched her step off into the shadows and fade into the darkness of the upper hall. He waited where he was until he heard her door close—a little too firmly—behind her.

Now he was too confused to sleep, but he wasn't in the mood either to pace his room while every thought he wanted to escape paraded through his weary brain. He had too many dangerous things to think about tonight, about loyalty and love, obligation and duty, and choices—too many choices.

He could take Fiona as wife—everyone said it, including her fiancé, his own brother. But what kind of a man takes his brother's woman—and his title, his position, and his place in life along with it? How would he break the news?

Thank you, brother; I'll have the house and the name and the girl, and you may take the kitchen cat and your old britches. I'll take everything else—after all, it's all my birthright. He gave a shudder of self-loathing.

To hell with dreams come true! he thought. *Or dreams of any kind.* Tonight, he decided, he'd drink until he had no room for thoughts and no choice but to sleep.

He wished Alfred hadn't gone. He wished Della hadn't already gone up to bed. For a moment, he considered tapping on her door. She was always understanding, always diverting. He wished she'd been the one he'd met again in the moonlight. But then he might be even more confused, he thought as he hurried back down the stairs.

The house was too quiet and his thoughts were too loud. He headed for the library, where he knew Justin kept a sideboard stocked with liquor. Once there, he paused, his hand on the door, because he heard laughter within—familiar laughter.

It was Della's laugh, those free, husky bell tones he'd know anywhere, quickly stifled to burbling giggles. It was the way she had laughed at home when they'd been up and talking far into the night while Alfred slept, the way she'd hushed her secret glee when he'd come home late from a trip and they talked about his experiences together, the way she'd laughed with him when they didn't want to rouse the rest of the household. But tonight it was accompanied by Justin's deep, muted laughter.

Jared's head tilted to the side as he listened to them, and a smile grew on his face. They thought they were the only ones awake in the whole house, in the whole dreaming world. He knew what a childish, wonderful feeling that could be. What fun it would be if he went in and joined them. Secrets in the night were always fun—like the nighttime raid on the kitchens to finish off the last of the pie that he'd made with Justin, a raid filled with hushed giggles and stubbed toes, a raid he remembered making as a boy. Like lying awake, reading a pamphlet by the light of a stolen candle carefully shielded under the covers when the master thought you were sleeping, your heart beating wildly at every false footstep heard, trembling lest the blankets catch fire, as he remembered doing when he'd been that other boy. . . . His hand dropped from the door.

He listened to them laughing, and his mouth drew into a thin, hard line. Justin had obviously come to terms with his losses and had maybe found an unexpected gain. So why should his brother mind? But somehow, he did.

Jared turned from the door and went up the stairs again, appalled and alone, wondering what sort of monster he was that he wanted everything his brother had, wondering why he'd come back, if it wasn't for everything that was happening now. Everything was spinning out of control, and yet going down every preordained path of his every dream, just as he'd always wanted. Just exactly as he'd always thought he'd wanted.

Chapter
14

〜

A word," Justin said, and Fiona turned.

"Yes?"

There had been a time, and not so long ago, he thought, when he would have gotten more than a politely interested *yes* from his fiancée when he first saw her in the morning—a smile or a pleasant word, at least. He didn't expect a kiss—their relationship was not, after all, that of young lovers; it never had been. That was something he'd hoped they'd grow into. But that never looked further from him than it did this morning.

"I wondered," he said, from where he stood in the hall in front of the dining room, where he'd intercepted her on her way to breakfast, "if you would care to share your plans for today with me? I understand you're going riding with my brother. Or so, at least, your further tells me. And that, my dear," he said with more emphasis, "is the only problem I have with it, I think."

"Indeed?" she asked, paying studious attention to brushing some nonexistent lint from her skirt.

"Fiona," he said, suddenly serious. "Let's have done with this nonsense. We've known each other too long to play games. Do you wish to be free of me?"

She didn't answer right away, which was answer enough for him. He nodded to himself, but she didn't see it. She was still too busy avoiding his eyes to see that, or his sudden pallor, or the convulsive way his throat moved as he swallowed.

"I hardly know what to say . . ." she began.

"You needn't," he said quickly. "So be it," he went on in a determinedly normal tone of voice. "I suppose there's nothing more to say, is there? Or do, for that matter. There's not even any need to put a notice about it in the papers, or to tell the vicar, either, because we never really set a date or made an announcement, did we? There was never any hurry to do what we both knew we were going to do."

"What we *had* to do," she said quickly, glancing up at him, and then, as quickly, looking down again.

"Ah yes," he said, going very still.

"We will have to say something to the neighbors, I suppose," she said, still keeping her eyes averted, "but I think we can trust my father to do that."

"Yes. Of that, I'm very sure," he said in agreement. "Fiona," he said softly, and there was something in his voice that made her look up into his cool blue gaze. "I wish you well; I really do, you know. Otherwise, I'd never let you go so easily, I think. But I can't hold what I never had, and shouldn't, no matter how I feel about you. Whatever happens, I don't think we can or should ever put what we had back together again. If nothing else, this has shown us we had nothing in the first place. So please understand I say what I do only out of concern for you— and him, because I care deeply for you both." Quietly, he added, "Fiona, be sure of what you want this time. But please, look at more than just what you want, too."

"Oh, I'm sure," she said quickly.

He felt odd, not so much lost or grieving just yet as relieved that it was finally out in the open, said and over and done. *Over and done?* He frowned. She stood there hesitantly before him, so lovely in her new amber-gold gown, so young and pretty—and so very uncomfortable with him.

A strange place for such a momentous decision, he found himself thinking as he looked down at her downcast eyes. *A sunny morning in the heart of my own beautiful house— my brother's beautiful house,* he corrected himself, *but home nevertheless, with the smell of bacon thick in the air around us. Shouldn't there be tempests, howling wolves, something cataclysmic to signal such a time, the death of my future? Maybe not,* he decided. Maybe this was no different than the ending of any other dream, and so ended the way all dreams did, when a man opened his eyes and left the most fantastic places to awake to an ordinary morning.

Fiona's gown was embroidered with little leaves. She thought she'd counted every one as he'd talked, but she couldn't remember how many she'd counted now. He looked so lost and hurt. She felt so bad, and yet good. She was free at last—free for the first time in her life, she realized. But not for very long, if she guessed right. Her father had made it very clear what he wanted, and, as usual, she very much agreed. Still, as he'd told her with a conspiratorial grin, this time it was her choice. And no matter how bad she felt for Justin, and how uncomfortable it was for herself, it was a heady feeling to know in this instant that, for this moment, she was as free as any young woman, with a new future. And it was even more dizzying to think that her future finally was her own to decide.

"I'm very sure," she said again, not really sure of what she said or of anything else except for the dazzling new notion that she was free. "I know what I want. And I hope you find what you want, Justin, I do," she blurted, "because you deserve it. You truly do, you know." She smiled up at him as though he were just any handsome young admirer of hers.

But although she had admirers to spare, she had never had any other real suitors, because she'd been promised to one man since birth—this man. She'd never looked at him as an admirer, and she supposed he'd never looked at her that way, either. Why court someone who was yours from the start? But oh, she loved being courted! Even now, she wasn't sure how Justin really felt about her, although he'd wanted to honor their bargain.

She gazed at him with new eyes. He was very handsome indeed, she thought, with his hair still damp from his morning toilette and his face so unusually solemn. The oddest thing was that now that he wasn't promised to her anymore, he looked better to her than he ever had before.

He offered her his arm to lead her into breakfast. She was relieved; trust Justin to be civilized about it. He wasn't angry with her—they'd always be friends, and now she could get on with her life. She felt a great weight lifted from her mind. She put her hand on his arm and walked with him, prattling merrily about the fineness of the day. She stopped only when they got into the room and saw the table laid, the sideboard filled with plates of breakfast foods, the footmen hovering over them, but no one else there but her parents and Della.

She was so beautiful. And such a lady. He ached for her to understand. He pleaded with her.

"Oh, please don't go—please don't," he cried.

She wore a blue gown with a fine frilly white lace apron over it that she couldn't possibly use for anything but decoration, so Jared had known even from afar that she was a lady.

"I am the earl of Alveston," he said desperately. "I am, I am. They stole me away from my home."

She turned away from him as people do in the worst dreams.

"Your pardon, mistress, for his disturbing you," his master said, huffing with the effort of running as he came to a halt in front of the fine couple, digging his fingers into Jared's shoulders to hold him still. *"He's my new bond-boy. Right off the boat, so to speak, and I paid a pretty penny for him, too. But I'll sell his papers in a minute. I ain't got a good day's work from him yet. You want him, you've got him. Still, none say I ain't an honest man, so I'd have to tell you to have a care. The lad's unhinged—'tis sad, but true."*

"Such a handsome lad," she said, and turned to the fine gentleman at her side, *"and how well he speaks! Can't we just take him, Lawrence? I'm sure we can find something for him to do at home."*

The gentleman looked down at her from his vast height. He was so tall, it was hard to see his expression, but his voice was warm and kind. Jared held his breath; his hope was too big to hold in any other way.

"Your tender heart does you credit, my dear," the kind man said, *"but the boy is obviously either a liar or quite mad. And neither will do. Besides—are you forgetting? We had plans for our own little lads before long, didn't we?"*

She laughed and turned her face up to the man, forgetting the boy. And then she turned farther and farther away, vanishing from his sight.

His master pulled him. *"Varmint!"* he growled. *"Run off, will you? Leave my side and go flyin' down the street, will you?"* As the man boxed his ears, it hurt so much that Jared turned his head from side to side on his pillow. *"Do that again and I'll break your head—runnin' through the town like a madman, bawlin', and pleadin' with a stranger. Makin' me look bad! Rot you. No dinner for you, no supper for you, no food for you, no water for you. . . ."*

The hunger ruptured his dream. He found himself sitting straight up in bed, staring into the empty dawn, still hungry—in more ways than one, knowing he could never really be full again.

"Sorry I'm late," Jared said as he strolled in to breakfast. "I overslept."

Della looked up, but it was Fiona who cried out, "I was so afraid you'd forgotten our ride, Jared! There are so many things I've yet to show you here!"

Justin said nothing, and Della looked down at her plate so it wouldn't look like she was waiting for an invitation to come along. But she was, and she sat very still, waiting.

After a while, when it was clear Jared had other things on his mind than invitations, she simply watched him. He was weary, she thought. His fine eyes were bleak and there was a tightness at the corners of his mouth. He sipped coffee and dawdled over toast, holding a piece in his graceful fingers longer than necessary as he carefully spread it with preserves. The Jared she knew could eat as much as a plowman. England's sun wasn't as warm as Virginia's, and he'd just been in London, so his deep tan was fading. But that didn't explain his loss of appetite. He listened to Fiona's plans for the day and smiled at her and nodded at her father's suggestions as well, but his mind seemed far away. That might be why he hadn't yet turned to her and asked her to go along with them, Della thought, as the lump in her throat got bigger and bigger.

"Have you seen the old mill?" Justin asked her.

She'd forgotten he was there, he was so quiet this morning. Her shoulders jumped at the sound of his voice and she looked at him guiltily, because she'd realized lately that he could read her thoughts where his brother was concerned. She was so startled by his question she could only shake her head no.

"It's a very old mill indeed," he said. "There's a wonderful story about it. In fact, we think it's the one behind that sad old folk tune about the wicked miller and the three sisters. But it's a beautiful spot. Jared and I used to sneak off there when we were young. . . . I say, Jared," he called, to get his brother's attention, "Della hasn't seen the old mill yet. Shall we take her there today? There's no saying how long the good weather will hold."

"Oh, but that's impossible. He promised he'd visit the Larkins with me," Fiona chirped, "and that's in the other direction. We're off to visit them, and then the Bakers and the Hardys—they have a new babe, you know. Does that make it seven? No matter; they're very proud. There's no sense slighting any of your tenants, my lord," she chided Jared, "and if one finds you've come to call on another and then didn't visit them, too, it could be an uncomfortable situation."

"No sense getting off on the wrong foot with tenants," Fiona's father said, agreeing.

"Are you sure you still want to go?" Jared asked Fiona. "The old mill sounds more exciting."

"Excitement shouldn't replace duty," she said reproachfully. "You promised to go, and they expect us."

"Yes, a promise is a promise," Jared said quietly, but he looked at his brother when he spoke.

"So it is," Justin said calmly. He turned to Della. "As they are already committed, would you care to go with me?"

Della looked at Jared. He didn't say anything, just stirred his coffee. He didn't ask her to come along with him to see the grounds and tenants. But why should he? she thought. They were part of his new life; she was a part of his old one. He obviously thought the time had come to separate the two. Wasn't that what she was here to see? Wasn't she seeing it, just as she'd expected? Then why did it hurt so much? It was hard for her to answer without crying. But she even managed to smile with what she hoped looked like delight. "Why, I'd love to," she said.

"Wonderful!" Fiona said merrily. "See how well it all works out?"

Della found it as beautiful as Justin said it would be— the weatherworn mill, the tranquil pond, and the rushing spillway that used to help turn the vanes and grind the grain. Now the spillway was slowed, and the old wheel spun slow and lazy in the autumn light, grinding up nothing but rainbows, spinning as slowly as the sun that traveled across the afternoon sky above them.

"They diverted the stream; it's better for an artist than a miller now," Justin explained after he helped her down from the gig. "I always thought this place was symbolic of the family fortunes. We don't need the money from the grain now. As the years went on, we Alvestons found more money in foreign investments than domestic ones. This is a symbol of that, I suppose. But we always had a healthy love of money."

"She's not *that* rich, is she?" Della asked, and then grew red at the surprised look on Justin's face. He couldn't have been more startled than she was when she realized she'd spoken aloud what she couldn't stop thinking about.

He threw back his head and laughed. That was good to hear, because he'd been so strangely quiet on the ride here she'd thought that maybe he had something terrible to tell her. But now his laughter paid for her embarrassment, and she thought it was a fair trade.

"No, she's not *that* rich," he said, sobering. "Fiona does bring money to the family, but I don't think it's the money in Jared's case. He may be one of the first earls of Alveston rich enough not to care. I, on the other hand, was dutiful enough not to even think about it."

"And you don't care now?" she asked incredulously, as she wouldn't have dared an hour before.

"I do care," he said solemnly, "but it doesn't matter anymore. You see, Fiona and I, we've come to an understanding—this morning, in fact. We are no longer promised to one another. It's over. She's free, Della. Doubtless, she's telling him about it now, just as I'm telling you. Ah, don't," he said, "don't."

Though she waved him off frantically, he moved to her to fold her in his arms as she tried to stop crying.

"Hush," he said into her curls, bending his head so she could hear his low murmurs of comfort.

"I'm trying to, but you're making it worse by being so n-nice," she wailed, and even though he grieved for her, he couldn't help smiling against her hair. When she got her tears under control, she gave him a gentle push, and he released her immediately. She took his handkerchief and tucked her own sodden one away. "I won't get this one wet," she said gruffly, and took a deep shuddering breath to ensure it. She finally raised her face to his and was immediately sorry, because his sympathy almost undid her.

He waited for her to speak, because he didn't want to set her off again. Her beautiful eyes were red and her face was stained by tears, but that couldn't make him forget that as he'd held her, he'd seen her dark curls capture blue-black whorls in the sunlight, and that she'd smelled of fresh spring flowers. She'd been light-boned and curved and warm in his arms. He'd been acutely aware of what a small and dainty feminine package it was that held such a lot of personality and courage.

"Well," she said with a sniffle, "fine fool I am. You knew what was going on with me, but I just spelled it out for you in big letters, didn't I?"

"Does it matter?" he asked. "If it makes you feel any better, was my problem any secret to you?"

"No, but you two were engaged, after all."

"That doesn't matter—in fact, that makes it even stranger," he said with a wry smile. "Considering our positions, our parents, and our heritage, it was unusual for me to care—for either of us to care, for that matter. You see, there's too much at stake for people like us to make our own choices in marriage. Vast properties and choice real estate's involved, so our parents make the arrangements before we even know our own names. Such marriages are the rule here for people like us."

Her face grew wistful. She was thinking about how nice it would have been if her father had extracted that kind of promise from Jared when she'd been a girl.

"No, it wouldn't be any solution," he said, and her eyes flew wide as she wondered if he'd been peeking into her mind. "Because infidelity is the rule in most of our marriages, too. We get to keep the property and glorify the name, but love is never part of the bargain. If it comes, it comes, and it's considered lucky—but unusual. Sometimes it comes from simply making the best of the bargain. That wouldn't be enough for you. I began to see it wouldn't have been for me, either."

"Well, we don't have many of those kinds of marriages at home," she said, considering the matter. "Names don't mean as much, and we don't have such vast holdings, either, I guess. Even if we do, there's always room for someone to come along and get even more. So if a bondboy can one day become as rich as the man he works for, there's no sense promising your daughter to the rich man's son, is there? We have lots of land and opportunities to get more from it; we have greater expectations altogether. No one knows what tomorrow will bring them." But then she thought of what tomorrow would bring her, and she had to stop talking and concentrate on not crying again.

"You colonials have brought us a new world, and new ideas with it," he said. "Come, let's walk for a while."

She took his arm and they followed the path that wound alongside the pond. He told her the old legend about the greedy miller and the jealous sisters, and then sang her the song in a clear tenor, and after a while she found herself listening to him and not her own sad thoughts.

He didn't mention those thoughts until he'd helped her up to the high seat of the one-horse gig again. Then he spoke, seriously and directly.

"It's early," he said, and she looked at him in surprise, because it was getting late and the autumn afternoon was turning to shadows around them. "Early, for us, I mean," he went on. "We're both confused and hurting. But it's never too early to know when you've found a friend, or even a friend you might want to be more someday. No, don't get frightened—there's nothing to fear, certainly not from me. I'm as turned-around as you are now. But I just wanted you to know—I just want to say . . . don't go home yet, Della," he said quickly. "Please. Not just yet. I know it hurts, and I know it's hard. None know that better than I. But if you could, please stay awhile longer. For me."

She looked everywhere but into his sad, intense gaze. His long, tanned hands held the reins tightly, and she saw that though his voice and face were only reminiscent of Jared's, their hands were very alike: big, strong, and well cared for. Her father always said you could tell a lot about a man from his hands. She could see the tension that knotted his now, turning his knuckles white. Finally, she nodded.

"I'll stay," she said, adding honestly, "but for me."

"Fair enough," he said, after a moment's thought. "So long as you stay." Then he raised the reins and clucked to the horse to start it down the long, twisting road back to the hall.

"Free?" Jared asked, as he felt his heart stumble.

Fiona nodded, gleeful. Her topaz eyes shone with more than the bright autumn sunlight. "We talked it out this morning, before breakfast," she confided, stealing a glance at the coachman driving their curricle. She lowered her voice so the man couldn't hear above the racket the wheels were making as they clattered over pebbles in the road. It also gave her a chance to lean as close to Jared as her wide skirt would permit. Close enough to breathe her warm, violet pastille–scented breath in his ear, close enough for him to look down to see the shadowed valley between the fine, firm white breasts tilted toward him.

"Not a tear or a fight or a wrangle at all," she said happily, her hand going to her white shoulder to adjust her gown and attract his eye there. "It was simple. We spoke about it and he released me, just like that. The engagement is over. I said it was fine, and then we went into breakfast. I'll wager you didn't even know, did you?" She chortled. "It's just over. There's nothing to publish, and nothing to do, because it was all in our fathers' minds and on a bit of paper that only they know about, anyway. Daddy's pleased, because he felt that since things have changed, the idea that I should marry Justin was really no longer valid, and not in anyone's best interests anymore. He didn't want to make an issue of it and was going to go along with whatever I decided. But I can tell he's glad, and even more happy because it was done so agreeably. He always said Justin was a gentleman. Mother agrees, and so there it is: I'm free! What do you say to that?" she asked triumphantly.

"I hardly know what to say," was all he could manage to tell her.

Jared found dinner unendurable, although, as host, he had to endure it. He smiled whenever Fiona seemed to have said something amusing, and nodded whenever anyone else appeared to be talking to him. That didn't discourage Fiona. She chattered on, her parents beamed at him, Della and Justin ignored him, and he didn't know where to look or what to say. Even talking to Fiona was difficult now, because since he'd found out she was free, it seemed his every word took on an extra meaning.

It was a relief when it got late enough for him to murmur some nonsense about all the fresh country air making him sleepy, so he could escape to his bed at an ungodly early hour. But he didn't sleep. It wasn't only because of the dark dreams he knew lay in wait for him. He was used to them, although they were coming more often now. In fact, it seemed that the farther he physically removed himself from his past, the closer it came in his dreams; now that he was back where he'd always dreamed of being, his sordid past occupied his every sleeping moment. He'd dreamed of the loss of his brother and his home when he'd been in the New World. Now that he was home and everything was restored to him, he couldn't stop dreaming about the dignity and freedom he'd lost in the Colonies.

But it wasn't the fear of dreams that kept him up tonight; tonight, his head buzzed like a beehive and he couldn't even lie still. He finally rose from his tangled bed and prowled his room.

It was very late. The moon had risen and flown overhead, and now he saw moonshadow crawling across the floorboards toward dawn. He slept free of clothes and blankets. Both Americans and English would find that odd, but the English would think his sleeping with his shutters opened to the night was just plain madness. They pulled heavy hangings around their beds, pulled their covers up over their heads, and locked their windows as though afraid of what might come flying in. He needed his windows open, and devil take what might fly in. Tonight, he wished he could fly out of them.

He drew a robe over his naked body because the night was chilled with first frost. But his heart was colder still. Fiona had broken off with his brother. He knew why. He had caused his brother to lose the woman he was going to marry. He'd taken Justin's house and title, and now knew the way was clear for him to take Justin's promised wife, too—if he wanted her.

He didn't want to think about that tonight.

What bothered him most now was the lack of sleep—or so he told himself. Still, in some part of his mind, he wondered if he was acting like a man he'd once seen watching his log house going up in smoke. The fellow had stood before his burning home, complaining because he wasn't wearing slippers, refusing to see his life going up in flames around him because it was simpler to worry about his naked toes.

Jared left his room, padded down the long corridor, and hurried down the beautiful, curving stairs. He'd forgotten his slippers, too, he thought with amusement. His feet were chilled by the cool, bare floors, but he didn't mind, because he began to think he didn't deserve to be comfortable in this house anyway. He got to the front hall and thought that he wanted to go to the front door and keep going. But he turned and went to the library instead, pausing at the last minute with his hand on the door, wondering if he'd hear them laughing softly inside again.

Then as he stood listening to nothing but his own heart beating, he realized he didn't have to feel this bad. After all, it looked like he minded more than his brother did. Justin had handed over the title and the estate, and was now handing over Fiona the same way. He wasn't mourning, not that Jared could see, at least.

Justin had sat with Della in the library until all hours just last night, hadn't he? And gone out with her for a drive today and come back smiling as if he had no troubles on his mind or heart, hadn't he? He and Della had kept laughing together at the same dinner he'd sat brooding at tonight. No, Justin wasn't grieving; it looked to Jared like he'd found himself a replacement already.

Leave it to Della to comfort the homeless and the loveless. She'd consoled him when she'd been a girl, Jared remembered, and now she comforted his brother. But there was a big difference. He'd been a boy; Justin was a man—very much a man. A man of elegance, humor, and self-sacrifice—with all that had happened, he'd never said a word in protest or anger.

But then, he had a wonderful distraction, didn't he? Jared thought, his eyes narrowing in the darkness. Della had laughed with him at dinner, her sparkling blue eyes fixed on his. As they'd left the table, Jared had seen Justin's strong hand close over Della's little white one as she'd placed it on his arm, and he'd seen the smile they'd given each other then. In that moment, he'd seen Della as he'd never seen her before: more than vivacious, she was a bewitching creature, tiny, but every inch of her dainty and curved, a darkly exotic woman in this land of blond women. *Woman?* he thought. *Yes, fully a woman.* It had been a strange revelation, even stranger to see Justin falling under her spell.

Did all brothers feel this way when their sisters grew up? It felt almost as though he'd envied Justin. But why? Della still loved him; she'd always love him, he knew. She'd had admirers before. Why should it disturb him now? Was it because Justin looked so much like himself? That was an odd, disquieting thought, and combined with all his other doubts made sleep impossible.

But unlike his other problems, this one he could deal with immediately. He only had to talk to her about it, to assure himself it was what she really wanted. Della was like a sister, and as her brother, he had to be sure she wasn't just feeling sorry for Justin. God knew, the girl had a tender heart and a place for every stray in it. He couldn't let her sacrifice herself out of pity for Justin. She was perfectly capable of doing it, too, he thought uneasily.

Justin was a good man—none better—and a good match. But Jared had to make sure she was thinking clearly. Bad enough it looked like Jared himself was about to steal his brother's wife; he couldn't pitchfork Della into a bad marriage by doing so, could he?

He'd talk to her in the morning, he decided as he strode barefoot into the darkened library to find the decanter of liquor he sought. He'd talk to her, reassure himself, and maybe then he could turn to other problems. He'd solve them, too, make decisions, and then maybe his heart wouldn't trouble him, his dreams would fade, and he could face the future as he faced the night tonight—daring it to bother him again.

But the liquor would definitely help.

He had downed two glasses and felt the cold leaving his feet, or at least felt them becoming as nicely numbed as the rest of him, and was yawning, thinking bed might not be such a bad idea, when the door opened. A tall, robed figure stole into the room as silently as he himself had a half-hour before. He hadn't bothered to light a fire or a lamp because he hadn't wanted any company. But though it was dark and shadowy, he knew who it was.

"Here, I've got it," he told Justin as he saw him bend to the sideboard. He squinted at the liquid in the decanter as he held it up. "And there's some left for you, too. But what the devil are you doing up at this hour?"

"Same as you, I suppose—looking for a drink. But not in an icehouse. Practicing economies already, brother?" Justin asked, looking at the cold hearth as Jared poured him a glass. "I know I was a free spender when I held the reins here, but I'm sure the estate can afford an extra log or two."

"I agree," Jared said as his brother tipped back his head and took a long swallow, "but I didn't think I'd be here long enough to need a fire. I'm surprised you didn't keep one burning all the time. You're the one who usually spends the night in this place, aren't you?"

"Only when the company is prettier," Justin said calmly, seating himself on the arm of a chair opposite his brother.

Jared grew still. He was glad of the darkness, because it meant he could avoid his brother's eyes. He took another drink from his glass and cleared his throat. "About that . . ." he said, and then changed his mind and said gruffly, "I heard about you and Fiona. I'm sorry, Justin, sorrier than I can say, and that's the truth. I can't help thinking that if I hadn't come back, or if I'd come a few months later . . ."

"We've been through this," Justin said wearily. "There's no point to it. Fiona's—very young. It's as well that I learned that now. And I wouldn't have postponed your return for anything."

"You make it harder," Jared said in a tight voice.

"Why? The simple truth is that her father has higher ambitions for her than marrying a second son, and he's a great influence on her. She's a very dutiful daughter, you know: she stayed with the bargain our parents made, in spite of all her other admirers, until I lost the title. What do you think my life would have been like if you returned *after* the wedding?"

"Are you trying to make it even harder?" Jared muttered.

"Want me to challenge you to a duel, then? But who's to say it's because she prefers you? You may fancy yourself an Adonis, but consider: once the word is out that she's free, she'll have a hoard of suitors trailing after her, some even richer than you. Unless, of course, I'm making a fool of myself because you're going to announce your betrothal to her now?"

"No," Jared said quickly.

"If you were, I wouldn't challenge you then, either. I can't hold what I don't have, I've told you that before— and I think it covers just about everything I had before you came here."

Tonight, in the dark, Jared thought his brother sounded too casual, too aloof and cold-blooded, too much an unapproachable aristocrat, nothing like the boy he remembered. He sounded alien and terse, nothing like the good-hearted boy he'd known or the good-natured man he'd come to know. But though neither knew it, they sounded very much alike now, so much so that they seemed to speak in the same voice. Both were tight-lipped; both now had reason to be glad of the concealing darkness.

"I think it would be easier if you were angrier," Jared said, gazing down into his glass.

"Would it be, for you? I mean, if you were me now?" Justin asked curiously.

"I don't know," Jared said. "Well," he said, letting out a deep, liquor-scented breath, "at least you're not brooding. In fact, seems to me, you're having a really good time these days—and nights."

"With Della? Yes."

"I see. Or do I?"

"Going to ask me my intentions?" Justin asked mockingly. "Why not? You say she's like your sister. Then rest easy. My intentions are honorable, my brother."

"Honorable?" Jared said in surprise. "Early days for a statement like that."

"Early? Not as early as being betrothed at birth, though, is it? This time, at least it would be my choice."

"*Especially* then," Jared said, swirling the last of the liquid in his glass. "I'd think you'd want to think about it a long time. Take your time, look around . . ."

"Look around? Why? I was engaged, not blind! Do you think I never looked?" Justin laughed. "I'm not a successful merchant like you are, brother, but I'm not a fool, either. It's not a matter of looking—it's finding, isn't it? Sometimes life looks out for you. You should know that."

"And you think you've found . . . Della?" The question hung in the darkness.

"Yes. Perhaps. Why so surprised? You know her like a sister. Think of her as a woman for a moment, if you can. Then tell me you're surprised."

There was a stillness. "You don't make it *any* easier," Jared finally murmured.

"Is it that you think I don't have enough money now?" Justin asked blandly. "Not as much as you, certainly. Not anymore. But still enough to make any bride blush, I'd think. Or is it that you disapprove of me?"

Jared made a sudden motion, then sat back. "Fool," he muttered.

"Mighty sullen, aren't we? Oh, I see: that is not your first glass, is it? Are you going to drink all night? Might I ask why?"

"No," Jared said tersely, and drained his glass.

Justin laughed and got up from the chair. "Sometimes a man needs to do that. If I can help, call me. But I'm tired now. I was reading late, but it's late enough now, I think. Good night, brother," he said pleasantly, and left.

It was only when he was out the door, with it closed firmly behind him, that Justin remembered to let out his breath and unclench his jaw. Though he was used to being a gentleman, he wasn't used to being an actor. He'd wanted a drink, and had gone to the library because it was always his best refuge in troubled times. That was why tonight it had been especially hard for him to remember that he hadn't the right, that it wasn't his house or his library or, strictly speaking, even his liquor anymore.

Jared sat in his library, in his house, in the dark, with everything he always wanted in his hand, or within his reach, and wondered if it was possible that if a man tried hard enough, he could actually hold back the dawn. Because he didn't know what he was going to do when it came.

He put down his glass and stared into the empty room. Then he put his head down on his folded arms.

That was why Della was sure no one was there when she cracked the door open, peered into the room, and then tiptoed in. And why she dropped her candle in surprise when Jared called her name out of the darkness.

He shot from the chair to help her search for the candlestick, but she didn't see that. The room was so dark, she had to drop to her knees, frantically feeling around the floor for the rolling candle, hoping she wouldn't see a glint of candle flame beginning to eat its way through the polished floor. She saw no flame; he felt no fire. But their hands met on the candleholder, and when they did, they remained there, knee to knee, like worshippers of a blind god, holding up a dark candle between them.

Chapter

15

〜

What the devil are you doing here?" Jared demanded.

"I didn't know it was forbidden," she snapped back, glad of an angry answer to lessen her shock at finding him here, when she'd only come down here to get a book to chase him from her mind in the first place.

"It's not," he said, "but you should be sleeping."

"I'm not, and I'm not ten anymore, so I don't have to be," she retorted.

He was very aware of *that* and so surprised that he didn't answer her right away—or move. Neither did she. They still knelt, knee to knee, looking into each other's faces as best they could in the darkness, until he grew aware of the hour, their silence, and the fact that they were entirely alone together in the night. That had happened too many times to count before, but after his conversation with his brother, everything suddenly seemed different.

He got to one knee, and then the cool air he felt on his naked thigh reminded him he was wearing nothing under his robe. Despite the darkness, he paused to quickly rewrap his robe around himself as prissily as any old spinster might, before he stood and gave her a hand to stand up beside him.

"Is anything bothering you?" he asked gruffly.

Everything was, but especially him, so she only shook her head. It was dark, but not so much so that he couldn't see that something was bothering her—her distress was obvious.

"Come on," he said in a gentler voice, "you can tell me, Dell. There's nothing you can't tell me, you know."

She swallowed hard and hung her head. Her hair was braided for the night, but some dark curls still tumbled across her face and concealed her expression—she hoped. There was so much she couldn't say she hardly knew what to say. His nearness, the actuality of him alone with her in the night, made it harder. But the darkness was her ally now. She tried for as much truth as she could, because the truth was always easiest for her.

"Nothing you can help me with, Jared. I know you always could help me with my problems before—with anything, actually. I remember how you even made death bearable for me. Remember? When Thomas died? You dried my tears and told me a story about rebirth. You had me watching for daffodils all through that winter and thinking there was some incredible miracle when spring came and they actually popped up out of the earth everywhere they'd been planted." She chuckled now, remembering, and then she sobered. "But that was then; this is now. There's nothing you can do for me now." *Except to love me,* she thought, *which would be an even greater miracle than daffodils in spring.*

"I'll always be ready to help you. If you don't think I can, I'm sorry. But I'm sorrier that there's something troubling you. Listen, Della . . ." He took a breath and put his hands on her shoulders. He felt how delicate those shoulders were, and his gentle grip grew tighter as he thought of how infinitely fragile and precious this little almost-sister of his was to him. "You may think you have to please me, but you don't. You should please only yourself. That's all I ever wanted. I know . . . that is, I think you might feel you have to . . . Ah, Lord. The sum of it is that maybe you think you have to please me by liking my brother, but we're two different men. And you don't have to show me that kind of loyalty. Do you understand?"

She didn't. Her eyes grew wide. "But I do like Justin; he's everything a gentleman should be."

"Yes, everything I'm not—I know. But the thing is—"

She didn't let him finish. She flew to his defense as always, even against himself. "You *are* a noble gentleman," she said, unconsciously putting a hand on his chest as though to put her thoughts right into his heart. "Always, in everything. I don't know why you think he's more of one than you are. You were raised the same; in fact, he says he's always looked up to you."

"Right—of course he does," he said bitterly. "Looks up to a man who once scrubbed out chamber pots and worried only whether he'd done it right. Looks up to a man who once ate table scraps and was glad he—instead of the pigs or the dog—got them. Looks up to a man who once was beaten if he dared look up to any other being full and steadily from both his eyes."

Della stamped her foot, then winced because her slippers were so thin. "Listen!" she said angrily, mad at herself and him and a world that had thrown them together only to pull them apart. "You just listen: a pig raised in a palace will grow up to be a pig no matter what you do for him. And a prince raised in a pigpen will grow up to be a prince, unless you kill him straight out. Enough! You *were* a bond-boy. You *were* hurt and abused. But you were never less than what you are. Never. And . . . and if you let any high-nosed, blue-blooded, pompous old Englishmen make you feel bad about what happened, then you're just—just plain stupid! But I don't think you are, and so . . . oh, Jared—you're good enough for her, you really are," she said, hating herself for having to say it. But she couldn't bear to see him suffer anymore.

There, she thought, looking up at him, feeling the warmth of his hard chest against her hand, feeling his steady heavy heartbeat pulsing against it. *I've done it. I've gone and said it straight out. I've given him permission and my blessing, and what a fool I am. But if it is to be done, then let it be done by my own hand. There.* She withdrew her hand and stood with her head down before him, defeated and bereft of what she wanted most from life.

But he laughed, and she raised her eyes in confusion.

"And if I murdered a king, you'd stand at the gallows and swear I was right to do it, too," he said, marveling.

"No, I would not. I'd weep for you, but that's all. I know your faults, Jared, and I regret them. But you do make too much of the past and not enough of yourself."

"Oh, you think I have faults, do you?" he asked with a smile.

"Of course. You think you're always right, you don't give me enough credit for being a grownup, you're wary of strangers, and . . . and . . ."—she closed her eyes as she listed all his faults—". . . and you won't eat a single lima bean, and you can't sing a tune on key for more than a minute, no matter what you say! And you say you don't hold grudges, but you never, ever forget a slight. Remember what you did to Old Man Potter's prize sow on market day?"

"Oh, Della!" he said, and laughed. He pulled her close and hugged her hard. "You'll never let me forget that, will you?"

She laughed with him then. But when they stopped, they realized they were in each other's arms, and neither wanted to be the first to pull away.

It had been a long time since he'd held a natural woman close, a woman without all the artifices of modern fashion.

She wore no hoop or stays, had on no stiffened bodice; there were no girdles, laces, padding, or petticoats between herself and him. The last time he'd held such a woman it had been Della—and he'd promised himself he'd never do it again. But he had, and now he couldn't bring himself to do more than stand with her in his embrace and wonder at it—as she seemed to be doing.

He became painfully aware that she had on nothing but a nightgown, a thin covering of cotton, and he, nothing but his silk brocade robe. He couldn't feel her robe or hers. He couldn't feel anything for feeling all those intricate, wonderful curves against him, all that firm softness pressed against his own body, all the sweet, warm, perfumed womanflesh of her. No, not womanflesh—Della. His own Della—infinitely precious, infinitely needed in this darkness—and needing. He knew it; it was in her body, in her quick silent breaths. She said nothing.

There was nothing she could say. She could only lie against him, breathing in the special scent of him, feeling him against her hard and real and everything she'd ever dreamed. Her Jared, this close—him, and only him, really him. She was stunned with pleasure. And so for that one sweet moment, she allowed herself to lie against him, knowing it was the first and last of him she'd ever know.

All too soon, he drew back, but only his head, tilting it away from her as he considered her. Every move he made was languid, dreamlike, easy, as he seemed to be considering her in a new, strangely exciting way. His breath was as soft as hers was. There was a new tenseness in his body, a new consideration in his hooded eyes. They regarded each other for several moments. His was the first move—he slowly lowered his head and brushed her lips with his. She turned her mouth blindly to his, dreaming, not wanting to be awakened.

His mouth opened against her searching lips. It tasted of new, bittersweet liquors beyond those he'd obviously had to drink. She squirmed against him, trying to get closer, and opened her mouth to drink his strange, liquid fire so it could course through her veins, turning her heart upside down, tingling in all her dark, forbidden places, making her burn everywhere.

His hand came to her breast, and she gasped against his mouth. His other hand came behind her head to cup it and hold her closer for his searching kiss, and she sighed into his mouth. She dared to put her hand on his chest again and found his robe had opened. She felt the soft hair on the hard wall of his chest and gasped again, but found she had no more breath, and her heart was beating too fast for her to draw another. She had to drink all her air from his mouth—she found she could live without breathing, without thinking, without anything but this enormous delicious ache of wanting—wanting him and having him so close. She had not believed anything in the world could be so wonderful.

He drowned in the dark joy of her. He fumbled at his belt and tugged it apart to let his robe fall open so he could feel the fullness of her body against all of his burning skin. He pressed against her; he writhed against her so he could feel every part of her. Her hair was silk in his hand; her breast was a wonder. His hands traced warm, incredibly shaped contours; he couldn't believe what he felt, so he stopped thinking and let himself feel only the heat and excitement and delight of it all. Her mouth was darkest wine, her neck sheer satin. The skin at her shoulder tasted sweet and cool and firm beneath his wandering mouth, the tip of her breast, beyond description. He had to pause for breath to go on. She was his entirely delicious Della.

. . . Della.

Nearly his sister.

Della—his former master's daughter—with all that implied.

Della! he thought, remembering.

He released her. His hand left her breast as though burned and moved to cover his own heart. Then he hastily drew his robe closed. He took his other hand from her hair and began to rake his own in consternation.

"By God! I'm sorry, Della," he said on a quick inhalation. "I'm sorry. The liquor—the lateness, the night—I don't know what I was thinking of. I'm sorry. I never meant to . . . Forgive me."

She swayed. Then she straightened herself and stood very still, because she couldn't believe what had happened, or what was happening now. She felt as though he'd wrenched more than himself away from her—she felt incomplete. She put her hand to her mouth; it was still damp from his.

"Forgive me," he said.

"For what?" she said—and prayed.

"For . . ."—he shrugged, confused and dismayed—"for . . . well," he said, half laughing, "if you don't know, then I suppose it's just as well, isn't it? I mean, if you . . ." He caught himself. His voice grew serious. "I won't try to pass it off as a joke. I'm sorry. I drank too much. I'm half dead with lack of sleep. And *you* are—as I've just thoroughly discovered—quite a woman, even though you're my little Della. I hadn't realized. But the feel of you—I'm sorry I forgot my responsibility to you. I won't say it's because of what I was or what I'm not. It's because I am a man. I'm sorry I lost my—sense of place. Do you understand?"

And what if she said no? she thought. What if she said *I wanted you, too, and the only thing I understand is that I still want you?* Would he ever be able to look her in the eye again? Could it have been only the liquor and the sleeplessness for him? Men were supposed to be different. She knew about the women he'd known in the past. Was it only that for him? A brushing of bodies—any body in the night—and too bad it was his "little" Della's? Too much liquor and I'm sorry? What if she made him face it? Consider it? But what if it *was* only that? Could she face him in the morning? Morning was coming quickly.

She drew her robe around herself like a shroud.

"It's all right," she said. "I understand." And the tragedy of it for her was that she did.

He walked her to the stairs and up them, then accompanied her down the corridor to her door. He seemed to want to say something important, but all he said was "Good night." All she could do was nod. When the door closed, shutting out his somber face, she turned and lay her back against it for long minutes, trying to breath, trying to think, trying to ride the waves of burning shame and keep her head above them so she could plan what to do next.

Then she straightened. Quickly, quietly, so as not to wake her maid, sleeping in the trundle bed, she walked to the wardrobe. Then she went to the chest near her bed. She began to take out her belongings and neatly, rapidly, started to pack her traveling bags.

Jared paced away what was left of the night, his mental—and physical—excitation so painful that he couldn't even lie down. As soon as dawn lightened the sky, he dressed and left the house at a run and awakened a sleepy stableboy to saddle a horse for him. He rode off into the growing morning light and stopped only when the sun was high above him and he felt the gelding falter beneath him; he realized he'd almost ridden him into the ground. He tethered the horse to a tree in a lush pasture as an apology, and then headed off down a nearby lane at a brisk clip. But he couldn't walk fast enough to escape his thoughts.

It hadn't been the liquor—or the night—or sleeplessness or confusion. It had been natural, undeniable, sure as the coming of the dawn. The moment he had touched her, his desire had flared, rampant. He still ached for her, as if no time at all had passed since he'd held her close. He'd never forget the way she fit into his arms, the scent and taste of her. He had known women before, but he'd never felt anything like he had last night. It hadn't been just her skin and eyes and face and figure that stunned him. Those were heady enough, but it had been the fact that he'd never stopped knowing that it was Della he held and touched and tasted and yearned for more of. His Della!

But he was supposed to protect her! He groaned aloud. Could it be that the wretched little bond-boy that lurked in his dreams had become a monster, stepping out of his miserable past to prove that now that he was a nobleman, he could have everything? Or had it begun before that?

When had he first found jet hair and blue eyes so beguiling? When had he known that just the touch of that small hand would excite him more than the bodies of all the available females in this world or the new one? When had he begun to lust after her? Exactly when had he started to betray his master's trust?

Maybe a long time ago. Maybe he'd never let himself know it because he'd never dared betray his master until he'd gained his own riches. Whenever it had begun, would he ever be able to look at her again without that longing? Should he? He burned for her. But what of his dream?

He walked on, unseeing, but he was seen. In time, he became aware of other people passing him on the road, on foot or in carts, and still others in the fields around him. He realized they were his people, workers on his estate, from the way they paused at whatever they were doing and bowed or touched their hats or foreheads when they saw him. He smiled back at them, not knowing whether he was supposed to wave or pause to talk. Justin would know, he thought bitterly. Justin was the lord here. He himself was just a curiosity, recognized because he looked so much like the earl of Alveston they'd always known.

"M'lord," one man said, ducking his head in greeting as he trudged past Jared, going in the other direction. He wore a rumpled, floppy hat and a countryman's smock and carried a hoe over one shoulder. A miniature of the man, dressed in the same baggy, dun-colored clothing, clung to his other hand and stared up at Jared, wide-eyed.

"Good morning . . . Robert, is it?" Jared asked, thinking he remembered the fellow's name from when he'd first toured the estate with Justin.

"Close enough, sir. 'Tis Richard, and this be me eldest boy, John. Make yer bow to the new lord, lad," he said, prodding his son.

The boy made an awkward bow, Jared somehow summoned a smile, and tenants and earl walked on in their own direction.

Lucky man, Jared thought, looking after them. *Lucky boy.* They had a roof over their heads, employment, food in the larder, and each other—and freedom. They were tied to the land, with little hope of doing more than their ancestors had done here, but their ancestors had been little more than slaves, while they were free. That made all the difference. They had never felt the sting of a master's whip or the shame of knowing they didn't own even their own skins. They'd never known the terrible moment of considering death as the only way to cheat their master and failing to seek it because the soul cried out for life even though the mind rejected it. And unlike their new master, they knew where they belonged. *Lucky people,* Jared thought.

He strode on until he realized he'd come to a rise that overlooked the hall. He finally paused at the crest of the little hill and took a long, shuddering breath, realizing his life now was a thing from which he couldn't ride or run or walk away.

He stared down at his heritage. The sight of it awed him as much now as it had the first time he'd seen it as a grown man. He saw the beauty and grace of the hall, the richness of it, the enormity of it—and saw it was more than he'd ever remembered it being. It was more than he'd remembered in those nights when, as a boy, he'd lain by himself, shivering and bleeding, consoling himself by conjuring up visions of his lost home, recalling it as a beautiful dream. Sometimes he'd thought it had been only that. Sometimes, in the depths of his misery, he'd started to believe he was mad to think he'd ever been an *earl*. Sometimes, he thought now, closing his eyes in pain, he still thought so.

He'd never really been happy, or allowed himself to be, since the night he'd left here. But he'd been a child then, a child who, to survive, couldn't let himself grieve for his parents. Whatever else he'd felt, he'd never felt complete since. Even though his days with Alfred and Della had almost masked his unhappiness, even then he'd been working toward his goal of returning here. Now he was here. And so what? Where was the completion? Where was the joy?

Would he ever feel worthy of this place? Of what was supposed to be his place?

Fiona accepted him. She was a lady, the born consort of the true earl of Alveston. With her, his doubts would cease—surely they would. She'd never doubted him, not for a minute. But neither had Della—and Della had known him as a beaten boy; she'd watched her father *buy* him. Jared's hands closed to fists, remembering it.

What was it he wanted? To be happy, of course, to be complete. To belong somewhere, certainly. To not hurt his brother anymore, definitely. To do the right thing for Della, of course—of course. And Fiona?

He lifted his face to the sky, but kept his eyes closed because he knew the answer would have to come from within. It would have to be the right one this time; he couldn't afford to make any more mistakes.

In the dark, he finally saw that he had one chance for true happiness and that he was no saint, because he wanted that above all else. He thought long and hard. Then he stopped thinking and searched his heart, because it occurred to him that he'd done enough thinking; his heart would show him the rest of the way.

It seemed to him, at the last, that he couldn't be false to himself, that Shakespeare was right: if he was true to himself, he couldn't be false to others. If he had the courage to do something worthwhile, and not just for himself, it was just possible that he might feel worthwhile himself. That would be the best thing for everyone, in the long run. *Yes,* he thought, opening his eyes. *Yes.*

Jared walked back to his horse and then began the long ride back to the hall. He had left in a flurry, but he rode back slowly. There was no need to hurry anymore.

"Something happened," Justin said as he strode into the library, where Della sat waiting for Jared. Bright sunlight illuminated the room and cast stark shadows on the truths she'd been thinking of as she'd waited.

"You weren't at breakfast or at lunch," Justin said, frowning. "I finally decided to stop waiting and hunt you down. You're spending the day alone here. Why? Something has happened, hasn't it?"

She didn't bother to deny it, but she kept her head down, as though she were studying her nails. "Where's Jared?" she asked.

"Riding all day, since dawn. He'll bring back that horse an inch shorter if he keeps it up. What happened?" he persisted.

She brushed away the question as though it were a gnat in front of her face and shook her head, not trusting her voice.

"Something between you and Jared?" he asked. "A dispute? Did it have anything to do with me?"

"You men," she said on a sob of a laugh. "You all think the world moves around you, don't you? Well, I guess it does. But no it was not about you. Not me, either. It's not important, that's what's important about it—oh, pay no mind to me. I'm deathly tired and not making any sense."

"Too much sense, I think," he said, coming to stand beside her chair. "Della?"

She looked into his strong, handsome face, so like his brother's, so unlike it, then looked away before he saw more in her own face.

He saw enough. She wore blue, and it was too apt a color for her today. Her black curls emphasized how ashen her skin was, and her blue eyes were shadowed. Her shapely lips, made for smiles, were held in a quavering line. She was always laughing, vivacious, vivid. Today, she didn't look her best, yet it added a new dimension to her, making her less beautiful and more lovely. She looked so tragically lost she broke his heart.

"I don't know what's happened," he said carefully, "and you obviously don't want to tell me. But at least . . . is it . . . Lord! Have they announced their engagement already?"

He didn't say whom he was talking about, but he didn't have to. Obviously they thought only of the same two people. She felt a surge of sympathy for him, as well as for herself. They were like two shadows thrown by others. What would he do if he knew she wasn't grieving because Jared had announced his engagement to another, but because he'd had too much to drink and had begun to make love to her? And not even because of that, but because he'd stopped making love to her—and then recoiled. It was even more terrible to think about Justin's reaction to that than her own sorrow. But it woke her up. She was right. She couldn't swim in such deep waters. She had to leave this place, and fast.

"No," she said, "nothing like that."

"If you won't tell me, at least tell me if there is anything I can do."

"No," she said and managed a smile. "Really. Nothing, thank you. It's all done. I—I sent word to my father up north. I'm leaving to join him now."

"You're joining him?" Justin echoed. "But I thought you didn't want to visit his family."

"No, I don't, and I won't. I'm meeting him in London. I'm going home."

He stared. Then he shook his head. "No," he said, "that I did not expect. Well, but who says life has to be what I expected?" he murmured as if to himself. "Especially since nothing has been as expected in the past weeks— nothing. You two arrived, and nothing's been the same since, has it? Della," he said, suddenly decisive, "we have to talk."

"I thought we were."

"No," he said with a lopsided smile so like Jared's that she wanted to look away even as she gazed at it hopelessly. "I came to offer comfort. I'm staying to offer more. Look, Della, this is a thing I've hinted at and promised to say sometime in the future, but the future has a way of arriving quickly these days. At any rate, it was a thing I'd hoped to say after weeks had flown by—after taking you to dances and dinners and parties and festivals, after quiet evenings and long afternoons. But the New World spins faster than the old—you colonials all move faster than we do.

"Here it is: don't leave. It's not so bad here. In fact, I think you could come to love it, and perhaps more than that. Stay here, Della—with me, as my wife."

She blinked, and he laughed, but not merrily. "I don't think you're that surprised, if you think about it," he said. "You had to know what I was getting at."

"I thought you were being kind," she said slowly. Then she gave him a free, warm, friendly smile. "I still think so. Thank you, Justin. But I do have a life of my own at home. And we don't move so fast—even there. Faster than here, that's true," she said, her head to the side as she thought about it, "but we don't normally leap into marriage after a few weeks, either, and we never do it as a favor. I guess that's just for English noblemen."

"Not even for them," he said, pacing toward the window and staring out distractedly. "I ask for your hand— for you, not for your sake. I know most men make proposals on their knees, gazing into their beloved's eyes. But it's not that way for us, so I can't pretend it. But it could be," he said urgently, turning to her again. She couldn't see his expression now, because he stood in front of the window and was outlined by light. It made him a dark figure with dazzling edges, and he spoke to her out of that blur of gold.

"We have something in common, Della. We both wanted what we couldn't have—and what we really didn't know. But we do know each other, and we like each other, and I believe it could be much, much more. I begin to think it already is, for me. I will strive to make it so for you, too. You are bright and beautiful, and for what it's worth, I think my brother will hate himself one day."

She stood and went to his side, standing in the brash light so he could see her face clearly. "It's not the same for us, Justin. I don't know how it was with you and Fiona, but I always knew what I wanted, always. I know him, and I don't think he can hate himself more than he already does. That's why he wants her, I think. He thinks that if she'll have him, he must be a true nobleman. With everything I could give him, I could never give him that. It's all he's ever wanted since I've known him. I don't think it will make him that happy, but we never want what we can have, do we?"

She stopped to hear herself and then giggled, sounding very young. "I've gotten very wise, haven't I? Maybe Dr. Franklin's right, and wisdom comes out of sorrow—or was that the Bible? Between them, they've said just about everything wise, haven't they? But that's not why I'm going to say no, Justin. It's for your sake—and mine, too.

"Wait!" she said, holding up a finger to silence whatever he was going to say. "Now you just listen. Look at yourself, Justin. You're handsome and smart as can be, a nobleman and a gentleman. Maybe you aren't rich as you were before, but you're still terribly rich by most folks' standards at home, and even here, I guess. You've got about everything a man could want, and yet you're willing to give it away to a woman you feel sorry for? I don't care what you say; that's what it is."

"I could come to love you, Della," he said seriously, "and you, me. I know it. I know I remind you of him. But that's because you don't really know me yet. It won't always make you sad to look at me, you know. And I need you, especially now."

The word *need* made her pause—it always had and always would. She tilted back her head to take a long, hard look at him. The autumn light was made for him: it highlighted his thick hair, his fair skin, his brilliant blue eyes. He was very handsome, and wholly good, and she hurt for him.

It was very good to be needed, too. She hadn't known how good that would feel until now. It was a true balm, because if it didn't heal, at least it soothed. She nodded slowly. Yes, now she understood how he felt, and now she needed someone like him, too. That was how she knew exactly what she had to tell him.

"I'd never, ever marry you, Justin," she said sadly, "because you remind me so much of him. Every time I'd see or hear you, I'd think of him. And that's just not fair—not to you or me. You're right. I guess in time I could come to love you; you're mighty lovable, you know. But then neither of us would ever know if I loved you for you or because of how much you remind me of him. That would be just awful. I could love you, Justin, but I won't. You're too good for that. And I am too, I guess. We two are just too blamed good, aren't we?" she asked, with a hint of her old grin.

"What we both need," she said, "is to move along and let it be. You'll find someone one day who'll love you so much that the thought of taking someone else who reminds her of you will chill her blood. You'll find someone you'll want not just for comforting, but because you'll know you'll never feel comfortable again without her. But for now, I really do thank you—because there's something else. I always thought it was just a foolish excuse that I had to say every now and then to suitors. Now I mean it: I hope you'll always be a friend to me, even if we never become lovers. I certainly could use a friend. This hurts a lot, you know. But you won't have to worry about that right now," she said briskly, "because I *am* going home. It's the right thing to do. Think about it. Isn't it?"

Even after all her reasonable arguments, in some lost part of her, she half hoped he'd say no, but he was just as smart and good as she'd thought he was.

"Yes," he finally said, "you're right. I do believe it is a very good idea. And, come to think of it, it might be a good time for me to take a long sea voyage, too. No, no—don't look so dismayed. I mean just what I said—a voyage, not a rout. I'm not going to run away forever, like an insulted boy. But my brother needs some time without me hovering at his shoulder, and Fiona . . . it would be an excellent time for a man to take a long journey, with a friend. May I accompany you and Alfred? I promise I won't plague you about our future, and it would be best—for everyone, I think."

She thought about it, nodded, and gave him a tremulous smile. He took her hand and kissed it. Then he bowed and left her, so she could finally cry.

When she was done, she wiped her eyes, saw that the brief, bright autumn day was growing old, and realized that though she'd just settled her whole life, she still had a lot to do. She'd told Justin she was leaving, but she had been careful not to say how soon. It would be today, but this was one trip she had to take alone. By the time she left London, she thought she'd be stronger; by then it wouldn't be such a tearful or shameful time for her, and so if he actually did go to Virginia with her, it would be easier for him by then, too. She'd leave him a note explaining it all. He'd understand. It was awful how well he always understood.

But first she had to be sure all the arrangements were made—the carriage and her maid ready to travel and everything packed before she said good-bye to Jared. Then she'd have to leave—quickly.

Chapter
16
∽

Della knew time was running out, so she hurried upstairs, head down, and looked up only when she heard a soft voice call her name. Fiona was there, obviously going down just as she was coming up the stairs.

Fiona was dressed for the outdoors and smiling brilliantly. Della ducked her head in a quick nod and tried to scurry past her, feeling like a kitchen maid caught out of place by the mistress of the house—which Fiona soon would be, she guessed. Della dammed up any threatened tears with her next thought, which was that she'd better hurry up—and then down again—if she wanted to catch Jared and say good-bye before he rode out again with Fiona.

"Have you seen Jared?" Fiona asked brightly. She was one step above Della, which was only fitting, Della thought numbly.

"No. Now, if you'll excuse me, Fiona . . ."

"Are you angry with me?" Fiona asked with what seemed real dismay.

"No, no," Della said wearily, pausing with one hand on the banister, looking up at the woman who had been born to be mistress of this house.

She looked every inch of it today. Her fair face was radiant; her fair hair was swept up into a neat bundle beneath a jaunty little riding hat. She wore a severely cut but dashing dark-green gown with yards of skirts and had flung a flowing green cape over it. She'd look the perfect lady of the manor as she rode out with Jared. But then, why not? She was, Della thought.

"Are you ill, then? You don't look very well, and that's the truth, Della."

"No, not ill. Just—I've just finally given up," Della said and her voice cracked as she said it. But it suddenly occurred to her that it didn't matter. It was as though she could already smell the salt sea air and see the waves rushing by beneath her feet as she sailed home again. She mightn't ever see this woman again—or at least by the time she did see her, they'd both be much older. She had a sudden, terrible vision of a still-smiling Fiona, with two little tow-haired children clutching the folds of that same beautiful green skirt and peering up at her. She blinked the children away in a faint wash of tears.

"I'm going home," Della said. "I've seen Jared in his new home, and I'm happy for him," she went on, rapidly inventing the tack she would have to take with everyone from now on, with family, friends from home—and the one she loved right here. "But England isn't my home. Virginia is. This is your life, but it's my—holiday. It's time I went back. I guess I'm homesick."

"Oh," Fiona said breathily, wide-eyed. "But then you'll miss the wed—the celebration—I mean," she said, coloring prettily, "the coronation and—any other festivities that might be coming up."

"You mean—like a wedding?" Della said, and watched

Fiona blush. "Yours, perhaps? But I thought you had broken with Justin."

"I have," Fiona said, uncomfortably, "but . . ."

But, indeed, Della thought bitterly.

Fiona bit her lip, and then her eyes opened wide on a new idea. "But everyone says the prince will be taking a bride at the same time he takes the crown; that's why it's taking so long," she said and then faltered. "But it's not only that. You're right. Jared would want you here to see . . ." She paused. "So why go? He'll probably invite you right back for the wedding."

"You're engaged?" Della asked in shock.

"Not yet," Fiona said, "but . . . oh, this is so difficult! But you know Jared came here to find his destiny and take over his inheritance. There's no denying I'm part of that. I can't say anything yet, but it seems clear to me, and to my parents. To Justin too, I suppose. And Jared . . . he's wonderful, isn't he? I'd hoped you and I could be friends, especially since he worries so much about you. I'm sure we'll see each other often. So we might as well be friends, isn't that right?"

Della couldn't answer right away, too busy grieving about what a shame it was that Jared should love a girl with no heart and less charity.

Fiona said a little more softly, "It can be done, you know. We can be friends." Her lovely, clear tea-colored eyes glowed soft with sympathy, but there was bright intelligence there too as she watched Della's expression. She seemed to come to some decision.

"There are things we women have to do to make life more pleasant," Fiona said rapidly. "If my own mama can be friends with Mistress Archer, who has been my father's mistress all these years, we two can certainly be pleasant to each other, can't we? Not that there's anything like that in your case, of course! Or even in Jared's mind. That's one of the things I like about him, and Justin too. They're not like that, nor were their parents, I'm told. I suppose that accounts for it. But I've seen enough of that sort of thing, and I didn't want it for myself. Besides, in our case, it's not just family wishes, as it was for my parents. Jared's far too independent to take orders from anyone, as you well know, and besides, his parents are dead. I know that sort of thing wasn't in your mind, either, which is wonderful, because I wouldn't tolerate it. But as he loves you as a sister, so shall I. If you let me?"

Not such a child then, Della thought, to slip a clear warning into all that happy babble. "Of course we can be friends," she answered, her chin coming up, "but I'm afraid it will have to be from afar, by letter. I'm going home soon as I can."

Fiona gazed at her thoughtfully. "I understand," she said, and Della's face grew hot, realizing that the girl did understand, and much more than she'd ever credited her with. "Yes, it's the right thing to do, I suppose," Fiona said. "But I'm sorry for it, really. You'll say good-bye?"

"I am," Della said, because that was all she could bear to say.

"Oh. Have you told Jared?"

"I will."

"Della," Fiona said, looking down at the smaller woman, putting one gloved hand on Della's shoulder, "somehow we never had time to get to know one another. That was my fault as well as yours, I suppose. I admire you tremendously, you know . . . perhaps that's why I was afraid to push myself at you, because you didn't seem to take to me, not that I blame you. . . . But that doesn't matter now. Now I want you to know I wish you luck and good fortune. I really do, otherwise I wouldn't say it here, when we're alone like this, when there's no one else to notice my good manners. I'm sorry you don't like me, but how could you? Neither of us can help this, can we? Have a good journey. Keep a good thought of me. I'm sure we'll meet again."

Della only nodded. She shivered and then fairly flew up

the stairs past Fiona, trying not to think about what Fiona had said or how much she knew. She began to worry, wondering if her head were made of sheer glass, so that her every secret had been open to all of them all along. She had to leave quickly, before she found out who else was pitying her.

Her maid had followed her instructions, packing her bags and leaving them in a neat row by her door. It surprised Della to see how little of her life she'd carried here with her, after all. It had once seemed like so much, but she supposed it had all been in her head and heart. And those were already overpacked with things to bedevil her during the long, weary journey home—a journey that for the first time in her life would not end with Jared waiting for her.

Della sat for a while in her room, holding back tears. When she felt more in command of herself, she was ready to leave the hall and everything in it. She went down the long stairs slowly this time, subdued and exhausted. She'd fought with herself and won. She would go home, though everything she wanted in life would be staying here. But if she could salvage nothing else, she was determined to leave with her pride.

Now she had to tell Jared. She wouldn't lie; she just wouldn't tell the truth. She'd certainly never let him know what she felt for him; that would be too embarrassing, too debasing. Besides, she thought wearily, it was likely Fiona would tell him soon enough—oh, but that meant she had to leave even more quickly, she thought with renewed panic. She feared shame more than death itself; death brought the possibility of resurrection, after all.

She wouldn't mention what had happened between them last night. Instead, she'd pretend she was just like a man and shrug it off as a thing that sometimes happened in the night between the sexes, although she'd never forget the shock and thrill of it—never. She would hug, close to her heart for all the lonely nights ahead, the memory of what it had felt like before he'd become ashamed. In time, she could forget the shame while remembering the wild pleasure of it—at least she'd try.

But she knew just what to say to him now if he brought it up: *This is England, after all. It's not as Puritan as it is at home, and as they say, "When in Rome . . ."* And then she'd laugh airily. Then she'd tell him to forget it, because she had—and she'd cross her fingers hard so she wouldn't be struck dead by lightning.

Because she'd never forget it, and never wanted to.

She'd go on to tell him that she'd seen his new state in life and was happy for him, but that now she had to get on with her own. That, he couldn't argue. She'd tell him her life would be at home from now on—*her* home, because however much he loved her, his home was not hers. That, he could not argue. She'd say she was leaving because she was homesick. That was unarguable, too, though she'd never tell him that the moment she left him she'd be homesick for the rest of her life.

She shivered a little as she thought of the conversation to come, but she wasn't a coward—only frightened.

She went down the stairs with her head high and her heart low. But she had to stop in midstep to prevent being run over or pushed over the side—Fiona was running up the stairs as fast as she could, not looking where she was going.

It was almost comical, because in order to run, Fiona had to hold her beautiful green skirt up, tilting the hoop so much it showed her legs and a great deal more than any lady should. All her elegant serenity was gone. She was panting because her bodice was so tight she couldn't draw a deep breath, and her face was set in a frown of concentration. She stopped only when she almost crashed into Della. When Fiona looked up and saw Della, her lovely eyes flashed with tears. Della thought in amazement that they looked like tears of anger, not sorrow—it was clear she was furious.

"He—" she cried the minute she saw Della. "He *dares* dismiss me! It's not even as if I asked for him—as if I even wanted him! As if I would! I wonder what he thinks of me. I wonder who he thinks he is! He didn't give me a chance to speak. He just called me in, said it was over, he was going, good-bye, and that was that."

Della gaped. Then she understood. Fiona was a great lady, a beautiful one, used to being petted and flattered since she'd been born. She mightn't want Justin anymore, but it probably still rankled that he was leaving her. She marveled at the woman's vanity, but almost envied it.

"But Fiona," she said, gently as she could, "try to see it his way. He knew you'd made your choice. You can't blame him; he's got too much pride to stay and see you marry his brother."

Fiona stared at her as if she'd gone mad. "He had the audacity to tell me to do just that!" she raged. "Not that I might not. . . ." She stopped and her eyes opened wide in horror. "Oh, but what if he won't forgive me? He has pride, too; Mother warned me, but Father said it didn't matter anymore—but it does. By God! Was there ever such a mess? How could he do this to me? How could he dare? You might say he doesn't know any better—but no, I suppose *you* wouldn't," she said, remembering who she was talking to and glaring at Della.

"I suppose you're laughing up your sleeve at me now," Fiona spat, her lovely features becoming disfigured by a sneer as she stared up at Della. "If *he* treats me like that, then I suppose I can't expect much sympathy from you. It's what comes of dealing with such people. . . . I should have known," she muttered to herself.

Now Della frowned. "You've got it all wrong," she said, her own anger growing, the more so because she felt guilty about Justin's going home with her. "Justin's going to Virginia with me for only a little while, only for a holiday."

"Justin's going to Virginia with you?" Della cried. "Oh,

before God, this is dreadful!" She tottered, and Della was afraid she would fall. But though her face was ashen, her eyes blazed with energy. "It's what comes from dealing with savages," Fiona raged, "no matter the title. Title—ha! We should have known better. It wasn't as if we didn't have warning. God's teeth! But he was a *bond-boy!* A slavey, a lackey, a bit of human offal—and God knows what else. I actually considered marrying—"

"Bond-boy? . . . Jared? You're talking about Jared? Not Justin?"

Fiona nodded, her eyes wild. "Of course! He—*he* had the audacity to dismiss me! Told me he hoped he had raised no expectations, but it was for the best—for the best! I should say so! I must have been mad. How could I have ever thought of him as eligible when he came from such low, base beginnings?"

"He comes from the same beginnings as you do," Della said, drawing herself up to her full height, which looked more impressive because she was now standing a full step above Fiona. And moreover, she thought with pride, Fiona still held her skirts up high over her knees and looked ridiculous. Della looked down her short nose at Fiona, and Fiona, realizing the sight she made, let go of her skirt so fast it bobbled as it settled around her ankles again. "Yes, the same beginnings," Della went on, "and he made much more of himself that you have of yourself, because he was forged in fire. *Low? Base?*" she said with her best imitation of a sneer. "Only in *your* low and base thoughts, *my lady,* because he is a nobleman born, and a gentleman to the bone."

"So say you," Fiona said, "and how else should you say? You've hankered after him since you were a babe, everyone knows that. And," she said with killing arrogance, "you are a *colonial.*" She collected herself, sniffed, and raised her chin. Because she was tall she could look Della in the eye. "I wouldn't be so smug, were I you," she said, "because this is as much of a surprise to you as it was to me, isn't it? More—because at least he told me. He never even consulted you. He doesn't want you, either, does he?"

"Well . . . well—why should he?" Della retorted, forcing herself to ignore the words that lanced through her like knives. "He can have *any* woman he wants, can't he?"

Fiona's eyes widened as the shot went home, and she gasped audibly. Then she closed her lips to a tight line. She turned to the side to avoid having her skirts touch Della's, and she followed her raised nose up the stairs. Della admired the fact that she didn't run again until she reached the corridor that led to her room. But she herself had nowhere to go but down, and that was where she must go now. She understood nothing and feared everything, but she still knew what she had to do.

There was no one in the great hall, so Della told a footman she was going to the library to see the earl, but that if he wasn't there, she'd wait. He'd be bound to come there eventually. He loved that room, with its rich, leather-bound volumes and its tall, mullioned windows; it was a place of refinement and light. It was a room fit for a nobleman, or any man who wanted to feel like one. She too loved it, because it was where he always sought shelter—and where he'd kissed her with real passion that she could pretend was love. Sooner or later he'd come home, and then she could go home, with him or without him. She didn't know where he was going; Fiona had been right about that. Why would he leave now? Because of what had happened between them last night? The thought brought her up short. That would be awful; there was no need for him to go, because she was leaving. She had to speak to him at once.

Once at the library, Della opened the door—and heard voices inside. She froze, her hand on the ornate knob, door ajar, when she heard her name. It wasn't being called, it was being spoken to someone else. Although she would have sworn she was an honest person without a drop of sneakery in her soul, she waited, holding her breath to hear the rest of it.

Eavesdroppers never heard good about themselves—she knew that. She knew she was wrong, but she couldn't help herself. She was confused and hurt. There was only so much will power she had left, though it wasn't really a matter of will: her body seemed to have taken over her mind—she found she couldn't walk away or announce her presence. She almost hoped someone would notice her standing there, in order to save her soul. And then she listened more closely and forgot about herself entirely.

They filled the room, just the two of them. Both brothers were big, vital men, each capable of dominating a room himself. They were so angry and frustrated with each other that their presence seemed to crowd even the spacious library. They didn't shout. They were too polite, their voices too controlled. The tension filled the room. Justin sat as if posed, too obviously not at ease in a chair by the fireplace. Jared stood by a window, looking out and not at his brother, although they were speaking to each other.

"No. I see nothing to make me change my mind," Justin said calmly.

"It doesn't matter," Jared answered. "I'm sorry you feel this way, but it's decided. I know what I have to do. I've thought it out. . . . No," he said, suddenly turning to look at his brother. "that's not true. I couldn't think at all for a while. I paced, then I rode, then I took pity on the horse and walked—halfway across the country, I think. And then, there it was. It just *was*, brother—like the sun after a storm. It was there, and so clear and simple and right. I didn't think it; it came to me. And I knew it for the truth."

"Revelations at Hawkstone Hall," Justin said sarcastically, crossing his long legs and sitting back. "How biblical."

Della winced at Justin's coldness. Jared didn't. "It doesn't matter what you think, Justin," he said. "It was a true revelation. I'm sorry you don't understand, but I know what to do now. Then as I said, I came back here to begin to do it and Fiona told me about Della! Can't you see? There's no more time for argument. I've made my decision; the thing is *done*."

"Only in your mind," Justin said, looking at his nails. "Or . . . did you tell Fiona?"

"Yes."

"Umm. That must have been a pretty sight," Justin said with a glimmer of a smile, but not a nice one. "But it makes no difference. It's absurd."

"It is *done*," Jared said. "Believe it. Accept it. It will be so."

He paced from the window, and when Della got a clear look at him she stifled a gasp of dismay. She'd never seen him so careless of his appearance. His long coat was open—his vest, too—and his shirt billowed out from his slender waist instead of being tucked smartly into his breeches. He had to keep brushing strands of his golden hair back from his face; it moved when he turned his head, because it had been loosed from its tie. Knowing his habit of running his hand through his hair when he was troubled, she suspected it wasn't mussed just from the wild ride or long walk he spoke about.

She'd never seen Justin so cold before, either. Gone was the friendly, gentle man she thought she knew. He was handsome, but almost inhumanly immaculate, his face so glacial he looked as if he would shatter or explode if anyone touched him. He was the complete English aristocrat, the kind the children jeered at, at home—a true mate for the Fiona she'd just met and battled with on the stairs. She didn't like what she saw. Even if she had wanted to speak from her shadowed corner, she wouldn't have dared now. The atmosphere was darkening, the storm not far off.

"Madness," Justin said, shaking his head. "I won't allow it."

"You can't stop it."

"Oh, can I not?" Justin asked with a glint in his eye. "I

can renounce you. And then the title, too, you know. And then, to whom does it go? Ah, yes, one of our wicked uncle's boys. That will be nice, won't it?"

Jared seemed stunned as Della was. Then he took a long breath. There was something in his face that she had not seen since the night she had seen Brown, his former master, call him a fraud: it was a look of utter despair. He held out his hands to his sides, as though to show he was unarmed.

"Justin," he said, "it's not easy. Do you think it is? Don't. I do what I must. Isn't that our family motto? I know how strange it must seem to you. Yes, I did fight to get back here all my life. It was a good thing, too—it kept me alive. I don't think anything else would have, at least in those first years. Obsession can sometimes be a good thing, but it can turn on you, too. I learned the hard way that blind ambition and thoughtless desire can keep a man going when it's not helpful for him to see or think, when the only important thing is to live to reach his goal. But that's the point: he doesn't see or think. He can't. The trouble is, once I had achieved my goal, I finally began to see *and* think."

He closed his eyes before he looked at his brother again. "I came to England looking for revenge," he said. "I found triumph, vindication, acceptance—love."

Della drew back a little, her heart knotting, wishing she hadn't stumbled into this, anguished to hear what she did but not breathing for fear of missing something.

"Indeed," Justin said tersely. "We've all had ample evidence of that."

"Have you?" Jared asked quietly.

"You claimed the title, and then my—your—promised bride. We both know you have her. What else do you want?" Justin asked in a hard voice.

"We were talking about Della . . ."

"So we were," Justin said, leaning forward, anger slowly fanning to fire from beneath his cold reserve, "and you weren't happy about what I said about her, either, were

you? So what else do you want now, brother? You have the
title, the estate, the lady-wife; you swept all to yourself.
Now you want the lovely disciple, too? There's to be
nothing for me, is there? You'll leave me nothing? Is it that
you've never forgiven me for not being the one who was
kidnapped? Or some other bizarre thing? You seemed
determined to take everything I had, as well as everything
I even wished to have. What if I make eyes at a serving
girl? Will you want her, too?"

"Good. So I've drawn blood, and the poison is finally
out. This is much better," Jared said approvingly, and he
didn't seem to be joking. "Let's lance the ugly thing; let's
have it in the open at last. I never really believed in the
damned saint I met, brother. Or if I did, it only made me
feel worse about myself."

"Saint?" Justin asked, shocked.

"Yes, saint. Saint Justin the divine. You never complained about my taking over the hall or anything else. I
came, I saw, I conquered. 'Take more, brother' was all you
said."

"How could I complain? I owed you everything! And
you took nothing that wasn't yours—until now."

"You don't understand," Jared said bitterly. "I might
have been lowly, and I knew it, but I also knew I could
never be as saintly as you were. It made me feel even
lowlier."

"*Lowly?*" Justin asked, his voice rising, breaking his
frigid calm at last, his hands tightening to fists as he rose
from his chair and confronted his brother. "Damnation!
How many times must you hear it? How many times
before it gets through your thick head? *No one cares that
you were an indentured servant.*"

"*I* do!" Jared shouted, his eyes bright with anger and
pain. "*I* care. I can't forget it—never, not for a minute,
nor can I believe anyone else can. Do you know what I
was, Justin? I was—nothing. Nothing at all."

"You were an innocent victim," Justin said in a voice
filled with suppressed rage. "Can't you understand?

You're returned to us, everyone's happy, all's right with the world at last. No one but yourself cares about that unhappy time—except those of us who grieved because it happened, and because it obviously still grieves you so.

"How many times do you think I've wished the boy they found that night and sold into bondage had been me?" Justin gave a bitter laugh. "You can't count that high, believe me. *Lowly?* Do you want to talk about feelings of unworthiness, brother? It was bad enough knowing I ruled here in your place even before I knew you'd survived. It was much worse finding out how you suffered in those years. Oh God, how I wished I bore your scars, real and imagined!"

Justin didn't seem to see Jared now that he'd started talking. "I have scars too," he said angrily. "Not spectacular ones like yours, of course. You must always have more of everything, mustn't you? But they thought I'd lost an eye that night. I thought so, too, but it was only that I couldn't see for all the blood. I fell on a rock, or the water pushed me into one—I don't know—and I was half blinded by the blood as I cowered there in the reeds. Yes, cowered. Do you think you're the only one with nightmares? I laid low, my face in the dirt, crying, praying they wouldn't find me. If I'd lifted my head, I might have found you or seen what happened to you, but I was afraid. Don't you think I've thought of that a thousand times since? You saved me from drowning, yet I couldn't even lift my cowardly eyes to see if you still lived. But all *I* have to show for it now is a thin line on my brow—they stitched me well—while you . . . I'm sorry for that, too."

"You were only six, Justin," Jared said quietly. "There's no such thing as cowardice at six. I would have done the same thing."

"You were only seven, and you *didn't,*" Justin spat it like an oath.

"It doesn't matter," Jared insisted. "That's what I've been trying to say. That's what I saw today, what I came to understand. I can't forget what I was. Maybe it's a shame, but you're right: it doesn't matter anymore. It all happened. I was a bond-boy, you became the earl, and you did it well. I might have, but I didn't. You see? You're right; let's bury the past. I'm tired of it. I need a future."

"And you want mine, too?" Justin asked bitterly. "You want Della now, too?

"No," Jared said, "no. I don't want Della."

Della felt her blood still in her veins and pool in her chest, a heavy, solid sorrow, too thick for tears and robbing her of breath. She wished herself thousands of miles away, taking cold comfort from the awful fact that that was where she soon would be.

"No," Jared said. "You don't understand; I don't want her—I need her."

"Oh, wordplay now," Justin said. "Excellent—games. Just what we needed. You want everything I ever had, anything I ever showed any interest in. 'Does Justin want it? Then it must be of value; I want it, too.' What will be next, my heart? My skin? Would you like that to hang on the wall? And when I ask why, you play with words. *Want, need*—it's all the same."

"No, it isn't. I'm not playing games. It's nothing but truth," Jared said. "I need her. Just that. I need her. It's simple; I need her more than the title, the hall, and the honors. They're nothing to me, after all. Isn't that amazing? After all these years, all my scrabbling, *that's* what I finally saw today. I was blind to everything but reclaiming what I'd lost. Until today, I didn't see that if I didn't have her, I'd have nothing, no matter what else I had. Can't you see? I'm giving it all back to you—you make a better earl than me anyway. I don't want it; I've found what I need. The rest was always a dream; when I lived it, I felt wrong in it.

"So take it back. Be the earl of Alveston again. I'm going back to the Colonies. It will be as though I've never been here, the way it was before I came, only this time you won't have to feel guilty about me. And you'll have someone to visit, if you ever want to. I'll be fine—more than fine. I have money and a profession and a place in Virginia. We don't hold with titles anyway, and I've got a good life there.

"I hand all the rest back to you, brother. All but the one thing I thought you were going to take from me. It was the possibility of losing that, that made me realize it was the one thing I had to have—absolutely—in order to live. In order to laugh, to have a future of any kind worth living— *my* heart, my Della."

In the hallway, Della felt her breath stop.

It seemed Jared could say no more. He turned abruptly back to the window so that the play of light on his gray eyes could account for their sudden brilliance, because they glistened now.

"But—I thought she was like your sister," Justin said, stunned.

"So did I. But she's not, thank God. She's closer. She's the other half of myself." Jared bent his head and busied himself by drawing invisible circles on the window with one long finger, to avoid his brother's eyes. "I'm not talking about saintly love, either. I'm talking about desire, too—a lot of desire, desire I denied for years. Don't fool yourself the way I tried to fool myself. I want to put the halves together—so I can be whole at last, in every way. I give you everything else, Justin, but you can't have her."

"And Fiona?" Justin asked in a hard voice.

The back of Jared's neck grew red, and he shrugged his wide shoulders. "I'm sorry. She came with the title, didn't she? We—never did anything but talk, for what that's worth. She'll recover; there was nothing of her heart in it."

"She has nothing of a heart," Justin said with a sigh, "but we all thought it was going to be a match. Della thought so, too. After the insult of that, do you really think she'll take you now?"

"I don't know anymore," Jared said, and his voice broke. He lowered his head and cleared his throat. Justin looked away, so caught between anger and pity that he couldn't speak, either.

"I've been a damned fool," Jared finally said, "and I have to try to convince her of that. I can't let you take her without a fight. I won't. I'd hoped we could be friends, but if we have to fight over this, so be it."

"I can't give her back to you . . ." Justin said slowly.

Jared stiffened, then swung around to his brother. They stood there, face to face, each with his hands fisted.

". . . because I never had her, in any way. She was always yours, brother," Justin said sadly, his hands uncurling, holding them up in surrender, "like everything else. How can I hold what was never mine? I asked for her hand today. She refused me—because I reminded her of you."

Jared's eyes widened.

"Don't look so anxious, my fool of a brother," Justin said with a huff of a laugh. "If she couldn't have the real thing, she decided she wouldn't settle for a replica. She said I deserved better. But I knew that it meant too that she could accept no substitute. She's beautiful and clever, but take care if you court her. You see, she's not perfect. The woman has either terrible vision or awful taste in men, doesn't she?"

He blew out a long breath, turned, and walked away from Jared. As he went toward the library door, he turned his head toward the shadow where Della stood. His eyes widened. "Ah, yes . . . mimosa," he said, "that accounts for it. I knew it wasn't spring. I wondered if I'd gone mad. But I always liked it when you wore it. . . . Of all of it," he called to Jared as he left the room, "this is the one right thing, brother. And the only thing in which I'll allow you to have your way."

Jared couldn't answer—he couldn't take his eyes from Della.

She felt as though she'd been sleeping and someone had ripped the covers off her, leaving her naked and blinking at the light. She wanted to flee; she wanted to see Jared—so she couldn't move at all. Until he spoke.

"Della?" Jared asked, looking at her in disbelief. "Della? You heard it all?"

"I'm sorry," she babbled, wringing her hands, backing up until she hit the door Justin had closed behind him. "I heard my name and I couldn't go away. I should have said something, but it was never the right time. I'm not a sneak. I . . ."

"I know you're not. I don't blame you," he said as he came toward her. He took her two hands in his to stop their shaking, and then he looked down into her eyes. "In fact, I'm glad you heard it. This way, I don't have to say it all over again. I don't know if I'll ever get it that right again. I meant every word. But if you want, I'll try to say it again: none of this inheritance matters—only you do.

"I love you every way there is to love a girl—a woman. I loved the child, and now I love the woman, but it's much more, because it's liking and loving all mixed together. I don't know what I'd do without you. I don't *want* to know. But I won't be an earl or have this grand house. Will you forgive me and have me anyway? Della?" he asked, as she lowered her gaze.

"I never even kissed her, Dell," he said a little desperately, when she didn't answer. "Honestly. Pretty as she was, I never did, though I never realized why. But how could I kiss her, when there was you? Always you. Everything else was only a substitute, as Justin said. How do you think I got this old without finding a wife? I'm not that bad-looking a fellow, am I?" he asked, hoping to make her laugh. "Surely someone would have had me—but I never even asked anyone else. It turns out that even when I didn't know my heart, it was true to itself. It wasn't until I saw you with Justin and I realized I wanted to rip out his— But—do you prefer him?"

She shook her head, and heard his sigh of relief.

"Then is it that you only think of me as a brother? But no, that can't be, not after last night. Is it because you doubt my constancy? Because it took me so long to know my heart, do you think I'd *ever* be untrue to you? Never! You are the other half of my heart. Della? At least say something, so I know what to say to you!"

"How can I?" she wailed, finally looking up at him with tear-filled eyes. "I'll make a fool of myself. It can't be true. It's because of what Fiona said, isn't it? You feel sorry for me. You feel indebted to my father. You're saying all this so you can—can repay him."

"No, I was wrong; I think I have to *stop* saying things to you," he muttered, then kissed her.

Chapter

17

~

He had meant it to be a persuasive kiss, a thing of passion and love, a kiss that would leave her with no doubts, though gentle enough not to frighten a young woman of her inexperience. Somewhere along the way, Jared had lost sight of what he had meant to do—he couldn't stop kissing her.

They'd clung together until they realized they couldn't stand anymore. Somehow they'd stumbled to a couch; somehow they got her gown off her shoulders, off her breasts; somehow she'd got her hands up under his shirt and on the warm skin over his heart, and that made him gasp as much as his lips on her breast made her sigh. But it was more than his heart involved now; it was something much more urgent and blinding than love, something both less and more than adoration, something so basic that he was wondering how to get that damned hoop off her— when he realized exactly what it was he was going to do when he did.

He broke from her and took a deep breath. Then he hastily buttoned his shirt. He gazed at her, winced at how she sat blinking, still dazzled with desire, her hands over her breasts, her mouth bruised to the color of peaches from his kisses. He took another breath, frustrated at his rekindled desire, because the latest fashion didn't lie about what it promised. The damned gown seemed to be purposely made so that her breasts could pop out easily enough, and they did. Her breasts were firm, tilted, and rosy tipped, and he had to swallow hard and brace himself until she came to her senses enough to cover them with more than her hands.

She just sat there, growing cold without his arms and hands and mouth to give her warmth. When she realized what he was staring at, she became hot with shame and confusion, and she crossed both arms in front of herself. But before she did another thing, she had to understand what was happening between them. There were a dozen things to say, but they all came out in one question.

"Just what *is* it that you want, Jared?"

"You, of course," he muttered, gazing at her partially covered breasts, "but not now."

Red-faced, she turned away. After a moment, she faced him again, her gown in place, her breasts covered by as much as fashion allowed. He felt safe again, until he looked at her face.

"I see. You obviously don't want me, no matter what you say. What is that you *do* want?" she asked haughtily, an effect that was ruined by the tears that started to course down her cheeks.

"Oh, Dell," he said, gathering her in his arms again, "you—"

He never got a chance to finish what he was saying. She pushed him away with surprising force. She ran the back of her hand under her nose, sniffled, and raised her head high. "Liar!" she said. "A man who wants a woman doesn't throw her away."

"I'm not throwing you away." He laughed in exasperation. "I'm *putting* you away, which isn't the same thing. I can't handle you—in every way, I guess," he added with a crooked grin. "Dell, the truth is that I can't control myself with you. It's all or nothing at all with us, every time I touch you. I care for you too much to consummate our love here in the library, with everyone knowing we're together here. But I think I lust for you too much to be content with merely kissing and cuddling. I never did understand bundling. . . .

"Nevertheless," he said with decision, rising from the couch to pace a few steps away, "I love you. Don't doubt it. We're going to be married as soon as we can; in the meantime, I flatly refuse to make you mine on a couch in the library, like a suitor in a bad farce. You see?" At her look of stubborn disbelief, he said, *"You don't?* Throw you away? Before God, Della, did I act like I wanted to? Do I look as though I want to now?"

She had to admit that he looked at the end of his rope. He hadn't been tidy when she'd first spied on him, and he looked on the ragged edge now. But oh! she thought, his hair did look wonderful unbound, framing his handsome face like cornsilk—it had felt that soft, too.

"And don't look at me like that. I have wonderful intentions. I don't plan to ruin them," he said distractedly, seeing her wistful look, that lovely, pouting pink mouth swollen from kisses.

He squared his shoulders, drew in his breath, tucked in his shirt, buttoned his vest, and shook out his cuffs.

"Now, then," he said with determination. "I think we should go to London as soon as possible. I understand you've already sent a note to your father. There's no point in sending another. London will suit our purposes. The sooner we're married and on the ship back to Virginia, the happier we'll be—all of us—you, me, Justin, and . . . Fiona."

"You just don't want to face her and her parents," Della said tartly.

"Well, would you, if you were me?"

"No. I don't even want to face them as me."

"But Jared!" she said in alarm, remembering. "What are we talking about? You can't leave; you're the earl of Alveston. You can't give it up—not the title and this wonderful place. It's everything you ever wanted. It's yours by right."

"No. If it was mine, it would be wrong," he said gravely. "Didn't you hear what I told Justin? I meant it. I've taken too much from him. Besides, I *was* the earl, and I felt like an impostor. It's not my life or place anymore. So I won't be the earl of Alveston—we'll hardly starve. I'm very rich, you know, and bound to become richer, even Alfred says so. But the title, this place—do they matter that much to you?"

"Not to me—to you. Can you ever really be happy if you give it up?"

"I'll be happy so long as I'm with you," he said, taking her hand and helping her rise. Then he brought her hand to his lips. He felt her fingers close over his and looked down into her troubled eyes. *Blue,* he thought, bemused, *blue as a jay's wing, blue as the part of the flame nearest the heart of the fire.*

"I don't know . . ." She frowned. "I don't know if I can bear being all that to you. What if something happens between us? Will you regret your bargain every time we fight? Married couples do fight sometimes, Jared; you know that's true. And what if anything happens to me?" she said fearfully. "There are fevers—there's childbearing; Jared, if you give all this up and anything terrible happens to me, you'll be left with nothing."

"That's true," he said. "If anything happens to you, I will have nothing—whether I have the title or not. Della, listen closely: I meant every word I said. Now you make me wonder about you. Don't you want me? If not, just say it. Justin will be glad to take you—"

She didn't let him finish. She pummeled his chest with her small fists until he laughed, and then she flung her arms around his neck and kissed him. He stopped laughing. Her mouth was eager, and he was delighted by how quickly she'd learned to seek his tongue with her own. And at how she made such soft noises in her throat as she did, how she pressed forward into his hands, how she . . .

"Della," he said shakily, putting her at arm's length, "we have to leave here as soon as possible. Your kisses are delicious, but they don't help right now—exactly the opposite. We have to find Justin immediately and tell him what we've decided. Then we'll say good-bye and leave in the morning."

"But Jared," she said, "does this—does this mean you won't touch me until we get to London?" Her teeth fretted at her lower lip, and she looked at her hands. "I—I don't want to seem forward, but if you don't want to kiss me, I can't believe you really want me. When you won't come near me, how am I to know?" she cried.

"Oh, Della." He sighed. "Here's how." He bent his head and kissed her. "I can't say it better than that," he said, drawing back. "Now, let's go tell Justin and set something other than my damnable lust in motion."

"Is it so bad that you want me?" she asked.

"Yes. Because we're not married yet, and I want you very much. Whatever else I do, I'll never betray your father's trust. We'll be together for an eternity, Della. A few more days won't make any difference."

She nodded, but wasn't sure she agreed. Jared was a man of strong ideals and a deep sense of duty. She couldn't help but worry and wonder if all this—even to his returning to Virginia, wasn't really for her father and Justin, no matter what he said. But he was determined once he made up his mind, and he obviously had. It was what he wanted, and he was all she wanted. She consoled herself with the thought that it would be only one more night here and then a carriage ride, and then London. Then they'd be married, and she'd know the bliss of his lovemaking, and though she could regret many things about what they were about to do, she could never regret that. Only a few more days, she told herself, and left the library with him.

"Are you mad?" Justin threw back his head and laughed. "It will take more than a few days to clear this up, Jared. You won't be able to leave for weeks."

He had said congratulations first, when he heard the news. He had hugged his brother hard, clapped him on the back, and then smiled down at Della and kissed her cheek very tenderly. But now he was roaring with laughter as Jared fumed.

"Legalities," he explained, when he stopped laughing. "You can't simply leave, leaving me holding the title. It wouldn't work. I won't do it. And there are the uncles to be told—and to argue with, unless I miss my guess. Then, if and when they agree—even if they don't—there are papers to be witnessed and signed, a judge or two to pocket your coins and mumble over the papers, look up any precedents, and make up some new ones if they have to."

"We can do that in London," Jared said.

"Oh. I see, desert the hall, and leave it with no owner, no one to oversee it?" Justin asked blandly.

"You own it, you have it, you can do it," Jared said tersely.

"No. It's not mine, not legally or otherwise. Now, if you want to know whose it will be, you'll have to do it legally. It's not so easy to give up a title. Oh," Justin said nonchalantly, seeing his brother's fierce expression, "I suppose it is if you don't care what happens to the estate or the poor soul who eventually takes it over. The barristers will certainly love you if you just leave. I imagine the entire estate will have to be sold just for there to be enough to pay them to decide who's entitled to own it then."

"You," Jared said angrily.

"No. I believe I already said no," Justin said. "Are you sure you don't want to send for Alfred? If you stay to see this through, I doubt you'll be able to leave for London for a while."

"Alfred's up north. By the time he gets the message and goes to London, we'll be there. Money can grease any wheels, even in England," Jared said. "I won't leave the title in jeopardy. And I won't leave it to anyone but you."

"I see. Can we argue about it after dinner?" Justin asked, glancing at the mantel clock. "I'm awfully hungry."

Not very much got eaten at dinner, or if it was, none of them paid much attention to what they were eating. The servants were shooed from the room once the food had been served, and then the brothers argued from soup to pastries. They and Della were the only ones there. Fiona and her parents had gone without a word of good-bye to Jared and Della. They had said some things to Justin, but he wouldn't discuss it. He'd only shrugged and said that Fiona was amazingly resilient, and that was very good for her, and then added thoughtfully that it wouldn't do her much good at Hawkstone Hall, though.

It wasn't until after dinner that Jared asked for a truce.

"I know what I'm going to do, brother," he said as he stood by the hearth and gazed into the fire. "I'm set on it. You might not know me well enough to know what that means, but Della can tell you. Poor girl, she's had to deal with it enough. She once said I had all the flexibility of an oak—so there's no sense arguing about it."

"Good," Justin said calmly, staring down into his glass of port, "because I know what I'm going to do, too. You mightn't know me that well, either, but anyone 'round here could tell you that we must be related—because once *my* mind is made up, it is graven in stone. But you're right. Let's not argue."

"You mean to say," Jared demanded, "that you'd pack up and leave the hall without a backward look—and let some miserable little toad spawned by our cursed uncle take over as the earl of Alveston?"

"No," Justin said calmly, "there'd be many a backward look, and a few manly tears to the bargain, I'd think. But

I'd leave it to Satan himself if he inherited it. I'll say it again: I don't deserve it while you live. And since I won't take it—or kill you, though sometimes your stubbornness tempts me—it will go to whomever it will go to. And that's the end of it."

"That's ridiculous!" Jared shouted.

"No more than your leaving is," Justin said grimly.

"I think it's time we went to bed," Della said.

It was the first thing the brothers agreed on all evening.

Della was in bed, but not asleep. She couldn't stop worrying. She loved the hall and grieved for Jared because after all he'd done, he still felt unworthy of it. She knew she was intricately tied up in his decision. She'd carry any burden for him gladly, but this was a huge one to take on for the rest of her life if she wasn't sure of his love. And she wasn't.

She wasn't even sure of his lust. His kisses had been impassioned. His touch had made her drunk with desire, but then, she thought worriedly, she'd always desired him. No wonder his touch set her afire. She'd kissed a few boys, but she really didn't know much more about men's desires than what she'd overheard other young women talking about. Men were supposed to be tinderboxes. They were supposed to actually ache if their desire was denied. Hadn't Molly Smith told all the young women at her house that night that Charles Bodine had said he was in pain when she finally insisted he stop? Of course, Molly was a baggage, and Charles a rogue. But it was generally agreed to be the truth. Many young men claimed it, and every young woman was warned that men had great passion, easily ignited and hard to subdue. They were set off by a touch, a kiss, a caress, and once passion was awakened, it was difficult, if not impossible, for men to stop.

Jared had drawn back, put her at arm's length, and while she couldn't even get two thoughts together had quietly told her to wait until they were married. He wasn't a cold man. A certain bar wench—and who knew how many others—could testify to that, Della thought darkly. So then it stood to reason that the fault didn't lay in the tinderbox, but in the tinder. With everything he'd said, still it seemed clear to her that she didn't really arouse him.

What a tragedy it would be if he left this place of his dreams and went back with her to live a life of sacrifice. *All for his damned—yes, damned!—sense of duty,* she thought rebelliously. She wanted him so badly she trembled with it, and *he* lay sleeping peacefully. That proved it. He was being so noble, and she, so— It would not do.

She crept down from her high bed and groped for her robe. She'd go to him now; she'd broach it to him now, while there was still time to right things. But what if—a small voice warned her—what if he really did desire her, and she went to him and he burst into flames as she did? It was nighttime; everyone knew men's passions ran highest in the night. She knew what happened between man and woman, and it was much more than sweet kisses and thrilling caresses. Some said it was painful, and everyone said it was shockingly intimate. She paused, her hand halfway into her sleeve. *Well then, good,* she thought—a little frightened, but undaunted. *At least I'll know.* Besides, she told herself as she shrugged the robe over her night-gown, she couldn't think of anything more wonderful than any kind of intimacy with him.

She might have some fears about making love for the first time, because she'd been well brought up and they weren't really married. But the thought of him gently, patiently, and calmly telling her to go back to her own bed was what really frightened her.

She slipped from her room and ran lightly down the hall, but she paused at his door. Her robe was made for warmth, not style, and her nightshift was plain and covered her from ankles to wrists. He was used to seeing desirable women in low-cut gowns and with their hair carefully curled and powdered—her hair! It was drawn back into one long plait for the night and fell to her waist like an inky rope, instead of rioting in masses of curls. She wondered whether she ought to loose it; he did seem to like her hair. *Yes, and why not put on powder and paint while you're at it?* she asked herself scornfully. *If you want to discover his real feelings toward you, get on with it.*

She raised her hand—and then stood worrying about whether she should tap or knock or scratch at the door. He mightn't even hear her with his bed hangings closed around him. Maybe he was sleeping, and she should just go in—but that would be very bold. She grew cold, in heart, mind, and body as she stood there, dithering. It wasn't until she thought she heard a noise that she acted.

This was the bad one.

It was very hot; he was sweating. The water in the pond looked cool. Best of all, he could hear that there were only other boys splashing and playing. They were around a bend, behind a bush. He had slipped away from his master—he could avoid them, too. He wanted just one moment in the cool, cool water.

It was wonderful. He lay on his back and looked up at the sky, and for a while as he lay drifting in the water—in his sleep—none of it mattered, not the loss, not the hardships. The water washed it all away and he stared into the sky as the earth turned beneath him. But then the cool water was gone and he found himself standing, looking for his clothes at the edge of the pond. He heard the sudden silence as though it were an explosion, and he looked up to see all the boys staring at him. Their faces shifted, magnified, becoming larger than life, caricatures of what they'd been, but just as true in their expressions of horror and fear.

He turned to see what they were staring at. He stared over at himself as if he were one of the gawking group. He gasped, shamed and frightened, because he saw the snakes

*on his back, too: twisting, writhing, thick white and red
snakes, stinging almost as much as they had when they
were lash strokes instead of the hideous scars they were
now.*

He ran—all the way into another dream.

There was to be no peace for him this night.

"I'll work long hours, and very hard, too," he said.

The woman looked doubtful.

"I promise; I give you my word on it," he vowed.

*He stood twisting his hat in his hands, because he knew
old Higgins could wake any minute and find him missing.
But he was only down the street, at the baker's. She needed
a boy. If he could just convince her—she had the money to
buy his bond. He was big now, and strong. She seemed to be
a kind person; her last boy had always been well fed and
clean. He'd bathe, too, if she'd allow him time and opportunity. He stole a glance around; it was a neat shop, swept
and orderly—not like the pigsty old Higgins lived in.*

*"Ah. Your word. There's the problem," she said with a
sigh. "You're the lad who says he's a nobleman born, ain't
you? An earl, no less. 'Tis a mad start, and makes me
terrible nervous, I can tell you. Still, you're a hard worker
with no harm in you, they all say. I tell you, lad . . ."*

*She looked at him. She was an ample woman with a
smiling mouth. He could be happy here for a while. He
could rest here, he could grow here, he thought, gain
strength and pride. It smelled like food and warmth and
comfort here. It looked like heaven. He waited.*

*"If you can tell me you'll give up that foolishness, and
never say you're a nobleman stole from the cradle or
whatnot again, why then, I'd be willin' to give you a try. You
speak well and work hard. I'm a fair woman, and I think
we'll suit. What do you say, lad? Tell the born truth, and
you've a position here."*

"I won't mention it again," he said promptly.

*"Ah, ah," she said, wagging a fat finger in front of his
face. "Not good enough. Not mentioning's not denyin' it,*

*and well you know it, you young scamp. Just tell me it's all
fudge so I don't have to worry about you being cracked, and
we'll talk to Higgins. Well?"*

*He wanted the job, the home, the chance to escape.
Higgins didn't use the lash, but he had a cruel mouth and a
heavy hand. The words were on his tongue; he wanted to say
them. But he didn't want to lose himself entirely, and he
knew that if he said them, he would. . . .*

"I . . ." he said. "I . . ."

Jared sat up in bed, his eyes wide. Something had
awakened him from his nightmare before his own despair
did, because it usually went on until he fought his way out
of the sack and up into the air again. Someone was in the
room with him; he realized he'd heard a gasp of shock. He
moved fast for a big man newly woken—he'd had to wake
in the midst of terror before.

"Ah! Got you!" he cried, reaching into the darkness and
wrapping his arms around the darker patch of black he saw
outlined in the dim glow of his opened window.

He released her a second later—and stood staring.
"Della?" he asked with shock. "By God, it is—Della!
What are you doing here, now? Something's the matter!"
he said in sudden horror when she didn't answer but only
stood shaking and staring back at him. "Tell me. God,
Della, please say something. I'll help; I just have to know
what to do!"

"Well," she finally said in a tiny, quavering voice, "you
could start by putting some clothes on."

He glanced down at himself, then swung around and
made a grab at something near the bed. She heard the
heavy rustle of silk as he drew on his robe. "Now, tell me;
what's wrong?" he asked, gripping her shoulders.

She couldn't answer right away. She was overwhelmed
at the nearness of him, the solid masculinity, the sight of
that warm, hard, naked body just inches away from her.
She swallowed. "Nothing," she said. "Oh everything," she
wailed, remembering that this was Jared, her Jared. "I

couldn't sleep. I was thinking—you can't give it all up for me; you can't. You've worked so hard—you belong here. What if I disappoint you? What if I already have?"

He was about to try to calm her fears, but her last question brought him up short. "What?" he asked.

"Well, but I—you—you don't seem to want . . . Jared, I know you said you love me. I do. But—do you find me desirable, too? Really?"

He wanted to hug her close, but he didn't trust his body tonight after the way it had reacted when he'd first held her. "How can you ask?" was all he could say.

"Because—because you keep turning me away after we kiss. That's supposed to be so hard for a man to do, but you do it so easily. You thought I was your sister for so long, I thought maybe the trouble was that you still do—and so you couldn't . . . you know."

"I know, and I could—oh, before God, I could," he said, and exhaled a long breath. "That's just it. Della, when you came in tonight, I was dreaming about shame and worthlessness; I'm plagued by those kind of dreams, because of what I was and what happened to me. It was hard to let you leave my arms—believe me, you can't know how hard—as hard as not touching you now. But we're not married, and I don't trust myself. Before God and man and Alfred, and especially myself, I have to prove I'm a worthy man. The bond-boy must be decent and repay Alfred's trust. I can't take your love while you're alone, under my protection. Can't you see that? I want you—but with honor. As my wife, and nothing less. I know that doesn't sound loverlike, but believe it or not, it means I love you more than myself or my desires."

She sniffed. It was eloquent. He lowered his head and feathered a kiss across her lips. The kiss was so light, so sweet, so extraordinarily sweet, that he leaned in toward her, and she toward him. This time, after a long time, when he raised his head, he held her close instead of away from him. But he didn't do more, and she felt his body shivering against hers. That wasn't all she felt against her before he let her go—which was precisely why he suddenly did.

"We have to be married soon," he said. "Now do you see? But for now, please, go to bed. Your own bed. And quickly."

She reached up on her toes and kissed his lips quickly, and then smiling, scampered back to her room. As she'd feared, he had told her to go back to her own bed. But she was very happy.

He took off his robe and settled back into bed—not to sleep, but to plan. Soon, he wouldn't have to sleep alone anymore. He frowned, realizing that meant that he wouldn't be able to sleep naked anymore, either. No woman had ever seen his back, and he certainly would never subject Della to such a sight. He decided nightshirts were a sacrifice he would just have to get used to—and it couldn't be soon enough for him.

The earl of Alveston stood at the window, looking out. The earl of Alveston stood by the vicar's desk, looking at him. They looked very alike, and the old minister was very confused—and not just by their request.

"But a special license is no easy thing to obtain," the old man said. "A quick wedding hasn't been possible since before fifty-two, when the marriage law went into effect. Now there are banns to be posted and a waiting period—a very good thing in all, my lords, do you see?"

"But there are special licenses," Justin said silkily, "obtainable in special circumstances. These are such. An earl, after all," he said in a confidential voice, looking at his brother, "and a young girl unchaperoned in his house, under his protection, and her absent father a baron. Let me see: that's an earl, an earl, and a baron involved, isn't it? Such a lot of highly placed persons to be inconvenienced by delay. And on our side, an additional marquis and a bishop as well who will be glad to hasten matters, I am sure."

"But why such haste, my lord?" the old man asked nervously.

"Aside from the fact that the lady in question is presently unchaperoned, through no fault of her own, in a house with two unwed men? My dear reverend sir," Justin said, lowering his voice to a whisper and indicating his brother, who was pacing now, "the earl, as you know, was raised in America."

The old man looked blank. Then comprehension dawned. "Oh, I see. A very savage land, is it not?"

"Yes, extremely. But settled by pilgrims . . . Puritans," Justin whispered.

"Ah!" the old vicar said. "Oh dear."

"Just so," Justin said smugly. "You perceive the tensions. A robust Englishman raised among Puritans in such a wild place—the conflicts, dear sir, the possibilities. Would you want that on your conscience?"

It was a quiet wedding. The bride carried the last roses of the autumn from the garden as one of the uncles of the groom escorted her down the aisle of the ancient church his ancestors had built for the people of their village. The groom's man stood at his side, looking so much like him that some villagers who had started celebrating early thought they were seeing double. But a closer look showed one man wore a smile of dazzled, disbelieving bliss, and the other, a sadder one.

They held the wedding dinner in the hall, but had arranged for feasts at the local inn and every cottager's humble home as well, because the earl had been generous, wanting everyone to share in this joyous occasion.

"And besides," Jared told Della as the two of them dined alone at the hall, "this way they'll all be too drunk to bother us with singing and such on the lawns tonight. Or so Justin said. That's why he and the uncles are dining at the inn right now instead of with us." *Or so he said,* Jared thought with the only trace of sadness he'd felt all day.

"Are you done?" he asked, looking at her still-full dinner plate with what he hoped was a casual smile.

"Absolutely," she said, looking at his dish, and seeing everything still on it. "Oh, isn't this silly?" She giggled. "As if we have to be nervous with each other just because we're finally married! We've had dinner a million times together before, I'd bet. How silly. Go on, finish."

"I am," he said, looking into her eyes.

"So am I," she said in a small voice.

They both felt foolish as they went up the stairs together, all alone in the vast hall except for servants, who were celebrating in the kitchens, way out of sight. It was awkward, certainly, when he led her into his chamber and closed the door behind them. There was no doubt it was a blush that rose in her cheeks when she saw her nightgown laid out on his high bed. He hesitated for a moment before he turned to her.

And then they touched.

"Before God!" Jared swore, his face in her hair, as he held her so close she could feel the heavy beat of his heart against hers through all their clothing. "I don't know what it is. I touch you and I fall apart."

"With no one else?" she whispered when she could.

"No one—never," he vowed, because it was true.

It took a while to remove their clothes. She was drugged by his kisses, clumsy with her buttons, and shy when at last her gown was to come off. He was slower getting his breeches off because he was so intent on helping her. And the kisses kept getting in the way, firing him and yet slowing his progress because they were incredibly delicious.

He stopped kissing her only when she was entirely bared to his gaze. She took his breath away. Slender and curved, all shades of rose and white, except for that jet patch she was so shy about, holding her hand over herself, looking like a representation of Venus rising from the waves he'd once seen. But she was his Della, and much more beautiful to him. Her breasts were high; her waist dipped and swelled out again in lithe curves that he reached out to touch so he could believe the perfection of them. He helped loose her hair into a dark, turbulent sea that made her skin glow by contrast. Then he kissed and caressed her until he could take no more and she looked as though she wasn't afraid of whatever more there would be. But he knew how much more was to come, and he gently bore her to his bed to show her.

He dazzled her; he was all warm gold and matte velvet to her touch. He smelled like sunshine and salt and soap and Jared, and she couldn't breath him in deeply enough. Her hands went under his shirt to his hard chest, tentatively—and then more boldly—stroking the firm contours of a superbly muscled body whose every line showed it had known strenuous labor. Broad chest and lean hips and flat abdomen with ridges of hard muscle— hard, but so sensitive he shivered when she touched them with her fingertips. He tried to keep his arousal from her sight because of her inexperience, but she saw and was wise enough to know that it was a tribute she saw, and she smiled and thought him altogether handsome, and told him so.

They made love with their eyes open, as if neither could get enough of the sight of the other in the shifting candlelight.

It was wonderful to make love to someone so beloved, Jared thought with dazed gratitude.

It was heaven; surely this was heaven; for this was Jared with her, Della thought over and over, really Jared.

But she was unaccustomed to loving and had been brought up to be innocent. He was wracked with desire, but he paced himself to her needs, and somehow found the grace to consider her expectations. When he touched her intimately and in spite of herself she gasped and closed her legs hard against him, he waited. Then he tried again, and he won her that way, slowly and with such control it almost undid him. She accepted all he gave after that— until he rose up on his elbows and began to position himself over her. Then she frowned. Her hands fell away from his wide shoulders, and she lay still, looking up at him as though she were waking from some dream of pleasure.

"Della, love, my Della," he whispered, his pulse racing as he held himself back against natural desire so forcefully he was breathless. "Relax. This will make us one. It won't hurt for long, and next time there'll be only pleasure."

"It's not that," she said. "I'm not afraid. But—take off your shirt. I feel strange, all naked, with you dressed for dinner."

His arms trembled as he pulled away. He was half out of his mind with desire, and she spoke as though they were in a drawing room. He had no intention of taking off his shirt, and he was surprised she'd asked. He was so frustrated he didn't see how she shivered when he moved away from her. "Della, my love, I can't," he said. "I . . . you don't want to . . . My back—it's ugly. Don't let it ruin the moment. Come, let me show you love."

"You do show me love," she said, her eyes brilliant with tears, "but not if you hide from me. Anyway, it's not fair. Hand me my gown, if you please," she said, sitting up, one hand covering breasts still damp from his kisses. He stared at her in disbelief. She blushed from her chest to her nose, but she held firm. "If you want to see my front, you have to show your back," she said as she held out a hand for her gown. "If not, I guess we'll do it this way. But as I understand, it's much better without clothes."

"I am hideously scarred," he said, his desire fading, his muscles tensed, and a hard knot in his throat. His stomach grew tight and he felt clammy with nausea. Was degradation a part of her pleasure? Was this really why the master's daughter had lusted for the bond-boy? If it was true, it would kill him. His hands clenched and his heart grew cold.

"I am your wife," she said obstinately.

He nodded slowly. He took her gown from the bed and flung it away with such force that her hand went to her mouth. Slowly, with set face and white lips, he dragged off his shirt and turned aside so she could see his back in the dancing candlelight. *Let her have her money's worth,* he thought numbly, closing his eyes.

After a while, he felt a little tug on his arm. "Aren't you coming back?" she asked in a little voice. "I didn't mean to make you angry."

"You wanted to see my back," he said bleakly.

"Well, not really," she said, and he recoiled, frantically looking for his shirt, wondering if a moment's foolishness on her part, taken too seriously by him, would now mean her lifetime avoidance of him.

"I saw it once, remember? When we were children. It looks much better now, by the way," she added. "They're not so red anymore, and since you've grown, the scars look smaller." She didn't lie, though she elaborated. The lash-marks still marred otherwise perfect skin, but they didn't mar the strength and power of the man. Lightning had struck here, but he had survived it. If anything, it made him dearer to her; that wasn't why she'd asked him to remove his shirt.

"That awful man," she said indignantly, dismissing his scars as the history they were to her. "I'd kill him if I could. I'm sorry if you think I was too bold," she said in a smaller voice, her head bowed, her hair covering her face. "All I meant was that it seemed it would be much—nicer if we were both undressed. I didn't know a man was supposed to keep his shirt on, so if you think it was sluttish of me, I didn't mean it. Put it back on, by all means. I—I just wanted to hold you the way you were holding me, with nothing between us."

He thought something broke within himself then, and he gathered her up and hugged her close so he wouldn't shatter to pieces.

"Nothing's between us," he vowed, "nothing."

It didn't take long for his body to remember what his suspicious mind had interrupted. Now there was such love that he could think of nothing beyond it, but it didn't matter—love gentled his desire and turned lust into something sublime. And she encouraged him every step of the way. They paused only once. When she feathered a touch over his ragged back, he shuddered, and she withdrew her hand hastily. "Have I hurt you?" she asked worriedly.

"No, how could you?" he murmured, distracted by her withdrawal. "They're only scars; scars don't hurt when they're healed," he said, and then he heard himself and laughed, and he reached for her once more. "And they are healed, my love," he said. "Thank you."

Then there was no time for speech—no breath for it, either. But they didn't have to speak. When he rose over her again, she smiled at him. When he entered her at last, she hugged him closer despite the discomfort, and there was some, because although she was eager to accept him, she'd never done such a thing before. Lust drove him forward, making him arch over her in ecstasy. Love filled him even as he finally broke against her. And with the loss of himself, he was finally whole.

She wept with the pleasure and pain and the realization of it all. He was hers—at last, at last. Different pleasure would come later for her—he had promised. But for now, this was almost too much. She was complete.

He didn't sleep, as she'd been told men were supposed to do after loving. Instead, he curled his body around her, kissing and caressing her as though he were still courting her.

"I have always loved you, always," she confessed.

"Forgive me. I thought you wanted to see my back in order to despise me," he admitted.

"Why should I despise you for your scars?" she asked, stroking his hair. "In a way—in an awful, terrible, selfish way—I'm glad of them. Because just think: if you were unscarred, if you had never been stolen and sold into bondage, how could I ever have met you? You'd be the earl of Alveston, with three children, at least, by now. You wouldn't have waited forever, like Justin. You'd never have come to Virginia, saved Thomas, and filled my life. Things happen for a reason, Jared. I hate those scars for your sake. But I have to love them, for mine."

When he didn't answer right away, she burrowed her face into his shoulder. "Are you shocked?" she whispered, nudging him with her nose. "It's true. I'll never lie to you again. I lived a lie for so long: I *hated* being your sister. I wanted so much to be—this."

He rose on an elbow and took her face in his hand. He stroked back her hair from her eyes, so he could look into them.

"You are both," he said. "'Behold, thou art fair, my love,'" he quoted. "'Thou art all fair, my love; there is no spot in thee. Thou hast ravished my heart, my sister, my spouse;'" he said, smiling down at her. "'Thy lips, O my spouse, drop as the honeycomb: honey and milk are under thy tongue. . . . A garden inclosed is my sister, my spouse . . . a fountain of gardens, a well of living waters . . .'"

She smiled through tears, and nodded. "I know my Bible—and my husband . . . my *husband,*" she said, and sighed with pure pleasure. "'His mouth is most sweet,'" she quoted in turn, touching his lips with trembling fingers. "'Yea, he is altogether lovely. This is my beloved, and this is my friend . . .'"

And then they spoke a different kind of poetry to each other, but one without words.

Chapter

18

London

He slept dreamlessly and awoke refreshed, as he had since the day they'd been married. He woke up desiring her again, too. But there was a morning ritual that came first. He watched her for a long time before he woke her. He lay on his side, propped on an elbow, watching her sleep. Since they'd married, Jared had found this to be one of his greatest secret pleasures. *His,* he thought, looking at her with pleasure and pride. She slept easy in his bed, and she was his wife. He still couldn't get used to the wonder of it.

When he saw first light change to sunlight and begin to stream in the window, he bent his head to kiss the nape of her neck. She stretched and sighed, and burrowed her face back into her pillow. He ran his lips down her neck and ran a hand down the sweetly curving lines of her back, pausing at her nicely rounded bottom. Her breathing changed. He smiled as she turned over and put her arms around his neck.

"Umm," she said. "Good morning, husband."

"Umm yourself, wife," Jared said, and kissed her awake.

Della loved it when he woke her this way, but then he surprised her by grinning ruefully and taking her arms down from his neck.

"Oh," she said, getting slightly pink, thinking about it. "Ah—just a moment; I'll go and wash my face and teeth."

"You taste like wine, beloved, even in the morning," he said. "Maybe because you really didn't get much sleep last night. Neither of us did, thank you. But that's not it. Don't you remember what today is?"

She frowned, trying to think, but was still befuddled by sleep and kisses. "Well, you said you'd show me the last of the shops on London Bridge. I think it's terrible that they're pulling them down. Modernization is very good, but there should be some room for the old ways. . . . Oh my, I've only been here a few months and I sound like an Englishwoman, don't I? But what's the hurry?" She smiled at him and wriggled into the plump feather mattress with sensual pleasure. "They won't all be gone today. There are much better things to do now, I think."

"So do I," he agreed, "but it's Wednesday, wife. Remember?"

Her eyes flew open wide. She sat straight up. "Oh, mercy! Wednesday! The ship! What time is it? We can't be late."

His amusement faded, and as he gazed at her in the morning light, his gray eyes grew smoky dark. She'd learned to sleep naked the way he did, and when she sat up so abruptly, the covers pooled around her. It looked as if her slender body were rising from a shining, satin sea. He took her in his arms and drew her back to the pillow.

"We won't be late," he breathed against her ear. "It won't sail until the first fair tide. That gives us time—*if,* that is, you'll promise not to take forever getting dressed."

"I'll go without dressing," she murmured against his mouth.

* * *

But in the end, they did have to hurry, because she'd wanted to look her best. She wore her best day gown of apple-blossom pink silk, with green satin panniers.

"I don't know why you dressed so carefully," he told her when their carriage finally stopped at the dockside. "You'll have to keep your cape closed anyway; the wind's cutting cold today."

"But it's clear, and that will make for a smoother sail, won't it?" she asked him with sudden fearfulness.

"Yes. Don't worry," he said. "The hurricane season's passed, and the great northern storms aren't due yet. It's a perfect time to sail, and the bright sky will make even smoky old London look beautiful as the ship puts out to sea. It will be a good sight to remember England by."

"Jared," she said, her eyes searching his, "you're sure this is what you want?"

"I have you; that's all I really want. As for the rest of it, now I'm sure that this is the way things must be. And you?"

She nodded and gave him her hand, so he could help her from the coach.

The ship was a splendid, great-masted vessel. There was a tumult of sailors loading livestock and last-minute cargo, and a confusion of passengers being registered and boarded and saying their farewells to a crowd of well-wishers. Jared and Della paused on the dock, looking for a familiar face. The one they found wasn't the one they were looking for.

Fiona came running down the plank and past them, her cloak trailing behind her like a sail. The ripping wind had pushed back her hood to show her eyes glittering with tears, and her fair face had two red spots high on her cheeks. Della didn't think they were caused by the wind. The wind could make a lady look like she was crying, but it didn't fill her face with disappointment and regret. She was going to say something to Fiona as she rushed past, but stopped when she felt Jared's hand on her arm.

"I think it would be best if we let her alone," he said quietly.

Della saw Fiona's father step out of a grand coach that had been waiting by the dockside and take his daughter in his embrace. Then the two disappeared into the coach.

"Yes," Della said. "Well, at least we know Justin's here already and hasn't changed his mind."

She gazed up at Jared as his eyes searched the deck of the great ship. In spite of his earlier comments, he had dressed as elegantly as she had today. The wind made his cloak swirl around him and it ruffled his glowing hair. She thought he had never looked so handsome, but then, so she thought every day. She held up her head, vowing to do him proud, and let him lead her up the gangplank.

They found Justin almost immediately. Few men were as tall as the two brothers. The wind made hats and wigs a jest today, and even elegant men found powder a waste, so the brothers' recent habit of going without wigs did not make their natural hair colors seem unusual. Justin's hair had slipped from his queue. It had grown out, and now it rippled to his shoulders. The wind brought high color to his face, but there was also vivid excitement in his expression when he saw them. Della thought he looked more like Jared today than she'd ever seen him look.

"Little sister!" Justin said with a broad smile, holding out his arms and enfolding her. "Brother!" he said, loosing her and hugging Jared hard. Jared embraced him in turn.

Della felt tears come to her eyes as she watched the two men. It was a capricious world, and she found herself wondering if they ever would see each other again. She banished the dangerous thought. When she saw her father beaming at her, she was glad to go straight into his comforting arms.

"Such a lot of hugging today," Alfred said, releasing her and running a hand beneath his nose. "Well, well. You look beautiful, my honey. I'm proud of you. You've done everything just right. Imagine, going through a wedding all over again here in London, and just for me. Or was it for the uncles? No matter, it was the talk of the town, you did me proud, as you always do."

She couldn't speak right away, she was trying so hard to be grown up and brave. She turned to the two brothers instead of answering, and listened to them saying their farewells as she composed herself.

"So, brother. I can't change your mind? There's still time."

"In a pig's eye, there is."

"You're sure?"

"We've been through this, time and again. I am. It's best for me, and you, and well you know it."

"So be it," Jared said, turning from his brother, "Della, before God! Get that look off your face! Alfred's going home, not to the end of the earth."

"Aye," Alfred said vigorously, "and it isn't as though I've lost a daughter either, for you know I've gained two sons!"

"My only hope is that I can be as good a one to you as my brother was," Justin said sincerely.

Alfred patted him on the back, "I don't expect that," he said, "for he wasn't like my Thomas at all, you know. But still he was altogether right for Jared, and about as fine a son as any man could ask, at that. I'm a lucky fellow. I know you'll be absolutely right for me as 'Justin,' too. Ah. See? You don't even flinch when I call you by your Christian name. You've gotten used to it already. You'll do well. Getting used to new things is the hallmark of success for a man in the New World."

"I'm used to it because it is my rightful name, now, as always. Jared's the lordship, and good luck to him," Justin said merrily. "I'm for a new world and a new life in it. You took my brother in as a boy, and gave us back a redoubtable man. I warn you, Alfred, I expect the same for myself."

"You have the same already," Alfred said with a laugh.

"So say you," Justin said, "but I don't know how to do things as Jared can. I don't know how to judge a beaver pelt, nor address a chief of the Indians, or even how to hew enough firewood for a really cold night—without cutting my toes off. Nor do I know a cotton boll from a tobacco leaf. And don't forget the caves you've said you'd show me, as well as the civilized delights of Williamsburg; or the men you said you'd introduce me to: from Dr. Franklin's friends to Hairy Pierre, the trapper. I want to be a trader and a plantation manager and a frontiersman, and good at all those trades, Alfred. So that when my arrogant, spoiled soft nobleman of a brother comes to visit me, with his many children, they can all wish they were like their wild and venturesome Uncle Justin."

"Even the girls?" Della said, laughing.

"Especially the girls," Justin said, smiling down at her, "if they're anything like their very wise mama, who always recognized a nobleman, whatever he was disguised as."

"Oh," Della said with a sigh, "how I wish there were two of me!"

They all laughed, because they *could* laugh about it now.

"I mean it, brother," Justin said. "It is exactly as I told you. You're a man now; your life made you one. I need to find what sort of man I am. Your New World's the place to do it, because there's room for all sorts of men there. Here, I would always and ever be Jared Alveston's brother. I'm proud of it, but that is all I would be—a man who stands high in the line of succession. I was born so. But there, Alfred assures me I shall have a chance to be Justin, a man who may stand as high as he wishes to, or can. Be glad for me."

"Glad?" Jared said. "God, man, when you say it like that, you make me want to push you overboard and take your place!"

Justin glanced at Della, into eyes blue as the sea he would soon cross, and smiled sadly. "Brother," he said, "no one could ever take your place, and woe to whoever tried. Because if you didn't get them, your fierce Della would. See that you take care of her, or you'll have to answer to me!"

"And see that *you* take care of my father!" Della said as a jest, but her voice faltered because she heard the call for visitors ashore.

"Take care of my brother," Jared told Alfred, with no jest in his voice.

"And you, mine," Justin told Della.

"I'm the only one who doesn't have to ask that favor," Alfred told Jared as he took his hand, "because you've already sworn to protect my daughter, and a long time before you stood before that preacher, lad. I remember. You've always been a man of your word, then as now. God keep you, son. You cannot know how happy I am to know you really are that to me now."

They all embraced and vowed to write, and then swore to see each other soon again. In the end, they had to be told very politely that visitors must leave the ship or they would sail with it.

Della and Jared stood on the wharf as the crowd dispersed, and they watched as a fine running wind carried the ship swiftly off into the horizon and away into a new day.

Only then did they turn to each other again.

"Have I done the right thing?" Jared asked her.

"If you wanted to make him happy? Yes. If you wanted to make me happy? Only if you've made yourself happy."

"You make me happy," he said, "but happiness isn't everything."

"Then what is?" she demanded, her hands on her hips. "And if you're going to go on about right and moral and just—well, you know what you've done is that, too. But if happiness isn't everything, I'd like to know what is."

He bent to her and whispered in her ear. Her knees grew weak and she put her arms around him and leaned against him.

"Oh," she said. "Well, yes—that. But surely that's a form of happiness?"

"Let's go home and discuss it," he suggested.

"Yes, please," she said.

They left the dockside together, as they had so many years ago in another time and place, on the opposite shore of this ocean. He helped her into a coach so he could carry her home, the way he had all those years before in that other world. She put her arms around his neck and told herself she'd never let him go, the way she had secretly promised herself then—the way she could at last promise him.